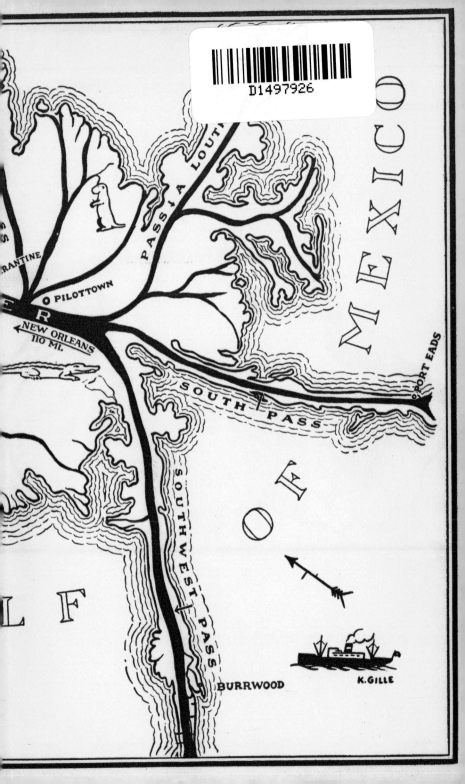

GREEN MARGINS

GREEN MARGINS

E. P. O'DONNELL

HOUGHTON MIFFLIN COMPANY · BOSTON

The Riverside Press Cambridge

1936

The Riverside Press
CAMBRIDGE · MASSACHUSETTS
PRINTED IN THE U.S.A.

GRATEFULLY DEDICATED TO
DOCTOR SIDNEY K. SIMON

These people and their doings are wholly imaginary, and in the making of the story, time and space were somewhat distorted to fit the writer's vision.

THE AUTHOR

CONTENTS

THE RIVER BRINGS

BOOK ONE

1

THE Delta blackness was deep and hollow. The girl shivering
on the deserted levee heard the wind's strange noises, the
troubled squeaking of floating hyacinth bulbs rubbing together
in the void, the thudding of driftwood logs, the swishing of unseen grasses. And farther out, the river's laughter, a ceaseless
bitter din.

She kept looking over her shoulder into the black north,
afraid. She crushed her cold young breasts to her, and blinked
the wind-tears from her eyes.

Was that a voice?

Every soul was asleep in the wooden houses along the winding
levee. The girl stood alone, yet unable to *feel* alone. And deep
in her being the cold had settled somewhere with a gnawing
pain, almost a burning.

Suddenly she could bear the cold no longer. She was too far
from home to go on. She took the plank-walk to the river, and
jumped aboard the boat moored there.

The man was picking a duck. He sat with his thighs apart
before a charcoal brazier with the fowl between his knees,
softly ripping away fingerfuls of down. She had never seen him
before in the flesh, but she often visualized his kind, strong and
strange, brought down casually by the river, which casually
brought many things. He wore a sleeveless undershirt. Both

his arms from the elbows upward were marbled by curious blue and green bruises, recently suffered. He was in pain, she saw — plucking his fowl with difficulty.

She would stay and warm herself and hear what he would say. It might be nice. She had never spoken to a stranger, except levee peddlers, and the cartridge drummer from the city.

She knocked her horseshoe-nail ring on the doorway and began mumbling an apology, peering into the cabin while she fought the wind that lashed her hair and the willow leaves pelting her.

The man looked at her, without much surprise.

'Come on down!' he invited. 'Your company'll pleasure me.'

'I thought this was Boy Chauvin's boat,' she said. 'A man I know with a gas-boat something like yours. This is his father's landing.'

'I knew this was somebody's landing,' he said, in a deep, even key that began to warm her, and with a curious oblique smile. 'Come by the fire. Your teeth are knockin' out there, and you've got goose bumps. Eat with me, if you're of a mind to. There's duck enough to meat the two of us, and more. Won't you eat?'

She saw the ducks. At the after end of the boat was an iridescent mound of slain mallards, full-breasted, open-eyed, piled in awkward attitudes as though they had just fallen in from the sky and lay paralyzed with surprise. The man closed the cabin door. They were alone in the boat.

The girl put her book on the table and drew close to the fire, wedging her skirt between her legs and shivering in the sudden warmth. The man kept examining her from under his lowered forehead. He was quite a big young fellow with partly closed eyes the same color as hers, throwing off honest and friendly brown gleams.

'I'm all stove up from shooting,' he said.

She could picture a fellow like this hunched over a table full of steaming food, driving off his great hunger after one of the hard bitter days that men outdoors stumble through — tearing at the bread, impaling huge forkfuls of meat, gulping the raw scalding coffee. She thought: 'He's not used to boats. He can't coil a rope. My! what big hands!' She could not understand it. It was exciting.

'What brought you away from home such stormy weather?' he asked. 'You don't even have a cape.'

'This ain't a storm,' she answered. She looked around her. The man stopped his work and smiled at her tenderly. He fondled his bruised arms. Sister said: 'This is just a blow, a nor'wester off the river, blew up when I was coming from Retreat. It was warm when I left home this morning. I'd better go now. Thank you for letting me get warm.'

'And you won't eat a bite with me?'

'No, sir. Where are you from?'

She sat on the stool.

'—— because I'd love to have you eat with me,' he said. 'Where is Retreat?'

'I'm making my first Communion Sunday.'

'You said coming from Retreat.'

'It's part of the Communion. We stay with the Sisters three days without talking or laughing, to get ready for God in Communion. Today's the first day.'

The man turned and looked at Sister's book on the table. The title said: 'Two Hundred Things a Bright Boy Can Make With Tools.'

'I'll tell you what,' he said. 'You cut up this here duck and I'll pick another one. It won't take us long. Yes, the wind caught me, too. I reckon we do send down a lot of cold snaps from our snows and freezes up home. I knew it was comin'. I taken notice it was a greenish sundown today.'

'Where did you come from?'

'Down the Pass by the Gulf, shooting these-here duck.

There's duck and then some, down there, Miss . . . what's your name? Mine's Bruce.'

'Nicolene, or Sister. Sister Kalavich.'

He studied her teeth flattening the sibilants through the dark full lips. His eyes sank to her waist, encircled by a wide ornamental belt made of tarpon scales.

He said: 'My grand-uncle used to say how the pigeons up home used to fly over, back in the old days, so thick you couldn't see indoors, the sky was so black with the wild pigeons. That's the way it was in the Pass yesterday with the duck. Black with duck, the sky. And everybody shooting till it sounded like a war-battle. God Almighty! Look at my arms here. Couldn't shoot no more with the right shoulder, so I switched to the left. My hands are still hampered. That's why I made this landing. With the wind and current, I couldn't steer another foot, and mind out for the injine. It's like red-hot needles progging at my shoulder meat.'

Sister finished butchering the duck. She returned to the fire and studied the man's broad back, stooped.

'Like red-hot needles,' he said, frowning with pain.

'I could pick that other duck,' said Sister.

He passed her the duck and watched her pluck it, more expertly than he had ever seen one picked before; and he resumed his talk, in that smooth deep key that relaxed her senses and at the same time impelled her to giggle, like immersion in some slow cool stream.

'I aim to hit New Orleans and the market tomorrow noon, barring accidents. If I keep usin' turps, my arms ought to loosen up by daylight, you think? I reckon turpentine'll drive in the bruised blood. That's all we use up our way for different complaints — turps. I lay you-all don't have turps down this far. No trees for it. For turps you want the pine. All your trees are sweet-sapped, such as the cypress and the orange. Good trees, but sweet-sapped. Up home there's a tang in most our saps, the rawsin and the different gums. You get it from the fireplace like you get it from the hills. Of a foggy mornin', open your window and sniff, and you feel the tang layin' on the air. Down here the air's softer like. Hard and salty by the Gulf, but behind the levees, sweet.'

Sister sat holding the forgotten duck with lips parted. 'Where is that — your home?' she heard herself asking faintly, as if from afar.

'Issaquena. It ain't a town, just a place, slanting away, away upwards, in the mountain country. Not exactly north, but it has more northernness than this-here. And our ways! God Almighty! There's a sight of difference from you-all's ways. For an instance, do you think I could row a boat up to my front gate like you can? Too shallow, our rivers, for boats, and full of rocks, colored rocks. Wouldn't no boat take her course up there.'

'What color rocks?'

'Green or gray, brindle or blue. Some red as your lips here.'

Every tissue in her body heard that. The man crossed the cabin, walking bigly. Now she could picture him striding tall and heavy in a room at home, searching as big men do for something that lay right under his nose. At a dance, he would make the parlor vases jump, swinging his partner until her skirts popped and crackled. His partner was laughing loudly, begging him to behave.

'In fact,' he went on, 'they're all colors. And our water's clear, a wonderful thing to look through, that-there, running among the rocks in different directions, different colored currents, like a piece of weavin', sunny and blotches of shade. Fine for trout, but the people don't know much about boats. My people's afraid of deep water. They think the deeper the water, the worse drownded you would get. But they're not afraid of high places like I reckon you-all are, like climbin' a thousand-foot rock 'way up and gone above the clouds. I reckon you'd be afraid of that-there, wouldn't you? A thousand-foot rock!'

Sister followed his gestures, speechless.

'And you just keep traveling around now?'

'Just around and around, you might say. Next week I'm liable to be 'way up the Atchafalaya River tradin' hardware for 'coon skins. I'm one of millions in this country, bred to home-stead, and no more frontiers left. I'll go back home some day, a long piece from here, and I aim to settle down for good. But not yet. I don't know. All our men was always great danger-lovers, messin' around through their youth, then moseying back to settle down, the Bruces. What would you'd rather do, settle or travel?'

She wished he would not keep steering the talk back to her. The wind outside howled brutally, belaboring the trees and flay-ing the river's mirthful surface, which tonight gave off a strong, wild, musky smell.

'I'd rather travel,' she said.

After the meal he walked with her to the levee. The invisible heavens above them were peopled with trumpeting wild geese crying thinly far up among the winds, in joy or in distress. The moon raced madly past a rent in a cloud.

'A body can see you ain't contented in this place,' said Bruce.

'No, and I'm leaving right now.'

He laughed and patted her shoulder with brotherly affection. She did not like brotherly affection. She hated being a girl.

'I'll pass with your coat at daylight going to Retreat,' she said, meaning she did not care to see him again.

'I'm glad we got acquainted,' he said.

'Thank you, sir.'

'I was right lonesome when you come. Listen that river pound the willows! I'm of a mind to stay here a spell; it appeals, in a way. I wonder could I sell my ducks around here against they spoil.'

'They sell them to the Bar Pilots.'

'At Pilot Town?'

'Yes, sir. Ask for the steward, Mr. Fortinberry, big bat-eyed man, a North fellow like you.'

'You might could come eat with me tomorrow night?'

'Maybe.'

'Could I kiss you good-night?'

'What for, kiss me?'

'Why shouldn't I?'

'I don't know.'

'Not even once?'

'No. I'm on Retreat.'

'Why not once?'

'You wouldn't be satisfied.'

He watched her moonlit lips fall into a hard curl, and he loved her.

'Let me see you home and meet your folks,' he suggested.

'There's nobody but my father and brother. Papa'll be mad at me for coming late. They don't like strangers here.'

'It's the same up my way. You've got no mother?'

'She was killed four years ago.'

'That's a terrible thing.'

'No. She's better off.'

'I see.'

'She wouldn't have much to live for but work.'

'May she rest in peace! Was it accidental?'

'A tarpon killed her. We were sailing home from the picnic on Saint John's Day. A tarpon jumped in Grampaw's boat and hit her. She didn't suffer.'

'Thank God! . . . The wind is getting stronger.'

'I've got to work on my Communion clothes tonight.'

'Good-night, then.'
'Good-night, and thank you.'

Sister walked backward against the wind. At home she hid Bruce's coat under her brother's pirogue lying bottom up under a fig tree. Inside her father sat by the fire with his battered hat on, and his thin brown fingers interlocked across his stomach. In the corner was an easel with a crayon of Sister's mother gazing ruefully at the fire. Her father was whistling between his teeth because the New Orleans cartridge drummer had brought him half a pint of whiskey, and because Sister was late, meriting chastisement. When Sister entered, he eyed her sideways without moving his face. Sister started to hang her hat on the deerhorns on the wall.

'Wait there,' said her father in Slavonian.

She turned and faced him. Whistling softly, he scrutinized her. Something was wrong. Sister looked somewhat happy. Her firelit reverie vexed him. His face was long, fine-textured, sensitive, with a noble expanse of brow, and burning, tuberculous eyes. Neither Sister, nor her brother mending a slingshot by the fire, resembled the father.

'What kept you?' Sister was asked.

She could not lie, because she had been on Retreat.

'I stopped and talked,' she answered in English.

'Who to?'

Sister hung up her hat and stood looking at the fire, tapping her foot in meditation.

Her brother Mocco said, 'I covered your cucumber vines, Sis, but I bet they'll freeze through the hay, with this wind.'

The father clicked his thumb-nails patiently. 'Who to, Nicolene?' he asked softly.

'A boy.'

'None of my business,' the father said sorrowfully.

'It don't matter, Pa.'

'What are you guilty of, then? Why do you look guilty? Have you been with Unga January again?'

'No, sir. I've been on Retreat all day. I learned all the Acts by heart.'

'I'm giving you a chance to talk. Remember I owe you the strap for wasting that bucket of water today.'

'I told you.'

'If you don't talk, I'm going to examine you.'

Sister grew taller. An expression of nausea appeared on her mouth. She threw a trapped glance at her brother whittling.

'Perhaps I'll examine you if you do talk,' said the father, thoughtfully poking the fire. 'I know this levee. I know these Grass Margin boys, and I know which ones have been with your bosom friend Unga. Your negro bosom friend.'

Mocco crossed the room for water. 'Let the kid alone, Pa,' he said in English.

The father turned. 'Get out, before I ——' He coughed hollowly, standing up. His body curved forward bonily, and seemed to be without chest or buttocks.

Mocco went to the kitchen door and turned. 'Never mind, Sis,' he said. 'He won't be examining you much longer,' and smiled bitterly.

Tony Kalavich called at the slammed door, 'I'll remember that and haunt you in your bed!' Then he turned to Sister. 'Come here!'

Sister advanced to the table.

'What have you and Unga January been doing? Tell your father. I saw her going up the road this evening with beet-juice on her cheeks.'

'I only met a boy and talked.'

'You only. You only.'

'Now, Pa, you're getting excited again.'

'You'll kill me, you two. The son is a loafer and the daughter is loose. A loose woman. I promised Mama I'd watch over you, and I owe it to God. Come.'

They circled the table in a kind of dance. Tony's pallid noble face was calm. He took hold of her wrists and she screamed harshly. Twisting her arm, he dragged her to a chair by the fire and examined her there.

Upstairs in her room Sister sewed on her Communion dress. She sat bowed over the snowy heap of lace and lawn until her fingers grew cold.

Tony decided to remove his shoes for bed tonight. He knelt devoutly by the driftwood fire and prayed for his wife's poor soul in purgatory, carefully lifting the air into his ruined lungs and expelling it in brittle Slavonian whispers to God. He was weak from the exertion, cold, trembling, panting. He was always cold. He hated to remove his hat and coat for bed. Without his wife he was lonely and afraid. The wind outside buffeted the trees, groaned and strained against the house like a dark avenger ...

In her bed Sister basked in the soft heat of the feather mattress saying her rosary, thinking of the tall stranger on the lugger, who somehow amused her. She heard thunder in the Gulf, a gentle neighborly sound in bed. It came like something thickly padded, like bales of oakum dropping. Or it was like the distant collapse of heavy walls. When the Cross reached her fingers, she balled the beads in her hand. The house trembled as if a giant hand were pushing it.

Sister smiled secretly in the dark. She closed her eyes and imagined she was lovely.

2

THE gray wind gathered force. The blurred sky was powdered with struggling fowl. It was fine goose weather. The men of Grass Margin abandoned their beds to make a last good kill for pickling in barrels before the geese went north. The women, left alone all day, talked on the levee, or shouted to one another across the twinkling patches of truck. Gray days in the Delta were rare and bracing. Between the seething orange trees the clotheslines flapped excitedly, and the chimneys uttered frantic smoke. Some old women (coarse, jolly temple-tenders) went with brickdust and soap to scrub the church for the First Communion.

Sister Kalavich went up the levee in the dark of morning. The nuns from New Orleans were holding the white children's Retreat in a vacant shrimp cannery four miles from her home. She stopped at daybreak at the Chauvin landing and hid the lugger man's coat in a log, then continued up to the store and sold the quart of honey she was carrying.

All day the children prayed and sang and listened to stories the nuns told of the life of Christ. The old nun in charge of the girls, while she related the story of Christ's death, looked steadily at Sister. Sister was the largest in the class and her face fascinated the nun, appearing at once wanton and saintly. Usually, when Sister Agnes instructed her, the young girl seemed totally unimpressed ... listening attentively, but only out of a sense of respect. Today, during the story a thrilling current of awareness flowed between the nun and the pupil. Sister was fascinated by the pale, wrinkled face nestling in the great white fluted bonnet, the thin dry lips shaping the phrases of the tale. The nun's tongue, too, sounded dry and bloodless.

Suddenly Sister despised the nun.

The other somehow perceived this at once. And her words, uttered in a bitten prophetic tone, full of malicious implication, bore a strange vindictiveness that seemed meant for Sister alone:

'... and a foul burly *soldier* stepped from the crowd. And he had a long sharp spear, the kind they used for slaying ferocious *boars*. And he looked up at his *God*, the great God of heaven and earth, bruised, beaten, *torn* by the nails. And he put the spear to our Savior's side. Then he drew back his burly shoulders and *leaned* on it, until it slipped between the ribs and deep, deep into that sacred flesh ...'

Sister shuddered, her eyes wild with terror. And she refused to hate the soldiers on Calvary.

The air in the building was musty with the smell of forgotten labors. Upon her dismissal Sister eagerly sought the sweet levee air, thinking Unga January might be waiting. She stopped at the store, where a group of black-booted trappers awaited the fur-buyer from New Orleans. With the coins received for the honey she bought a pair of stockings and a ready-made bow of yellow for her hair.

The levee wind was provocatively bold. Down the long empty road, Sister kept thinking of the nun's parched face, and she thought of her father sick abed at home.

And Jesus crucified had cried out to his Father on such an evening.

The western sky — garishly illumined by colossal streaks of orange and green, incredibly bright and yet casting only pale spectral shadows — was silent as the voice of God. Sister felt alone, alone on a vast darkening sphere whose shaggy surface was raveled by demoniac winds. And ahead was her home, containing no central glow, no abiding kernel of warmth. Gripped by a sudden twilight-fear, she began to run. Her flesh vibrated to the sudden blare of a nearby bull. Freshened by some secret store of energy, she sped fast and farther; and when her destination drew near she was wild-eyed and spent, tingling with joy and defiance.

She found the coat in the log and went to return it to the stranger on the lugger.

The man was waiting. He had turned the lamp low because of a shortage of kerosene, he said. He had a mess of boiled crabs, cooked as the peddler had instructed, with bay leaf, thyme, onions, lemon, and little red peppers. In the dim light Sister was shy. She sat, not next to him but at the farthest end of the table. The man, too, was self-conscious. Bruce's arms were stiff now. He was in great pain.

'A crab's got thorns exactly like a rose,' he said. 'That's for protection, same as the rose. Your fingernails are your thorns. And your teeth too. I lay you could use them well.'

'I suppose you know all about the river up north,' she said.

'Nobody knows all. Some that get their bread from it don't know ne'er thing. A long and a fearful and a headstrong river, this Mis'sippi.'

'Think of the States it crosses!'

'A whole passel o' States, takin' its time, dividin' some strange breeds of men, older than anybody can recollect in the books or hearsay, swingin' to east or west ever' now and then to catch the drainin's well.'

'We don't feel American. I don't.'

'There's others don't, plenty others in hidden places like here.'

'How does the river look up north?'

'Different. Accordin' to the lay of the land. I've been by Des Moines in Ioway and past Saint Paul, the Twin Cities on this-here stream, most to Canada, same route as the first Frinchmen, the Catholics, and that's a wonderful thing to see, not because it's me. This river's made bread for many and many a man through the pages of history, and gnawed off many a proud town when it taken the notion. . . . Tribes of paddlin' savages! God Almighty! Ten-acre rafts of timber usin' up a whole green spring floatin' south, I was readin'. Boats with music in them glidin' down from the iron country — before the railroads, that was. That-there's all gone, and I wish it wasn't.'

Sister thought: 'Grampaw said they've got to be tall up there to see over the mountains. This man has tang. He aims to hit New Orleans. He *aims* for places and things. His eyes are like a woman's, sad about the past.'

Bruce said: 'I've been by the wheat country, past the coal, tobacco, and the timber States on this river. And the Missouri, this one's right bower but a sight different — never no tall waves like here . . . And now I'm down to the Gulf I used to dream about when I was drivin' home the cow. But I can't get my bearin's nor hardly point north in the night. So much clouds and distance! The distance eats your voice. And I can't understand the people talk. This is a lazy man's country, with a great deal of bogginess to be redeemed, I judge. The people walk lazy. I've watched them in their land. God gave 'em the richest land on earth, I was readin'. Looks like they're waitin' for God to plow it. *You're* the only — the first one I've met, the first ——'

Something lay behind his soft words and his large slow kindness that she could not identify. First, she could see nothing in herself worthy of flattery. He wanted something. And his tenderness was almost womanish. Sister was accustomed to masculine advances, but these had always been

playful, sportive, never proffered with such soft earnestness.
This man watched her out of soft placid dog-like eyes. It made
her sorry for him, and at the same time sorry for herself,
aware of all her premature woes and yearnings.

Suddenly she laughed aloud. The meal was finished. She
ran to the companionway. The man stood bewildered, his
large eyes wide in the dimness.

'Listen!' she whispered, standing with the stars at her back,
rolling her eyes from side to side. 'A screech owl!'

The big man obediently cocked his head and followed the
sound far outside with his great shining eyes. Sister uttered
a peal of laughter.

'You look like an owl yourself!' she giggled, 'good-night!'
and was gone. Far down the levee the wind brought her his
faint call: 'Come back tomorrow!'

Sister relieved Mocco at her father's bedside, sitting at the
fire to finish her Communion clothes. Tony Kalavich had had
another hemorrhage. Mocco had sent for the Army doctor
at the forts, who was unable to come. A physician at Quarantine Station down the river had sent some pills which had
thrown Tony into light sleep. Around his face there seemed
to hover a soft pale glow. Now Mocco went to his room to
rest until midnight. The wind outside nudged the panes.

Later there came a secretive tapping at the window, and a
face. Sister motioned Unga January to enter. Unga tiptoed
in. She carried a small oil-can, and wore white stockings
all flecked with blood where she had slapped mosquitoes.
She stopped suddenly in the middle of the room like a cautious
deer, lifting her white, finely moulded face and swinging her
nostrils about.

'Sacré nom!' she whispered. 'What smell lak dat?'

'Medicine,' said Sister. 'Lung drops.'

'Non!'

'I don't smell anything.' Sister peered under the bed. . . . Mocco had forgotten to dispose of the basin of hemorrhage blood.

The girls spoke in whispers. Unga had brought two large pickles from the store. Sister bit into hers with a delicious shiver as her saliva began to flow. Unga was morose, concerned over Sister's tale of the man on the boat. Once she put her hand over Sister's needle.

'Ef you go back to dat boat again — ef you ——'

'I'm going tomorrow.'

'Dawn let him touch you, cher! Thank the Virgin his hands is cripple! Did he play off lak single, or married? Where his home is at, dat North fellow, hein?'

'In the mountains — big high bumps of rock. People live on them, and trees, in the north.'

'I seen rocks already. They got rocks down on the jetties. Be caffle, cher. Be caffle from dat North fellow.'

'Careful of what, silly?'

'Get yourself knocked up and so forth. You too pretty for a tramp man, Jolie!'

'Sh-h-h!'

'They gone run me away, blame it on me, you get seduced. Yo' paw run me off de Margin, you get in trouble. You wants um to run me away?'

'Unga, I think he's going to die this time. He sang a hymn this morning in Tocko language.'

'Oui, po' fellow, he done suffered . . . Jolie, you sho' gone look pretty than everybody for Communion, you. Listen, cher, you gone mind out wid dat lugger man? Christ heppus! Me I'm glad his hands is cripple, but I'm gone be worried, me, till dat mast-pole go 'way from Chauvin's landing.'

Tony Kalavich stirred and sighed deeply. Quickly Unga melted behind the curtain with her oil-can.

'Mocco!' Tony called weakly.

'Yes, sir. This is me, Sister.'

'What time is it?'

'The pilot boat just passed, father of mine,' she replied in Slavonian.

'I'm going to die tonight. Is Claiborne in the stable and fed?'

'Yes, sir.'

'Good-night, Mocco.'

'Good-night, Father.'

Unga reached the door in a quick fluid bound. She placed her hand to her cheek, briefly raised her dark eyes in anguish, and disappeared. Sister smoothed her father's blanket, then took the basin of blood to the river. Its contents slid away in the dark smoothly, and struck the water with a dull slap. Sister spat in disgust, but her heart was heavy, because it was her father's blood.

The last day of the Retreat was quiet and balmy, and in the night the waters were dappled green with starlight. Tony Kalavich was improved, constantly craving nourishment. Many returned marsh trappers in the saloon far back by the rear canal made a great noise, but the levee was deserted, the people housecleaning and weeding their roses in preparation for Communion Day. Sister made her confession in church with the other children.

In a rear pew she sat alone with her sins, awaiting her turn, hearing the tipsy trappers singing and shouting afar; and these voices blent in her mind with her tense, abased, almost audible contrition. To recall her sins in the confessional, she used her fingers, each finger representing a grievous offense. Her thumb was for the water she had often wasted when the cistern at home was almost dry.

'I am guilty of hating my father,' she told the priest.

'Honor thy father and mother.'

'He does not honor me, and —'

'Enough! Your own sins, please. You are now committing the sin of pride. What else?'

'I took olives from the store.'

'A venial sin. These grow into mortal ones. Repay the store-keeper for what you took. What else?'

'I coveted a girl's dress and hat. I had bad thoughts. In church.'

'What!'

'In church. A boy —'

'Ah! The biggest sin you fished out so far!' Father Sam smacked his lips. 'A sacrilege! The first I got today. Don't worry about it. I will take it from your soul.'

'Thanks. I am guilty of dirty things four times.'

'Things?'

'Actions.'

'A mortal sin. Hate this sin instead of your father. Was it with the same boy?'

'Two different ones.'

'Dreadful! In thought or deed?'

'Deed.'

'A fine ticket! They touched you, eh? Why didn't you stop them?'

'I don't know.'

'Watch the hands of men. Why can't you girls *ever* learn that! Honest hands are often weak and vile. Hate it — the sin and not the boys. Guard the sanctity of your body, the wonderful house God gave you to live in. Remember that — the *sanctity* of your body.'

Laboriously Sister approached her most grievous sin, the one she saved for last, on the left little finger.

'I think I committed another sacrilege, Father. I called one of the nuns a — name in my mind.'

'One of the nuns!'

'Sister Agnes, Father. I called her...'

'Well?'

'A son-of-a-bitch.'

Father Sam blew his nose violently. He lectured Sister about the nuns who had given up all pleasures to serve humanity, and imposed a penance of ten Ave Marias.

Now Sister on the road skipped and whirled joyfully. She felt glad of the dusty earth and its vigorous growths and stirring waters. From the row of pointed shacks along the way, there came curious tokens, friendly signs of mankind dwelling peacefully under the skies — a lullaby hummed in time with the croaking of a porch rocker; farther on, a sudden smell of new leather; then a crippled man carrying a smoky lantern through his yard, slapping the ground vigorously with his lame foot; and from far ahead the drowsy clement bleating of a goat. Sister sped down the levee to see her friend on the lugger, and together they made a good supper, roasting two fat marsh hens with new potatoes.

Bruce was leaving next morning. He told her he disliked the idea of departing, and in various indirect ways tried to learn how she felt about his going. She did not know what to say. Bruce was still a very large stranger, invested with a glow of unreality, cast into her life by a strange river. (There was about him no challenge — only this heavy, agreeable yet embarrassing semblance of dog-like devotion — the soft gravity of his gaze, softly persistent and knowing, as if capable of and bent upon searching out the very quivering fibers of her compassion.) She would not think of his going. She wanted tonight to keep the exalted mood of the confessional, as a preliminary of her first taste of the body and blood of the Divine Victim, for which she still felt somewhat unworthy.

Bruce asked questions about her people. He called them ancestors.

Sister looked at him, aroused. The word 'ancestors' sounded honorable, deeply significant, vaguely associated with the girl's present ritualistic mood.

But it yielded no coherent impressions. Searching her mind, she found little of interest to tell the man. Her mother's people had been Acadians, driven to Louisiana from Nova Scotia by the British long ago. Cajins, they were called. Her father's people were Dalmatians — 'Tockos.' Her father was a dying man. Before her mother's death he had been sober and industrious. Now he was a drunkard.

Bruce sat admiring the tanned and pensive oval of Sister's face. Her eyes, dark as coffee, were usually lit by quaint heats and joys. Now they gazed calmly at the deck, searching for something to remember about her ancestors, realizing that some day she, herself, would become an ancestor. Bruce folded his arms, on which the bruises had turned black and yellow, and leaned back.

'You ain't got much of a future here,' he said thoughtfully.

'How do you mean — future?' she asked, sobered by the heavy seriousness of this statement.

Bruce gave her his slow grin and said: 'I mean, do you aim to live here and die in this far place, if it's a fair thing to ask? Most folks dream of escaping that's prisoned.'

'I don't aim for things. I ——' She wanted to say she groped for things, but she did not have that word. And discussing herself and her secret needs was a new and an awkward thing. Prisoned! Was she prisoned here, where a person might run or paddle until he dropped of hunger? Was she prisoned who had just been freed from sin and sorrow?

'But you know for certain you'd rather travel,' said Bruce.

'Yes, sir. It's a way of thinking. I never traveled north of Lacroix.'

'You ain't contented here. Your kinfolks are nice people enough, I lay, but it looks like they don't appreciate you.

They sure wouldn't let you jeopard your health if they did. They'd send you a cape on a nasty night.'

He walked to the companionway and faced the mirthful waves. Now Sister was losing the exalted mood of the confessional, and against her will she was thinking with Bruce, of herself, her lonely lot — prisoned.

He turned. 'Why couldn't you come travel with me?' he asked in a bantering tone but with a kindling hope in his eyes. 'You're sort of like me anyhow. Wouldn't it fun you — shummickin' around the rivers?'

'Well ——'

'But I suppose you've got a beau,' the man said quietly. Sister turned her head away.

The food in the pot was scorching. They both hurried to rescue it. Bruce fetched another pot, and transferred the food. Sister put water into the burned pot. They worked mechanically, as if his proposal had not been uttered, though the daring words still gripped their two minds. Afterwards he sat on a bench caressing his bruises. The turpentine odor of him filled the place. Sister felt weak in the limbs, and there was something in her throat, beating. She wanted to cry, but the heaviness in her limbs was pleasant. She would have liked to sink with her sinless soul into some waiting chasm of forgetfulness, without knowing what was to be forgotten. But there was this other throbbing of the living blood, the lonely blood, impelling her to yearn, not so much toward her companion as toward something he represented, some latent need his words had made urgent and vocal.

Eating the meal in silence, they felt the man's audacious words still about them. Bruce had sunk into a bewildered silence, fumbling with his food with slow disabled hands. He could not manage his knife.

Sister washed the dishes while the man toyed with her prayer book. She was afraid to suggest leaving: he might detain her with his fatal gaze. Once while drying a pan she heard him cross the cabin and stand behind her, close enough for his warmth to flow.

'You're pretty as a picture,' he murmured near her hair. It held her again, the vibration of his voice in her hair, and the desire to relax rushed over her.

He said: 'Why have you got to leave me and I'll be livin' a sad, sad life without you? Who is it — what is it, that says you can't travel with me like you want to, as my wife, away from this country of lazy waters and lazy people?'

'Behave yourself, silly!' Her voice could achieve no more than a quavering half-whisper.

'What is it sent you here in the night — that night?'

'Behave, damn it!'

'Washing my dishes like a thing in a dream!'

'Mr. Bruce!'

'Like a made-up thing and if I touched you it would melt away! Who are you? What are you? A proud bog-flower bloomin' amongst the unredeemed?'

She swung, facing him with her child's eyes — at bay, yet wanting to read his face. There was a scream inside her, ready. It would have brought out the occupants of the Chauvin dwelling. She did not vent it. The man could not grasp her in his arms. They hung now at his sides bruised and helpless; and his great heavy helplessness went like a dirk to a strange new part of her heart. She pushed at his chest, not wanting to hurt his arms. His breast seemed padded with folds of hot stone.

'They don't appreciate you,' he said. Her hand lay on his chest with no force exerted now. He took her into his discolored arms, wincing, turning angry with pain, grunting an oath. Sister hung annihilated among his bruises, as though swung high among the branches of some storm-tossed tree. 'Have you got a beau?' he asked.

'Mr. Bruce!'

'Have you?'

'Yes, sir.'

He held her close and they swayed with the boat, both seemingly suspended in space, rocking.

'Do you love him, or like him?'

'Yes, sir.'

'What? You love him?'

'Yes,' she answered, responding to his kiss.

'You're all bruised up too,' he said to her on the couch. 'Who beat you there?'

'My father.'

'What for, he beats you?'

'Talking to soldiers from the forts. Wasting cistern water.'

When she left the boat she found herself still clutching the damp dishcloth. Her neck and shoulders smarted from contact with turpentine. Gaining the levee she heard Bruce's call: 'Come back! Come go with me in the morning!'

With the eagerness of a cunning plunderer she sped home. The stars lay fixed and watchful in the river where they had fallen.

3

THE Chinee runners had smuggled in from a Honduran
vessel in the Gulf eight scared Chinamen. These were delivered
to the New Orleans schooner waiting at Dutch Scenery. The
smugglers stayed in Dutch Scenery to get drunk and dance
with the mulatto girls — all except Mitch Holt. Mitch paddled
across the dawn to Grass Margin. At his father's palmetto
shack on the bank, he dragged his pirogue high up where
steamer waves would not bother it, and tied it to a young
cypress. He bounded lithely up the long stairs from the
wharf, singing loudly.

'Wake up the dead!' grumbled his sleepy father, who was
cooking eels at the stove. 'How many Chinks you bring in?'

'Eight,' answered Mitch, hanging his pistol on a nail.

'Eight times fifty's four hundred.'

'We'll get fifteen next trip from Martinique.'

Mitch stripped and ran down to take a bath. The father
resented Mitch's audacity in earning big money. He put
on his denim jumper and blew out the light, burning in a
glass of grease from a tallow tree behind the shack. 'Eight
times fifty. Four hundred dollars. I skull-drag two weeks
for that kind of money, pullin' a pirogue through the stinkin'
marsh. I guess he diced it away already.'

Mitch rubbed his body all over with river mud. The texture of the sand was like that of creamy fudge. Its color

was soft reddish yellow, smooth, presenting in sunlight a fine tawny sheen. Rubbed on the skin, it was bland as salve, and more effective than soap for bathing, imparting to the skin much of its own rosy silken glow.

Coated with mud, polished like metal, Mitch climbed an old piling that leaned high out over the water. Thus perched, he raised his hands toward the opposite shore, where the marsh had just disgorged a plump misshapen sun. He yelled into the glorious burning void and waited for the echo, then dived.

His father glimpsed through the window the toughly moulded young body poised like a bronze statue, and chuckled deeply. Then the old man, who was lonely and impotent, thought of women — dark women melting into river cabin doorways with a backward glance; plump rosy orange pickers laughing down out of reddened trees; ripe-breasted figures humming on wharves in the dusk, waiting for his son ...

'I guess you diced it away already, the money,' he said to Mitch at breakfast. 'Most of it, anyhow. I saw a Government cutter going down Wednesday, looking over here with the glasses, like they were looking for you. You talk too much, Mitchell. They always look over here lately.'

'Let them look!' Mitch smiled cocksurely. 'We saw 'em outside, but they didn't see us. We kept circling South-South Mud-lump. Here! Get you a shave, o' man, I'm ashamed of you. You're not in the marsh hunting minks.'

The father took the ten-dollar bill. 'I'll get barbered when I'm damn gooden ready,' he said.

'Drink it up, then.'

Mitch left the table and picked up a large otter skin from a corner.

'Put it back,' said his father.

Mitch went to the window and shook the skin in the light of the risen sun. He blew circles of breath into it. The fur gave off soft waves of red flame. The same sort of fire kindled Mitch's eyes. He pictured Sister Kalavich smiling in the fur.

'You leave it where you found it,' complained the old man. 'I'm afraid I've got to buy it for my baby's cape.'

'Which baby? You better keep away from Sister. She's joining church today, I heard.'

'Sure!' exclaimed Mitch, waving the fur and dancing about until the shack trembled. 'I'm going to see her make her First Communion or something. I never saw how they make that stuff. How do I look, o' man?' Mitch passed his hands over the fine serge that covered his muscular breast.

'My God! How does he look, he asks. How do you always look? Like a Lafourche Cajin on All Saints' Day, with your Roebuck suit.'

Mitch grinned and winked at his father. He was blondly neat and happy and handsome, pleasingly shaped out of much activity and indolence — and he knew it. The one man on the lower river who was exciting to all women, in a bold, ironic way. Sister Kalavich was known on every beach and bayou as the girl who could marry Mitch Holt.

On the levee road, Mitch plucked a late orange from an overhanging branch, a single remaining fruit which no one had taken because it was too high to reach. At the church Mitch heard a subdued dice game in the canebrakes behind the building. He pushed through the crowd waiting before the church and joined the circle of unshaven trappers at dice. He stood undecided. He had resolved to tell Sister today that he was finished with gambling. He stood sucking the orange through a hole. He picked the cockleburrs from his newly pressed trousers. Then he knelt and joined the game, blowing on the dice and pouring them over the sand with a grunt. The trappers after their big season had lots of money, so Mitch lost a hundred dollars. Then he went whistling to the levee and joined the crowd waiting for the Communion procession. He spoke to some friends about his last trip in the Gulf. A ragged barefooted stranger standing nearby edged closer to Mitch and began examining the church steeple, then sauntered off casually.

'Who is that?' Mitch asked.

'A new swimp trawler,' someone explained. 'He say he come from Biloxi to trawl swimp, him. He lives 'cross duh river on his boat.'

'He look lak Government man,' someone else said.

'Oui, he mind his business too much for me.'

'Did he hear me say anything?' Mitch asked.

'You call duh name of duh mud lump where your boat hide.'

'Me, I'm gone watch dat fellow,' said another.

'You better be caffle how you talk, yes,' the first man warned.

'Hell with 'em,' said Mitch indifferently.

Mocco dripped the coffee. Tony Kalavich lay at the window with his slack wasted face propped up to see the procession of singing Communion girls marching by on the levee. He smiled at old Sister Agnes hobbling ahead, throwing clamshells at the stray dogs and kicking the fiddler crabs from the road. Tony was glad to have lived through the slow night. Death would hardly come for him during the day. The swollen river was pale blue. The front yard was white with wet fragrant Easter lilies, at least a dozen huge blooms on each tall stalk, which Sister had covered during the cold spell. He would get well once more, maybe, and take good care of himself. The virgin morning, the drenched orange trees, glittered with hope and pain. A cold bright tear slid down the point of Tony's jaw, and hung quivering.

'There she is!' he called to Mocco weakly. 'Come see your sister. Lagging behind the others, dreaming, I suppose.

She'll be another Durot, the image of your Aunt Girlie. You'd think it was her funeral.'

'She's the biggest,' said Mocco in English. 'That's why they put her last. You come to her gradually, and she don't look so big.'

To Sister the day was a painted dream. The impact of the crystalline morning had not awakened her fully. She went softly, with the tender tread of a sleepwalker, inwardly smiling her soft cunning smile. Ahead of her the sun made a winding white nebula of the mistily veiled girls, all carrying their tall candles that gleamed like sabres of ivory; and their timid chanting was lost in the great glassy calm of morning. Sister Agnes reached out and pulled Sister's sleeve. 'Sing!' she whispered.

Sister sang with the others the tender unreal words of the hymn, which she seemed to know without ever having heard before. They were at the Chauvin landing.

In the mass of hyacinth bulbs in the water an oval clearing gaped, where Bruce's boat had lately lain. Sister lingered a moment with dilated eyes, then turned and walked away with the others.

'Sing!' the nun whispered.

There was now a great crowd before the church, and at the landing scores of varicolored boats and pirogues. The people were of all shades of black, brown, yellow, cream, and white. Many of the mulattoes had copper-colored skins, reddish hair, light spectral eyes.

The crowd opened in halves like gates before the procession, and closed behind its passage. On either side, dark warm eyes watched Sister Kalavich, her dragging footsteps and cold hard young face. Most of the whites present were relatives of hers on the Durot side. The blacks laughed in the morning, and wore their brightly hued clothing like proud gay plumage . . .

Among the silent faces radiant with festive devotion, Sister was frightened. She felt like scampering home. The church was like a huge trap, baited with the Host. It waited filled with the thick cold smell of flowers, deeply soundless after the filling of the pews, save for the occasional pious clearing of a throat. Among the densely banked roses on the altar the candles with their hot gold buds grew tall and stern. The organ breathed an ancient tune.

When the ranks formed for the visit to the Communion rail, Sister Kalavich remained in her pew with eyes downcast, picking at the mother-of-pearl cover of her book. She was nauseated. The rank of girls stood near her in the aisle. Sister Agnes hobbled to the pew, entered, and sat with Sister.

'I can't receive Communion,' Sister said.

'Why? Did you eat after midnight? Are you sick? Look at me, child.'

'I made a sin last night.'

'Why didn't you confess it this morning?'

'I am not sorry for it, Sister Agnes.'

'*What?*' The nun stared incredulously. She made a dry noise in her throat. The little girls in the aisle knelt with veiled backs curved, listening. Their mothers would question them about this.

'This is your First Communion day, you little...' The nun made the dry noise again. 'Say an Act of Contrition quick. God will forgive if you realize you offended Him. Come!'

Sister allowed herself to be urged from the pew. The girls all looked at her with childish flower-like faces lifted. The congregation craned its neck to see.

'Go on!' said the nun. 'Say your Act. Be sorry for your little sin. God will forgive.'

Sister could not be sorry. The sin had been too strange and delightful. She was not sorry. She wanted to get away. Her stomach sickness was rising to her throat. When the rank advanced toward the altar, she stood alone a moment, then turned and walked in the opposite direction, toward the door. Halfway out of church she felt herself stumble into soft black oblivion.

Mocco had been watching. He sprang from his pew and lifted her. Mitch Holt was hurrying from the rear. 'Give her here!' he called to Mocco. 'Come on, Bud.' Mocco looked at Mitch dazedly. 'Give her!' said Mitch. He took hold of Sister in his arms and walked away. Mocco returned to his pew, darkly flushed and pouting. Sister, borne from the church, opened her eyes. 'Fix my dress,' she murmured. 'My legs ——'

'Your legs are grand,' Mitch said. The dark faces swimming past stared with wide shocked eyes.

Mitch carried her over the levee to the river's fringe. He set her down where the briers and willows formed a verdant tent. He did not ask questions. His face was tender and satanic, making Sister feel unimportant and very desirable.

'Mitch, I'm bad,' she murmured. Mitch dipped some river water in his new hat and Sister drank.

'Sure you're bad,' he said. He removed her wreath and veil. 'I ought to willow-switch your behind, studying catechism a year and not letting me touch you above the elbow, and now you're not worthy.' His gay young laughter routed three touseled buntings from the leaves. Sister gazed past him at an early lizard mounting the blurred boughs and leaning out between leaps to smile down at them.

'I'm not worthy of Communion,' she said.

'But you're worthy of me.'

Mitch fished out a roll of bills from his pocket. 'Go give this to Father Sam. He'll let you take Communion. We got eight Chinamen. Let the priest send this to the Chinese Mission, and marry us.'

'Mister Smart Aleck!'

'Your legs are grand. Let's marry. Then I'll behave.'

'Maybe when you stop making fun of God.'

'Make Him quit making fun of me. Listen — you'll be proud to live with me now. The Federal Government's watching me.'

'I don't feel like being proud today.'

'Will you marry me?'

'Maybe if you keep away from women for a year.'

'You'll have to talk to them about that.'

'Such conceit! And you think I want to be another one of your women?'

'You're my *good* girl, for the home and family. What's the matter?'

'Nothing. Let me go before they come out of church.'

'Communion girl! Communion girl!' shouted some little children as Sister walked up the levee alone. 'Let's go touch her veil!'

The sunny river lay barely a yard from the levee's crown. A clouded donkey eyed Sister from the weeds, and turned to flee her veiled approach. She laughed aloud. The trees were full of clamorous indigo buntings. Sister turned to look at the church rising sharp as a thorn behind her. She could see the brown crowd pressing out. She walked faster. She was happy. She had been saved from a sinful First Communion. None of the other communicants was as happy as she! Bruce had given her a river, its slow bigness flowing from far North, swinging to east or west every now and then to catch the drainings well.... She hurried home with this secret. Before entering the house, behind the cistern she dried her eyes on her petticoat, which was her Communion present from a neighbor. According to the custom, everything she wore or carried this day had been given by a relative or friend, for good luck.

She went into the house humming casually. The constant

surveillance of her father had taught Sister a certain ability to dissimulate. When he questioned her about her Communion she had ready a calm lie.

In the night Sister went to a cousin's Communion party down the road. She and Mocco rode the mule, Claiborne, because Mocco's pirogue had needed caulking for some months. There was plenty of wine and whiskey at the party and the men were all tipsy, singing, wrestling, and playing pillow-kisses with the women. Some trappers were having a knife-throwing contest for large stakes. The whole house smelled of boiled crawfish, and one's nostrils smarted from the stinging fumes of red pepper. Jean Prieur, an old toothless Cajin alligator hunter, sang a Creole ballad of fifty stanzas. Hearing this old song of bayou love and intrigue, Sister grew conscious of her Acadian blood, her mother's dark passionate people.

Mitch Holt went about with a king snake up his sleeve, frightening the girls. He and Mocco had been over the river earlier in the day, and had shot a wild hog, which was now being roasted by the levee. Sister did not enjoy the affair. She danced only twice, with Mitch Holt, then retired into a corner to watch the goings-on, drinking very little wine and speaking to no one. None of the women asked her why she had not taken Communion. This was very strange. As usual, none of the men teased her or rubbed their whiskers on her face. For this she did not know whether to feel honored or slighted.

She left the party early, taking the mule. Unga January was outside in an orange tree, peering in at the dancing. She went a short distance up the road with Sister, swinging her half-gallon oil-can. Sister told Unga everything that had happened the previous night on the lugger.

'I knowed it!' Unga said. 'I could tell by yo' face in church. And you was the pretties' one in duh church. Now I guess you gone have a baby for dat man.'

'We were only together one night,' said Sister.

'What's duh different? You can get baby lak dat, you. Animals does it. And look Inez wid a baby, and her husband was snake-bit nex' day of duh weddin', fo' God sake! Me, I'm glad he's gone, dat North fellow. An' his hands was cripple! Father Sam all duh time say watch out for duh hands, hein? But you pray lak hell for it not to be a baby, cher, Saint Theresa and Saint Boniface. And pray to plain God, you, and me I'm gone find out from Aunt Little Popo what's duh saint for bad girls, ef dey got a saint for dat. Mussy-ful God heppus! Dawn tell a soul, 'specially duh womans. Duh good married womans gone backbite you off duh levee from Homeplace to clear out Pass à la Outre. Look, dat mule-back gone mess up yo' pretty drawers, cher.'

'He's clean. I washed him in the river.'

'Yo' paw hear 'bout dis, he gone run me off duh Margin, Jolie. But everybody mus' know you done badness and couldn't receive Communion. Dey thinks it was wid Mitch Holt you commit dat. Again dey seen him carry you out duh church.'

'How do they know what to think, silly?'

'Duh womans knows what to think. What you tole yo' paw duh matter with you was?'

'I told him I forgot and drank water after midnight.'

'All duh time duh right answer you got, you. But pray, cherie, you ought to be prayin' right now for no baby, you.'

Sister went up the road, keeping the mule in pace with a slow, gently breathing steamer ploughing upstream. She did not pray. She could not believe she might have a baby, because she was not married.

Unga kept in touch with Sister. Every day while Tony Kalavich was in his afternoon nap, she sneaked through the orange trees to talk. Or she would wade through the dismal cypress marsh in the rear while Sister worked in the field, in the morning, making a circuit of a mile to avoid being glimpsed by Tony. Here the huge buttressed cypresses were draped with long gray drippings of Spanish moss. The brown water was mottled with patches of bright green slime floating about with imperceptible slowness, resolving itself into slow, curious, ever-changing patterns. And there was a silence so deep that the tick of a worm or the swish of feathers overhead sounded inordinately loud. Unga would move in cold terror, stepping gingerly and expecting at each step to meet the Congo — the cottonmouthed moccasin. . . . She wanted to find out if Sister were pregnant. Unga's head was filled with stubborn forebodings. Her color was no darker than a faded magnolia's. She and Sister were the only attractive girls in Grass Margin. Between them, the usual hidden current of primitive animosity had not yet reached the point of awareness. Unga's devotion to Sister was warm but physically distant. She seldom embraced Sister or fondled her as other girls were inclined to do. Sister unconsciously appreciated this absence of familiarity.

One day Sister was patching a cast-net by the river. Unga paddled up to her, left the pirogue with her oil-can, and sat beside Sister. (The woman for whom Unga worked, in order to prevent the neighbors from discovering she was a tippler, would send to the store for whiskey in the oil-can.)

'Il est bon heur,' said Unga.

'Hi, Unga.'

'How you feel?'

'Fine. Why?'

'I dreamed you was carryin' a parasol. Dat means trouble.'

They sat in complete silence for a long time. Unga January was angry. A store loafer at Jule's had just insulted her. He had slyly offered her a banana. In Grass Margin it was a vulgar prank, offering a girl a banana.

Sister preferred to be alone. She was depressed. Tony had been drinking, and Mocco had been compelled to tie him in bed. The river stupidly laved the gray driftwood with milky ripples gurgling like cream. It was ridiculous, such tiny waves from so great a stream.

Sister spat impulsively in the river, leaning over to watch the foaming dab of spittle dance away among the hyacinths. The day was cruel with silent light, and the futile dull quarreling of gulls. Unga beside her had a grave young face, already somewhat startled by the impact of two strong races clashing. Unga should have been happy, with no fixed home, no responsibility. Yet she was seldom happy. Her favorite occupation was making artificial flowers for sale on All Saints' Day. She loved to sit in the dim room, smelling the wax boiling, and thinking about troubles. Her folks lived far down the river. Her mother was a jovial kindly yellow woman with well-mannered daughters of all colors by various jovial men. Unga, the daughter of a soldier from Fort St. Philip whose enlistment had expired before Unga was born, was an itinerant domestic. She earned her keep and clothes helping white women incapacitated by childbirth. She had seen much suffering. With men she was viciously chaste. She did not cultivate the paradoxical virtues of seductiveness and chastity as her sisters did. She never tried to appear seductive. The fingernails of her right hand, her 'rape-nails,' were kept dangerously pointed. Her assertive breasts, that seemed ready to burst with pride in life, were carried with pride only among women. Passing a group of men in the wind, Unga would draw her bosom inward, closing her throat against the insistent air. Yet since Sister's adventure with the man on the lugger, Unga had begun to think more of men and secretly to examine them, pained by their stout legs scrambling up the levee, wounded by their tough live arms flogging a mule . . .

'You felt well when you got up dis morning?' she asked Sister.

Sister did not answer. She thought, 'I believe she *wants* me to have a baby.'

Unga put her arms around Sister. Her fingers lay along the other's resilient young ribs. A sea-bound steamer opened a gash in the river, like a spear with a smoking point. A feeling of languor crept over Sister, a lassitude seemingly emanated by Unga's hot solicitous flesh, lulling Sister's mind into a half-pleasant state of sad inertia. This was what Unga loved — dreaming over heavy troubles. Sister suddenly disengaged herself.

'If it's a baby, I want you to nurse me,' said Sister in jest. She enjoyed teasing Unga, who took every statement seriously.

Unga flushed with pleasure, and snatched Sister's hand to her. Suddenly she cast the hand aside and looked away, weeping.

'Go 'way from me, you!' she sobbed. 'Go!'

Unga rose to her feet. 'You bad, bad girl!' she exclaimed, and hurried to her pirogue. Sister fell to stitching her net with a smile on her face.

That night by the fireside as Sister was dreaming over the strange shapes and colors of the driftwood flames, her father suddenly spoke to her in Slavonian, so gently that she was startled.

'Little girl, tell Father something.'

'What, Pa?'

'Are you going to make your Communion soon, our Nicolene?'

'Yes, father of mine.' She spoke in Slavonian. 'Why?'

He stroked his powerful, sensitive chin and gazed with her into the fire. His hand was long, thin, transparent, incapable longer of making a formidable fist or grasping a heavy tool. 'I want you tomorrow to paddle over with a message to Grampaw in a pirogue you can borrow from Jule. But you must not cross the river unless you are in the State of Grace. Can you not confess tomorrow morning and take your Communion?'

Sister stared at the fire with her eyes widely opened, showing a twin reflection of the play of the flames.

'I know I can paddle the river without upsetting, my father. I have done that in a full gale,' she said gently.

And Tony was even more gentle and reasonable than she. He smiled benevolently, a twinkle in his eyes. 'Why don't you wish to receive Communion now, our Nicolene? Tell Father, please.'

'Yes, I'll tell you, Father. It is because I cannot get Absolution. I am not sorry for the sin. Not yet.'

'Ah! A sin! I was afraid of that. You committed a sin the night before Communion, didn't you, our Nicolene?'

'Yes, Father.'

'It is a great pity, indeed. I have done that very thing myself. What kind of a sin was it, my daughter?'

'The sin belongs to me, Father.'

Tony reached out his shaking hands and took hold of her dress at the bosom. Weakly he shook her. 'Liar! Telling me you drank water and couldn't receive! Unrepentant liar and degenerate!'

Sister savagely clawed off the scrawny hands. 'Keep your filthy sick hands off!' she commanded. 'Don't handle me any more!' She quaked from head to foot in the throes of a strange new capacity for loathing. Tony's mouth went slack with surprise. A half-appreciative spark illumined his eyes. He found no words until Sister began to walk from the room.

'I'll find out!' he called after her. 'The truth always comes out.'

'Find out, then!' she answered defiantly. But in her bed waiting for sleep she was possessed by unutterable loneliness, because she would never be able to approach her father again.

4

ONE night Mitch Holt called on Sister. It was Monday, the night he usually came. On Sundays Mitch gambled at Dutch Scenery. When he was penniless, he always visited Sister. He had lost all his money the night before. He walked into the kitchen where Mocco was sandpapering a sawfish snout, and Sister sat dreaming over the mail-order catalogue. Mitch straddled a chair and folded his arms on its back. He was shaven, and wore a new tie. He made a great business of ignoring Sister.

Sister began to whistle, and went out into the back yard. She peered into the side window a long time, until she saw Mitch leave his seat to follow her. Then she darted to the front of the house and entered softly through the river door. Mitch looked all over the back yard for Sister and went about among the orange trees calling her name. When Mitch strolled in from the back yard some time later, Sister was quietly perusing the catalogue. Mitch winked at Mocco. His eyes moving toward Sister's back were glinting with deviltry. He tiptoed over and dangled a brightly painted silk handkerchief over her shoulder. He opened his fingers and the handkerchief floated down, covering Sister's book. The humorous green dragon on the handkerchief looked up at Sister sideways, curling its scarlet tongue and smiling waggishly. Sister loved the dragon. She smiled and brushed it away.

'Wrap your hard little heart in that,' said Mitch, 'and give it to me.'

'You've got too many hearts for your own good.'

'Throw it in the river, then.'

Sister felt the black nervous river quivering beneath the stars, with a lonely hound baying on a far shore. 'I could give it to someone else,' she said.

'Try it. Try it and see what happens,' said Mitch close to her ear, the immaculate bit of pink flesh whose glow made him want to grind his teeth. 'I'd tear him to pieces, anybody took your heart.'

A flood of pleasure laved her breast. The painted silk was soft and cruelly lustrous, smelling elusively of a long journey. A grateful Chinaman had given it to Mitch. (Mitch had intended presenting it to another girl, of whose favor he was certain, but he had forgotten to do so.) Sister tucked it into her bosom. It lay against her skin in a deliciously cold crisp wad. She would have liked to sleep in silk, to have heaps of it in gorgeous colors to shake out around her ... 'What did you say?' she asked Mitch.

'I asked you what you were thinking about.'

'China.'

'You're always thinking here lately. I come here to play and your thoughts go around to the other side of the world. Why do you want me to come see you?'

'I get tired looking at Papa and Mocco.'

She turned primly to the catalogue. Mitch sat beside her. Under the table his hand toyed with her kneecap, sliding it to and fro under the skin. She pulled the hairs of his wrist until he let go.

Mocco went toward the next room. Passing Mitch he playfully rumpled the other's combed hair. The two began to wrestle, overturning a chair and knocking down from the wall some brightly scoured pans. Sister sprang from her chair and joined the scuffle. She grasped Mitch from behind and tickled his ribs. Mitch tripped Mocco to the floor and turned to attend to Sister. The dog outside began to fume, and in the next room Tony called weakly in Slavonian. Instantly there was a deep silence, but Sister's laughter escaped through her nose. Mitch backed her into a corner and kissed her. Sister laughingly fought him, viciously pounding his stomach. She turned and opened the window, and when Mocco came to her aid they lifted Mitch and pushed him out into the dark. He was not a heavy man.

Mitch returned the following night. Sister was alone with her father. Unseen by Sister, Mitch slipped Tony a flask containing a good drink of whiskey. At the kitchen table, Sister and Mitch looked at the mail-order catalogue. When Sister came to the pictures of pretty women in underwear, Mitch attempted to hold the book open at that place. They scuffled until the page was torn. Sister turned to the household furnishings.

On the levee, Mocco was on his way inside when he found Unga waiting in the dark.

'Tell Jolie I wants to see her, me,' said Unga.

'Don't you see that horse?' he answered. 'She's got company.'

'*Merci*, I see her tomorrow. Good-night, Mocco, honey.'

Mocco stood in her path and groped for her hand. 'Listen honey, don't run off,' he pleaded. Unga crushed his hand avidly, grinding the bones together. But she backed away. Mocco sped behind her, but she swung her oil-can and it hummed past his head.

Sister and Mitch were looking at the household goods in the catalogue.

'Take your pick,' said Mitch.

'I'll take the big chair and the bookcase — full of books.'

He covered her hand with his. His hand had scars on it, some small and some large in the lamplight. The little finger, which she loved, was twisted awry by some mishap in childhood which Sister did not know about; but she knew the interesting history of each of the scars.

Mitch's voice above the tough adventurous hand came very softly: 'I'm through playing around, Nicolene. I swear to God!'

'Until the next time.'

Mitch had dealt scars to many people, in anger and in play.

'I'm through playing around. I'm through with the girls.'

'Now you want to get through with me.'

'That would rest with you. Let's take the chance. I'm ready. I'll give you a good home, first-class, everything. Don't you care for me? I wish you'd realize this is serious. Don't you care?'

'I don't know, Mitchell.'

'You don't need to know. Take my word, we'll have fun. Here you are already seventeen.'

'Too young.'

'All your friends are married that's going to be.'

'Too young. I'm different from them.'

'Something else is bothering you.'

'It's not exactly bothering me.'

'What's not?'

'A certain little thing. I'd tell you all about it.'

'What thing?'

'A certain thing. It's nothing. Mitchell, you're sweet tonight. Can't you always be that way? You're always so rough and wild. And you're lazy sometimes, too, like the others. Not lazy, but——'

'Listen, I don't care what you've got in your head against me — this certain little thing. Me lazy? Hell, I'm going outside tomorrow night again. We expect a dozen Chinks. Two-three more trips and I'll have the money for our house. Will you think it over serious? Will you let yourself love me?'

'I don't know. I'm too small. I'd be playing all the time. I think you're sweet — you can be sweet when you remember your manners.'

They made a fire in the charcoal furnace and broiled mullets. Mitch assisted with this, peeling and mincing the garlic and stirring it in the glass of olive oil. He took his turn at the broiler, turning the fish over and over until the skin was pungently scorched. In the ruby glow of the coals his face was hardened by triumph, thinking, 'If I'm not the damndest fool!'

After the meal, when they were merry with wine, Tony Kalavich commanded Sister to go to bed. Mitch took his hat and went to the door. He drew Sister out on the landing. They stood beneath the huge liquid stars. Sister listened to the silence. Mitch took her to him and fumbled for her lips. When she drew away she heard his strong teeth grinding. The bugles at the two forts far up the river were blowing keen silvery notes.

'You do want me!' Mitch whispered upon her cheek.

'I don't know.'

'Don't it feel good when I kiss you?'

'It feels good when anybody does.'

He grasped her angrily and pressed violent kisses upon her. Sister knew one defense against this — laughter. She began to giggle. Tony Kalavich was screaming at Sister inside.

'I've been too nice to you!' Mitch said. 'I'm going to make you love me. From now on, watch out!'

'Go on, you big dangerous man,' Sister laughed. 'Papa's getting excited.'

Mitch jumped from the landing into the dark. 'From now on!' he cried, and laughed loudly in the darkness.

Sister thought, 'Tomorrow he will forget everything he said.' She blew out the kitchen light. Although the night was warm, Tony hugged the fire, rubbing the harsh dry knuckles and grumbling.

'Bitch!' he said to Mocco. 'If you're interested in your sister, that's what she is. Water-wasting bitch!'

Mocco scratched his armpit. He wanted a woman tonight, any woman.

'The men handle her like a side of beef,' said Tony.

Sister gazed down at Tony with a face grave and unperturbed. She let down her rich black bright hair. 'Drink your egg and milk,' she told her father. She plunged her hands into the warm opulent mass of hair, fingering the tough scalp, dreamily prolonging the play of live silken hair among her fingers.

'Like a side of beef,' said Tony. 'When I die, don't you dare wash my bones.'

'Drink your egg and milk.'

Mocco dozed. Sister was gone to her room. Tony furtively poured his egg and milk into the slop-jar. The house uttered loud clockticks. Tony did not like being alone with Mocco. He disliked the boy because Mocco had been his mother's favorite.

He leaned over and fingered Mocco's sleeve. 'Mocco!' he whispered. 'Go and get your father a little whiskey.'

Mocco glanced up toward Sister's room. 'No,' he said. 'The doctor forbid.'

'One drink, Mocco. Get it at Jule's. Second-best sour mash. Father feels weak.'

'Where's the money?'

There was rarely any money in the house, save occasional bits of cash — a donation from Grampaw, or the sale of honey or vegetables — that appeared just in time to fill some urgent need. The proceeds of the orange crop were used for taxes and clothing.

'Come, you've got money,' said Tony. 'What of the three aigrets you killed?'

'Shh! Do you want her to hear? You'll get me put to jail with your talking some day, the way the Government's watching the people.'

'You sold those plumes to Jule! Don't say you did not. Where's that feather money?'

'Shh!' Mocco produced from his pocket a thick sheaf of long white feathers. 'Look! Does this look like I sold them?' He shook the misty plumes in the firelight and passed them across his cheek dreamily. 'I'm saving these. When I get enough I'm going to make a trip to New Orleans. I'm going to get me a job there and take up telegraph at night school. Sam Gruden took up telegraph. He's making big money.'

'Who says you are going?'

'You promised. You said when I'm twenty.'

Tony dropped his palsied hands and stared at the boy from head to foot in bewilderment. It was as though he had never before perceived that Mocco had grown larger than he.

Mocco swaggered to the mantelpiece. 'Sure I'm twenty!' he said. 'Ask Sister.'

Mocco talked in English. His accent was somewhat purer than Sister's. Tony continued watching the fresh untried youth standing very tough and physical, with his cleanly hewn features, bold expressive eyes, crop of fine black hair drooping unmanageably down his brow. And the dark pliant skin, the sound articulate members capable of leaning far backward to deal a blow, of swinging a great burden to the shoulders, of trudging tirelessly through miles of sodden marsh. Good God, was it possible?

Now Mocco would go away and leave him by the fire rubbing his hands. No respect for the old folks, these Americans with their big money. What would become of *him?* Sister, the American daughter, would want her own home when she married. Tony looked about him at the walls and furniture, at his wife smiling on the easel. He pocketed his hands and drew his knees together, shivering forlornly.

'Not for a while, I won't be leaving,' said Mocco. 'Just so you know I'm going. I've got to learn the code first, dots and dashes. That's what the job is, sending out dots and dashes all day, very important messages about death and race-horses. People send tips on the race-horses and you can read them and go play the horse. Sam won ten dollars that way. He talks over the wire to a girl in Texas he never saw, but he's got her picture.'

Tony watched Mocco speechlessly. *He* had never had the courage to leave his father. Mocco had been getting restless for the past month, because of a disappointment. All his life, Mocco had wanted to be a river pilot. At the age of ten he had known every pilot's name, every steamship company's emblem. As a small boy he had waved to the pilots on passing ships; or in high river when they passed close to shore, the pilots had thrown him pennies or comic supplements. Finally, when old enough, he had managed to secure a job as boatman for the River Pilots' Association at Pilot Town, to serve his apprenticeship in preparation for the examination. Then it was discovered that Mocco was color-blind. The discovery came about in a strange way. Mocco was helping the negro cook at pilot headquarters to clean some chickens, and once the negro said to Mocco: 'Look, son, you done bruk de gawl in dat bird. Look all over yo' hand! Dat bird's done ruint!' Mocco looked at the fluid that stained his hand. 'That's only blood,' he said. To his eyes, gall and blood were the same color. When this became known, Mocco lost his job. Since then he had been restless.

'You said yourself there's nothing here for a young man with any brains,' said Mocco.

'I don't know what will become of the place,' said Tony

fretfully. 'The orange trees need spraying right now. First your mother goes, then your grandfather, now you. That leaves two people in this big house.'

'You and Sister can go with Grampaw.'

'Weeds and vines will cover the place in a month, growing as they do in this accursed country. Weeds and vines ... This was the finest orchard in Grass Margin once. I remember ...'

'—— before you ruined your health ——'

'Yes. Before I did that.'

'—— drinking.'

'Yes, God forgive me. But you haven't worked the place as you should, Mocco, you will admit. I'm afraid you are a bit lazy.'

'I guess that's true. I just don't like hard work, Pa. It's no pleasure to me.'

The two fell into thoughtfulness. Tony once moved slightly closer to his son, as if for warmth, and simultaneously Mocco made a barely perceptible movement toward his father. The great quiet house with its loud clock-ticks hovered over them. The vague ancient shapes of the furniture gleamed about them like neutral witnesses of the squandered years. Outside, the broad earth lay pulseless in the benign darkness. And Sister, the proud virtuous one, detested because of some quality of good or evil that placed her beyond them, was asleep in her room. Tony and Mocco were drawn together in a strange haven of solace, a feeling of mutual culpability which in the bright hard glare of the next morning would become intolerable to either.

After Mocco went to bed, Tony sat pensively by the fire, sunken in abysmal melancholy. He thought of his boyhood in a little Dalmatian village, how he had helped gather grapes for the wine. And he thought of his buried wife. Lying in her grave, she was still his wife. He never thought of her in any other way. She was unable to produce meals or babies, but she was still his, in a coffin in the dark vault, turning dark, growing hard, shriveling. After all the years, the coffin would be falling apart. A big ship would pass near shore, and as its propeller vibration shook the cemetery, a metal handle would fall from the coffin.

Tony heaped driftwood on the fire until a great friendly blaze lighted the room. He read his Slavonian newspaper awhile. But his blood was torturing him for alcohol, the caustic fiend that was friend and his foe.

Taking his rubber raincoat, he went outside with a lantern. He crossed through the cold orange trees to the rear canebrake marsh. Shivering, wet to the knees, he took out his knife and cut a small canebrake. Then he returned to the packing shed, where two barrels of orange wine were fermenting. He removed the cheesecloth cover from a bunghole, and made the sign of the Cross over the hole; then on his knees he inserted the cane, took the other end between his lips and sucked out a mouthful of the wine. The stuff had been working only three weeks. Swallowing it he shuddered and retched twice, but the rank potion remained in his stomach and warmed him at once. The second drink was more palatable.

Mocco's pet otter came and snuggled into Tony's lap.

Tony got drunk in the packing shed. He slept on a folded trammel net, covered with a pirogue sail, and the otter lying against him kept him warm and alive.

5

BRUCE returned a few nights later to marry Sister.

Tony Kalavich disliked Bruce at once, because after knocking decorously and being told to come in, Bruce opened the door so timidly and stood in the open doorway so long that hundreds of mosquitoes flew in. Tony was under the lamp weaving a palmetto basket, while Sister and Mocco lay on their stomachs on the kitchen floor playing with the otter.

'Tchut door!' Tony growled at Bruce in English. 'Look mosquito comit in room. Tham bashits gun' bite us a' night. 'At you wunt?'

Bruce, all scrubbed and shaven, smiled his amiable smile. 'I'd love to see Sister. Nicolene. Air you her father, please, sir?'

'Go in kitchen.'

'I thank you, sir.'

"At you wunt for Nicolene?"

Sister stood in the kitchen door fingering her hair.

'Who is this one?' asked Tony in Slavonian, 'this hour of night.'

Sister replied in her father's tongue, 'A friend of mine. A — hunter from up the river.' She smoothed her dress and drew up a chair for the visitor, awkward and ashamed of her father.

'Didn't you come off that lugger, the *Wanderer?*' Mocco asked.

'This is my father,' said Sister, 'and my brother Mocco, Mr. Bruce.'

'I seen your lugger by Chauvin's,' said Mocco.

'I've been to New Orleans, and I just got back,' said Bruce. Tony's face was pointed at his weaving, but his eyes were fixed upon Bruce. He slapped a mosquito from his ankle and grumbled.

Sister sat looking at the fire, still overcome by surprise. Bruce and Mocco talked about the *Wanderer's* engine, then there was a constrained silence. Bruce's heavy-lidded eyes returned again and again to Sister, searching for the cause of her indifferent welcome. Sister's cheeks had dark spots in the firelight, and the corners of her mouth kept twitching upward. Bruce could not decide whether she was smiling or not.

'Could we take a little walk?' he asked her.

'No valk!' said Tony. 'Bedtime.' In Slavonian he said: 'What does he want, this stranger? Is he a soldier?'

'I told you he's a hunter and a friend. What *could* he want? Can't you be more polite until he leaves?'

Bruce watched the strange words coming from their mouths. Then he began talking pleasantly with Mocco, who wanted to know about New Orleans. Presently another awkward silence fell, with Tony implacably weaving his basket and repeatedly staring at the stranger with open hostility.

'Bedtime, Nicolene!' he said.

'Do you want me to help you to bed?' Sister asked.

Bruce glanced coldly at Tony. He reached for his watch. Eight-thirty. He spoke to Sister in a low tone: 'Don't be tetchious. Don't be scared. Let me 'tend to this.' He took a sheet of paper from his pocket and handed it to Sister. It was a marriage license, issued in Lacroix that day.

Tony crossed the room and snatched the paper from Sister. 'Mind out, please, sir!' said Bruce. Tony returned to his chair.

Mocco, reading over Tony's shoulder, told him in Slavonian what the paper was for. Tony did not know what to do. Bruce was rolling a cigarette. Tony had a coughing fit. The other occupants of the room turned to watch him in fascination. Tony looked for a place to spit. He would not spit in the fire, because he believed that to do so would cause his lungs to wither. He sat holding the phlegm in his mouth, and panting.

'She belongs to me,' said Bruce slowly, smiling proudly at the floor. Sister turned and glared at Bruce, amazed. 'We love each other,' Bruce went on, 'and we'd thank you for your consent. I hope you-all won't get tetchious, although come to pullin' the bung, I'd hardly blame you. Still, I'm fixed to look after her. She'll never go near a battlin' block nor tote home e'er turn of firewood with me around. I've got lavish cash with me that I worked for, Mr. Kalavich, and a good boat to earn more. I come of a family proud as yourn. My pap's goin' to be rearin' mad too, I reckon, till he comes to know Sister better, and confidence her ways. But we can't mess with true love. Not the way we're wropped up in one another.'

Tony spat on the floor.

'No understand,' he said.

Bruce, studying Sister's perplexed face, thought, 'Poor little thing does not realize we've got to be married.'

Mocco translated to Tony: 'They love one another. He wants to take her away.'

'Tell him I want to do the right thing like a man. He'll see her married before she leaves,' Bruce interposed.

Sister edged away from Bruce. He seemed to her as he had one night on the boat — big and noble, like a great faithful dog who would follow her everywhere. Bruce sat very sure of himself, radiating his high resolve.

'He wants to do the right thing by her like a man,' Mocco said.

'I see,' said Tony softly, almost solicitously. 'Of course. He wants to do right. Ask him when he had her.'

Her father watched Sister, noting with magisterial obeisance the slight shifting of her facial muscles produced by his words. Tony smiled crookedly. His own face was turning yellowish. The eyes burned toward Sister craftily, and the lines about his mouth twitched. He uttered a cackling laugh.

'And you, our Nicolene,' he said suavely, 'our pretty little prostitute — what would *you* say? Do you want to marry the tramp?'

'No,' Sister said.

'Of course you don't! No prostitute wants to marry. But you are going to marry him tomorrow at the eight o'clock Mass, since you are ruined.'

'Ruined for what? Ruined for what?'

'At the eight o'clock Mass. Tell him I consent.'

'I think you're all crazy.'

'Never mind what you think. You understand what you're to do?'

'Anything to get away from here!'

'Mocco, tell the tramp he can have our little girl. Don't tell him she's a prostitute. Let him find out himself.'

'You can marry Sister tomorrow,' Mocco told Bruce.

Bruce walked over and shook hands with Tony, and squeezed his bony shoulder.

'Good gel!' Tony said. 'Fine gel! Tche makit good vife.' Then he turned to Sister. 'Don't tell him you're a prostitute, do you hear me?'

'No, sir, I won't tell him.'

'Get yourself ready to go with him to the priest tomorrow. You either marry him or go to the House of Good Shepherd in the city. For your mother's sake, I will ask your brother to mention this to nobody.'

Sister walked out of the house. Tony broke down, weeping

hot tears before his wife's portrait. Then he went out for a drink of green orange wine.

Bruce followed Sister to the levee. They sat on the levee bench. He put his arm around her waist. Sister made no protest. She wanted to laugh.

'God Almighty warn us!' Bruce exclaimed. 'I've suffered the tortures of the cave o' tears. The thought that I wronged the little dream girl that I love. I never did a thing like that in my life. I never despoiled a good girl in my life. Will you forgive? Will you let me make up for what I did, darlin'?' His big hands groped about her shoulders, hips, ribs. 'I don't wonder you disgust me, stayin' away so long. I had to sell my oranges and buy some clothes. But I'm sorry, darlin', God knows.'

'Sorry for what?'

'I feel like a dirty low-down cur-dog! You just don't understand it yet.' Bruce fell to his knees, burying his big face in her lap, weighing her down toward the levee mud. Sister was deeply embarrassed. She was again impelled to laugh. A moon was out, and the night was softly purple by the river under the gently traced willows, but Sister felt no magic tenderness. She could have laughed at the big man kneeling in the dust, but her heart felt cheated, and whatever magic she had gleaned from the affair with Bruce was gone. She was trapped.

'Get up,' she said. 'I've got to go.'

'What's the matter, darlin'? Ain't you glad I'm here? Don't you want to travel with me and make my life happy? Don't you forgive?'

'Yes, I'll forgive.'

'I don't blame you for disgusting me. I disgust myself. I feel like a cur-dog.'

She wanted to tell him that he looked like one. 'Go, now,'

she said. 'Go to your boat and come back early in the morning. We've got to go and see the priest.'

'Say that you forgive me, then.'

'Forgive what? Forgive what? You haven't done me anything! I went to your boat because I wanted to. It's a — joke, you coming back here thinking *you're* responsible. Let me go! Go now to your boat. If I'm here in the morning I'll marry you.'

'All right, darlin',' said Bruce meekly. 'Get you a good rest. You need it. You're all het up and don't know what you're sayin' tonight.'

Sister went down the levee to look for Mitch Holt. When she reached the poolroom she stood looking into the place. Once a man emerged carrying a pair of wild geese. Sister engaged him in conversation. He informed her that Mitch's schooner was in the Gulf. It should have returned the day before, with a load of Chinamen.

'How you feel, you?' the man asked.

'I'm all right.'

'When you gone make yo' Communion, Sister?'

'I don't know. Sometime...'

The man had a queer look on his face. Walking away from her, he turned once and looked back.

At the rickety wharf a tall schooner was being loaded with barrels of lettuce for icing at Lacroix and shipment north. The thick bowed negroes in the lantern light dumbly climbed the resilient gangplank, all in rhythm with the rise and fall of the plank, which lifted and sank in time with the chanter's tune. Sister conceived a plan. She would ask the schooner captain to take her to New Orleans. She had three dollars secreted at home. She approached the boat, but presently saw that it was the *Hail Mary*, operated by Captain George-Pete, an old family friend, who would never consent to take her away...

Halfway home she heard a voice coming on the levee. She stopped in the road and glanced about for a hiding-place. It was her father. The drunken bellowing was echoed by the rear cypress swamp. Sister hid in the willows. In the starlight as he passed she glimpsed his disheveled hair, his long wild face lifted, his head rolling about, and the white tail of his shirt dangling in the rear.

'Unga January!' he howled.

All along the levee windows were pushed up; voices and laughter followed his passage. A woman at a cabin farther down was alternately blowing a conch-shell and screaming for her children to hurry home.

'Unga January!' Tony roared. 'Unga January, I keel you!' He sat in the road opposite Sister, sobbing and coughing, then resumed his reeling journey. 'Unga January! Dutty bashit nigger winch make whore out my lilly gel! By goh, you no can get avay. I keel you, put fork in belly for you, dutty no good bashit nigger winch, come out! Come out!' Tony was followed by a group of levee loungers, four black giggling shapes. Sister sped home.

When he came to the home of Cyprian St. Germain, the deputy sheriff, for whose pregnant wife Unga was working, Tony turned and cursed away the men who were following him. Then he raised his fist and screamed at the house:

'Unga January! Come out! Oh-h-h-h! Dutty nigger winch make whore out my *mala-divojka!* Come out!'

'She ain't here, no!' someone called from the house.

Later St. Germain appeared on the levee and informed Tony that Unga had already left with all her belongings.

Unga, with a mealsack full of clothes, clutching a small crucifix carved from a shark tooth, stole from orchard to orchard along the river, pausing at intervals to make herself known in whispers to a barking dog. There were no fences to impede her. When she found herself in the orange grove of Octave Leroy, the poolroom man, she crawled up the sloping levee.

The cook of the *Hail Mary*, an aged negro, promised to conceal her in his room until the schooner reached New Orleans. Going up the black river he played songs for her on a mouthorgan with notes made weirdly discordant by bits of tobacco dust from his pocket. When the schooner slipped past the Kalavich house on the port tack, Unga was peering from the porthole. She bared her fine teeth whispering tender **profanity.**

6

WHEN the *Hail Mary* stopped at Dutch Scenery, Grampaw Kalavich boarded the schooner. He had come from Bay Saint Francis to see his friend Captain George-Pete. The two talked on the dock, and the captain told Grampaw that Tony Kalavich was drunk and threatening to kill a negro woman in Grass Margin.

The next morning before dawn, Grampaw, neatly dressed in brown corduroy and sharkskin slippers, paddled across the river to visit Tony.

Grampaw's paddle arm was sinewy as a youth's, and his back was thick and supple. His pirogue forged through the maze of driftwood in the dark in powerful lunges. Grampaw was a vigorous man, bookish and contemptuous of luxury and women. He looked like a brother to his son Tony, not much older. He once had been an officer in the Austrian cavalry. His pirogue bore him like a fiery steed, taking each wave like a barrier ardently vaulted.

He had been in Louisiana thirty years. When he arrived from Dalmatia with his wife and son, the east shore of the river, the vicinity of Dutch Scenery, was a region of fertile groves and fields. Beginning as a trader of muskrats, mink, and other peltries, he had prospered. Investing in extensive orange lands near Fort Saint Philip, he had lived in peace for years until his holdings were ravaged by tidal inundations. After burying his wife, he had gone to live with his son in Grass Margin. He had been very fond of his daughter-in-law, Sister's mother. After her tragic death and Tony's lapse into habitual drunkenness, Grampaw had returned to the eastern side and made his home among the Dalmatian oyster fishermen of Bay Saint Francis, far behind the levee of Dutch Scenery.

Sister remembered his departure. She had watched him carefully crating his books on the levee. 'When you get married I will come and live with you,' he had told her. 'Tsave me a place to tsit in tsun. That will be the kernel of my life. This is only the rind.' He spoke excellent English, using that tongue in preference to three others he knew.

Sister had slept badly, most of the night staring through the dark at the momentous fact of matrimony. She woke shortly after dawn and heard Grampaw below, his resonant voice lecturing Mocco in the kitchen:

'We always gave tsome of our crop money back to the trees that earned it. Then they work harder for you. Hoe them well. Thoroughly. Clip off the dead wood regularly, just as you must trim your own hair and nails. Give the trees a relief from the dead wood they're trying to throw off. Tsome time before blossom. Have you done that yet this year? And spray them carefully. High up and low down. Every leaf wet. Once in winter after breaking your fruit, and again when the baby fruit takes hold in tsummer. But hoe them well! Not too deeply but thoroughly. Give them your big back muscles. Right up to the trunk. For tsweetening out your ground, letting in air to the baby roots, keeping off alligator grass, there's nothing like the hoe. Where is Nicolene?'

There was no reply. That meant Mocco had shrugged his shoulders.

Then she heard Grampaw out at the chopping-block, opening some oysters. He never visited them without bringing a mess of delicious natural reef oysters, the wild ones that grew in inaccessible places.

'Where is Nicolene?' she heard him repeat from the chopping-block.

There was no reply. He repeated his question. Mocco answered that he guessed Sister was asleep. Tony said nothing. Sister dreaded to have Grampaw learn of her forthcoming marriage. He would perhaps denounce her. Suddenly she sprang from her bed, tore off her gown, and began to dress, singing wildly and defiantly:

> What de ole lady say when she come to die,
> Han' on her hip an' han' on her thigh?
> Um-m Lawd have mussy Lawd,
> Um-m Lawd have mussy!

Afterwards she saw Grampaw from her window. Now that day had broken, he was examining the orchard. He kicked at the ground about him, which had not been hoed for two years. He broke a long gray dead branch from a grapefruit tree, shook his head to himself, and walked off meditatively.

But his shoulders were erect. His hips swung freely with a quality of youthfulness which he had never relinquished — a tanned alert abhorrence toward slothfulness and inertia. The ruin he saw about him, the thorny creepers and thistles blanketing the place, roused him into a cold fury. After his inspection he strode into the house and stood looking this way and that. When angry, Grampaw would attempt to look in every direction at once. He pretended not to see Sister, frying the oysters at the stove.

Mocco, sensing trouble, had gone up the road. Grampaw walked into the next room, where Tony lay with his face to the wall, grunting with pain, burning with fever.

'Where is Mocco?' Grampaw asked. 'That good-for-nothing lout!'

'You wait till I am dying to come see me,' Tony mumbled.

Grampaw went and put his hand to Tony's forehead. He grew calm and troubled. He went into the kitchen and sat at the table. He examined Sister, whom he had not seen for a year, squinting his large black eyes.

'How's the little black devil?' he asked her. 'Turn around. You're as tall as I am, and tsprouting out as well as up.'

'I'm fine, thank you, sir,' said Sister respectfully for her father's ears. But she smiled audaciously and wrinkled her nose at Grampaw. He leaned backward and chuckled appreciatively. He continued watching her, the fine warm sheen of her skin, the peculiar erect bearing, too erect — a Kalavich characteristic.

'She's a prostitute now!' Tony called from the bed.

In the long silence Grampaw's steady black eyes gazed tranquilly into the next room. His face was shaped somewhat like an ape's — clear-seeing, restless, yet readily falling into nobly pensive lines, with powerful hard-biting jaws and fine sensitive nostrils.

'He's delirious, your father,' he said. 'Have you had a doctor?'

'I don't know what he is, and I don't care!' Sister said with such harsh bitterness that Grampaw straightened up in his chair and glared with eyes fiercely roused.

'A little prostitute!' Tony called. 'Ask the boys on the levee, the soldiers from the Forts. This is her last day under this roof.'

Sister shrugged her shoulders and walked outside with lips curled. She puttered around the packing shed, making a bundle of sweet bay leaves and sassafras roots to take with her on Bruce's lugger. Then she went to her patch of cucumbers in the rear of the orchard. Here among the faintly greened willows, huge canebrakes like gaunt mad disputants gesticulated in the salt spring wind. A thin soundless rain slanted out of the east. The climbing sun was swaddled in a silken pall. She would give the cucumber patch to Mocco. He would neglect it. The cu-

cumbers would lie on the vines until they grew red and swollen.
... The shy star-like leaves were already pushing through their
coverlet of hay, sending forth pale curly tendrils. To raise the
earliest cucumbers on the Margin and realize from their sale
sufficient money for some extra summer clothes, Sister had
lavished her care upon these plants. Once when a nor'wester
had blown up in the night she had left her bed to cover them
with hay by lantern-light.

Grampaw came out of the house. He strode casually toward
Sister. He began picking some wild greens near her. He was
very thoughtful, saying nothing, tugging at his belt, brushing
from his sleeve the misty rain, which immediately returned.
His mouth was puckered very reasonably, like a thoughtful
ape's. His eyes blinked with simian alertness. The clouds of his
curly gray hair were densely jeweled with beads of rain.

A lame wild goose left the orchard and limped past them disdainfully, and went into the canebrakes quanking fretfully.
Once a hunter who wounded the goose had brought him to Sister. She had fed and tamed him.

'What's wrong with Jerry this morning?' Grampaw asked.

'The spring. He hears the other geese flying back home.'

'Yes. I heard a bee ... And Jerry tstill acts that way?'

'Yes, sir, every spring.' The geese somewhere overhead were
trumpeting madly, plunging northward. Jerry, born in Baffin
Land, heard them and answered. After three years his call
had lost its wild clearness. 'He won't let me go near him. He
walks around so — so ——'

'Disconsolately. Look! the canes are budding out. There's
honey dew! On that weed! Tsummer will be here tomorrow.
Tstop your crying. Don't be a baby. Help me gather some *kostric* and boneset for tea.'

Together they gathered a great heap of dandelion for salad,
and enough boneset to fill Grampaw's pockets.

'We'll take this over to my camp,' he told her.

'Am I going to your camp?'

'Yes. Quick as we can get away.'

'Thank you, sir.'

'You don't want to marry that lugger fellow.'

'No, sir.'

'Your father's got no tsense.'

'He's been terrible lately. What did he tell you?'

'All about it. You come with me for a while. This is no place for you. Accursed! Accursed! Tsince your mother died. It's tchameful, that orchard. Those trees waiting for the hoe. The highest land on this Margin. I remember during the big hurricane, the deer. A hundred deer huddled right here. And tsnakes, 'possum, otter. All mixed up, waiting for the deluge to recede. Tchameful! A disgrace before God, wherever He is. You come over with me. You will be in my charge. Cook. Tscrub. Tsew and wash. Make your Communion later. Forget the lugger man. It's not important, honey. Almost every young girl ... A good woman is one who never got caught. Get your tstuff together now. We'll cross before the barbarian from the north comes to claim his booty. What's wrong with him?'

'I don't know, sir.'

'Is he too ugly?'

'No, sir. I don't know. He's too big and — good. He makes me feel funny.'

Grampaw laughed thickly in the rain, bitterly. Sister smiled and loved him, who had never before treated her as a grown-up. He was like a bitter gray god, full of sharp sour compassionate grimaces, with a youngish, unbeaten face that had commanded many men — bright, clean, watchful, at once malignant and compassionate.

'What about papa?' Sister asked.

'I've tsent for a doctor and a nigger woman to nurse him.'

In the house she gathered her belongings, and stuffed them into a mealsack. She had a few clothes, her *Tales From Shakespeare*, a wild-goose-down mattress which had been her mother's, and a large mirror. The mirror was a handsome ornamental one which made a bright unreal fretted gold frame for her face. She had purchased it with a ten-dollar school prize won for gathering marsh fowl eggs for the State Museum.

Downstairs, Grampaw was arguing with Tony about Sister. Tony, still his father's obedient son, at length acceded to Grampaw's desire to take her away. Tony said he hoped he would never see her again.

The rain was gone. The sun smote the treetops with joyous fire. Sister looked over the orange trees at the swift gay surface of the river, mottled with miles and miles of flashing black driftwood — the great yearly purging of the stream, which always vaguely stirred her. On one log a lone tern was riding seaward, gazing ahead with comical pomposity, as though he were directing the vast movement of drift.

Sister smiled and vented a hiss of a laugh through her nose.

Now she could see the oyster camps far behind the opposite shore, a group of dark dots scattered about the shimmering water of the bay. She knew Grampaw had a telescope at his camp. Through this she would be able to look back upon the Grass Margin housetops; and at night the lighthouse at Port Eads by the Gulf, the great spokes of light revolving around a jeweled hub. Soon, too, she would smell the orange blossoms of Grass Margin when the wind was west. Their fragrance traveled for miles.

Mocco was lingering about her room. He was quite downcast. Sister began perversely to sing. He looked in at her, somewhat awed. She nonchalantly handed him a bag of marbles from her drawer.

'Here are your real agates, Mocco.'

'They're not mine. You won them off me.'

'Take them. What do I want with agates? They've been here a year.'

'What'll I tell Mr. Bruce?' Mocco asked.

Sister felt very much grown-up. 'Tell him I left because it could never be. I would only ruin his life. And I don't care to have him following me. Will you take my things to the pirogue, please? I'll take the mirror.'

Sister felt wicked today like a wanton outcast. She enjoyed the feeling. She turned the mirror to her face. In the bright gold frame her countenance looked wicked. After the grown-up things that had happened to her in the last month, her cheeks had sunk. The blue morning glare cast the hollows of her face into deep shadow. The outgrown dress she wore flaunted the untimely maturity of her body. Her polished hair was drawn back tight. Her eyes burned back at her deeply from the pale worn face. She gazed up the levee road absently, with a pleased sigh.

Bruce was coming. She discovered him far up the road, dressed in a black suit. He walked as if he were still full of noble intentions, carefully examining a house, trying to identify Sister's home, which he had never seen by daylight.

Sister hurried to the levee with her mirror, bidding no one good-bye. She would be back to see them some time. Tony did not care. He had grown very weak. He must lie quiet, thinking: 'I must save my strength and get well. I am still a young man. I can marry again and fix up the place. I'll show the worthless little bitch! She does not even say good-bye, and I am most probably dying at this moment ... Let me lie without thinking of the future ... I've never done the things I planned to do. My life is black and white, swinging back and forth, bright sin and dark remorse. What will become of the place now? This big cold lonely house! Weeds and vines! Frogs and crickets! God, please help me! God, please help us all!'

Grampaw paddled away the yellow water. He dug careful strokes, because the wind was brisk, the frail pirogue deeply laden and unruly. In the glittering important morning Sister watched Mocco on the levee growing smaller and smaller. She felt small, helpless, ruled by men, utterly content. She saw Bruce's boat lying far up the river at the Chauvin landing, a sad white speck in the trees. With the deep river under her she relaxed, some newborn part of her soothed by its dark ponderous flow.

She must never forget this journey. Behind her forever was her mother's side of the river. The Durots had settled here long ago on a narrow ridge and thrived, tending their fecund trees, trapping marsh animals, taking alligators, frogs, and terrapin, guiding city hunters about the Delta, readily intermarrying and begetting hordes of dark babies. And they were deeply superstitious, intolerant toward innovation, passionate, jealous of their white blood.

The opposite shore, beyond which lay her future home, was her father's people's side of the river. It was barren of all growth save marsh grasses, wild indigo that rattled in its dry pods on winter nights, and stunted dun-colored mangroves. On that side the sun rose. The wide lonely mud-flats were peopled by screaming waterfowl, and the Gulf tides salted the land. But the Dalmatians had planted oysters, sowing the seed shells in the low water and cultivating the beds with curses and songs. The succulent harvests were shipped to New Orleans in their shells, or farther up the valley in cans. The Dalmatians were tough vigorous sea-peasants of frugal habits, still consuming inordinate quantities of olive oil and wine. And they were fond of music and women, but only after their work was done.

Between these two shores, moving in bronze laughter, was the broad impartial river, heavy now with an arresting musky odor that hinted of the potent secretions of infinitely remote hills.

The Big Marsh

BOOK TWO

7

THE oyster settlement far ahead sprawled peacefully in the briny sunlight. Cavorting waterfowl, egrets and herons and gulls, greeted the occupants of the pirogue with many kinds of cries. Huge plump clouds wallowed slowly by. With barely a sound Grampaw paddled out the canal that connected Dutch Scenery with Bay Saint Francis, the big oyster fishery. Just ahead a swift otter clove the stream with the water between his teeth. To Sister, all was a breezy vision, from the polished brown water to the richly painted heavens. Colonies of mossy oysters grew on either side of the canal. As the pirogue approached and disturbed their meditations, the oysters quickly closed their shells, each squirting up into the sunshine a vexed blue javelin of juice. Sister laughed.

The sparsely scattered oyster camps, painted in various vivid hues, were perched on tall posts driven into the mud, and all faced the canal that wound aimlessly toward the distant bay. Under each camp a firm footing had been provided by oyster shells dumped several feet thick.

Grampaw's camp was the smartest of all, painted tan with green trimmings. On the shell-mound beneath it were briskly singing hens and two pigs, all of which were carried upstairs to a pen on the broad porch whenever a storm threatened to flood their home. (Grampaw was a lover of good food. Like most other Delta girls, Sister was skilled at Creole cookery. He would appreciate her cooking! Nor would he attempt to direct her kitchen activities, or idle about her stove!) Behind the camp was a tall green cistern — plenty of rain water! And under the camp, behind a palmetto screen, a bath! She remembered Grampaw taking his cold bath on winter mornings. The lugger and skiff in the bayou were immaculately scoured. A fish-car for storing live fish floated by the landing. The camp was equipped with a lightning-rod, and had a bird-house on a bamboo pole — the only camp possessing such things.

Over the front door were the antlers of the largest buck Grampaw had ever killed. (When they were put there, these antlers caused many a smile from oyster fishermen poling their oysters past the camp. In the Delta, when a man's wife was found to have a secret lover, one of the husband's friends might warn him by placing deer-horns on his door during the night. Concerning the antlers over his door Grampaw had explained that God, wherever He was, had finally deprived him of his wife.) Beside the horns were a barometer and thermometer, and a loaded shotgun in a waterproof cypress case which Grampaw had devised. Spying a flock of ducks or geese flying low toward his camp, Grampaw had only to hurry to this stationary case and press a button, whereupon a cover would fly open and the gun slide down into his hands.

While Grampaw unloaded the pirogue Sister mounted the high stairs and stood on the porch. She saw the earth lying below her. Her blood stopped flowing a moment. She turned her head first to one side, then to the other. Nothing obstructed the view — nothing but the sheer naked circle of the horizon. The earth was inconceivably broad and flat and silent, made of rich heady muds skimmed from the northern lands, borne down by the river and deposited here by ancient floods — now densely grassed, dappled green and brown, gorgeously spattered with shimmering blue pools of brine.

So this, at last, was as much as one might see of the world!

How flat it was! And yet the earth, the whole earth, was round! Sister could now feel the awful bulk, the tremendous inert weight of the earth. But how much vaster was the sky — even the clouds were vast, this slow ponderous movement of gigantic vapors heaped on vapors. Now she could visualize the puny earth hanging barely visible in the fathomless sky, swathed in clouds of trailing mist.

She would be lonely here. There would be people, visitors, coming and going; but in this prairie people shrank in size. Their voices and their houses shrank in size. There was little need of their drawing close to each other. One's voice might be heard across the bayou in a whisper. People moved about timidly, approached each other warily, as animals do.

She wanted to be lonely.

How silent! She heard a faint gurgle from her digesting food. The echoes of her living heart could be felt passing out through her finger-tips. The sun seemed to seep through her flesh and find the bones. There was warmth here, but not the gregarious, intimate, human-warmth of Grass Margin.

She had thoughts to think, while working — bright important thoughts which she had not been able to think in Grass Margin, whose loneliness had been crowded and confused.

Grampaw came and opened the door. The sudden clean smell of cypress was wafted out. The floor of heart pine was scrubbed white. She perceived it was knee-scrubbing, and not done with a broom. She grew momentarily confused, thinking of a man like Grampaw scrubbing a floor. . . . They discarded their shoes at the door. The tables, chairs, beds, closets, shelves, were of cypress. These and other household fixtures had been made by Grampaw himself, during the summer, when the oyster fisherman has some spare time.

Sister could not contain her happiness. She leaped upward and swung by her fingers on a rafter. She moved along the timber hand over hand like a monkey, humming weirdly with joy.

Her hair fell in wild disarray. With her toes she plucked Grampaw's hat from his head and tossed it up into the loft. Grampaw opened a drawer.

'Look! A doll I carved!' he said.

Sister fell with a loud thud. She snatched to her the little
toy, a defiant pathetic driftwood doll with two oyster pearls for
eyes staring at her fiercely, and three big buttons down his fat
belly.

'I love him!' she cried, and kissed the doll. She stood the little idol on the floor and lay before it gazing dreamily, wor-
shipping, adoring its screwed-up face twisted sourly in protest,
its bulging brow and sunken temples where Grampaw had actually managed to carve sinuous veins.

'I began him as Doctor Johnson,' said Grampaw, 'but he
turned out to be William Blake. What will you cook for tsupper?'

'What have you to cook?'

'Beans, green shoulder, rice, eggs, fish, crabs, oysters . . .'

There was a fat keg of olive oil by the wine barrel, and a
large mealsack of hardtack. He took her to the back porch and
pointed. She saw a long trough containing rich brown silt.

'Where on earth did the river sand come from?' she asked.

'I hauled it from the river,' he said.

There were tomatoes growing in the trough, covered with glass!

Sister took Grampaw's hands, forcing him to skip about with
her.

'Have you an omelette pan?' she asked.

'Yes. One big one that hasn't been used since Gramaw died.'

'Then we'll have tomato omelette, for one thing.'

'Ahhh!' Grampaw smacked his lips. 'Thanks! Now tomorrow
you may paddle to Dutch Tscenery for any new pots and pans
you need. You'll find tsome money in my coat pocket.'

'I've got some money too,' she said.

'Go tspend it for ribbons. Give it away. No thrift allowed
here. Thrift is for the tstupid bees.'

They ate a good lunch of ripe olives, hardtack, and wine. Grampaw spent the afternoon at his little charcoal forge mending a pair of oyster tongs. Sister explored her new home, the hundreds of fine books, and the dim clean loft, where the sun's warmth flowed like potent liquid through the cypress shingles. There was a place here where she could lie on a folded sailcloth and watch the spiders hanging snares for the succulent gnats — an ideal retreat for lying coiled in soft thought... but not today! She could not think clearly today. Her blood was plagued by the rank wild salt of liberation.

With a cautious, secretive thrill she explored the shell island under the camp, a strange region full of thick blue shadows and triangular patches of sun, roofed by fragrant creosoted timbers, hemmed in by the contorted and gnome-like old mangroves. The creamy mud among the mangroves was tracked in spots with curious tender footprints, where some little wild thing seemed to have been dancing. A blue heron in the leaves fixed her with a mild brave look. She dipped a toe into the bayou. Crabs basking on the shallow bottom darted away in every direction. From among the wharf piling came a strange sound which some underwater creature was repeatedly uttering, a brief elusive twang, like the plucking of a banjo string...

In the evening the bayou's surface was furrowed again and again by swift mullet escaping to sea with the tide. Grampaw waited on the wharf with his cast-net held in teeth and hands. A large school of fish darted past the wharf. The thrown net whirled out and dropped in a neat circle. The fish were heavy with roe. Grampaw took out the roe with his knife and threw the fish into the bayou, where they were immediately gulped by the waiting gars.

Sister fried the roe for supper. Then with some trepidation she began work on the tomato omelette. She minced and fried half an onion. To beaten eggs she added a tomato cut fine, some condensed milk, and salt. Then she stirred in the fried onion, and dumped the mixture into one side of the pan. When the omelette's crust had formed all over, she allowed it to cook slowly, watching it with bated breath for a long time, until the pan cover began to rise. The omelette was juicy, tender, and light as foam.

'Eat it before it falls!' she warned Grampaw.

He took a forkful. She watched the movement of his jaws. Presently he raised his eyes to her and smiled delightedly. Grampaw devoured another portion, opening and closing his eyes contentedly. Sister flushed with pleasure. She had been accepted.

After a few days Grampaw said, 'There are two young girls in Radovich's camp.' This was the nearest camp to Grampaw's, about a quarter of a mile east. Sister had heard a baby crying there in the night, and an accordion playing.

'I saw them pass in a skiff yesterday,' she answered.

'Would you like to know them? I might take you over there tonight.'

'No, sir. Not yet.'

'Don't you like their looks?'

'They look all right. They stared at me until they rounded the bend.'

'You are good to tstare at. They never see tstrangers. Don't mind that. They are children. Don't you tstare?'

'Not at people. At animals and things like that I do.'

'People do not interest you?'

'Two or three I know do.'

He went on knitting his net. After a while he spoke again: 'Are you going to have a child?'

'Yes, sir, I think so.'

He looked deeply into the calm round orbs of her eyes. He wiggled a finger in his ear, then resumed his knitting.

'Do you want to?' Grampaw asked.

'I don't know, sir.'

Grampaw made several stitches. Suddenly they looked **at** each other and smiled.

Later Grampaw was drinking wine by the window. He had been rather dour that day. He saw Sister scrubbing the cypress table, her quick elastic arms and back driving the hissing brush filled with sand. She reminded him of his dead wife toiling in their first home in ancient Ragusa on the Adriatic. His tipsy face lighted up, then grew stony and proud.

'Have you too much to do?' he asked, wrinkling his brow sternly.

'Too much?'

'Around here.'

'Shucks! I thought you had *lots* of work here! Move, please, before you get splashed.'

Obediently he moved his chair. He frowned at her over his piercing eyes. 'A baby will be fun in this camp,' he said.

'There'll be lots to do then,' said Sister.

'But it is nice.'

'Yes.'

'Crying and playing.'

'Yes.'

'You are participating in a great mystery. We tseldom think of that.

'How?'

He looked out of the window, as if to pick the answer from the sky. 'We are all conceived in rapture,' he said. 'Everybody. Humanity. In rapture.' He waited for his words to reach her, then, hopefully: 'I am sure you feel reverence for that.'

'I don't understand it,' said Sister, perceiving and not perceiving.

Grampaw violently ducked his head and flung his hands out sideways. 'Nor I!' he exclaimed. 'Nor I! Is that material?

Do we need to understand? No! Only feel! Don't you *feel*
reverence for it, like you do for — for God, or two and two making always four, or birds knowing where to migrate?' His nose
was but a foot from hers, his face red.

'Don't yell!' she said, smiling. She returned to her work
thoughtfully, stubbornly, keeping silent. She would not be lectured to so emphatically. But her eyes had brightened. He had
caused her mind to tingle — his words — their sound, not their
sense. He waited for her to speak. She turned, her face illumined by a bright responsive glow. 'Yes!' she said. 'So great
and strange a thing to happen — to me.'

And Grampaw beamed. 'Exactly!'

'But . . .' Sister's face clouded. She turned away, brooding.
'But I don't care about the man — the father — Bruce. He
don't seem to be — in it at all.'

'Good!' Grampaw laughed and patted her tenderly. 'You
tsee? You respect the mystery and not the man. I am proud!'

'Oh,' she murmured. 'Thanks.' She dipped another brush-
ful of sand.

On another day Grampaw brought from Dutch Scenery a
package, and a letter from Mocco. The package contained a
pound of caramels bought in New Orleans. She read Mocco's
letter:

Dear little Nicolene:
    Papa has to lay still with the windows all open. I keep the
mosquito bar around him. Mr. Bruce and I are good friends
now. He is a fine fellow. We are using his boat to take orders
up and down the river for Pelcher's Ox Physic and these new
heaters that burn insurance oil and can be moved around your
house. We sold three bottles Ox Physic. This is a bad time for
heaters. Now Sis you must not be too hard on Mr. Bruce. He
is good as gold and loves Humanity. I am sending you a package, something from Mr. Bruce. He is expecting you to soon get
over your Fit and send for him.
                    Your loving bro.
                            Mocco

Grampaw did not like candy, so while reading *Gulliver's Travels* by the stove that night Sister ate all the caramels, spitting out the bits of wax paper.

Grampaw said, 'You are going to live a new kind of life here.'

'Yes, sir.'

'You are going to change. You might be happy.'

'I am happy.'

'You are going to get knowledge. Learn the tseasons. Birds. Fish. Animals. Breathe tsalt. Play. And well-bred countrymen of mine from the city come here to hunt and fish. My books are the best ever written. When you get lonesome realize this, that there is nothing for you in Grass Margin. No decent home. No friends. No one to marry. Nothing.'

'I could marry. Mitchell Holt wants me.'

'No.'

'He said so.'

'Try to forget him. We'll talk about him later.'

Grampaw had learned in Dutch Scenery that morning that Mitch and his confederates had been taken by Government men in the Gulf after a chase and fight in which several had been wounded. Mitch would get a long sentence in Atlanta Prison.

8

WHEN the Gulf tide was moving in the canal, it was easy paddling to Dutch Scenery, under two miles. Sister went often to the village on the river, and there she would wander carelessly. Packets and schooners stopped at Dutch Scenery, but no ships. These tremendous bulks of iron, mostly larger than the village itself, rushed past very close to shore, puffing gently and dousing the mounds of tangled driftwood with golden roars of spray. Men gathered always under the few trees and the oyster shed, because of the cool. Slow cows kept the levee grass clipped and richened. Evenings, babies crept through the dust; girls sat stringing four-o'clocks, boys splashed about a raft of planks. On the porches, accordions wheezed, producing worn rhapsodies or waltzes. Mateo Lucich climbed the ladder to light the Range Light. The Government paid him twelve dollars monthly for that.

Sister once found an empty barge, a big ancient hulk. Probably it had once brought coal down river to New Orleans, and was set adrift there in the old days, when oak was plentiful. Its timbers were worn by the elements, ragged with splinters, chewed by the shovels of old. Sister intended to climb into it some day.

One day she heard a humming sound inside the barge, a pleasant languid humming. She climbed the spikes to the top. Inside the hulk was a young negress. This was Carrie Longmire, a village girl who was mentally unbalanced. Carrie was naked. Except for a few inches of water in its bottom and Carrie's clothes on a stick, the old barge was a vast empty hollow, with the black girl in the middle, washing herself. Sister straddled the bulwark and studied the girl below, her strange wonderful blackness, completely black.

'Hi, Carrie!' she called.

The girl was not startled at all. She did not look up. Sister climbed down the ladder and stood in the warm water. How strange it was, utterly shut off from the world! The barge was pallid gray under the deep blue sky, nothing visible but its rising walls, and the sky. And the shape of the barge changed the quality of one's voice, and the movement of disturbed water sounded queer, unreal. And the black girl had not yet looked. Carrie rubbed her armpits with brown soap, and playfully squeezed her hand over the hollow, which emitted soapy gurgles.

'Can you do dat?' Carrie asked, not yet having seen the intruder.

'Where is your mother, Carrie?'

Carrie rose to her feet and looked at Sister. She was all smeared with white lather. Her face was vacant a moment, then she seemed trying to recognize Sister. Suddenly she put her hand over the juncture of her thighs, turned sideways, and raised her shoulder to her chin, smiling shyly.

'Where's your mother, Carrie?'

'I hopes she gone to de valley of de passengers on de east of de sea!'

Carrie was angry. She turned her back, stooped, and splashed herself with water.

'Do you want to be left alone, Carrie?' Sister asked.

'No, wait! I show you my dance. You gone clap for me?'

The negress stamped the water, dancing sideways around

Sister, who began to clap her hands slowly. Carrie kept time, chanting:

> Ba-doom! Ba-doom!
> Doom-doom!
> Ba-doom! Ba-doom!
> Doom-doom!

She snapped her fingers. Her pelvis seemed an independent part of her skeleton as it ground away a revolving rhythm of its own. After a while Carrie grasped Sister's hands, and Sister fell into the movement. Ba-doom! Ba-doom! Doom-doom! In the barge Carrie's voice sounded unreal, as though from far off. The water splashed Sister's clothes and trickled down her legs. Carrie chanted:

> Ba-doom! Ba-doom!
> Bap-tize!

Sister joined in the chanting, and stamped the water as vigorously as Carrie did. Very soon she was wet to the waist.

> Ba-doom! Ba-doom!
> *Bap*-tize!

Sister was laughing without restraint. Some drops of water sailed skyward, glittering in the sun. Once Carrie stopped dead, listening. 'Shh! Somebodday comin!' Carrie's listening face wore a trapped look, with a kind of snarl around the mouth. Someone was climbing the outside of the barge. A man's face appeared over the bulwark.

It was André Laval, the constable. He wore a greenish beard, and had only one eye. Sister thought him very funny, squinting down at them, rapidly chewing his tobacco. Carrie was again washing herself, soaping her belly. Laval spat into the water.

'Go away, whoever you are,' Sister told the man. 'Let us be.'

'I go. I'm gone tell you something, but that is not right, dancing in dat bodge.'

'How, not right? What harm are we doing?'

The constable sat on the bulwark without a word, squinting down.

'Who are you?' Sister asked.

The one eye gazed down, unblinking, rather kindly, the eyebrow lifted high.

'What have you to do with us?' Sister asked.

'Is not right. That's all. Don't talk back. Is not decent.'

'Not decent! Who says that? Who are you? Where do you work? You and your not decent!'

'Me? Where *I* work? I work for the pipple! *All* the pipple, you and her too. Mais don't I know your Grampaw? Ask him! I work for the pipple!'

The glaring eye stared down, reddish. Sister kept her gaze fixed upon the single eye. Suddenly Carrie splashed across the barge, grabbed her drawers, slipped into them, took her clothes, and climbed the far ladder. On top of the barge she called: 'Put a bridle in his jaws! Thank you, mam!' and disappeared. Sister looked around. The constable's face was gone. Sister began to giggle.

When she passed through the village a group of men standing around the constable waited on the levee to see her pass. They regarded her curiously. Sister was smiling inwardly at the row of solemn faces. . . .

Now Sister went regularly to the village for groceries. The little blue store was a fascinating place, deep pine shavings on its floor whose odor mingled with the smells of oakum, calico, whale-oil soap, ripe olives in a big stained box. Mateo Lucich owned the store, the cannery, the tiny saloon where motley idlers and fishermen's guides haunted the cool. Afternoons, sun reflections wriggled in off the river, casting dancing filaments of light up among the dim rafters hung with oddly shaped boat fittings, vivid cartridge advertisements, bright waterproof jackets. From the window one could see the thick verdant smear of willows across on the Margin. The white cemetery looked curiously gay from afar, the bright clustered tombs forming a kind of flower with snowy petals, where Sister's mother lay neatly stored away among the dead. Passengers on ships pointed to the cemetery with its orange blossoms, pampas grass, hibiscus bushes a dozen feet tall. In Dutch Scenery there was no cemetery, no ground high enough. It was an ancient joke that a fellow had no place to bring his girl at night. In some indefinable way, the lack of a cemetery made Dutch Scenery less attractive to Sister.

Mrs. Lucich, the grocery woman, was a slow, dumpy, harassed mother of daughters. Her bosom looked like huge partly deflated balloons, and her apron was dirty around the stomach. She gave Sister her change, and thanked her, looking elsewhere. She never looked into anyone's face, but generally seemed searching for something on the floor. She was slightly cross-eyed. Her husband waddled out and gave Sister some peppermint candies for *lagniappe*. Mateo was a fat Slavonian with an oily Mongolian face. He was making money and raising girls.

'Don't you come see us sometime, Nicolene?' he asked. 'Our gels ass for you all time. My vife and gels like you whole lot.'

The wife wiped the counter and smiled. She had big tough hands.

'I'll come some time, thanks,' Sister said.

'You live at camp all time?'

'Yes, sir.'

'No get lonesome?'

'No, I like the camp. Lonesome for what?'

Mateo's beady eyes followed her to the canal. All through

the village, net-menders turned to look. Sister was aloof and pleased. Men were so queer, happy while at work in the wind, bubbling over with staunch coarse tenderness, so wild and safe, eager to be noticed.

Women were not safe — for her. She instinctively felt that. How did Mateo know his women liked her? Sister knew they had not yet judged her. They wanted her in their little circle of mutual cunning and consolation; but only because her isolation gave her an advantage, in some way. It was very strange.

At the canal Sister discovered Mrs. Lucich had given her too much change. She returned to the store.

'How much is butter?' she asked Mrs. Lucich.

'Twenty cents pound.'

Sister examined the groceries in her arms. 'I think you gave me too much change.'

Mrs. Lucich stared at Sister's shoes in alarm. She began marking down the price of the articles, and drew an impatient line beneath her figures. After adding the column, she took the broom and resumed sweeping. 'No wrong,' she said. 'Right change.'

Sister went as far as the door, counting. She lingered, then returned. 'I think it is wrong, Mrs. Lucich.' She put down the change. 'The things add up fifty cents, don't they?'

Mrs. Lucich got a damp rag to wipe the counter, then a dry one. She spread a paper, and began listing the items, loudly calling out each one, then checking them back. Slowly she added the column, calling out her additions and carefully marking the figure to be carried. The result was fifty cents. She had given sixty cents change from a dollar.

She threw away her rag and went into the saloon for a chair. Seating herself, she turned over the paper and began calculating again. Four customers had arrived, and Joe the bar-keeper was looking over her shoulder, counting with her. 'I don't even cheat *customers*, how can I cheat *myself?*' she asked them, counting and recounting.

'It's only a mistake,' said Sister. 'Here's the dime.'

'Don't want dime! Don't want dime! I count again.'

The articles were put on the counter. She opened a bag to see that it contained split peas.

'Don't remember bottle catsup!' she announced. 'Maybe you take catsup off counter from mistake. That's all right, anybody make mistake. Maybe you mix up dime with my change you had already, put other dime with change from mistake. I don't make mistake never. Ask Joe if I cheat. Ask anybody. I swear to Jesus I am sorry you make mistake but is terrible, telling all this people I cheat myself. All right, I take your dime, pass it to the poor.'

Mateo came in. When told what was amiss he pushed his wife from behind the counter and smiled at Sister. 'She make mistake all time,' he said. 'Sure. Is crazy. She wants to chase away good customers.'

As she went out, Sister heard Mrs. Lucich, who was now her eternal enemy, whining: '*She* crazy, comit back with too much change! She got it in for me. I never done her nothing!'

But Sister felt strangely obliged to visit the Lucich family, in spite of the incident, or perhaps because of it. Some obscure impulse of pity or contempt drew her to the crosseyed woman's home.

The eldest daughter, Natasha, received her warmly, exclaimed effusively over her hair, and wanted a pattern of her dress. Olga, the remaining girl who was through with school, was busy skinning a mink she had caught. Sister and Natasha took a stroll. Sister pointed to a little wood far down the river. 'Let's go there,' she suggested, 'and see what's there.' The trees were tall and strange, casting dim shadows that invited and repelled. Sister had often sat on the levee in Grass Margin looking across at the fascinating grove.

'I wouldn't go there for anything!' said Natasha. 'They say wild bulls are in the trees.'

'Pshaw! I don't believe it! Anyhow, we could climb a tree.' Sister shuddered at the thought of bulls. She could close her eyes and feel their hot breath on her shoulder. But her heart urged her forward. Natasha edged away from Sister. The sloping river-bank was broad as they approached the grove — clean and lonely, dotted with meditative cattle, some knee-deep in water, with spots on them shaped like maps.

'Come on!' Sister whispered.

'No! Not on your life!'

Sister stood listening. The river whispered deeply. The placid fathomless heavens bore not a shred of cloud, and over the water the sinking sun hung red as a blotch of gore. Sister's dilated eyes stared down and down, into the very molten core of the hot bold sun.

'I'm going to see! I must see!'

'See what, Nicolene?'

'In there! Come on!'

'I'm a-scared! It's already getting dark in there! Are you a-scared?'

'Pshaw, come on!'

'Nicolene, you *are* a-scared!'

Sister went down the levee and across the damp pulpy meadow. She stopped, listening. A bright gathering of gnats whirled about her head. Suddenly she sped into the grove. She began to tiptoe noiselessly. Once Natasha on the bank called. In the pure and profound silence the voice sounded infinitely remote, and rather sad. Sister was strangely happy. The ground was trampled everywhere with hoofmarks all filled with rain, forming burnished cloven pools of light. A gaunt dark fowl rose suddenly beside her, and an instinctive scream tore out of her throat. The bird, a frightened ragged night heron, watched her from a perch. Sister smiled. Her heart grew calm. The tree-trunks were immense. She had never seen such huge ones before — tall, taller than her thoughts could reach, and seemingly swaying in unison, describing great slow arcs. And they grew cunningly, having placed their branches so that all air space was taken, yet no tree touched its fellows. She placed her ear against one of the trunks, pretending she could hear the sap coursing past. There were no wild bulls, she saw almost with disappointment — only cardinals and buntings, and everywhere big hidden frogs calling each other through their noses.

But voices approached on the levee, many of them, talking excitedly. Sister hid behind a tree and peered out.

The approaching party was composed of a couple of men and a dozen small boys, and led by André Laval.

Laval motioned the others to stay behind, and approached the grove cautiously with his hand in his hip pocket. Sister came out and met him.

'What you do in deh, you?' he asked. 'You know them bull could buck you, and dat's not belonk to you, dat property?'

'You still working for the people?' she asked. She walked back toward Dutch Scenery at the head of the long procession. No one said a word. The boys regarded her with open mouths Sister suddenly sat in the grass to allow them to pass her. Each eyed her curiously as he went past.

Laval said, 'Me, I got a mind to tell you grampaw, you trespas with that man property and them dangus bull could kill you dead.' But he walked on with the others. His rubber boots plodded hollowly, all caked with earth and manure. The boots seemed very pathetic to Sister. He turned to look back, and his single sad eye glanced apprehensively from her to the grove.

Sister returned to Dutch Scenery. A group of idlers stood

before the store, Laval among them. Mrs. Lucich was in the doorway, with her bloated bosom and her gnarled hands folded across the big round stain on her stomach. She looked at a sleeping hound beneath the tree and whined: 'See that? Hiding in bull-woods! Is she got right mind? Bringing back too much change? Dancing with Crazy Carrie?'

Natasha met Sister at the canal.

'I'm sorry,' she said. 'I didn't tell them. Olga told Mama. She sent for André.'

'Oh, I don't mind, Natasha. It's nothing.'

'But the constable! I thought he'd arrest me. He really thinks you're crazy.'

Sister looked gravely at Natasha. She turned and her puzzled eyes rested on the people before the store, who were still watching her.

'I don't know,' she said softly, and walked to the pirogue.

At home she asked Grampaw, 'Do I look sane to you always?'

'No,' he said quickly, without raising his eyes from his book.

'I'm not sane? You really think that?'

'I hope that. Devoutly. There is no danger. Let us give thanks.'

Sister stuffed a chunk of wood in the stove and began to sing.

The Lucich girls, five of them, called at Grampaw's the next week. They owed Sister a call. Sister was ill. Grampaw entertained them, carving dolls from vegetables. After several weeks Sister visited the Lucich home. It was a Sunday afternoon. The father was over-amiable to Sister. The wife eyed Mateo sharply, no longer looking at the floor. The elder daughters, Natasha and Olga, were giddy today, square-bodied peasants who talked incessantly of men and giggled over empty jests.

On pretense of looking for thistle buds (which Delta girls used for powder-puffs) they paraded Sister up and down the levee. They wanted to linger wherever men were gathered, inviting the banter of the men. Sister walked stiffly, casting reproachful glances at her companions.

Presently, losing patience, she asked, 'Must we make a holy show of ourselves?'

They did not understand that. They were young girls, seventeen and eighteen. Olga was sprouting a fine pair of little breasts. She did not care to bother humoring the insane. When the three parted, the two girls bade Sister farewell in a distant manner.

'Stuck-up thing!' said Olga to Natasha when they were out of hearing. 'Just because her fellow's under the jail.'

The two burst into loud laughter. Sister did not look back.

One day a handsome young man from the city, in Dutch Scenery for fishing, assisted Sister in loading her pirogue. He detained her, talking about himself, not perceiving Sister was inattentive. (She was thinking of her baby. From one of Grampaw's books she had learned the baby's form at this time resembled that of a curious fish or reptile.)

'Who made your pretty belt?' she heard the stranger ask.

'I made it — out of tarpon scales.'

He reached out to finger the belt. She removed it and handed it to him. 'Do you want it?' asked Sister.

'I'd love to take it to someone I know.'

'Take it! I'm getting tired of it.' She was attached to the belt, but preferred to think of it being in the city, worn by a strange beautiful girl.

'What are you doing tomorrow night?' he asked airily. She looked at him. The young man had a mustache. He was pinching, or trying to pinch, the mustache. Its hairs were stiff and whitish, pointing in many different directions.

'How do you mean?' Sister asked. 'I'll be making a kite then.'

'A kite! That's funny. I might come out and help you make it.'

'You might!' Sister eyed him from head to foot. She had to smile at his sudden abashment. She liked him, chiefly on account of the mustache. Grampaw had said Europeans wore mustaches to have something to do with their hands while talking to a woman.

'May I, then?' he asked, mollified.

'You must bring your accordion. Then I can dance — with Grampaw. He is a nice old man.'

The young man could not play. He owned no accordion. Sister insisted he should learn. He promised to do so the next day. He sensed he was unwelcome. Sister knew he was not over-anxious to fight the tide. They made a joke of it.

Next time in Dutch Scenery, as she left the store to return to her pirogue, she saw the window of a shack open on the grinning face of an old fisherman playing an accordion. Farther on, a fat negro on a porch began blowing a harmonica. Another window still farther banged open and she heard a phonograph. Soon the entire village was a din of music. Sister flushed and smiled, enjoying the prank. When she reached the canal there was a group of girls sitting on a log on the levee with the young man from town. Among the group were the two elder Lucich girls. The entire party began to laugh uproariously.

Sister's mouth continued to smile. The remainder of her face tightened, and her eyes took on a narrow fierce light. Her body tautened and the blood rushed against her scalp. In her hand was a large can half full of green deck-paint. She sucked in her breath and heaved the can. The thing sailed neatly, tumbling through the air. It dropped near the log, brightly spattering the shrieking girls, who fell over pellmell with their upturned legs or underwear exposed to the howling village men.

Half a mile out the canal paddling homeward she could hear the sough of distant laughter.

'Where's the paint?' Grampaw asked.

She told him. He examined her out of quiet level eyes through the pipe smoke. (Sister had come to trust the old man implicitly. They were becoming friends. The relationship was an odd one, almost devoid of words but rich in tense or humorous signals. At times for days Grampaw was morose. Then he grew loquacious for a day. On rare occasions he drank and talked half the night, or read aloud from Montaigne, Blake, or the Old Testament poets — the bilious prophets, he called them.)

He attended her tale of the paint-throwing. At the end his eyes danced. Afterwards he was silent and thoughtful, frequently pinching his flabby jowls, whistling between his teeth. Cobbling a pair of shoes for winter, he carefully drove home each peg. Sister brooded, slow, sullen, a woman unsure.

After supper Grampaw called her to the porch to sit with him. He had built a kind of screened cage there, to sit and smoke, and hear the vicious mosquitoes swarming on the screen a few inches away, whining for his blood. This enhanced his pleasure, thwarting the pests. Sister curled up at his feet. His breath was rank with wine.

'Do you hear from Mitch?' he asked.

'No, sir. I write every month.'

'How long until he gets out?'

'I don't know. Three years.'

'He will be ready to settle down.'

Something warm rushed down her trunk and past her thighs, almost a pain. She did not understand it.

'He will be changed, Mitch.'

'Yes,' she answered. 'But he won't settle. Not him. Not for long.'

'Mitch is proud. He needs to lead. Tell him that. Fire him with it. Do you understand me, little minx? Lead others. Lead men.'

'How?'

'I don't know,' Grampaw mused. 'Well — this is a big country! Rich! Tso rich! Rich in challenges. Meadows tsweet and waters aswarm. Mitch could make the people move. He talked here tsome nights.'

'Here! To you?'

'Yes. He is proud. Perhaps he is one of the good-proud.'

'How? Who are they, the good-proud?'

Grampaw yawned. He looked at the sky. 'Do you still love the Scorpion, Nicolene?'

'Yes, sir.'

'And you don't like the Lucich girls!'

'I'd rather the Scorpion.'

'Morbid. Why dislike them? They are no better than you.'

'You don't understand.' (Grampaw laughed and pinched her ear.) 'They are stupid,' she went on. 'Ignorant! Like cows!' she asserted vehemently. 'Hugging and kissing each other! Getting silly and — frisky when men are around.'

'Wonderful! Wonderful! It is nice, this play of boys and girls, young animals. Alive! Functioning! Devouring good meals! Drugged with tsleep! Things of the mind are beautiful, but the healthy body is the tstrong wise minion of the honorable old instincts. They want babies and tsome tsuffering. The men want families. It makes them important. I am talking nonsense. Remember it well in other years. Pride is the tstar above the Cross. Jesus knew. He worshipped His father the tsun.'

Sister settled more comfortably in expectation of one of Grampaw's talkative moods, the ripe kindly philosophy, the noble platitudes. She did not care to hear about the girls, but about Mitch, for whom at this time she bore a pleasant hatred.

'Ignorance is the tstate of ignoring,' said Grampaw.

'What were you saying about Mitch?'

'You had better have the present baby first and think of him later.'

'You said the good-proud. He might be one of the good-proud.'

'Perhaps and perhaps. The devil gave Mitch to his father and tsaid, "Here, it is my treat!" I mean the Lucifer-devil of Milton, whom I respect, not your modern devil who sweats when you bless yourself. Later, when he finds something to do, Mitch might become one of the good-proud.'

'But what does it mean? What will he be like then?'

'The good-proud are those whom — chance has endowed with the — vitality and curiosity to — go on.'

'How — go on?'

'With a task. With a chosen or fated task.'

'Fighting enemies?'

'Fighting *all* forms of death. Expecting no reward.'

Sister's heart sank.

'But *he* would expect a reward!' she said.

'Who? Who are you talking about?'

'Mitch.'

'To hell with Mitch! Listen to me! Expecting no reward, I tsay, no reward but — the little — delights that tsweeten the blood.'

But her visit to the grove had sweetened her blood, and the heaving of the can of paint, and her escapade with Bruce.

'And insolence,' Grampaw went on. 'The tsweet insolence of having dared filch their measure of rapture from the tstupidity and tstagnation around them. I never did that. Not quite. Tsomewhat — yes ... They know the cosmos would never miss them. But they would never miss the cosmos. They do not look for truth. They *are* truth. And are they ever alarmed? Are they alarmed by tseeing that in the flow of custom and the flux of tseasons cruelty does not matter? I tsay no, and I am full of wine! Because they have humor! They dream but never yearn. They keep the curiosity of their childhood. Are you awake?' ·

'Yes, sir. Mitch will never be all of those hard things.'

'They are aware. Ignorance is the tstate of ignoring. Always aware! They never preach as I am doing now, an old man full of wine. Wine makes me old . . .'

The old words had little meaning for her. But she would listen more with senses than sense, as one basks in the flow of well-woven music. Then in bed she would lie awake for an hour, dimly feeling the vague margin of another stratum of life, a region of boundless richness. And she came to feel this Infinity with which Grampaw was so much concerned. She felt it, not as a place somewhere back of the stars and beyond the centuries, but as a reverent feeling — exemplified, for her, by the flow of waters, or the patience of a tree, or even by the label of a can of Anderson's jam showing a jolly monk holding a can of jam bearing another jolly monk displaying still another — infinity. And when Grampaw told her things in the Infinite grew larger instead of smaller, she lifted her hands and gave up. But she ached alone, alone, toward some veiled insistent need. Often in her exquisite confusion she called upon God for light, the Giver of light, or merely relaxed her will and her soul into His hands, wondering whether He knew.

She talked to her baby. The sweet insolence.

Through the summer they worked and played. For the few dimes in cash they needed, they took speckled trout for the market up river, and Grampaw daily paddled the fish to the river for icing.

Despite his frequent periods of gruffness when Sister felt she was unwanted (as she was), she became aware that she and Grampaw were alike in temperament. He never questioned her conduct past or present, and during discourse rejected or applauded her embryo opinions, using two kinds of laughter, the bitter and the sweet, but laughter always. When she was too naïve, it caused him a kind of pain to enlighten her. He was now carving an entire community of wooden dolls — a fat policeman leaning down to answer a child's question, a mayor of New Orleans, a bad boy studying his lessons, the usual obscure winner of the Irish Sweepstakes, a scullery maid with a mop. Sister began to save questions to ask him. When he was in the proper mood she put her query. Why do sharks lay square eggs? What makes the oil travel up the wick? Sometimes her question would precipitate a long discourse veering into many anecdotal byways; or it would result in some meaty utterance one could ponder a long time.

They had music. Grampaw had a phonograph with a morning-glory horn, and he taught Sister some of the strange dances of the Balkan mountains. He had nearly a hundred cylindrical records sent by countrymen in New York who wrote bulky letters and shipped pungent sausages in tin-foil. Some of these tunes were the melodies upon which noted composers had based parts of their works.

Frequently they went visiting to remote camps, out near the Gulf. There was considerable social intercourse that year on Bay Saint Francis. Hundreds of fishermen, discouraged by the low price of oysters, had decided to remain idle during the summer rather than work for a pittance. So while Grampaw talked and drank in a camp, Sister would be free, alone or with friendly children, to explore new regions — beaches of driven white sand; grassy islands blinking like emeralds on a pounded shield; jagged coves where the waves spent themselves in the rushes, and the lean sure frigate-hawks whirled in fleet black legions.

Sister loved children. They believed in magic. They took her restless wanderings and her fits of torpor for granted. They never asked her what she was hunting for. In adult company Sister sometimes giggled with the children, or at least did not show that she disapproved of their mischievousness — and this at a time when she should have been interested in the women's talk, practicing their wiles and imbibing their lore.

She grew strong and brown, with a shy white smile, and remembered Grass Margin only on Sunday when the faint dong of church bells came to her and she could picture the wild games in the orchards and the vividly clad negroes courting on the levee.

She continued to go visiting with Grampaw until her body grew larger.

9

IN THE summer Mocco Kalavich was restless. He caulked his old pirogue with cotton, and paddled up and down the river looking for a girl. There were one or two nice ones in Lacroix, terminus of the Lower River Railway; but their fathers and brothers were too watchful. Mocco attended dances at Pilot Town, the lighthouse station at Port Eads, the River Engineers' settlement at Burrwood. He wanted a pretty girl, blonde, refined, who loved sunsets, long walks, letter-writing. He thought of many interesting sentiments that might be used in letters.

He needed someone to encourage his ambitions. At this time he wanted to be an inventor. Inventors everywhere in America were making fortunes with their airplanes, moving pictures, gas engines. Mocco believed the water hyacinths that clogged the bayous might be used for making fiber bags. People said the lower River needed only one big man endowed with brains to wake the natives up to the possibilities of the Delta's bountiful resources. Mocco aspired to be that man.

He found a job once, selling lottery tickets for the lottery in Lacroix. There was a negro lottery and a white one. Many white customers asked for negro tickets. Working diligently for a week, Mocco was awarded the agency in Grass Margin for both lotteries. He began visiting Forts Jackson and Saint Philip on pay-days. The soldiers were ardent gamblers. So he began to earn quite an income. But once the chaplain found Mocco smoking in the right place but at the wrong hour. He was reported to the commander, and ordered off the reservation.

He paddled downstream against a vicious south wind and arrived home at dusk weary and disheartened, to find his father had grown worse. The room was full of neighbors, each suggesting some root or weed as a *remède*. Melia, the negro servant, had prepared no supper. Weak and giddy with hunger, Mocco went to the river and hauled in the shrimp trap. The box contained but a handful of shrimp, which he boiled and ate with hardtack and a bowl of *kostric*. He found the honey-jar empty. Melia was fond of honey. She could eat a tumblerful, swallowing the wax.

Presently Pretty John's wife brought a bowl of catfish soup for Tony. After taking it, he told Mocco to chase the people out.

'How do you feel now?' Mocco asked.

'Always the same. God punishes the uncomplaining. Your sister is the cause of all. Did you go see her today?'

'Not yet. What did you eat for dinner?'

'Bread and grits, I think.'

'An' butter,' said Melia, tenderly rearranging the pillows. She sat by the bed with hands folded on her huge stomach. Melia had a head cold. She hoped Tony would last until winter. (She was appropriating to her own use half the money Grampaw sent Tony for food.)

Tony would not allow them to wash him or to raise the window shades. Sunlight annoyed him. His tongue was furry. He watched a fly crawling to and fro on his hand. The insect mounted a knuckle and began vigorously to roll its head between its paws, then wandered leisurely about the back of the hand, apparently in search of something. Melia sat sniffling dolefully, waiting to be dismissed for the night.

Mocco took a grass mosquito-brush and went down the

levee. He swung the brush in circles. He could see waving currents of insects washing past the big jaundiced moon. On a passing ship he heard big Sam Watts, a pilot, singing a song. This was the pilot who had insisted Mocco should be discharged by the Association when it was discovered Mocco was color-blind. On that fateful day he had carefully tested Mocco's sight in the presence of others, using a green necktie and a red curtain. Now Mocco studied the port and starboard bridge lights of the ship. When he looked at the lights together there seemed some difference in the colors, but when viewed one at a time they appeared the same. Mocco's heart was black with youthful bitterness.

He cupped his hands and shouted at the ship, 'Hello! Sam Watts!'

First the echo came over the water, then a voice on the bridge: 'Hello!'

'You're a dirty no-good pig-faced bastard!' Mocco shouted.

There was no reply. The singing on the bridge was not resumed. The immense black ship went swiftly by, leaving a roar of waves among the willows. Mosquitoes flowed past the lonely moon.

Mocco proceeded down the levee until he reached the home of St. Germain, the deputy. He stole in among the tomato bushes and groped through the leaves. That very day, he had seen the bushes drooping with large ripe tomatoes. Now he could find none. They had been picked that afternoon. Only hard ones remained. With curses and tears Mocco searched and searched. He went back home hungry. Melia was sitting by the bed as he had left her, not a muscle changed.

He lit his bull's-eye lamp and fastened it to his hat. With his gun he crossed the orchard to the melon patch. The young melons, he saw with his light, had been gnawed by rabbits. He went to the ditch-bank and waited, swinging his head to and fro to play the lightbeam over the patch. Mosquitos collected on his hands and neck in a thick fuzz, which he occasionally smeared off.

The deep quiet night brought puffs of swampy breeze, and hints of distant well-fed voices wrangling cheerfully. In the trees the roosting chickens stamped their feet continually, to dislodge mosquitoes. Mocco was unbearably lonely, and a hard lump rose in his throat. The bugle was blowing at Fort Jackson. There was a dance there tonight. What was Sister doing now? She had written him a letter. He had not replied. What was there to tell her? Was she at this moment bustling between Grampaw's stove and table with dishes of broiled mullet, or pot-roasted clapper rails, or her savory shark-fin soup?

His sweeping bull's-eye picked from the darkness a glowing red eye. He aimed at the ruddy glow and fired; but when he crossed the patch and looked, there was no rabbit, only a shattered watermelon, its pulp tough and unripe. But there was a scampering of tender little feet in the dark. Rabbits seemed to be scurrying off in all directions. On a blade of grass was the creature whose eye had caused him to fire — a huge black spider, looking up at him calmly. He reached down and crushed the insect. He went through the dewy trees to the house, dismissed Melia and went to bed hungry.

Some days later he met Sister in Dutch Scenery. Sister was down on the river edge filling a mealsack with silt for her garden in the camp.

'Just in time to carry this to the canal for me,' she said, cheerfully, but her heart felt a pang to see how Mocco looked, bearing himself with exaggerated casualness, his derby hat cocked, his body thinner than she had ever seen it before. His skin was burned almost black. He wore a yellowish celluloid collar. Suddenly Sister felt an acute longing for Grass Margin and home.

'What are you doing with yourself?' asked Mocco.

'Working and playing.'

'Playing! In that camp?'

'I raise little chicks. I make kites and fly them. I weave palmetto stars and crosses. I look through the telescope when ships pass in the river and see the women's styles. I read books and dress dolls.'

'You're drifting off from your home and people. I can tell.'

'How?'

'I don't know. You're — different. You look high-toned. You talk different.'

'What are you doing, Mocco?'

'Selling lottery tickets. What else can I do?'

'You were selling egret feathers.'

'They're going out of style. I had a wonderful chance there. Now they change the styles.'

'You could still make a stand of beans.'

'Root the ground for some commission merchant in Chicago? Have him write me a letter the stuff spoiled on the way? I want brain work. Wait till I get to town. I'll show all of you.'

Mocco whistled courageously, pushing back the greenish derby hat. The day was three colors, blue, green, and the nameless magic hue of the river, streaked with bluish backwater from the Gulf. The wind kneaded the water into slow fat swells lumbering upstream. There were some girls playing in an empty shell-barge. Their voices came against the thick wind, singing. They held hands and danced in a circle with one in the middle. This was a joke on Mocco. The middle girl was a wizened hunchback. She and the others smiled at Mocco as they sang a song that linked the cripple with Mocco:

> Rain rain high and the wind blows cold,
> The snow is a-flashing through and through,
> And Miss Pearly says she'll die
> For the sake of the land and the Roman sky!

> She's handsome, she's a beauty,
> She's a counter one, two, three,
> So please tell us who she loves!
>
> M. K. says he loves her,
> All the boys are fighting for her.
> Let them all say what they will
> For M. K. loves her still!

Mocco looked like his father, smiling with his mouth only, and the way his nostrils went white. It startled Sister. She took his sleeve and they moved to a bench under a fig tree. Figs lay thickly strewn about the ground, some of them covered with ants.

'Do you ever get sick of living?' Mocco asked.

Sister felt a strange power rise within her and flow to Mocco. She laughed. 'You're a big baby! Don't mind those girls. Who are they, after all?' But she was dreadfully lonely too, here with Mocco.

'Hell, it's not the girls!' Mocco said. 'It's everything. I *hate* it here!'

'They couldn't pull you away with sugar mules.'

'Do you still make devil's-food cake, Sis? Remember you, me and Mitch in the kitchen at home? Jeezam, we had good times! How is Mitch? Nobody hears from him.'

'I wrote to him twice, and no answer.'

'And Bruce?'

'He wrote a long time ago from Lacroix. Said he'd leave the country in three days if I didn't answer.'

'Jeezam, everybody's separated from each other.'

'He sent me some pink soap and a scrapbook, Bruce.'

'You made a big mistake. Bruce was a real friend to me.'

'Why didn't he take you along?'

'How could I leave, with Papa still alive?'

This was the first mention they had made of Tony Kalavich.

'How is Papa?' Sister asked.

'You can't tell. One day I thought he was gone. He took the Sacraments. Melia even went and told the bees, and Uncle Placide came for Claiborne. Papa owes him twelve dollars. He wanted the mule.'

'The nasty skinflint! Don't you let anyone take Claiborne! I'll send Placide Durot the money, or Grampaw will. Does Claiborne still like you for not working him?'

'He's lots of company. Jule says Papa might live for years. A fine life for me! Bruce was willing to live with us and work the place if you'd married him. Now he's gone. Mitch is gone. You'll be an old maid. I'm going through hell without a decent meal. Unga's gone, too. You played hell, Sis.'

'Unga's gone where?' Sister asked in a dull, miserable voice.

'Nobody knows. Papa scared her away that night.'

'She's in New Orleans!' said Sister, reflecting. 'I'm sure she left on the *Hail Mary* that night.' She leaned her head against the tree, her soft young throat arched back. The crazy jumble of events involving her almost stupefied her. Mocco seemed waiting for her help or suggestions. Was Unga alone in town without money?

'Let's go to New Orleans, Mocco. I've got our fare! To hell with it! You'll find work, I'll keep house!'

'You're crazy, Sis.'

The bright vision of city towers faded from Sister's mind.

'I'm crazy and you're afraid ... well, come eat supper with us.'

Mocco chewed a spray of pepper grass and his dark harassed eyes swept the prairie, sprawling fine and free, away and away into the verdant distance. Far out the winding canal the camps gleamed, each stocked with good food and wine. High above the camps many twinkling kites danced and flapped their dainty tails. The oyster people did not like Mocco. He and a companion once had been caught stealing oysters from the beds, fishing them from a pirogue with gloved hands.

'Come eat with us, Mocco.'

'They're expecting me at home. Somebody's got to keep an eye on Papa. Jeezam, I could use some of your steamed cabbage this minute!'

'I can tell you how to cook it.'

'Write it down.'

They went to the store. Sister asked for paper and pencil. From the post-office wall Mateo Lucich ripped away the picture of one of the mail robbers, a fellow with a mischievous pug-nosed face. Sister wrote the recipe on the back of this circular. Mocco sat in the store doorway and fell asleep. Sister included all details. The cabbage was to be shredded and steamed in tomato and onion sauce with a little garlic and a mess of fried pork cubes, and served with rice. She awakened Mocco to give him the paper, but just then a man passing on the levee called to Mocco. Mocco left Sister standing in the doorway and joined the man. Sister looked after them in a bewildered manner until they disappeared in a distant saloon.

'Better you take chair to wait for him,' said Mateo. 'He drink in Numa's place. Mocco don't like my whiskey. Like Tocko oysters, no like Tocko whiskey. Take chair.'

'No, thanks. Give him this paper when he comes back, please.'

Mocco forgot about the recipe. A week later Mrs. Lucich found it lying on the counter. Seeing the feminine handwriting she scolded Mateo in the presence of the customers, and thereafter prepared her cabbage as directed on the paper.

10

SISTER went past the cannery, deserted now for the summer. Beside its hot red oblong bulk rose a tall heap of blinding white oyster shells in the form of a cone. Near this were the rickety negro shanties, smelling of rancid greases, fenced with festoons of blackened Spanish moss curing in the sun. Sister walked among the shanties inquiring for Carrie Longmire. The girl was not at home; but turning away Sister saw her coming off the levee with a huge basket of washing on her head. On top the basket of clothes was the girl's straw hat. Carrie was peeling a banana, smiling, chanting to herself in a sweet doleful voice. She appeared not to see Sister.

'Good evening, Carrie.'

Carrie stopped, swaying her torso to balance the basket. Her great dry lower lip sagged outward; her mad eyes gazed with sad vacancy at Sister's throat. 'When de clouds move same direction wid de river, what do dat mean?' she asked in a voice thick and rich. 'See can you remember what I done tole you.'

'Carrie, what happened to Unga January?'

'Ah'm wearin' mah crown o' thorns today. No time fo' debment.'

'Listen, Carrie! Where is Unga? Tell Sister.'

'She overcharged in de works of de earth.'

'Tell Nicolene all about it, then.'

'Nickel, Nicolene. Gimme nickel, white folks. Gimme one po' lil hambone nickel, wearin' mah crown o' thorns.'

'Think, Carrie! Where is Unga? In town? In New Orleans?'

'Gimme nickel Ah'm gon' do my trick. Watch dis!' Carrie snapped her entire body around to face the opposite direction without changing the position of the basket on her head. Once again she pivoted herself about, and the basket did not budge. 'Ain' dis worths a nickel, white folks?' Sister handed her a nickel, which she placed carefully in her ear, and crossed herself. She eyed Sister's throat blankly.

'Tell me about Unga,' said Sister. 'Carrie's a good girl.'

'Amen!'

'Carrie'll tell Sister what the boys on the mail-boat say about poor Unga who was run off the Margin. Carrie's a sweet girl!'

'Amen, by God! Carray never tracks up de Lawd's scrubbin'.'

'Carrie's ——'

'Carray woshed in de blood of de Lamb! Bound for de land of vision!' Carrie walked away, down the hot plank-walk. She had no hips, and her tough dry feet scraped harshly and plopped. Sister followed her to her doorstep, thinking, 'Washed but not rinsed.'

'Please tell me, Carrie!' Sister begged.

Carrie's mother was in the window. She was a great fat yellow woman with a grease-coated chin, chewing something. She left the window and appeared on the porch with a shark-skin strap as wide as her wrist. 'You Carray! Tell Miss Nicolene what she ax you! You wants me to lay you out, playin' off crazy than you is?'

'Ah see wicked inventions,' Carrie grumbled. She put the basket down. Sister and Carrie sat in the deep grass. Dragonflies circled about them, some blue and some green. Carrie took

Sister's hand and stared into space. She talked in a rough dry whisper through her enormous loose-hung lips:

'Shonuff. Big news today for you. Yes mam. You got a girl friend made a big exodus lookin' for de bud of renown. You know somethin'? God saved her alive. Amen! She livin' on Dumaine Street wid a Pullman po'tah and his wife, to her own bruisin', overcharged in de works of de earth. Set still! Ah see wicked inventions, double money. She got a hatred on you. You go right smack home and pray you some prayers. Take up a lamentation!'

'Who told you this?' Sister asked. 'Is this true?' But she did not doubt the veracity of Carrie, who knew all of the things which white people were not supposed to hear.

'Amen! Unga, she wukkin' in de Maternity Hospital, Parish of Orleans, a pittaful place, full of words lak de groans of de slain, and lamps turned low. Set still! She livin' by the river. She 'fraid to live nowhere excep' close to de landin' where she got off de *Hail Mary* full of grace. She 'fraid to go deep in de town where people gets run over by de horses and dey's no place to set down and res'. She waitin' fo' de news ole man Tony gone to de noble vale. Den she come back home. She thinks in de window. Long about dark she hangs in de window studyin' 'bout yo' ravish-baby. Yo' po' lil ravish-baby, got no paw! How come you didn't tell Carray 'bout dat? Ain't dat's a fine way to treat po' Carray? Is you takin' up a lamentation? Is you beatin' yo' wayward breas' an' is you heppin' de po'?'

'Who told you this?'

'Amen, amen!'

'Who saw Unga in town? I want to talk to them. Is it the boys on the schooner?'

'Amen! Is you castin' down yo' eyes, an' is you heppin' de po'?'

'I want her address. Get me Unga's address on a paper.

I'll give you a quarter. Five nickels. Carrie's a sweet girl. Carrie knows everything.'

'Amen!'

Sister paddled home thoughtfully. She was troubled because she could not feel sorry for Unga. She was only depressed and awed by a sense of the ponderous ruthlessness of events.

After supper she and Grampaw were on the porch, Grampaw with a book on zoology and Sister with her kite, which had been in the air, flying in different directions as the wind shifted, for three days and nights. The kite tugged valiantly on the string. The sky flamed in varied tones of red. Grampaw would stop reading at intervals and blink at the gorgeous sky, holding his place on the page with a thick blunt forefinger. The skin of his hand was mottled and creased in the manner of brightly tinted scales. Sister's gaze wandered idly up the long curve of the string and rested on the kite, hanging motionless and stately against the flaming clouds. She loved a kite! The strong smooth drone of the hummers flowed down the string to her fingers linking her blood with the deep reaches of pure space.

And through Grampaw's telescope she could bring the kite suddenly near. How strange it looked in its own element, magically endowed with life! And she saw other kites, the sky was full of them, of all colors, like blowing sky-blossoms, even away over Grass Margin were some. She felt another prick of homesickness for the place which she hated.

In the night the house was full of strong dark fishermen talking on the floor until a late hour. They wore stiff black or cinnamon-colored suits and strangely shaped boots of foreign make. There were three Dalmatians, a Serbian, and a Montenegrin called Turk, who wore a fez and watched Sister with reddish eyes set deeply between humps of bone. She returned his stare with a still, feline sort of defiance, feeling herself an object of black, foreign desire. One of her forefathers had been a

Turk, she had heard — a roving Christian Turk, renegade to his Prophet.

Grampaw pounded the floor with his glass and spoke sharply. He was trying to induce the oyster fishermen to organize and protect themselves against exploitation by the canners and Northern dealers. His eyes flashed above the group, and the Slavic phrases rattled sharply from between his grim lips:

'Own your oyster bedding grounds! Own yourselves! By God! Here you are! You settled here! Nobody else would! The sun's too hot! Too many mosquitoes! No dry earth to walk on! Too lonesome! The work's too hard! But you came from Europe and do it! Your fingers are stiff and your backs humped from the oyster tongs and pushing poles! You gather fine harvests and the rich waters are yours! You young fellows! Investing your sweat! Investing in the — hell! are you cows and sheep? Wake up! Wake up! This is America, the land of promise!'

Sister, crawling into bed while the talk seethed on, lay confused, excited, lonely. She peered through her jumbled thoughts trying to find Unga, swallowed by the city, searching for a place to sit down and rest. She thought of Bruce, large and well-meaning, roaming the rivers with a stricken heart. And Mocco, ill-fed and despondent. Her dying father at home, refusing to talk. And deep in the unknown darkness of her body the growing baby which, Grampaw had said, already contained within itself the seeds of future men and women.

What had started all this? she wondered.

Back to the source she groped. Was it she, herself? Or was it Bruce, seeking shelter on the west instead of the east shore that night?

She would never know! No one would ever know! She knew enough about things to see that. There *was* a first cause, but it was hard and hidden and gone — into the past. She felt the past. She *heard* it — a cold faint droning. It was vast and be-

wildering to her, composed of all the things that had ever happened.

During the greater part of the night she lay sorting out her
thoughts, staring at the dark, feeling herself intensely alive and
part of what Grampaw called the fascinating spectacle of existence. It was as though she had only just realized her identity
as an individual. She was a woman! She was concerned in
strangely important events! She became acutely aware of her
relaxed body throbbing of its own accord, fashioned to move in
curves of play and angles of work, capable of chiding or consol-
ing itself, of uttering a command or forgiving a fault. She
cupped her tough hot breasts in her hands and breathed deeply
of the strong salt wind blowing through her mosquito-bar.
She would soon be sitting by the fire with a bosom full of
milk . . .

But for many days her mind toyed with the notion that there
was a dark culpable cause of the events which had lately involved her and the others. And at length she decided to let it
be the wind — the nor'wester that had driven her to Bruce's
boat that first night. Yes, it was the wind that had blown their
lives awry, the dark Northern visitor.

11

SISTER worked and played and waited for her baby. The newly born, rapidly maturing part of her seldom forgot the approaching hour. As one who expects a strange but valued guest, she asked: 'What will you look like? Will we be friends?' She did not mind if the little one should look like its father, if only it would not be like him — possessing his soft, cloying humility. Whenever she thought of Bruce now, it was with healthy, clear-seeing contempt, almost mirthfully.

She wearied of the long wait. For a time she lived dumbly alone, solaced only by the magic flow of the gorgeous days, ignoring the now palpitating presence within her. Then unexpectedly the child would kick her — an uncanny impact jarring her ripening vitals like a great heart leaping. She would place her hand tenderly to the spot and smile inwardly, filled with a dark potent knowing sense of well-being . . .

Now grown large, heavy, and slow, she moved with tender deliberateness. Yet the floor seemed to give beneath her powerful tread. Her habits were almost animal-like. While sinking into the utter slumber that came each night, she stretched her stoutened legs deliciously, turning about and about, literally wallowing on the cool sheet. She drank deeply of the rainwater. The cistern overflowed daily with the thunderous midday showers. The flavor of oil and ripe olives assumed a new fullness. Always a bright golden stalk of bananas hung under the camp. Softshell crabs, sheepshead, drumfish were plentiful. Visitors brought shrimp, terrapin, pairs of tender summer duck; Grampaw bagged many marsh hens, and the two broods of chicks had reached broiler size.

The brightly scoured, disorderly camp with its books lying everywhere was filled with salty breeze and Grampaw's opulent laughter. Life took on a certain largeness, tolerance — an easily flowing quality dictated by Grampaw's hale contempt for petty concerns. The clock stood unwound. Grampaw was always alert and ready, yet never in the way — as unobtrusive as a shadow. When not laughing or telling stories of his youth he was fuming, in his half-serious way. At this time he was busily mingling with his neighbors, endeavoring to rouse them into organizing a fisherman's co-operative group against the approaching oyster season. He rose daily before dawn. She heard him splashing himself with water and puffing like a porpoise. He left hurriedly, and often returned late at night, to lie smoking in his mosquito-proof cage on the porch. Or he would pace the kitchen, talking to his granddaughter but not for her, voicing the surplus notions of his seething brain ...

Father Sam, the Grass Margin priest, came one night. Sister secreted herself in her room; she was not yet ready to see the priest. A long time she lay listening to them. The two men had resumed the argument they had been engaged in for twenty years, concerning the nature of man and of God. As usual, Grampaw had conceived many new ideas and discovered passages in his reading in support of his agnosticism. The men talked courteously, yet eagerly and with guarded incisiveness.

'I thank the Supreme Being for his blessing,' Grampaw said, 'and I condemn him for the tsuffering he has caused. If he is omnipotent, he foresaw the coming of evil. Before creation he foresaw it. Christians exploiting and butchering one another. Floods and plagues. Poverty. His church afraid to denounce wealth and war. If a God made me I didn't ask him to. I came here with inherited tendencies I didn't ask for, into an environment I did not choose.'

Sister was startled, incredulous. She grew afraid — of some obscure new peril in life — and at the same time filled with a sense of awe toward Grampaw, who could calmly express such insolence. Through a crack in the door she saw him at his methodical knitting, erect before the net. His body was bare to the waist, the skin white and satiny under the bronzed wrinkled throat, the chest tufted with wild silvery hair... And Father Sam's noble benevolent face slightly bowed, hesitant, sad, heavy as if with the sins of the whole community, and his hand half-lifted in a gesture of restraint.

Sister suffered for days from the shock of Grampaw's assertions. This knowledge that he doubted God lay heavily upon her. What did he mean — '*if* a God made me...' What could this mean? She shrank from asking him. Was there any doubt of the reality of the wise and watchful God — speaking to one through twilight silences, gazing at one from the eyes of playful birds and beasts? A panic seized her. She herself had conceived odd notions regarding her Creator — wondering about His daily habits, the language He spoke, and whether He was not lonely, with no one wise to comfort Him, and nothing to be comforted in — soft, silly thoughts that she could smile at now. But they had resulted from her *love* of God, a desire to know Him... And she also loved Grampaw, the wise erect one whose pride was very sad. She loved Grampaw, and Grampaw doubted God! It was unbearable, unbearable.

Secretly she went to his books for enlightenment, the volumes of philosophy, science, religion — written, she knew, by writers he loved. Searching through these for weeks, however, she found nothing that interested her, nothing that enlightened. She quit the task filled with childish misgivings. Some sweet vital spark of hope and trust which she had always borne within

her now seemed dead forever, forever. Her mind was only be-
numbed by the deep, persistent, mocking music of vaguely remembered words. For a time she avoided comradely contact
with her grandfather, watching him with pained or puzzled
eyes from a great distance. And he, briskly and with his usual
dexterity, went on performing his tasks — doubting God! She
would never understand him, never!

Now her child was growing more active. Sister was working
unusually hard, cooking more elaborate meals for the increasing number of visiting fishermen; preserving quantities of figs
and watermelon rind. When she lay down to rest, the child
kicked incessantly, as though urging her to bestir herself. 'Damn
it, be still!' she exclaimed out of sheer impatience. But when she
slept, the child slept, and they awoke together. How good! the
refreshed awakening after a small nap! It was mid-afternoon,
hardly time to cook. She could watch the skies from where she
lay, day by day ripening and growing full, as she was growing
full. The huge flat-round earth under an inflamed sky was
smoothly wind-washed and fruitless, devoid of reddening fruit,
barren of mellowing seed. But the sky was gloriously fertile,
ploughed back and across by virile winds, bearing transitory
clouds like cool frosted forests, brief gray gardens, ruddy heaps
of blowing grain. And the quivering green waters were fertile.
Fisher-boats crept punctually through the canal, miraculously
heaped to bulging with silver harvests for the waiting city.
The earth-colored fishermen cursed cheerfully, or chanted
brave discordant songs.

'Doctor Dobravich will be on the next boat,' Grampaw said.
'I invited him down from New Orleans.'

'Who is he?' she asked.

'You will like him. A famous and jolly physician. His father
and I were together in Franz Josef's cavalry. His grandfather,
Wolfgang Andreas Dobravich, was one of the Emperor's doctors.'

'How do you know I will like him?' she asked, with the self-assertiveness Grampaw had encouraged her to cultivate.

'Because he will like you. He will imitate a steamboat, and tell you all about the tsalt mines.'

The next boat brought the doctor, with many fishing-poles and a shooting outfit. With him was an attractive golden-haired woman. The little camp was the scene of a confused, noisy welcome. Grampaw laughed loudly, brought out wine, olives, hardtack, and played the phonograph. Sister was quickly drawn into the merry group. She danced with Doctor Dobravich, who sang through his nose the words of the old waltz.

Mrs. Dobravich danced beautifully with Grampaw, who was an excellent waltzer. Tall and effortless, she was wafted by the music like a reed in the wind. Sister watched her dark, luscious lower lip, held between her teeth. Her full greenish eyes shifted with tender negligence, wandering listlessly through the screechy mechanical tune, gazing at nothing, seeing nothing. To Sister she seemed wholly at home — though the camp must have offered her many novel sights. And she made Sister feel at home in her own house.

'Show my Loretta where to rest,' said the doctor after lunch. 'My incomparable darling is tired, but the flat marshes will rest her. Maybe we'll put some health into her out here. Her ribs are beginning to show. All dressed up and no place to go. Another rhyme!'

'Don't trouble,' said Loretta. 'I mean to look after myself this once.' Her quiet distinct voice was quite cool beneath its warmth.

The doctor took Sister's hand. 'You're splendid! I like you! Soon I will go like a steamboat for you. You're like your poor mother — much prettier than I thought you'd be when I saw you attired in a morning diaper. And now it seems you're having a brat of your own! The first? I'm beginning to understand why Grampaw invited me here to fish. Was there a mission at the church? Since leaving Lacroix I've seen a dozen pregnant women. Whenever there is a mission here ——'

'Nikolai!' Mrs. Dobravich interrupted. 'I think I'll ask ——' She turned toward Sister a lovely face that seemed at once vital and wan.

'Nicolene,' said Sister.

'—— Nicolene to show me around the place.'

'You're a tactless bungler!' cried the doctor, raising one finger above him, 'devoid of discernment, intellectual hardihood, sympathy toward ——'

Mrs. Dobravich checked his words with a kiss, and rumpled his hair. He protested, sputtering:

'Did I hold this child when she was a month old and sucked my tie for an hour? Why not come to the point? A stitch in the bush is the mother of prevention.' The doctor was shorter in height than his wife — grotesque, nervous, bandy-legged. His enormous eyes swam in pools of merriment. He rolled them mischievously at Sister as she went out.

'Did you see my Tony on the Margin?' Grampaw asked.

'Tony needs air and food. He might get well. Part of the bad lung's still there. He's got the Kalavich resistance. Nicolene has it too. You see that belly?'

'What belly?'

'Hers. It sets in a fine square box.'

'Don't tell her that.'

'—— strongly buttressed, structurally perfect. Look how she carries it! That's what I call built to stand. Most women are. You and I are built to run. She's made for motherhood, Nicolene.'

'Tche ails. Beginning to think. That age! Tche heard me telling Father Sam about God, tsome foolishness . . .'

'That's bad — thinking. Get her functioning as a whole.'

'I am not her husband.'

The doctor had his shoes off. He rubbed his bare soles gratefully on the clean smooth floor. 'I'll bet they say you are—some of them.'

'Yes,' said Grampaw bitterly. 'Tsome will think the child is mine.'

'What the hell.'

'Yes. What the hell.'

'Don't let her think too much. What can it lead to down here?'

'Give me advice. I need your advice.'

'Never mind. I'm telling you what to do for the present. Keep her busy. The baby will come smaller then. Plenty to do, and variety in diet. Plenty oily fish. I'll be here to deliver it, provided the tarpon are biting, or at least the reds... Tony might get well. Give him more food and keep his window open. He's starving and suffocating.'

'That lout Mocco! Tselfish idiot!'

'I like Mocco. Loretta likes him. He's raising mushrooms. A money-making scheme.'

'Money! What can he do with money? I'll go over and tstraighten him out. Mushrooms!'

'He needs a girl pretty soon. The boy's trying to reach for something. He's fighting the mud that flows in his blood. Another rhyme! How do you feel yourself?'

'Fine! Why not? Am I not an old man? I have another calling. I will live to raise my great-grandchild. Perhaps until he's able to look after Nicolene.'

'It could be a girl.'

'Girl or boy, I'll leave them comfortable. I want to make tsome money now. A little hobby for my descendants. My books are a little dull. I have read everything five times, and reached the point of mature ignorance. I want to do tsomething. I tshall lease more oyster beds. Hire men. I am making a large oyster association to bring good profit to those who raise the oysters. Things will change out here.'

'This rich country needs a leader. That's been the legend.'
'I have known that.'
'And you are that man?'
'I'll be that man.'

During the afternoon the men would hear the laughter out-side — soft, tremulous, guarded. Sister was entertaining for her guest. Loretta had grown animated. She stood with the telescope, examining the distant camps.

'I see a blue man painting a boat,' she said. 'Now a woman emptying a tub. Another one combing a little girl's hair. In that farthest camp, the one with the white kite, two boys are playing with a dog. The dog is barking, so close I could almost touch him, and no sound comes from his yapping mouth!' She laughed softly. Her garments were faintly perfumed, her fingernails polished. Her entire person suggested a delicate, softly tinted, flowerlike newness, strangely sprung from a city's grime and disorder. Sister had never before seen manicured nails. They were too pretty for scratching one's self. There was a sadness about Loretta, a tired appealing sadness. She swung the telescope about to see the snug rooftops far over on the Margin; the grassy battlements of Fort Saint Philip miles northward; and far over the prairie the fat slow bulk of a deeply burdened liner seeking the sea. This too amused her — the ship seemingly groping through the marsh grass, with no river visible. She held the telescope delicately, with fingers spread outward, as she had held her fork at lunch.

'The big Delta!' she exclaimed. 'So splendidly forlorn! Peace — but no place to walk. This is a place to be passed through — to be looked at over one's shoulder. And it is real to you! You feel permanently a part of this! You feel secure here! See the grass and grass, and smell the sea! I have a friend, a painter from New York. He would like to paint here. The mud is brown and the wind is clean. I'll tell René Davidson about this place. Could we build a camp here, Nick and I?'

'Anywhere you please.'

'Like yours?'

'Yes, mam.'

Loretta called to her husband. Nikolai's hair was in disorder, his face redly suffused. He and Grampaw were arguing about bygone civilizations. 'Nick! Come see something!'

'I'm mad at you!' Nikolai answered. He winked at Grampaw. His eye remained closed a long time.

'He's getting tipsy,' said Loretta. 'I want him to build a camp right over there.' She pointed the round long arm, the imperious polished fingernail on the end, and beyond the fingernail a green place by the canal where the camp would surely be. The vague rare fragrance emanated by her clothing gave authority to her words. She had pointed at many coveted objects. She looked at her husband through the reversed telescope. 'Nick, my little man! I want us to have a camp built right across the canal. You can come to escape your practice and I my dull friends.'

'A camp!' Nikolai answered. 'Well, will you pay for it? Grampaw orders the material tomorrow. What does my darlin' Nicolene say?'

'She will visit us every day.'

'Order the nails and wood!'

Loretta squeezed Sister's hand. Her eyes flashed happily.

Nikolai said, 'You'd better see how Grampaw feels about having you for a neighbor.'

'I'm sure he won't mind,' said Loretta.

Grampaw pointed his pipe at Nikolai. 'With our machines and sanitation,' he said, 'and their seasoned philosophy, the Chinese might produce a civilization that . . .'

Loretta took Sister's arm and led her away.

'I wish you wouldn't be hard on poor Loretta,' said Nikolai.

'Tsince when is she poor?' Grampaw asked.

'If only she could have a baby!' said Nikolai. 'You would see a happy woman. I've got my work. She's got nothing, poor child, nothing but me.'

'It is very tsad. But you must not get maudlin. You insult my wine.'

'You insult my wife.'

'We can't drink your wife'

'Tell me about your storms, then,' said Loretta.

'I've never seen one here,' Sister answered. 'I saw one big one on the Margin.'

'I suppose they're beautiful.'

'No. You get frightened. They pull the trees over and rumple the houses so the windows won't open. Snakes came in our house that time.'

'Snakes!'

'From the swamp out back. The tide came in and drove them to the river. There were moccasins in our house, and ground rattlers, the bad little vipers.'

Loretta was not hearing Sister. She was looking fixedly through the window at Grampaw. There was a small quizzical frown between her eyes. Behind Grampaw on the wall was his cavalry saddle, forty years old, the same color as his face. Sister thought: 'These two are enemies, but they have seen each other only three times. The dislike is his, not hers. I don't dislike her. But I had better not show her the dolls. Perhaps the dislike is hers. Perhaps she has seen him blow his nose without a handkerchief. Ah, her beautiful hands for a man to kiss! What things do they do?'

The women wandered about the shell island under the camp, and Loretta asked many questions. She was interested mainly in the curious aspects of the Delta — the huge floating islands moving in the wind with men working on them; the brief rain-showers that pass on a clear day, close enough to be heard; the birds that drop from the sky into the water and reappear long afterwards at unpredictable places; the insect-devouring plants; the peculiar fish, the tchoupique, which can live ashore in the soil. Loretta had taken biology at school. She could identify the classes, orders, and families of the mollusks or crustaceans they found. But Sister knew the creatures' daily traits. (Living with Grampaw, she was already dimly aware of the dramatic play of life in and on and above the earth.) Finding Loretta as ignorant of her mind and life as she was of Loretta's, Sister vanquished her timidity. Because this well-bred and educated woman found her words interesting, her self-confidence took speedy growth. It was an important hour.

Loretta would go barefooted as Sister was. She considered this a rare lark, and called Nick to see. The hairs on her legs were pale and fine. The feet were well-shaped, but the toes were crooked, crushed sadly together. Sister smiled to herself at the toes that had trodden many alien soils. In the water they still huddled together as if for comfort.

'In my camp I'll go barefooted and get my big feet as brown as yours,' said Loretta.

'You really mean you'll build a camp?'

'Of course! Whom shall we get to build it? Does your husband happen to be a carpenter?'

Sister turned to the other, her eyes round with surprise: 'Husband! I've got no ——'

Almost at once Loretta leaned over and whispered, 'You may have mine, if you'll give me the baby.' They laughed together. Then both were silent for a long while. Sister tossed a shell at a basking crab. She was ready to dislike Loretta. She almost wanted to, but the other would not provoke her. A huge bronze and purple dragonfly had settled on Loretta's toe. Her hand stole quietly out, reaching for the gorgeous insect. Her face was wistful, half-smiling, thrust out as delicately as a poised trapezist's. Sister tried to envision a deep quiet friendship between them, such as the classical friendships of which she had read. And the thought was exciting, the hour important, deeply significant to Sister beneath its show of light decorum.

Sister began at once to cause the ritual of hospitality to move about herself. She gave the visitors her room and laid a straw mattress for herself in the loft. And through the day the Dobraviches conferred upon Sister the tacit prerogatives good breeding accords a hostess. Sister's mind excitedly fingered the honorable old word which she had encountered often in her reading — hospitality! The word was alive — as full of meaning as Bruce's word 'ancestors' had been. Nikolai praised the supper extravagantly. Loretta took a recipe for her own cook.

'Let me wash the dishes, it will be fun!' Loretta exclaimed.

'You'll ruin your hands!' said Sister.

'Oh, I want to ruin them! Can't I, if I want to?'

The polished nails went into the dishpan.

'I wish the ladies of the Wrought Iron Club could see you now!' said Nikolai. 'They'd give birth ——'

'Shut up!' Loretta interrupted, scraping a dish with her lovely nails. 'You're supposed to entertain us.'

'Yes, tell us about the salt mines!' Sister suggested.

'What — what ——' the doctor sputtered, and gave Grampaw a savage look. 'Are you telling everybody about that?' he asked Grampaw, and threw a sofa-pillow at the old man.

'Tell us! Tell us!' Sister pleaded.

'There's nothing to tell, except that I bought a lot of bogus stock in a salt mine that melted away.'

'And you tried your best to get *me* into it,' said Grampaw, 'and fell out with me when I laughed at it. Tsalt mines in Tennessee!'

'Talk about your travels, then,' Sister said.

Presently Nikolai told them a story of his student days in Vienna. He had lived in poverty in a garret with no friend but a pet cockroach. During the long hours of night study, this roach had assisted him, he explained, by keeping other roaches away from him. Hugo, as he called the roach, would move back and forth across the book page to lead Nikolai's eyes from word to word, and while Nikolai wrote his notes Hugo would hold the place in the book. If Nikolai dozed, Hugo would fly up and tickle his nose.

The Dobraviches would leave in three days, then return in a month to await the baby. Loretta would assist Nikolai in the delivery, at least 'morally.' 'Tomorrow,' said Nikolai, 'we'll see if the pelvis is all right — although the Kalavich pelvis is known in the old country as being equalled in size only by the ——'

'Nick!' exclaimed Loretta.

'—— by the thickness of the Kalavich skull. Do you feel well, sweetheart?'

'Yes, sir,' Sister answered.

'No pain, eh?'

'Discomfort on the waist,' said Grampaw.

'Skin pain, Nicolene?'

'Yes, sir.'

'Rub with olive oil. Loretta, will you show her how?'

'Of course, darling.'

In the night an enormous ruddy moon came through the glistening reeds. There was the muffled booming of distant alligators, and in the canal the tinkle of pursued mullet. Grampaw and Nikolai went out with torches to spear flounder. Sister lay on the bed and Loretta rubbed her with warm oil. Loretta's hand, coated thickly with the bland liquid, clung to Sister's body, slid around the firm live bulge of the abdomen, where the skin had been stretched and pitted with deep raw gaps. The women were silent.

Sister watched Loretta's revolving arm. Circling between lamplight and shadow it glowed alternately nebulous and vivid, like some evanescent wand, exerting but faint pressure, and charged with solicitude and pain. Sister did not observe the barren woman's face hanging above her, wise and hapless in the shadow. She only lay half-drowsily contemplating the odd wordless moment, quaintly soothed all through by the sorcery of oil. And the gruff forebodings of her flesh were assuaged by some hint of fatality, smooth benignant fatality, in the passage of the clinging hand tracing its great oiled circles.

Long afterwards in bed her mind revolved in those vast slow circles without need of goal or comprehension, and she saw herself once more the ragged secretive creature of the circling seasons prowling the harsh grasses of yesterday, or the fragrant groves. Or she was the core of it all, the quick ripe core of a whirl of fantastic events stirred into motion by the wind on a dark fabulous night long ago.

12

LORETTA returned in a week. Grampaw met her with civility. She brought Sister some back numbers of smart magazines showing handsome photographs of well-known women lounging on yachts, fondling sleek dogs or horses, sitting on garden seats. One magazine devoted considerable space to views of Loretta's country home on the Mississippi Coast. In one of these Loretta sat under a huge live oak, smiling prettily.

'You look like the pictures of the other women,' said Sister. She crossed the kitchen and returned with the freshly picked carcass of a hen. It was plump and bluish, with rich globules of fat visible here and there through the immaculate skin.

Loretta raised her eyebrows, shifted her gaze from Sister to the fowl's body and back. 'They're silly,' she murmured, 'but ... oh, well ... you'll enjoy the satirical articles.'

Sister deftly slit the fowl's belly. She flashed a friendly smile at Loretta. 'I don't know what I mean,' she said. 'The pictures seem all alike, sort of, and you with them. I mean the way they sit, I guess.'

'Yes. The thing is to be casual. Never get excited. But they *are* excited, appearing in *Country Hostess*.'

Sister's busy hand came out of the hen's body full of brightly hued entrails. 'Are *you* excited, then?' she asked. The iridescent blue gizzard was heavily encrusted with fat, like a big gold-fretted jewel. Loretta shrank away a pace, turned her head, did not answer Sister's question.

'You're not angry?' Sister asked.

Loretta would not approach the table with its pile of entrails. She smiled amiably. 'No, of course not, dear!' she said. She sauntered toward the breezy window. 'Can I do anything — help you with anything?'

Grampaw, sitting on the floor in a corner, raised his eyes and stared at her back over a wrinkled nose.

'Wash the chicken if you want to,' said Sister. She handed Loretta the pan of dismembered fowl. Loretta had brought along some 'house' clothes, figured washable garments, and an apron, the first she had ever worn. Gingerly she carried the pan to the cistern. Sister flung the offal through the window. In the canal outside a splash was heard, then a loud rush of agitated waters. With her face screwed up and her lips compressed and white, Loretta washed the raw meat.

Loretta stayed a week. She begged Sister to allow her to attend to the housework while Sister made dresses from the material she had brought from New Orleans. So Sister busied herself only with cooking and sewing. Grampaw absented himself, except during mealtime. Loretta was quite excited, cleaning windows, dusting furniture, paddling her hands about in hot soapy water. 'It's as much fun cleaning dishes as soiling them,' she said. She ate plenty of fruit, slept at night more soundly than ever before. She would get sleepy around nine o'clock, earlier than Sister would. The moon was good, the nightly bath, the dripping nakedness under the camp beneath the moon's bold gaze, then the firm sweet bed and the drowsy purr of the distant sea.

Never before had Sister talked so much to anyone. Grampaw did not join this talk. He and Sister had little to say to each other that week. Sister was blossoming out a woman now, he thought, in her element. Hearing her unconsciously mimicking Loretta's precise articulation, he gritted his teeth angrily.

The women chattered incessantly. Whenever he came in he found them at it again. The details of household economy which had never concerned her at home seemed now to fascinate Loretta — such problems as contriving means of using table leftovers; methods of removing stains and eliminating odors; and the housewife's vigilant warfare against flies, roaches, ants, moths, even bed vermin, which might at any time appear seemingly out of nowhere to breed in the home of the unwary.

Sister made a trip to Dutch Scenery with Grampaw. He was alert and taciturn. On their way home Sister said, 'Loretta wants me to go and stay with her until the baby comes.'

Grampaw at the oars made no answer.

'Well? May I?' Sister asked.

'No.'

She was startled. He looked into her eyes and smiled.

'I don't see why not,' she said, pouting.

'I have good reasons. Next year you may go. If tche wants you then, you understand?'

'Yes, sir.'

Sister rowed Loretta to Dutch Scenery to board the packet for home. When the whistle blew, Loretta took her hand fondly.

'Good-bye, dear. It's been the grandest thing ever happened to me. May I come again?'

'Whenever you want to.'

'Oh, I do hate to leave! But I'll be back soon again, for another dose of wholesome work and — reality.'

Sister did not quite understand those words.

While they talked, Sister saw Mrs. Lucich in the window of the store, leaning on her bloated bosom watching them. When Sister passed on her way to the canal, Mrs. Lucich called, 'Goot *evening*, Mrs. — Miss Kalavich!' and bowed in an exaggerated manner. Sister flushed and bowed cordially. She restrained herself from telling the store woman to go to hell. It would have been bad manners.

Loretta Dobravich visited Sister several times that summer. After her second visit, she did not rise in the morning until breakfast. Sister made new curtains for 'Loretta's' room, and she was crocheting a spread for the bed. She repainted all the walls in the camp, ordered a bright new reading-lamp to surprise Loretta, and made hanging baskets of willow for ferns on the front porch. A pair of rocking-chairs was bought.

In the soft quiet evenings the women sat on the porch, which Sister had induced Grampaw to screen. Mosquitoes wailed on the wire. Far across the marsh blackness the beams of Port Eads Light revolved in silence.

Loretta yawned contentedly again and again, deep, grateful yawns that renewed the air in every lung-cell and brought moisture to her eyes. 'Tomorrow I want to polish the stove,' she said sleepily.

'You'll do no such thing!'

'Oh, but I must! I *must* polish a stove, I tell you.'

'All right. All right.'

'I'm too lazy to go to bed. Please you get up first.'

'It's early.'

Loretta laughed, and snuggled down in the rocker, sighing.

Sister thought: 'Heat lightning over Chandelier Islands. Last year this time Mitch Holt brought me the first watermelon of the season and we sat on the levee eating melon and seed-fighting in the heat lightning. Is this a dream of a dream? What is Loretta doing here? Is there a baby inside me? Will the banana I ate today form little eyebrows? Was Unga conceived in rapture among the willows? Are we all dreaming? Our Father who art in heaven! God, God, are you there? It doesn't *have* to be a place in the sky! Pregnant. Pregnanted. Knocked up. Is it up? Knocked. All conceived in rapture, humanity. Here comes Radovich in his skiff. Man in heat lightning pulling his oars, bothering no one, attending to his business. Grampaw says this is religious. All work is religious. What does this mean? I don't love my baby yet. Why is Loretta here? Did I cause that? Yes, Grampaw sent for the doctor because I got pregnant. Where will this lead? *This*, tonight, what is next? Am I right at this minute bringing something else about? Should I say to hell with it? Should we mind our business and let what happen will and tomorrow's another day? *Why* does he say thinking of one's self is bad? It looks religious, yes, the man pulling oars in the heat lightning, not bothering anyone, tired, sincere, only wanting to get home, minding his business. Stars and flowers mind their business. Thoreau worships Hebe, cup-bearer of Jupiter and daughter of Juno and wild lettuce. And where she walked it was spring. Thoreau: "I have a great deal of company in my house, especially in the morning when nobody calls."'

She turned to Loretta and pointed toward the distant revolving light: 'Loretta, down there is Baptiste Colette. It is a pass from the river to the sea. Once there was a man, Baptiste Colette. He wanted to get to the sea without dragging his pirogue over the marsh. He took a shovel, they say, and cut a little ditch. Every year the river scoured it wider. Today it is a big swift pass. It helps take high river away. The man is dead.'

'There are strange things around here,' said Loretta. 'A trapper on the boat told me he found in the marshes all of the metal things that go in a household, rusting among the reeds. Decay is quick.'

'Except the cypress.'

'In twenty years nothing left of a big village but a mound of oyster shells. It is like centuries of decay occurring in a few years. I daresay it's lonely down by this Baptiste Colette.'

'Very lonely,' Sister murmured absently.

'The loneliest of places.'
'The loneliest of places is a womb.'
'Or a grave.'
'A womb.'

13

NEAR the end of October Loretta and Nikolai came for the baby's delivery. Sister saw them coming in the skiff when Loretta was a dainty blue speck. Half-dazedly she remembered why they were coming. Wearily she smoothed her hair. This was four days before Sister's time. She received them quietly, with little emotion. She was without humor, curiosity, vitality. Her shoulders sagged and her mind was torpid. During the previous weeks of fitful winds and crazy rains, she had conceived a certain dour black self-aversion — a final desperate marshaling of hostility against the stupidness of past events and the irksome obscurity of the future.

But now, her hour approaching, she was resigned, quiescent — feeling like an inert, shuffling, undreaming mass of hot swollen flesh, incapable of laughter, wrath, or pain. And what did it matter? What did anything matter? She ran her leaden fingers through her hair. They came away joyless and damp, and she did not care. Her leg, propped ungracefully on a chairedge, would slide off and thud inertly on the floor, like wood, and she did not care. She wanted only to be let alone, not to be talked to, not to be looked at. It was indecent to be compelled to endure the presence of others. There should be a lair for her to crawl into, hidden from people and things. Events were meaningless.

The day following the doctor's arrival was strangely filled with incident; yet to Sister all was remote and unreal.

Nikolai was whining and cursing with an infected arm caused by a sawgrass cut the previous day which he had neglected to doctor. Grampaw was highly amused by this, and Loretta was worried. Sister sat unmoved by her friend's antics, mechanically throwing stitches into her net.

Then in the afternoon a letter came, delivered by Carrie Longmire's brother. It was from Unga January in New Orleans. Some amanuensis had written it for Unga — in French. It was all decorated with quotation marks, underscorings, exclamation points, brackets, dashes. Unga T. January. Sister had been trying to communicate with Unga for months. She gazed at the letter, the quaint signature, with dull eyes.

'Unga writes to me in French,' she murmured.

'Who?' asked Loretta. The two were alone. The men were under the camp in the cool.

'Unga. My girl friend. She knew I can't write French. We used to . . .'

'Surely,' said Loretta softly. 'Shall I read it for you, dear?' The rosary slipped from Sister's lap. She straightened her spine, trying to draw more air into her cramped bosom. It was a still torrid day. Her chin and forehead were thickly dewed with sweat. A heavy obsession lay back of her mind, harassing her vaguely — an irritating awareness of the vast, blue, windless day outside, of stolid frogs too comfortable to croak, struggling fowl purposelessly cleaving the thick heat, and everywhere the lifeless waters congealed, fixed to reflect the image of interminably curving reeds. She raised her eyes to the waiting negro, who was also stupid and intrusive.

'Shall I, dear?' Loretta asked.

Sister frowned and nodded her head and shoulders.

'Unga is well. She sends love and happiness in your baby. She gets the news from men on the boats. She is to be married on the seventh of November. She loves her husband . . . He loves her dearly. He works in the car-barn. To get married she requires about eight more dollars, for pillows and music and small things.'

'I haven't got eight dollars.'

'We'll send her a check. Shall we surprise her with a nice generous check, dear?'

'I have no check.'

'I'll attend to that, dear.'

'All right. If you . . .'

They sent the check by messenger, one hundred dollars. Sister gave no further thought to the check or to Unga.

Finally, in the afternoon, Mocco came. With him was Mitch Holt's father, who waited outside, talking to Grampaw from the pirogue. Mocco clumped cheerfully up the stairs, whistling. He shook Loretta's hand awkwardly. He saw Sister. He stood dumbfounded by her bigness, and her aged, worn face. No one had told him there was to be a baby. He was indignant. He unbuttoned his new coat and glanced about the camp. He was disgraced. Suddenly his face brightened.

'You know who's here?' he asked Sister. 'Guess who's on the Margin! . . . Mr. Bruce! He wants you to let him come over here. He had an idea you might need him now, and he came down.'

Loretta rose and sauntered casually from the room, waving her small sandalwood fan.

'Talk English,' Sister said.

'I'm just telling you. Jeezam, Sis! How do you feel, Sis? He's got a new boat — well. Twenty horsepower!'

'I feel . . .'

'I'll go tell him to come over. Don't you want him?'

'No.'

'You don't need — don't want to see him?'

'Who?'

'Him.'

'I told you no. What time is it? You look well — bigger and more tidy. Kiss me, why don't you?'

Mocco picked up the rosary and hung it on the chair-back. Sister's lifted face was jaded, glistening with moisture, like the countenance of one emerging from the deeps possessing some insupportable secret. Mocco walked away. On the back porch Mocco leaned on the rail, staring over the vast incandescent sheen of the marsh. Presently he went in. He kissed his sister and turned away. Sister paid him no further heed. On his way out he took a banana. He smiled at Loretta on the front porch, and stuffed a third of the banana into his mouth. There were tears on his face. He swallowed the banana with difficulty and smiled, the great brilliant tears oozing from his eyes. Loretta did not know what to say.

'How are the mushrooms?' she asked.

'F — fine! I shipped——' His cheek was puffed out with banana and he was weeping copiously. 'I shipped a hundred pounds yesterday. Good-bye. Take — care of her.' He hurried down the steps. The banana peel dropped and Loretta kicked it into the canal. She looked in at Sister slowly throwing stitches. Loretta was barefooted like the others, and immaculately clad in starched white muslin. She was not perspiring. She was lapsing into a half-stupor from the long hours of heat.

She went in and sat by Sister. She folded her pale hands and leaned back, relaxing, with bare feet crossed and lowered eyelids dyed by the hot blue window glare. Now she began to talk dreamily in her low, precise articulation:

'Visit us with your baby. The city will amuse you. We have a small nursery at home. It was there when we bought the house. I can never have children. I came from a family of twelve, the tenth. All of my sisters have large noisy families.' She was smiling. She saw that Sister hardly heard her remarks, but worked on as though deaf or insensate. Grampaw beneath the camp was heard to laugh heartily at something Nikolai had said.

'Your grandfather is a superior man,' said Loretta. 'You must try to get his secret, although you have a secret yourself, strange and remarkable serenity when you are well. Last week I had four vacant days. I tried to crochet. The next day I made that.' She pointed. It was a jacket she had knitted for the baby, hanging on the wall. Under the jacket on the table was a geographical globe she had bought for Sister. The globe shone like a newly born planet. 'On the same day I thought of the globe for you. I knew you'd like a terrestrial globe. The next day I went for a long drive.' She smiled brightly, then her face fell into pensiveness, but Sister was not attentive, so she went on: 'I passed the clinic for Nick. The clinic was crowded. The poor! The dumb, hollow-eyed poor! Those faces, watching my carriage, drained of hope and gladness, swam before my eyes all night. And nothing can be done. What could I do, with my paltry fortune?'

Sister was looking at the globe. Loretta closed her eyes. The unhurried sun now shone through the window, flooding her misshapen toes with rosy light. 'I dream that some day someone will need me. Nick doesn't. In town he's hardly aware of my existence ... So the day after the jacket I thought it would be nice to have the house done over. I tried to discuss it with Nick. He makes a joke of it. You see I had books, catalogues, magazines, samples of the fabric. He wanted to get downstairs to his rabbits. "Anything you decide will suit me. You go on and have your fun." I said: "Darling, please show some interest. This is our home." He said: "I took interest last time. You were very enthusiastic the first day, then you lost interest and the decorator couldn't find you, telephoning my office." I suppose he's right, but perhaps if he'd show interest I would be different. See the condition of the poor darling's arm today! A little dab of iodine would have prevented that. He neglects his diet, eating those heavy Creole breakfasts. He neglects his friends, never remembers the date, overworks himself, brings home the most dreadful people. When he cooks for them he prepares the queerest stews and hashes, dormitory recipes, burning with pepper that he warns his patients never to use.'

'What time is it?' Sister asked.

'Almost four.'

'Would you please rub me?'

Two days later the baby was born. There was a cool white breeze of wind. Everyone in the camp was more cheerful. During the first pains, the small ones that seized her like gently tugging threads, Sister smiled, made wry faces, and even chatted with Nick. All the mental dullness was gone. Her body was alert, girded for the bright final encounter. She joked with Nikolai, whose temper had improved since his arm was somewhat better.

Sister had been jarring figs. The air was still sharp with the odor of cloves. Throughout the afternoon occasional fishermen poled by. They glanced up gravely at the neat dwelling perched aloofly, the source of the now harsh screams that carried half a mile. They would raise a slow hand, saluting Grampaw on the porch with his knitting, or they touched their cap to Loretta, who waited with her cheek in her hand. No wives of the settlement came. They had not been sent for. No one had known the child was expected. No one understood any aspect of the affair, save the certitude of Nicolene's queerness and the probability of her bearing an idiot. While on Grass Margin it was believed the child was Mitch Holt's, the Slavonians of Dutch Scenery, being unfamiliar with Sister's life on the Margin, had little basis for conjecture. The more conservative and pious ones thought Grampaw was perhaps the father, but few were bold enough to say so. Yet the suspicion, propelled now by an intuitive glance and then by a laconic deprecatory allusion, was spreading — flowing from mind to mind like a murky permeation beneath a limpid stream.

Loretta said to Grampaw, 'I would adopt the child later on, if she were willing.'

Grampaw stared, blinking, as if he had never seen Loretta before. The woman, realizing her mistake, felt utterly annihilated. 'Adopt what child?' Grampaw asked.

'Adopt Sister's child and give it — well, an education and so forth. I'd promise to give it good care, every advantage.'

Grampaw spat. He rubbed his cloud of silvery hair with both hands. His bright reasonable eyes traveled from his work to Loretta and back, several times.

In the camp the laboring girl uttered through the silence a long, savage, unnatural screech of rage, like a powerful beast throttled. Loretta paled. Her throat was getting raw from hearing the screams.

'Is that what you've been sitting there thinking about?' Grampaw asked Loretta. 'Why don't you read a book or take another bath?'

'Is it so inconceivable to you?' Loretta queried gently with her soft look. 'Is it inconceivable Sister might be handicapped in a stern world? Or that the child might be entitled to a chance — a richer life, broader ——'

'I don't understand. If I could know what's behind or under your ideas! What are you up to? What is it, beg pardon? You tspeak of a richer life. Do you mean richer than Sister's here? Did you talk to Nikolai about this? God pity poor Nikolai!'

Loretta looked away, cut to the heart. She looked down at her hands.

'Then you tspeak of being handicapped. Handicapped in what, please?'

'Well, I mean the usual difficulties. We cannot ignore the stigma.'

Grampaw laughed at the awaited word. 'The tstigma! And you will adopt the tstigma too? No! The tstigma will not hurt her. We can fight the tstigma!'

'I didn't know you feel that way. Last night you told Nick and me the feeling around here about you and Sister might give you trouble in your oyster association scheme. I gathered you were angry. I feel that all this will be a hard burden for you. So . . .'

Grampaw's jaw hardened. He glared moodily over the lush and vacant plain. His face, bilked and trampled by the years, seemed for a moment as tired and puzzled as the woman's. Then, 'Yes,' he said. 'I was angry. By Christ, it will be a valuable fight! My last and my sweetest!' She heard him chuckling zestfully behind his dark brutal frown.

Suddenly they heard a baby. There was a baby in the camp, squalling angrily! Loretta's face sprang into light and color like a flower. Nikolai met her in the doorway. He carried a towel.

'A deckhand!' he crowed. He clenched his freckled hand and flexed his unbandaged arm playfully. 'A burly Tocko deckhand with genuine Tocko organs! Go grease him, my sweetheart.'

'Yes,' said Grampaw. 'Tshow her the little tstigma. Find her tsomething to do. I'll kill and tsoup a cockerel for the mother.'

Loretta's eager shadow swept past Sister's bed to rest across the cypress cradle. Her face, radiant with pain, sank low; and her nostrils met briefly the very odor of birth, the faint archaic rankness of nascent flesh. 'Baby!' she cried. 'Darling ugly little man! Make him let me stay here always! Make him let me!'

Her oiled hands traveled over and over the tough quick torso of the baby, and up and down the struggling members, clinging; and her deep throaty laughter was rich as poured gold. Once Grampaw came and stood behind the kneeling woman. It was a noiseless visit, but she felt him there, wide-legged and thoughtful.

Nikolai went to bed. He had rigged up with cords and pads

and pulleys an apparatus to hold his infected arm high. He grumbled that he had been cheated out of his tarpon fishing. From where he lay he could see a big tarpon lying in wait for passing mullet, occasionally leaping with a great crystal splash. Nikolai was nearing the end of his three-month vacation, his first in six years. He had visited many fishing resorts, but had caught no fish, because always there had been a clinic near by, or a colleague with rabbits or passable wine.

'You poor darling!' said Loretta. 'Is there anything you want?'

'Yes, put a sail on me and get me a compass. I want to go home.'

Loretta took his hand, but just then the baby in the next room stirred, and she hurriedly left her husband . . .

Sister slept deeply.

14

LORETTA returned in five days, alone. She brought many gifts for the baby, and fine dress-goods for Sister, who had sent away the hired negress and was doing the housework. Loretta stayed for a week, a gay and memorable one. The two women were alone all day, Grampaw being out fishing and cutting willow channel markers. Loretta bathed the child by the roaring wood-stove. She carried it about possessively, following Sister at her work. Afternoons she tended the little crib on the south side of the camp, carefully guarding the child from the sun and wind. Loretta knew all about babies, even the proper songs to sing, a certain song for each occasion. And intuitively interpreting the child's sounds and gestures, she was constantly mindful of its veering moods and aware of its every need. When the baby was being fed she lingered near. She moved softly, yet without her wonted genteel weariness, at intervals casting a pale vigilant glance at the eager working of the infant's jaw. Sister smiled. She was glad to share the child. Because of the baby, Loretta would return again, and talk about the French Opera, and the great David Warfield at the Tulane Theatre, and the brilliant balls and gay parties of the social season, and the racetrack with its hoarse throngs and galloping colors, and René Davidson the artist. When holding the baby Loretta spoke interminably of herself, her past life, and of people she knew. With the child in her arms she seemed older. Her face, so close to the pink countenance of the child, now lacked something of its usual unsullied freshness, and bore faint signs of ravages wrought not so much by care as by its absence.

The baby rarely cried. Innumerable passersby and people in adjacent camps marveled at that strange thing. Visitors emboldened by a desire to learn whom the child resembled were struck by the serious, almost contemplative look with which he stared into space. Sister herself wondered, what was the child remembering?

Loretta returned again and again, always laden with gifts. The loft was cluttered with gifts, most of them packed away in their boxes, toys and trinkets the child was too young to use. As soon as Loretta arrived at the camp, before even removing her hat, she possessed herself of the baby. For an hour she would talk and coo to the child, holding it on its back in her cupped hands like some rare fruit or vital potion upon which she longed to feed.

To Sister the baby was not yet wholly real. Often she half-fancied he might droop and die, like a flower of which she was the rugged stalk. How could a thing endure that was so strangely begotten? She could not recall the father's face. All of her remembered meetings with Bruce had become merged in her mind into one blurred night, full of wind and laughing waters. The cries of the geese struggling overhead were perceived more clearly than Bruce's arresting phrases. Did she love the child? She did not know. Since bringing it forth she was again confronted by her own problems, beholding her own resumed growth, attending former promptings which now recurred with added insistence, visualizing the busy world without, groping for God.

But did she love the child? There he lay, freshly powdered and healthy, flailing the air with resolute manly fists . . . She did not know.

Spring was coming. The sweet long days of good growth,

music in the camps, and in the sky the long-awaited golden plover. But did she love the child? She ought to know that! A nameless fear took root in her mind. Then she shrugged her shoulders. She must not dwell upon herself while spring approached. She turned to Grampaw:

'Let's read Shakespeare!'

The stove's warmth had set Grampaw dozing. He had worked hard since dawn. 'Do what?' he asked.

'You're tired. I'll warm you a punch. Are the fishermen coming for the meeting?'

Now that the busy oyster season was closing, Grampaw was again preoccupied with his association. He had written many letters to authorities concerning similar ventures elsewhere, and received some answers. His association had not progressed beyond the stage of discussion. Some fishermen had confidence in Grampaw and assented to the moral justice of his idea, but they were reluctant, afraid, in this strange land, to band themselves against their exploiters. Others had somehow cooled in their attitude since the birth of Sister's baby.

'Two fishermen were coming,' said Grampaw. 'If the lantern on the wharf tstill burns, put it out. They are not coming.' Sister was glad. She disliked these meetings, dreaded the quizzical stares of strangers eyeing her with hidden thoughts in their eyes.

'Do you need anything for your kitchen or baby?' Grampaw asked. 'I am going in tomorrow morning to mail tsome money to the bank.'

'You're putting money in the bank?'

'Well?'

'But — it's so funny. I never knew you to save. You said it's a bad habit.'

'Tsummer is coming.'

'"Sumer is icumen in."'

'You — we will need things. For winter. Perhaps we will earn nothing in the summer. Perhaps the trout ——'

'Is that bothering you? Are you starting to worry about —
us?'

Grampaw laughed and rumpled her hair, but she saw his
eyes. From his brave battered face they were looking far beyond
her, far beyond the walls.

'I hope you won't start worrying about us, Grampaw. After
raising one family ——'

'Don't take it so tseriously!' he said, chuckling.

When he walked to his room, his shoulders were very straight.
She heard him settle into bed, grunting with great relief.

In the morning he awakened her and the baby, chanting an
old song of the Austrian troopers. Later he returned from Dutch
Scenery with Sister's daily letter from Loretta. Sister had a
thick packet of these. Each was a sort of chapter in an in-
genuous narrative of Loretta's doings. Loretta was an affection-
ate and facile writer. Sister loved to compose the answer, writing with extreme vigor, but little facility. In this her first cor-
respondence of consequence, she was gradually acquiring skill
and solace, tracking down her elusive impressions. But the captured phrases, once confined to paragraphs, seemed little more
than footprints of her thoughts. Never, never would she be
able to convey the image and the essence of her feelings. Nor
did she care to. In one letter she told Loretta about her per-
plexities concerning God, her growing inability to commune
with Him satisfactorily. Reading over the letter, she tore it up
forthwith. It seemed rather silly and pointless.

'Nick lost a patient yesterday,' Loretta wrote. 'And can you
imagine, he's *angry* about it — impatient even with me. Is the
baby all right? You didn't even mention him in your letter.
Are you concealing anything to spare me, darling? I am worried. It is so windy and draughty down there, really pneumonia
is one thing that would give us trouble, so far from medical aid.
Today is dank and heavy, not a ray of sun. My andirons gleam
cozily, but I cannot read. I have been lonely, far lonelier than

down there. I have an army of friends, none interesting except the few truly brilliant and charming ones, who are obscure people, not of my world. They are dear to me, but when on rare occasions they seek me out I catch myself wondering, "Who am I to attract such a one? What does she want of me? How does he plan to use me?" Ah, darling, how rich you are! What a rich life you lead! If you knew! I sent you by mail a little bottle of drops. If he develops a head cold, put two drops in each little nostril, and don't laugh at my precautions or tell Grandpa, darling.'

The earth was growing warm. Everywhere the bristling reeds rose and sank in the wind, as under madly prancing feet. Sister, thinking by the dripping cistern, saw the distant clotheslines flapping gaily. Far down west a blue rainstorm had gathered somewhere into livid sheaves; but the soft infinity overhead bore only a scattered few tiny clouds drifting like loosened bits of some giant migrant's plumage. She wrote to Loretta:

'Do not be worried about the baby. He is full of joy and hunger. I have people here too, all around me, that I don't want to mingle with. That's why I stay to myself. Loretta, why don't you find something to do? Why don't you travel or something?'

At breakfast Sister and Grampaw heard a strange far cry in the wind:

'Wah-eeeeeeeeeeee-oooo!'

They looked at each other, waiting.

'Wah-eeeeeeeeeeee-oooo!'

The call was strong and clear, imperative yet plaintive.

'A whooping crane?' Sister asked.

'Yes. In trouble. I have not seen one in years.'

'I must see it!'

'Wait! That fellow's at least a mile away. No use looking.'

Sister had heard of this huge noble bird, that is as big as a small man. When her mother was a girl one of these great white creatures had stalked past the cemetery on All Saints' Day night, and the people gathered among the blessed candles burning on the graves had jumped the fence like maniacs, many brave fathers leaving behind their children and swooning wives.

'Hist!' Grampaw cautioned. But the cry came no more. Sister's heart kept pounding throughout the meal. Her eyes shone with excitement.

Suddenly she tossed her head and said: 'I like Loretta.'

'What does that pertain to?'

'Loretta. Nick's wife. I like her.'

'I know that well. She is a nice person.'

'You don't like her.'

'I am Slavonian. At least I was. I have been in the cavalry, riding all over the Empire. I have known women.'

'What does that pertain to?'

'Nick's woman. We have returned to the tstarting place. Let us go elsewhere.'

'You needn't like her.'

'I like her. She likes you, too. Tspeaks highly of you. You will be a wonderful woman, feeling many things. The deep kind, living at the tsource, tsuffering to laugh to tsuffer. Loretta has much tsense.'

'I think she's *very* nice.'

'Good! I understand. She has money, culture. Tsweet disposition. Nice manners. She can't have babies, so she has artists. She has taught you to curb your profanity, and fix your hair, and where to put the seeds from your olives. A good friend for you to keep, for a time.'

He smiled at her, his sharp kindly face a cryptic expanse of shrewd fissures, the ape-like eyes clear and reassuring, yet glittering, burning, dancing with some alien, seasoned, hard-won judgment withheld. Sister was exasperated.

'You don't like her!' she said. 'Why? She loves books. She has traveled everywhere. She ——'

'What do you want me to say? The woman is not important. Pleasant and virtuous. Important — no! I joke with her. I admire her. But to think on her — hell! What truth or law does one deduce from her?'

'And you go around deducing laws!'

'I go around living! I am not defending myself to you!' He turned away. Sister's face was scarlet, but her eyes flashed after him, full of spirit. Grampaw returned.

'You have neglected your knitting for three days, Nicolene.' He smiled, but his tone was not without sternness.

It had been agreed that Sister would spend some time each day working on a net. It was the only task Grampaw insisted she should perform. She must cultivate this habit.

For a long time she sat grim and rebellious, knitting. Soon, she was contented, at one with the other women of the region who knitted in dignity. Grampaw thought: 'I am an old fool! Sister will never be corrupted by the tame conformists.'

And at supper he was jovial. 'Perhaps,' he said, 'Mrs. Dobravich will invite you to town. She has a fine house and carriages.'

Sister began gathering the dishes. He watched her back. He could feel her wits floundering. His eyes twinkled. In a rather shrewish tone she said: 'Why talk about Mrs. Dobravich?'

'We are taking this too tseriously, Jolie. I have nothing grave against her and the other millions like her. If you insist, I have tsomething against her civilization, her age, her period in history.' Now Sister was interested. She had drawn him out into what she considered to be deeper waters. 'It is not entirely Loretta's fault,' he continued, 'that she goes around in rings, picking things up and dropping them. It is her civilization, our civilization. Built with slaves and doomed to crumble as all slave civilizations have. That is not for you — yet. The thought for you is this: what is Loretta *for*? And this: everything she considers important is probably not important. And this: what does she *do*? Is it not very tsad? How can she be real? She does nothing! How old are you?'

'Over eighteen.'

'Bah! Bah and dog-damn! Your pardon! . . . what is she for? Like the poor fellow holding the tspear in the play.'

Sister bit her lip to keep from smiling. Whenever he grew pompous and sententious, Grampaw's face looked like the swaggering, comical doll he had carved to represent Doctor Johnson. But Sister thought: 'Loretta comforts her valuable husband. She laughs at his jokes. She keeps him merry and couraged. She is the other half of the great doctor.'

Grampaw said: 'You are thinking tche is a useful wife! She helps Nikolai very little. She probably makes him a little afraid of things.'

'How — afraid of things? What things?' Sister's eyes were big and imperative.

Grampaw glared darkly away, his face a gloomy mask. 'Things. Life.'

'What things?' she insisted.

'I don't know. All of it. She makes Nikolai — makes him careful. A little. I'm afraid he's slipping. It's a tshame. A doctor who knows that in addition to valves and chambers the human heart also has cockles. Slipping comfortably into the status quo.' Grampaw was no longer talking to Sister. There was rain outside moving in bunched gusts, laving the shingles like dim hoarse breaths. 'The insipid glutinous status quo that nurtures the race but starves the man. Nikolai is slipping. Loretta does not know.'

'I don't understand,' said Sister.

'Nor I.'

Sister went to her room and wrote to Mitch Holt in prison. The letter discussed Mrs. Dobravich, but not the baby. 'I have a new friend, an interesting rich woman from town. She has been to China.' Sister decided not to mail the letter she had written to Loretta. She was confused regarding Loretta. Before bed she sat near the crisp chill rain to remember Mitch Holt under the kitchen lamp eating devil's-food cake with a bandaged hand.

She wrote a note to Mocco, inquiring whether anyone had heard from Unga or Mitch Holt.

In Grass Margin, Mocco was crawling under the mosquito-bar beside his father. Tony's breathing was irregular. The room was stifling hot. Moths dancing about the lamp threw gyrating shadows the size of a man's head. Mocco slept, but was awakened in the night by a terrific banging in the stable. Claiborne, the mule, maddened by mosquitoes, was kicking the walls. Mocco left bed and went out to attend to the stable door, which he had neglected to close at bedtime. As soon as Mocco closed the door, Claiborne stopped kicking. The mule knew when those mosquitoes left in the stable had filled themselves with his blood, he would have peace.

Mocco lay in bed sweating, thinking: 'Sister and Grampaw don't care what happens this side the river. Why does God Almighty play with father like this when he is better dead? In New Orleans I could easily find a job, and a girl too. There the houses are side by side, miles and miles of houses full of people. Thousands of nice girls sit on the steps at night. They walk through the parks at night singing, holding each other around the waist, turning to look back at the boys. Mornings they go up Royal Street to work in droves with their little lunches in their hands, laughing and flirting, and their little heels make such a happy noise on the bricks. Trolley-cars, doorsteps, parks, all packed with girls, girls, girls!'

Mocco looked at his father. Tony's lips in sleep were puckered like a spoiled child's, stubbornly, as if he meant to lie there forever, neither living nor dying. The eye-sockets had grown dark and immense; the sharp gaunt angles of the face slanted grotesquely downward from the pale dome of the brow ...

15

WHEN Loretta came again in August, Nikolai was with her. He had a little ten-cent harmonica which he was learning to play. He wanted Sister to teach him. She played well, and they all sang the words:

> It's sad when you think of a wasted life,
> For youth cannot mate with age.

And Loretta sang her part to the baby in her arms.

In the afternoon Grampaw sailed them all to sea. He took them to one of the enormous mud-lumps off the mouth of the river, and showed them a huge crater through which the earth breathed, belching large mud-bubbles of gas. They struck matches and tossed them in, to see the gas burst into flame. And everywhere the ground was strewn with nests of pelican eggs, mottled laughing-gull eggs, and the handsome speckled eggs of the royal tern. Between the eggs and the clouds, hundreds of vociferous fowl whirled about, and the husky waves climbed the dazzling shore. Grampaw and Nikolai went off a ways in the boat to fish bull-redfish. The bright sunny desolation, the wild wind, the huge caravans of clouds forging through the sky, fairly robbed the women of all desire to talk. They sat on the water's edge, dreaming. The baby sucked greedily, fighting sleep.

'René Davidson must see this place,' said Loretta. 'He would build a palmetto shack and live alone here for a week.'

'Does he like reading?'

'Very much. His taste is exacting. He does not care particularly for the classics.'

Sister did not understand. She said nothing.

Loretta lay relaxed, thinking, 'They will like each other, two such complete individuals. Has he ever known anyone like Sister? Perhaps they will fall in love! How sweet! René loves the primitive. She would want marriage. Would René marry? She might be the very one to share his haphazard life. Would she enjoy traveling? I might arrange to have his pictures bought without his knowledge. They could go about as they please! But would she leave the baby with me?'

Sailing homeward, Loretta held the baby, tenderly shielding him with her cloak. Grampaw and Nikolai discussed their anthropology, and Sister sat wordless. She thought of René Davidson, who was obviously about to come into her life. What kind of man was he, and in which way would he change the color of her days? Then her mind told off the other motley figures that peopled her life, wandering idly from Loretta to Grampaw to Mitch Holt to Unga January.

She said to Loretta: 'I have more news from Unga. A man on the city schooner said she married a Scandinavian who used to be a ship fireman. He passed Grass Margin in ships for years. She lives near the wharf in a cottage surrounded by thick figs, with a red brick banquette. She is thin and worried, has no friends and wants none.'

But Loretta was engrossed in the baby in her arms. 'Yes?' she said. Then, absently, 'Why does Unga behave so strangely?'

'I think it's on account of the husband. Perhaps she didn't tell him she's colored, and someone else may tell him at any time.'

Loretta stared at Sister, her face under the crisp aureate hair turning sallow, and no longer beautiful. She could not talk. She turned her head, to think. 'I believe I told you that,' said Sister.

'That Unga is *colored?* I don't think so.'

'Well, it's not important.'

'You told me you had been intimate friends, but——' Loretta clutched her cloak nervously and looked away.

'I'm sorry to embarrass you,' said Sister, but she lifted her chin primly.

'Perhaps — after all,' Loretta floundered, '— that is, I suppose it's not unusual in such an isolated place ——'

'It is unusual. Our friendship caused Unga lots of trouble. Of course her people didn't approve.'

'But — what about *you?* What about *your* friends?'

'I didn't want their approval.'

The boat tacked eagerly through a seething narrows and headed for home, with Grampaw at the tiller. Nikolai was asleep, curled up like an untidy boy. Loretta's eyes brooded upon Sister's valiant tan profile. She thought: 'Does she mean that? Does she care nothing for people's approval? I doubt it. Yet her life proves it. Her intimate friend a negress! Revolting! But my lips dare not affirm my heart's revulsion ... Yes, René will like her. She has many madnesses, and is not a slave to this cheap maternal instinct. I see what Nikolai means now. She is like the grandfather. How did I become entangled with these people? The old man has changed. He is losing his color. He seems in pain. His left arm probably rheumatic ... Unga a negress! ...'

At the camp they found Mocco waiting. He had brought a present for the baby, a little rocker with a strap across the seat, and sides representing a dappled horse with a mane of Spanish moss. He had made the toy himself. Loretta was surprised to learn that Mocco was skillful with his hands.

Mocco watched Loretta examine the rocker, his eyes glow

ing with homage. He was quite sober today, shaven and neatly attired, with his shoes polished behind as well as in front.

'He's a good carpenter,' said Sister. 'Did you see the house he helped build on the Margin?'

'You helped build a house!' Loretta exclaimed.

'Shucks!' said Mocco blushing deeply, 'that was a long time ago. A little old three-room cottage for mulattoes.' But he strutted about with casual cockiness.

In the night, while Nikolai and Grampaw visited the Radoviches, Mocco sat inside with the women. Loretta was drying the dishes for Sister. At the table, Mocco sipped wine and toyed with a pencil and paper while he recounted bits of news from the Margin.

Old Man Holt had received a letter from Mitch in Atlanta. Mitch, who had been to high school in New Orleans, was now a clerk in the prison office. His letter had contained no message for any of his friends. (Sister sniffed disdainfully, but in her heart she felt hurt.)

Tony Kalavich was still confined to his bed, no better, no worse. He had consented to have the windows open, and was drinking two quarts of milk daily.

The oranges were starting to bloom. (Sister heard this with a pang. She hoped there would soon be a west wind to bring her the smell.) The previous orange crop had fetched only fair prices. Florida was beginning to produce quantities of fruit. People all along the river were complaining of hard times. Rice and sugar prices were falling. No one knew why. Only the fur-trappers were prosperous. There was persistent talk of forthcoming game laws, limiting a man's kill of ducks and geese. No one feared a law so easy to evade; but there was also to be a law prohibiting shipment of game for the market, which would deprive many hunters of a livelihood.

A band of soldiers from the Forts had broken up a dance at Pilot Town.

Two shrimp trawlers had been lost off South Pass Lightship.

As he talked, Mocco was idly sketching a picture of a house (for the benefit of Loretta). Once Loretta stopped to watch him. His fingers trembled. He scratched the pencil over the drawing and brushed it aside. 'May I see it?' she asked, and took the paper.

'What are you doing these days?' Sister asked him.

'Waiting for a job hauling logs for the levee contractor.'

'With Claiborne?'

'Yes.'

'Don't work that mule too hard, Mocco.'

Mocco sat drawing circles on the wooden table. He was very handsome in the lamplight. He had recently grown heavier; his neck and wrists had thickened; his voice was as deep as Grampaw's. Sister's heart ached toward Mocco. He looked so forlorn! He now strongly resembled Sister, though he lacked her earthy badinage and the burning inner vitality of her eyes. Mocco's were Cajin eyes, soft and haunting and indolently shrewd.

'Mocco,' said Loretta, 'you seem to be good with tools. Do you amuse yourself with tools?'

'Amuse myself?'

She waved her fine white hand. 'You know. Do you work with them often and like it?'

He looked at her with naive abashment, trying to see the connection between amusement and physical work. 'A little, yes. But I'm pretty lazy, you know.' Sister was surprised, hearing him admit to his chief fault. 'Especially after dinner,' he went on. 'I get drowsy, when it's hot or damp.'

Loretta reflected, then suddenly: 'Would you like to build me a camp across the canal? *Can* you do it? A large comfortable place with four bedrooms? Perhaps this would give you a start in a business of your own — contractor or something.'

Mocco was dumbfounded. Sister, her hands limp in the dishpan, watched him with wide urgent eyes. A long silence passed. Mocco's heart was clamorous; his body felt light as air.

'He can do it!' Sister said. 'He can.'

'Well ——' Mocco looked at his sister.

'You know right well you can, Mocco!'

'*Four* bedrooms?' Mocco did not yet believe his ears. He had always worshiped Loretta from a distance, but...

'Go on, tell him what you want, Loretta,' said Sister.

Loretta raised her sad green eyes, thinking. Mocco thought she resembled a new sort of blonde Virgin, so clear-eyed and tranquil. 'I'd want the bedrooms, wide porches, living and music room ——'

'Kitchen,' said Sister.

'Yes, that. And big porch with plenty of soil from the river for flowers and vines. And a wharf for boats, so my guests might come in through the Mississippi Sound and Gulf.'

'Two by sixes on creosoted piling,' said Mocco judicially.

Sister dried her arms excitedly, picturing the guests coming in from the Gulf... a piano in the living room... laughter... She hurriedly brought a fresh sheet of paper. 'Here, Mocco! Let's draw a sketch!' She began to sketch, but her roof leaned askew.

'Too much pitch!' said Mocco. He snatched the pencil from her, which was what she wanted him to do. He began to draw, hesitantly at first, then more and more surely. Loretta leaned close to him. Her perfume was prowling about his head.

'Wonderful!' exclaimed Loretta. 'Grand!'

So it was decided. Mocco would build the camp. He knew two good helpers he might hire. Under the lamp the three sat a long time fashioning the plan until the structure stood forth in their minds as a finished whole. Mocco had never been so excited before. He gnawed the pencil as if it contained a stimulant imperatively required. He mopped his brow. He pulled his hair into a wild state, and frequently vented a deep sigh.

'My, this is so exciting!' exclaimed Loretta. 'Shall we make the roof green shingles?'

'Oh, yes!' Sister assented.

'I don't know — yet,' Mocco decided. 'I'll think about that. Maybe we'll use palmettoes — covered thick with them. Thatching, they call it. That will look like a camp, and keep out the heat. Over the shingles — eh?'

'Fine!' Loretta agreed. Sister, too, approved, rather dubiously. She glanced doubtfully at Loretta, who nodded at her behind Mocco's back and smiled indulgently. Loretta had once told Sister she detested palmetto roofs because the lizards bred in them. Sister was now somewhat puzzled.

Mocco sat making notes for material and taking names of supply firms which Loretta gave him. Over the protests of the women, he insisted upon returning home that night. He had many things to attend to in the morning.

Sister and Loretta sat on the porch in the darkness. There was the gruff booming of alligators everywhere among the stars and waters, the wandering, fugitive smells of fermenting vegetation, and faint music at the distant Fort — very unreal, the music over the prairie.

'And now I'll have my camp, right close by you!' said Loretta. 'We'll fix it up together. How I wish it were already built!'

'You've made Mocco happier than he's ever been,' Sister answered. 'You're too good to be true, so kind to us. I wish . . .'

'What, dear?'

'I wish I knew how to be grateful.'

'I'm weary of receiving gratitude. In this case the gratitude is mine. This has been the rarest, most wholesome experience of my life. And you let me love your baby! How could I possibly repay you? It seems I've always been helpless to give anybody anything that involved personal sacrifice.'

'It's a sacrifice to come here so often, riding that bumpy train to Lacroix, the crazy little boats, the mosquitoes — all to visit a — fishwife in the marshes.'

'The marshes make me feel alive, the decay, the slow tempo make *me* feel strong, stronger than any health resort has ever. Calling yourself a *fishwife!* A fishwife, darling, carries a basket through the alleys of Europe screaming for customers.'

'I've done that here, on the Margin, that very thing. I've sold terrapin to get a dance dress, and Mitch Holt helped me.'

'Who is Mitch Holt?'

'He was my beau. He's in prison.'

Loretta slumped back in her chair, as if throttled by an unseen hand. Sister began to hum. She sat with her strong thighs wide apart, wench-like, beating her foot on the floor, and sang in a rather weird key:

> Terrap'! Terrap'!
> *Here's* your sweet lil —
> *Here's* your tender lil —
> *Here's* your juicy lil —
> Friday terrapin cheap!
> Oh, buy your rice from the grocery sto-o-ore!
> Buy your terrap' from me-e-e-e-e!

'Mitch sang the song,' said Sister. 'I rode the mule. It was fun.'

'Yes,' said Loretta. She wanted to ask why Mitch was in prison. It was all so unutterably sad! The barefooted girl under the willows, the sad dust under the mule's slow hoofs! Her heart went out to Sister and to the boy far away in his cell. Just then the baby in the camp cried. Sister's breasts were full, each cell swollen tight. When given the breast, the hungry child groped over-eagerly for the nipple, so that he could not find it. Sister laughed like a child herself, to see the infant so vexed; but soon the dripping nipple was gulped and the child grunted and uttered in its throat a rhythmical croaking. The vast purple world of wind and stars lay calmly salubrious about them, distant lamps gleaming reassurance and the saurian disquiet of the quagmire strangely quelled.

'I wish you would come live with me — always,' said Loretta. 'Wouldn't it be nice, for the summers at least? We might send your father to a good sanatorium, and you and the baby come with us. I'd love Nikolai to have a baby around.'

But now there was a boundary between them, in Sister's eyes. It was there, fixed and strange. They were sprung from alien roots. It was not yet time for honest, guileless affection between them. It was not a question of any difference in *value* between their respective stations. It was another, an obscure factor, one that Sister with her native insight felt but could not identify.

'You are so kind!' said Sister.

'Will you think over my suggestion?'

'I don't know.'

'I suppose you have your own plans.'

'What plans?'

'For yourself. For the future.'

'No. Should one have plans?' She rocked in her chair and mused quaintly. 'Did you — do you have plans?'

'Why ——' Loretta turned her star-blurred face to Sister. 'Yes, I had plans once.' She gave a low laugh in the dark, and in her voice at last there was bitterness.

'It's hard to plan,' said Sister. 'I should hate to be caught.'

'Caught how?'

'By whatever's coming. I don't know.'

'Surely. But "caught"! One would think you'd been awfully knocked about for your age. I think you have everything.'

'If you knew what's coming you'd know how to plan, I mean.'

'Ah!'

'But it wouldn't be fun, eh?'

'It isn't fun now — for most of us.'

'Oh yes, I think it's lots of fun.'

A paddled lantern was approaching in the canal — Grampaw and Nikolai returning. Grampaw's laughter floated in, somewhat barbarous, somewhat sad. Sister felt a rush of gladness. Across the darkness she hallooed. Grampaw responded gruffly. Then Nikolai was heard uttering incredibly convincing barnyard sounds — bleating, cackling, mooing, crowing. Then he mimicked a dog-fight. Finally he mimicked a steamboat. It was so realistic Sister burst out laughing and leaped about delightedly, awakening the baby.

'Give him here,' said Loretta to Sister and reached for the child. 'Yes! Bad ole mother! Yes! Waking the young man up! Yes! Yes! Wants Loretta, that's what he wants. That's what he wants! That's what he wants! That's what he wants!'

Early in the morning, before dawn, Sister planned a surprise for Loretta. She paddled to the black swamp below Dutch Scenery for a mess of young *grosbec*.[1] In the swamp she jumped from root to root among the saplings, or she waded waist-deep in the black water, keeping sharp watch for the deadly cottonmouth moccasin, the only snake that will not flee when approached. It was a difficult task for a woman. One shakes the tree and the nestlings tumble down like some strange plump feathered fruit. Then, unable to fly, but hopping away frantically, the birds must be caught by the hunter, who leaps through the deep water among the twisted roots and strange vivid growths. The black swamp was full of men and boys hunting *grosbec*, flashing eyes, hungry hands reaching, all shouting and splashing about happily gathering this rare delicacy. When Sister had taken six, she turned homeward.

[1] Night herons.

She arrived at the camp after sunrise, utterly fagged, wet to the waist, with bits of twigs chafing her between the legs and her breasts painfully swollen with milk.

The baby was crying lustily. Loretta was still in her room. Grampaw, waiting for breakfast, said nothing, but he was plainly irritated. Sister, bathed and freshly attired, sang at her stove, broiling the delicious birds in olive oil.

'What is this?' Loretta asked at breakfast.

'*Grosbec!*' Nikolai exclaimed. '*Grosbec!* Eat it!'

Loretta had the baby on her lap. She was a little reluctant about eating new kinds of food. She did not care very much for this exotic meat, but managed to eat one of the legs of a bird. She was much preoccupied with the child. She contorted her face to amuse him, and produced the strangest sounds with her tongue and throat. Oddly, the child knew Loretta very well.

Grampaw and Nikolai feasted upon every last vestige of the *grosbec*. Sister blushed when Nikolai praised the dish.

16

MOCCO bought overalls. He came each morning in a skiff with his two helpers to work on the camp. In a few days they completed the placing of the creosoted piling, a heartbreaking task involving many bruises and creosote burns on the sweating skin. They filled the site with white oyster shells, until it resembled a gaunt unroofed temple with black columns reflected in the water. They patiently barged the lumber from Dutch Scenery, the sills and plates and joists, all bright new heart pine milled in Mississippi.

All day Sister across the canal was aware of the pounding and clatter, the cheery bustle and grumbling of busy men. How happy and gruff Mocco was! She loved to watch men at a heavy task, revealing their true simple selves. She was always stirred by the irrevocable finality of a burden strongly borne, a nail driven home neatly. She shared Mocco's pride in the work. And she enjoyed feeding the three grimy workers at noon, great helpings of strong food. Afterwards they lay about the porch to rest and smoke. Grampaw was in New Orleans, gone to see the doctor about a queer, intense pain that had troubled his breast and left arm. During the noon rest Mocco sat contemplating the raw skeletal frame over the canal, his hair full of sawdust and a pencil behind his ear. He had a lot on his mind. He should have demanded a written contract — well, not of Loretta, but of her husband. Since starting the

work he had had no contact with the owner. All material
was ordered charged to her, and arrived with undue prompt-
ness . . .

'Did you write and tell her the framing's finished?' he asked
Sister.

'I told her a long time ago it was started.'

'What did she have to say?'

'Good gracious! I can't remember.'

'When is she coming down?'

'Soon, I suppose. Go on, finish the thing! She's not interested in that mess of raw lumber.'

'Mess! A lot you know about architecture! You see only
the mess.'

'We don't expect the *architect* to see the mess.'

'Never mind. I'll prove there's some brains in this family.'

'It's time somebody did.'

The two helpers eyed Sister with dark puzzled glances,
awed by her curious absorption in the formidable-looking geographical globe which she dreamily examined while nursing
her child — like a clairvoyant searching a crystal.

Grampaw returned late one night. Sister heard the grinding
of the oars. She left her bed to bring lanterns to the wharf.
It was pitchy black outside. A sweet quiet summer rain fell.
She lifted her head, offering her face to the clean lonely
rain.

'*Pozdravlyen!*' she called — the Slavonian greeting to a
welcome returner. 'Hurry and let me see you.'

'Catch this box,' said Grampaw in the skiff. 'Careful, it's
books!'

She would not forfeit the joy of welcoming him noisily. She
laid aside the precious box to embrace him, his thick powerful
shoulders and the damp woolly coat that had traveled far.

He shook himself loose like a pleased mastiff, and rumpled her hair roughly.

They sat up till nearly daylight. Grampaw's face was rosy from rain, his eyes bright with devilment. In his starched white shirt and trimmed hair, he was a vigorous, handsome figure. But somehow she longed to see him again attired in his rough and careless everyday clothes.

He told her about the new moving pictures, the first he had ever seen. He showed her a long list he had obtained, of the names of retail dealers to whom his association would ship oysters.

'I have learned much,' he said. 'We will improve our oyster grading. Mateo Lucich is going to join us. You are my tsecretary. I bought you a typewriter. Later the association will have an office here. Hire a woman to tscrub and cook. Attend to the kid. You wait and tsee!'

'What did the doctor say?'

'Hell with him. Will you be my tsecretary?'

'Of course. But what did he say?'

'He gave me drops. I am all right. Do I look sick? I pulled the river tonight and the canal. Nikolai called in his partner to tsee my muscles. Ha! If they could have seen my father at ninety! I saw your father tonight. He improves — a little.'

'Of course he sent me his blessing!' Sister laughed.

'He sent no curse.'

'He's improving more than a little. How is Loretta?'

'You tshould know that. She writes every day — or she used to.'

'Was she well?'

'I didn't notice.'

'Did Nikolai say anything about the camp?'

'Nothing.'

Sister had expected tidings of Loretta. She had not heard from her friend in three weeks.

Later she went to her room and read over the last note Loretta had written:

'Darling,— Tell our baby Loretta is kept running frantic between town and country house by stupid duties. But I'll not go abroad this year, and see you both soon. How is he? And you? I do miss you dreadfully.'

There was no mention of the camp... Since receiving this note, Sister had written twice. She could not understand Loretta's odd silence. She took her pad and began:

'Loretta dear,— Are you all right ——'

She looked from the window thoughtfully. Herons outside were stirring, and the rainy east had paled. Grampaw, bailing out the skiff below, chanted fragments of an old song...

Sister took a fresh sheet and wrote:

'Dear Loretta, — Did you receive my recipe? Mocco is going ahead splendidly with your camp. He wants to know ——'

She felt too self-conscious to go on. 'Let her answer my letters,' she thought, and hurried to work, because day had broken full.

Week by week the camp over the canal took shape. The silt in the flower troughs waited for seed. Sister cleaned her own flower-boxes and ordered fall seeds. Loretta's camp stood squarely in the center of Sister's view through the front door from her stove — a place of habitation, where friendly forms would soon appear, and sounds occur. It enhanced her prospect of the blank green prairie, yet sometimes she found it vaguely disturbing, she knew not why... She frowned and returned to her preserving.

Mocco arrived for his afternoon coffee and hardtack.

'I ordered the paint,' he said.

Sister said, 'I wish you'd bring river sand for my flowers.'

Sipping his coffee, he continuously surveyed the new camp, slanting his head critically.

'Now I'm glad she stayed away,' he said. 'Now I hope she waits until it's all finished.'

Sister said nothing. Mocco finished his coffee. He lingered, drifting from window to window restlessly.

'Maybe Loretta's mad,' he said.

'Mad at what, for goodness' sake?'

'How do I know? Don't she want to come down any more and exercise herself — doing housework? I thought she enjoyed helping you. Maybe she's waiting for you to write.'

'I'm waiting for her to write. Listen, Mocco, I've told you it's a pretty job, but Loretta's seen lots of pretty things. She's sick of pretty things. Aren't you getting your money? Anyway, why do you come to me with this — this business business?'

'Both of you were mighty interested at first. You two got me started on this.'

Sister slammed the pot cover viciously, thinking, 'What the hell *is* Loretta up to?' She could picture Loretta in town walking negligently through a fine garden — conveying as always this exciting yet ominous sense of multitudes of sure-footed rulers and workers, this feeling of thickly carpeted chambers and firelit retreats, unobtrusive sounds and perfumes, half-tasted dainties and the mingling of chimes and urbane repartee... Sister fought a momentary sense of woe descending upon her like a bludgeon from the void. 'What *is* the matter here?' she wondered. 'Is this woman's good-will after all so important to me?' She felt utterly hollow and lifeless, and yet so full, so burdened! She sat on her leg, gazing across at Loretta's costly retreat with the great calm eyes of a child. Suddenly, with a sigh of self-contempt, she jumped up and feverishly resumed her work. And soon she was singing again.

She said to Mocco: 'There's an old book on the bed you

ought to take home and read. It's a fine book. I threw it aside when I was small because the hero has a beard!'

Within ten days the camp was completed except for a few finishing touches that Mocco was intentionally protracting. They were building the wharf. Still Sister had no word from Loretta. The handsome building, painted white and green, was always before her, audaciously bright and silent. Sister could not bring herself to write to Loretta again. She was waiting for Grampaw to write to Nikolai. One day when at last Grampaw sat down to scribble a note to the doctor, she said, 'Grampaw, a little postscript, if you don't mind. Please, please tell Nikolai the damned *camp* is finished. Mocco is very anxious to know what kind of flowers Loretta wants planted. Ask him if anything's wrong with Loretta,' she added. Grampaw raised his hoary eyebrows and his mouth twitched humorously. He asked no questions. Sister was immensely relieved, to have shed this irksome burden.

Two more weeks passed. The job was done. Mocco continued to spend his time around Grampaw's camp. He no longer asked Sister for news. He would haul additional shells to widen the island. This would keep him cheerfully occupied for a while. The surrounding island was very wide now, and squared off neatly. But he left two of the piles unpainted, in order that he might be still engaged in the job when Loretta came.

One day he scoured all the window panes and built a birdhouse like Grampaw's. Just as he finished Sister returned from Dutch Scenery with the mail. Immediately he rowed over to Grampaw's camp and loitered about the kitchen where Sister was beginning supper. He waited, but Sister did not speak. After a while he put on his shoes and started off.

'I won't see you tomorrow,' he said. 'There's nothing more to do.'

'You're all through, then?'

'I've *been* through, for God's sake.'

'A fine job, Mocco!' said Sister. 'I'm so proud! Now I suppose you're anxious to get back home and look for another contract.'

Mocco shuffled off, scratching his head and glancing at the sky. 'I'll see you sometime, Sis.'

He did not come next day. Grampaw, too, was away. Sister felt uneasy all day, alone with the new camp. In the afternoon she was on the back porch flying a new kite. Suddenly she heard a startling cry behind her:

'Wah-eeeeeee-oooooo!'

The whooping crane! She hurried to the front. The great crane, as tall as she, was over on Loretta's wharf, walking back and forth, limping. The bird was hurt — probably the same one they had heard one night. She watched the creature, fascinated. Once the bird stayed motionless for at least half an hour. The sun moved on, so hot and silent! The crane stood on the edge of the wharf looking toward Dutch Scenery, a gaunt, nearsighted old man of property waiting for visitors who would never appear. Sister laughed so loudly that the startled bird flew away... But later another bird came, a swallow this time, circling the strange bird-house, careening deliriously, then perching on the roof. But the swallow, too, spied Sister's alert red form, and flew away. Sister was suddenly touched by a sharp feeling of sadness or regret. That was deep in the evening, when the marsh was a great darkening void, the sky brushed with twirling scrolls of flame.

Next morning shortly after Grampaw brought the mail Mocco wandered into the camp. He said he had come for some oysters. He took a pair of tongs and left. Soon he returned with a sack of oysters. He was all splashed with mud.

He had never learned the knack of oyster fishing. He would bring up large quantities of mud.... He lingered near Sister at the washtub, played with the baby, picked up a book and scanned the pictures.

'Did Grampaw get an answer?' he finally asked.

'I don't think so,' Sister replied. 'Why don't you ask him?'

'You'd know if he did. As if you're not as anxious as I am to hear from her!'

Sister wrung a shirt. 'I've got other things to think of.'

'All I've got to say, I don't understand this. I don't understand it a bit. Ain't she ever coming down to — to accept the job?'

Grimy, fatigued, sullen, Mocco leaned in the door. Sister was reminded of the day he had returned to Grass Margin to tell her he could never become a river pilot — pathetically in need of sympathy yet somehow beyond her aid or comfort. She felt if she could place a sisterly hand on his shoulder he would begin to cry. Perhaps she herself would cry.

'Why don't you go hunt some work?' she asked Mocco. 'Quit bothering me. Forget Loretta. It's ridiculous. You're in business now, Mocco. A contractor! You have other jobs to do. Business! Look at Grampaw how he runs around, no time for reading or talking or playing. Saving his money! Fussing with little pieces of paper! Everywhere you look around here, little pieces of paper! You've got to be like him! Forget Loretta. You've got your money. Business is business!'

'I'm not bothered about the money,' said Mocco. 'Hell with her money! But jeezam, Sis, it looks like she'd ——'

'I know. I understand.'

Mocco jammed on his hat and strode off impulsively. He returned and said, 'If she does come here, you tell her I'm over the river! I can't be hanging around here waiting. That's final!'

'Fair enough!' Sister said cheerfully. She hitched up her

skirt and spat over the rail like a decisive man. 'But scrape that mud off your behind!' she called.

Weeks passed. The earth was growing cold at night, the muds and waters. Alligators back in the fresh marsh were quiet, settling into their winter sleep. Afternoons Sister heard the muffled crack of cannon at the forts, the soldiers playing at war. Following each dim report there came a peculiar heavy grunt as the shell struck the surface of some distant bay. During these weeks of scoured heavens and hissing waters and fugitive clouds, Loretta's camp over the way stood vacant, bright and emphatic in the sun, and in the moonlight pallid, hollow, unreal as a disturbing dream. Birds visited it. They hopped about the roof and the empty verandah; but curiously none stayed. A gale of wind once loosened a bit of the palmetto thatching, which now continually flapped in the wind, a first token of neglect.

Another afternoon Mocco drifted in. He greeted Sister gruffly. The sun was gone. Grampaw was in Dutch Scenery on business. Sister and Mocco ate supper in the silence of faintly clattering utensils. Mocco was washed and combed. 'Perhaps after papa dies,' Sister thought, 'Mocco will come and live with us.' It might be nice, another man around the place. She would keep him hard at work, see that he rinsed his feet each night. She closed her eyes that were tired from knitting. Grampaw's saddle, freshly oiled, was on the wall. Beneath it, the terrestrial globe on the table shone as brightly. The two objects emphasized each other in an odd, fascinating way.

Suddenly Mocco said, 'I got a mind to burn it down, Loretta's camp.'

'Don't be foolish,' Sister laughed. 'She wants her camp to come to, sometime, I suppose.'

'She's been playing with us. To her this camp means as

much as a postage stamp to us. I know, don't fret. I know what she wants from us — from you.'

'I wish you'd tell me, then.'

'She wants your kid.'

Sister raised her face alertly.

'I know what I caught her doing one day back on the porch,' he went on.

'What was she doing?'

'Letting the baby suck. I'll tell you. What do I care now?'

Sister looked out of the window where stars were appearing. Mocco looked away too, chewing vigorously. Sister waited. Mocco swallowed and took another forkful. Sister busily fed the child, spooning the rice into his mouth. 'I don't understand,' she murmured.

'Her breast.'

Sister wiped the child's greasy chin. She looked at Mocco steadily, and clicked her tongue. During the past months Sister's face had grown rather mature. Her mouth smiled briefly, faintly, and the pallor of her skin made her anguished eyes seem darker than black.

'A little white breast,' said Mocco, giggling nervously. 'No sap.'

Sister reached over to push back the child's bright curls.

After two weeks, Sister received a letter from Loretta. She scanned it eagerly:

'... must write instantly ... ashamed of myself, but ... and the days fly so fast ... convention with Nick ... your own judgment about the flowers for Mocco's camp ... pleasant evening we spent planning it ... little picture-books for baby ... good care of yourself ... go and see you before winter ...'

Winter had come. The tarpon and sharks were gone with the tropical birds. The baby pointed to a flock of geese flung over the sky in the form of a writhing lariat. Grampaw aimed a broom and made a noise like a gun. Grampaw was in high fettle. His oyster association had made a first tentative shipment north. Sister showed him the letter. They had never discussed Loretta's silence, nor the matter of the vacant camp.

Grampaw folded the letter and dropped it on the table. They waited for each other to speak.

'Tche writes a pretty hand,' said Grampaw, with one of his hard wise laughs. Sister hated him who had doubtless foreseen all of this. Afterwards he sat with an open book gazing thoughtfully at the vacant camp. Sister sat on the arm of his chair, no longer hating him.

'Tell me what you think of it,' Sister asked.

'I would say it is all over. You no longer amuse her. Or I frightened her away. Tsomething like that.'

'She's dropped me?'

'You tstill like her?'

'Yes, sir.'

'I tsee. Good!'

'No, that's not true. I'm hard towards her. I feel hard, and amused, toward her and everyone else, because of this.'

'Preserve your little core of hardness. A tsweet little core of it. Let us give thanks! Tche gave you that. And tche taught you manners and how to dress. But you had a close call. A close tchave that time! Tche damned near made a lady out of you.'

They feasted with all their old joy in life. Sister dismissed Loretta from her mind, thinking, musing. ' . . . a little core of hardness . . .' But she wished the camp across the canal might blow down.

All day Mocco lounged from place to place. For hours he would sit alone on the levee bench opposite Jule's store. He wandered the levee in sun and rain with his left hand in his pocket, holding the roll of bills earned on Loretta's camp. He had not yet spent one cent of the money. He had put up a sign on the Kalavich Landing:

M. KALAVICH, CONTRACTOR
BUILDING AND REPAIRS

Jule the Postmaster had promised to help him find a construction job, but — 'This is no place for a contractor,' Mocco thought. 'All morning only four people have passed my sign — a nigger and three Cajins. I am a Cajin. I am not a Cajin. I am American. But to *her* I am just another Cajin down here living on shrimp and rice. What do I care? I built her a good camp. Huh! Old enough to be my mother! I wonder what she's doing today. Running around with other beautiful women, clean pale girls, dressing and smelling like her. When I go to town I'll get her to introduce me to one. Just one! Then to hell with Loretta. Loretta! I never even got a chance to call her that!'

Tony Kalavich dozed in his chair. He now weighed about ninety pounds. His tendons twitched and he woke to see Mocco thinking in the doorway. He studied Mocco a long time.

'Mocco!' he called weakly.

'What do you want?'

'When are you going to see Jule about that job?'

'What for? There's no jobs here.'

'Why don't you fix the stable if you are a contractor? The mosquitoes are eating Claiborne up, and he keeps me awake kicking.'

Mocco said nothing. He stood in the door until the brown twilight had risen from the earth. A green grass fire was burning fitfully near the doorstep. Mosquitoes on the Margin were more numerous than they had ever been before. At dusk they prowled about in huge whirling masses, dense wandering clouds darker than the dusk, whose smooth sweet whine was audible from a long distance. Children stayed away from school, indoors all day. The fields were dotted with lonely fires where the tormented cattle huddled. Some mules and cows, maddened by the insects, had run into the river to perish, or dashed their brains out against barns or trees ... Somewhere a horse screamed. An answering scream came faintly from another direction. Tony pointed his chin at Mocco and his voice quavered in Slavonian: 'Boy, don't stand there thinking about the city.'

'I'm not.'

'Don't. Promise me something, boy. Tell me you will not leave until I am dead. It will not be long.'

'I haven't got enough money. I should have charged her more.'

'Do you promise?'

'Don't worry.'

'Thank you. I'll try to make it soon.'

Mocco went and propped the stable door closed. He hung burlap sacks over the cracks. Claiborne kept snorting, blowing the mosquitoes out of his nostrils. A ship was coming. Mocco went to the levee. A passenger ship approached, blazing with lights. But Mocco looked only at the signal lights on the bridge, red and green, which he saw as one color, one color. He narrowed his eyes. He ground his teeth and clenched his fists in the dark, holding his breath and tensing the muscles of his throat. But he could not see two colors ...

When once he had begun to spend the money, it disappeared quickly. There was a place in Lacroix for that, a house of girls, dark languid young women who slept each day until noon and lived on sandwiches from the store. In this house Mocco learned to make love, to touch a woman's rich hairless

flesh without trembling. He stayed in Lacroix four days, and
went home a man, strong and drunk. He spent the remainder
of his money in Grass Margin. Though very drunk, his head
was heavy with the strong peculiar smell of the women, which
somehow resembled that of the sea. His breast was sad.
Prowling the Margin day and night, his uncertain legs led
him past many smoking chimneys, gay clotheslines, stooped
workers, boats with brave white sails. People on the road
made room for him. Mulatto girls bowed gravely and shrank
from his grasp. Children looked up from their play with round
gentle faces. His father whined and whined, or snarled from
his dark corner.

'What have I done, what have I done to be punished so?'
he asked aloud. 'And not a drop of liquor for his dying father!
I will be dead in the night, and no one to wash my poor bones.'

On the last day of his big drunk Mocco was lying in the
weeds by the road when the packet *Bonita* tied up at Jule's
landing. The roustabouts filed down the plank with their
burdens, and soon straggled back one by one from the store.
One of them, a tall rawboned negro, left the line and stooped
over Mocco's apparently lifeless form. With a long bony
hand he turned Mocco over. When Mocco opened his eyes
the negro smiled.

"Smattah, Bud?' he asked. 'You layin' in a gang of briers,
get yo'self all to'n up.'

'Take me home,' said Mocco.

'Ah got a boat-job to hol'.'

'Take me home.'

'Capm whistlin' fo' me now. Where at you live, Bud?'

The captain was blowing the whistle angrily, and the hands
were pulling in the gangway.

'Right down road,' said Mocco. He held the big negro's
hand. 'Hell with your job. I'll give you job. I'm big contractor

here. Mocco Kalavich. Take me home. Melia roast you nice goose. Good place to sleep in packing shed.'

The negro lifted Mocco to his feet. The packet captain was cursing. Now a second negro and his wife were fishing on the wharf. The packet captain called to this negro, offering him the job of Mocco's negro. At once the second negro threw away his fishing-pole and ran to the boat. The wife overtook him and tried to hold him, but he shook her off and jumped aboard the boat. The packet steamed off. All the roustabouts laughed at the negro woman standing with her hands on her hips watching the departing packet. Then the black wife smiled broadly and waved her hand. The rawboned negro helped Mocco home and put him to bed, and lived with the Kalaviches.

He was called Bonus, and Mocco liked him because he had been many places and enjoyed talking about his adventures. While waiting for Mocco to get a construction job, Bonus repaired the stable and daily curried Claiborne the mule. He helped to break the oranges for shipping, and to plant a vegetable garden. In the kitchen he laughed with Melia, who was now cooking delicious meals. When laughing, Bonus tilted his skull until its base met his spine, and his face snapped open into ruddy halves edged with dazzling white, giving out a prolonged, raucous, deafening howl. From his corner in the next room, Tony Kalavich would begin to snarl.

'Hesh up, Capm Tony,' Bonus said.

The household was taking on life. Every afternoon Bonus and Melia lay on the porch answering the calls of the passersby; and at night Mocco, spending all his evenings at home, played cards or checkers with Bonus in the packing shed. Bonus had managed to make the shed rather cozy. From unknown sources on the Margin he had acquired a stove, a hammock, and a few articles of battered furniture.

Tony was left alone most of the time. He had nothing more to think about, so his life consisted merely of drinking milk and breathing. Now and then he grumbled, but his grumbling somehow added to the new cheerful aspect of the house.

Bonus was fond of Mocco. With an expertness acquired while employed as a Pullman porter, he kept Mocco's shoes polished and his clothes pressed. He also trimmed Mocco's hair regularly. And soon Mocco became the only neatly dressed man on the Margin. Now he looked the part of a big contractor. But there were no contracts. And nobody cared. There was plenty to eat — sea food, game, and the vegetables Bonus raised.

In the packing shed at night, Bonus talked and talked, in a low musical voice:

'But Ah didn't like de East. Ever'body tryin' to make time. Lunchrooms, lunchrooms ever'where. Don't nobody sell cat-fish. People all de time eatin' out de little slot-boxes. Ever' post got a slot-box, one cent for piece of candy in New York. Po' people so tired dey sleeps in de subway train. . . . So de nex' day Ah quits mah job and come back-on-down South. Den Ah gets a job rat-catchin'. Ever'body was scared 'bout de plague in dat town, rats bringin' in de plague from de Fah East. Bo'ad of Health put all these men out catchin' rats, nickel a rat, all sizes. Had a big silveh badge, goin' 'round settin' traps in people's houses, no boss-man around. Plenty people give you lil somethin', piece of money or stuff lef' over from de table, sometime make axtry piece of money doin' odd jobs, drowndin' puppies and so foath. Good jawb, but you had to step, wentah an' summah, rainy days an' all, totin' them rats and dodgin' dat plague.'

'You had any women there?'

'Ah had um ef I wanted, but Ah didn't wunt.'

'No kind, you didn't want?'

'Nawser.'

'That's a damned lie.'

'They'll mess you up, Bud.'

'You mean winches'll do that.'

'Mess you up. White or black. All debment comes from de same devil. Stands to reason a woman gon' pester a man 'cause he don' need her excep' at night time, an' she needs him night an' day. Ef you fin' a woman you need too much, you quit stoppin' at her station. Sometime Ah'm gon' tell you 'bout de piece Ah thought Ah could trus'. Ain' none of um you can trus', podnah.'

'I'm not bothered about trusting them. I want to know how to get them.'

'You wants free booty, and the bes' is de free. Well — you got to make lak you don't need um too much. Come to pullin' de bung, you don't need money wid a woman and you don't need clothes, but you got to make plenty fun. What she care how rich or handsome you is, or educated, long as you do things she ain' never seen an' say things she ain' never heard. I see a woman go to lovin' a man jus' by de way he set on a sugar-mule.'

'We had a fellow here,' said Mocco. 'I remember what you say is true. Friend of mine, Mitch Holt. He had all the women he wanted, except one . . . He's in the penitentiary.'

'Ah been in de pen. It was all account of dat liver-lip woman I thought Ah could trus'. Ah'll tell you about it sometime.'

This new knowledge of women Mocco carried with him on his idle jaunts to Irishtown, Venice, and among the back alleys of Lacroix, where the cannery girls, smelling strongly of shrimp, went to work with irises in their hair. He bore his knowledge to his bed, sat under the willows with it, in the hot brief afternoons, turning his head deliberately away from the occasional barefooted girl who came along kicking up alternate clouds of dust. At a dance he fancied himself strong and disdainful. This was easy; but he was having difficulty inventing things to say and do that the girls had never seen or heard. He tried to be boisterously funny; but being unable to convince himself that his attempts were amusing, he impressed no one else.

At length he told himself that these girls knew him too well. Later on, when he reached the city, he would try all of Bonus's lore on strangers.

He watched Bonus work his will with the black, brown, and yellow Margin girls — how his geniality and his childish, grotesque capers attracted them. Bonus never hemmed and hawed with women. For them he always had an amusing answer to return, as quickly and effortlessly as a bounced ball.

In the night, the sentient darkness of spring, girls frequently visited Bonus's cozy domicile in the trees. Mocco tried his hand at winning one of these, a little pale yellow child of fifteen — skinny, as skinny as Bonus, but with none of his pointed angles and sharp edges — who was oddly endowed with a mature bosom. He sat by her on the bench. 'You're a pretty girl, Poline,' he said, resting his hand on her knee. His words came thickly out of a throat already clogged with blood. He could think of nothing funny to say. He gathered her close to him. Poline submitted. Her lips were near — waiting and not waiting. He saw that she was looking through the window thinking of something else. His trembling hands prowled blindly. Poline gazed through the window, grave and still while Mocco's hands traveled farther and farther. The girl sat like a captive resigned to her jailer's search. Suddenly Mocco moved away from her violently, the inferior creature who was his dignified superior. Poline stroked her skirts into place.

'Where Bonus passed to?' she asked with a hot proud gleam in her eye.

Mocco buried his fingers in his belt and sighed gloomily.

Bonus came in and looked at Mocco. There was an eel in Bonus's hand someone had given him, wrapped in bright angry convolutions about his wrist and fingers. Bonus seldom returned from his peregrinations empty-handed. He went to get the hatchet, walking with a slow, soundless, gliding motion, moving only his resilient lower limbs. Bonus crushed the eel's head. Poline vented a curious giggle. She and Bonus looked at each other, smiling, as if amused at some secret knowledge they shared, to Mocco's exclusion.

'Poline, you been treatin' mah podnah right?' Bonus asked.
'Assah.'

'Don' lemme catch you crown-o'-thornin' mah podnah, you hear me?'

'Eh bien!'

Mocco strode savagely to the door and turned, his big dark eyes stern in the haggard face. 'Who do you niggers think you are around here?' he said, 'asking *her* to treat *me* right. You better be careful I don't run you off this property.' He walked out.

But before a week had passed Mocco was again spending his evenings with Bonus. Mocco loved a human gathering-place, relaxed listeners to his plans. Further, there pervaded Bonus's dwelling an air of fleshy languorous mystery — dim uncertain light, vagrant smells, the growing array of assorted objects Bonus had accumulated from nameless sources on the Margin, the variously colored healthy females that drifted in and out. And the absence of physical overtures on Bonus's part toward these visitors. Sometimes these evenings were very quiet, Bonus lying across his bunk like an austere and emaciated head-cultist, with bare feet dangling and soft raucous voice recounting a tale whose sentences were old and smoothed by usage. But usually there was the continuous rise and ebb of joyous fleshy laughter, dominated by Bonus's great strident peals of mirth.

17

AT THE proper time Mocco heard Bonus's story — the tale of the liver-lipped woman whom Bonus had thought he could trust.

'Ef you got long ground to cover, the Nickel Plate's de road to ride,' said Bonus.

'I pull in town on de Nickel Plate. I walk in Evelyn's house. Who I see but Frank St. Green, my old time podnah, settin' at de table pickin' his teet' wid my woman.

' "Hello, Frank!"

' "Hello, Bonus!"

'He didn't change color. Frank was de same color of Evelyn, bright custard yolla, but straight hair, and been to college. Coal-chute niggers called him a fruit. He was too gentleman.

'You ever come home find another mule in yo' stall?

'But we was friends. I say, "What you yollas doin' — two-timin' me?" Den we all laugh.

'Den Frank got me a job on de coal-chute, de night trick. He was on de day.

'After dat Evelyn look lak she love me mo' than ever. Hot almighty! An' she begin showin' me new tricks. Where dem tricks come from? I didn't think to ax. Jes' keppa givin' her all my money, three dollars a day, an' she give me lil somethin' on a Sadday fo' gamble.

'Look lak Frank start spendin' mo' money hisself. Where dat

money was comin' from? I didn't think to ax. He always
lendin' me money.

'Say, "Bonus podnah, it's rainin', le's go fling us some
dice."

'I say, "Man, I'm broke!"

'Say, "You gon' give de shirt off yo' back to dat liver-lip
woman, an' you works so hard I hates to see it. She ain' wuth
it. Take dis ten dollars. Le's pitch dice."

'An' de presents he give me! Clothes he ain' wo' but twice,
suits an' shoes. Frank was de dress-upin'es' nigger you ever
saw. Didn' nobody lak him fo' dat excep' de women, but I
did and still does, 'cause Frank wasn't happy bein' yolla and
educated.

'Monday mornin' he climb up top of de coal-chute to relieve
me. I ax him for nickel for carfare. He hands me a smooth
halfa dollar wid a nick in de edge. Den I remember I given dat
same fo' bits to Evelyn de day befo'.

'I look at Frank, I say, "Frank, I done got you."

'He say, "Bonus, you done got me. What we gon' do 'bout
dis?"

'I say, "Frank, we gon' fight."

'Frank's knife was out.

'Ah look up, Ah say, "God heppus," an' I lets him have it
wid de lef' hand.

'Way down underneath us was de Broadway Flyer waitin'
for coal, ingineer an' fireman runnin' across de track for cup o'
coffee.

'Frank fall backward an' hit dat coal-tender right plunk on
his haid an' smash de skull crooked.

'What you want me to do?

'I pulls de coad an' down comes de coal and buries my bosom
enemy. De train pull out and I stand on top de coal-chute, I
say, "Now, you two-timin' rascal, you gon' be blacker than me."

'I went to de pen for manslaughter, 'count of they found his

knife in his hand, an' I had de fo' bits. Mos' ever' time I see
him, Frank tells me to hold on to dat fo' bits.'

Mocco looked at Bonus. 'How do you mean — tells you?'

Bonus chuckled. 'Oh, I sees him ever' now and then. His
spirit comes befo' me ever' time I stay out in de hot sun. Never
at night, only de hot sun, one of these bright hot days. He give
me good advice. Soon as I gets in trouble he come back an'
say, "Be caffle, podnah, don' hit nobody wid yo' hand, you'll
kill him sho'." I speck he still feels dat lick. Yassuh, he's de one
advised me to quit de boat dat day and stay down here wid
you. When I pick you up dat day an' begin to tote you Frank
come out dem hot weeds an' smile an' keepa noddin' his head.'

'How — how does he look?' Mocco asked.

'Oh, he look fine! What you look so church-eyed about,
Bud? He don' come to nobody but me, jus' a po' spirit ho-
boin' aroun' peepin' out de tall grass.'

'He talks to you?'

'He talks, but I don't *hear* it. I jus' *understand* it. But it ain'
no educated talk, lak he used to talk. De first time he come
back, he begin talkin' jus' lak I do, an' he was black and ugly
as me, an' stayed black an' ugly, wid his hair turned kinky and
raggedy clothes on, but Lawd! he sho' is happy! You ought to
see him laugh!'

18

ONE spring night while Bonus and Mocco were entertaining three mulatto girls, there was a knock.

Some arresting quality in the sound caused Mocco himself to leave his chair and open the door. They had been playing cards. Mocco had brought the lamp from the house, because Bonus's lamp was broken.

When he opened the door Sister was standing there, all in white, holding her baby, blinded by the light. The sudden incongruous radiance of her printed against the blackness shocked Mocco into complete bewilderment.

'There's no light in the house,' Sister said. 'We can't find the light.'

'But — but ——' Mocco foundered for words.

They walked toward the house, Mocco bearing the light.

Sister asked, 'Honey, who are those people?'

'Some friends of Bonus's, the boy that works for me. We — I was talking to him about a job. What are you doing here? Is Loretta — did Loretta ——?'

'Grampaw's with me. I'm going to have the baby christened tomorrow.'

Mocco was happy to see Sister. He sent Bonus to Jule's for a piece of ice. Sister had been saving her thirst all afternoon for ice-water. The mulatto girls gathered by the kitchen window to look in at Sister and whisper excitedly about her pretty clothes, and the new way she had done her hair. Just behind the white immaculate curve of Sister pouring wine, they could see old man Tony sitting up very straight and disheveled, looking at Sister with tears in his eyes. Sister was a big young lady now, and she looked virginal and strong and sure of herself, an American version of the alert and supple girls of the Dalmatian mountains. All was forgiven her.

Grampaw brought in the phonograph, fetched along for the christening celebration, and played a new Slavonian record from New York. Tony's interest in life seemed to revive. 'Play that again, please, Father,' he begged. It was a song of the stone-masons, said to have been sung by medieval workmen of Ragusa. Grampaw wound the machine and played the record again. He removed his coat and shirt and paced the floor, singing. He had a deep, sweet, though uncultivated voice. To Tony, Grampaw seemed actually stronger and fresher than on his last visit.

'I hope you will stay with us awhile, Father,' said Tony.

'I must leave after the christening.'

'What?' A christening! Is that why you came, and not to visit me?' Tony did not know Sister had a child. The baby was asleep in the front room. 'A christening . . .'

'I go up on the *Hail Mary* tomorrow. Business. Five men to see. Sixty good fishermen compose our association. Those who were laggards are dying to join. We will keep them waiting a while.' Grampaw laughed. Tony tried to smile. His laughing muscles were almost numb. He grunted. How had Grampaw managed to keep tough and young? 'Hurry up and get well,' said the older man. 'Come in the oyster business with us. We are getting fifty cents a sack.'

Tony closed his eyes, trying to orient himself. He was rendered speechless by a sense of life going on without him — Sister grown up, happily pressing Grampaw's 'good' suit for the morrow; Grampaw, hale and ruddy, engineer of important

transactions, stroking the otter on his lap; Mocco, the contractor — was Mocco building any houses now? Tony could
not remember. What a dim jumble of events life was, going on
without him.

Sister and Mocco took a walk to the store. She wanted him
to help her plan the christening celebration tomorrow. There
was no one on the road. The stars glittered fiercely. Sister
peered gratefully through the dimness at the remembered
contours of the levee, the tall feathery willows, the strong black
river racing past the groves. She was intensely alive and restless to be walking again on the good hard dry Margin where
she was born. She skipped down the levee into someone's
orchard. Among the damp sweet leaves she could have wept
for joy. She called to Mocco, but when he approached she
moved to another tree, eluding him.
'Where are you, Sis?' he called.
'Here, silly!'
When he came she moved away again, and watched him
fumble about in the starlight. She plucked a grapefruit and
threw it at him, then ran for the levee. At the base of the embankment Sister waited behind a tree, and when Mocco passed
she grabbed his leg and yelped like a dog. Mocco clutched her
arm and himself gave a sudden loud bark, so realistic that
Sister was frightened. 'My breath jumped back at me!' she
laughed. All around them, dogs began to bark. They ran down
the road together hand in hand, leaving the barking far behind. They sat on an upturned skiff to plan the christening.
Sister had thirty dollars to spend for music, liquor, and frogs'
legs.
Returning home, Sister said, 'Don't hurry so!'
'Why?'
'Let them be together a little while at home.'
'How — together?'

'But they want to be together sometime.'

'I keep forgetting Grampaw's his father.'

'We're all mixed up, this family. Who'd think I'm any kin to Papa, for instance, or you to Grampaw. A hell of a family.' She laughed.

'Why don't you stop that, Sis?'

'It's true. We hardly know one another.'

'I mean cursing. Cursing with those nice clothes on.'

'Do I look nice? Hooray! Let me tickle you!'

'You're all changed, Sis.'

'You said that a year ago. Say something nice.'

'Changed again. You know something? You can dress.'

'I saw this dress through the telescope on a passenger boat.'

'You don't act like a Margin girl. You're brown?'

'Brown all through. Too much sun. Sick of the sun, even the sky, sometimes. I don't mean that.'

'I wish Mr. Bruce could see you. Did you ever hear from him again?'

'Don't spoil the christening.'

'What are you naming your baby?'

'Raymond after the saint. Middle name Bruce. We'll call him that — Bruce.'

'After him? I thought you didn't like Bruce.'

'Don't think. Tell me what you've been doing. . . . I didn't say I liked Bruce, but I must remember him. He started me living. I broke with Unga — met Loretta and almost became a lady — Grampaw's going to be the leader of all the Tockos — your life is all changed too. Bruce is close to us as our cousin.'

'I wish Mitch was out. That's the man for you, Sis.'

Mocco walked slowly, to let Sister talk. She would not talk like this except in the dark.

'What's going to happen to us, Sis? Where will all this end up, I wonder?'

Sister was unwell. She was happy and sad. She felt like

fleeing down the road with loosened hair, or finding a place to lie on the earth to weep, or plunging her hands among the stars. 'What difference does it make what happens to us?' she asked. She raised her face and found the star she wanted — red Mars. She lifted herself on her toes and drank in the night air. It was not too bitter.

When they passed the kitchen window Grampaw was bent over the kitchen table, showing some figures to Tony. Tony kept nodding his head, but understanding none of the figures.

'His association again,' said Sister to Mocco. 'That's all he thinks about.'

'Well, he enjoys it,' said Mocco, 'and we've got one big man in the family anyhow.'

When they entered the kitchen, Grampaw folded up his papers. He rubbed his hands and chuckled to Sister. 'Some news for you, little minx! Your father's going to come and live with us. We'll enlarge the camp.'

'And I can go to New Orleans!' Mocco exclaimed.

Tony hobbled over and sat on the bench next to Sister. She had not yet touched her father. He had a strange smell, vaguely suggestive of decay. With an effort Sister remained at his side.

'And you are learning to typewrite, little one?' he asked in Slavonian.

'Yes, sir, I'm trying.'

'And you are being a good girl now?'

'Did he see your baby?' Grampaw asked.

Sister's face fell into the lines of a white stone mask. She had hoped Grampaw would tell Tony while she was absent. Tony gripped the arms of the chair rigidly, as if to prevent himself from bounding into the air. He looked at Grampaw, his mouth an oval hole in the oblong face.

Grampaw sat with the otter in his lap, stroking the animal's plump bright shoulder. He flashed a strong calm smile at his son. 'Of course!' he said. 'The prettiest little rascal! Go get the baby, Nicolene. We are going to have four generations living in one camp. The kernel of my life at last!'

Sister rose reluctantly, but Tony clutched her arm, trying to see her face. She dreamily pried away his fingers and walked into the next room.

'*Her* baby!' Tony whimpered. His chin with its tinseled rill of spittle began to quiver violently. 'No one told me! She is not married!'

Sister came in with her sleeping child. Tony uttered a croaking sound and flung his face into the point of his arm. Sister went and sat beside Grampaw. She jounced her baby gently, looking down at the child with pride or with anguish. Tony was crumpled now, utterly undone, voicing a thin, hardly audible sobbing — a bootless dirge of weariness and woe that wrenched their several hearts. The silence lay like a clamorous stream suddenly halted, when slowly, almost reverently, Mocco advanced through the fatal stillness and placed his hand on his father's shoulder.

At once Tony rose and shuffled toward the adjoining room, slowly dragging his bony dangling legs behind him. Presently he returned. He had a shotgun.

Grampaw opened his legs and the otter thumped to the floor. The faces in the room were all white, silent, frozen. In the doorway Tony worked his twitching lips.

'I have been a bad man,' he began, 'but — but ——' He whimpered incoherently and raised the gun toward Sister and the child. All the time the girl was watching him with a pale and frightful smile, curiously prepared for the leap into bright cool death, and the gun was nearly leveled. Suddenly Grampaw was heard to utter a sharp, quickly drawn, almost tender sigh. They saw his thick torso topple sideways as slowly as a collapsing tower, then turn forward and drop in a neatly bundled heap, with his hands tightly crossed on his bosom and his knees drawn up, somewhat like a baby not yet born.

19

TONY knelt by his father. 'Father! Get up, please, I didn't mean to frighten you.' His hands wandered about the great relaxed breast, as if searching for some imperative document or object. He looked up at Sister curiously, and saw her staring eyes and the working of her throat.

'Water!' Tony cried. 'Quick, some water!'

Mocco looked down at Grampaw's surprised face, the open mouth and eyes clouded faintly. 'I think he's dead,' he told his father, and began to weep.

'No! Get a doctor, you stupid! A doctor, quick!' He lifted his head and howled like a lonely beagle. 'Oh, please God, my father! My only father! Oh! Oh! How did it happen?' He turned to Sister, now kneeling with her child. 'I didn't touch him!' Tony wailed. 'I didn't shoot the gun or touch him! Both of you saw! Not a mark on him! Oh, God, please, my father!'

Mocco straightened the limbs and closed the eyes. He went to the packing-shed with the gun. Bonus and the mulatto girls were still there talking and laughing in the dark. Mocco called Bonus and they walked to the levee. He handed Bonus the gun. 'Fire three shots in the air,' he said. 'My grandfather is dead. He dropped dead, just now. No relative of his can shoot the signal. Go ahead, Bonus, three shots.'

Bonus seemed not at all surprised. He fired the shots and returned the gun to Mocco. It was as if he had been expecting Grampaw to die, as if there were a plague killing many people. Now that the old ritual of the marshes was done, Mocco began to cry. Bonus helped him down the levee by the arm, soothing him: 'Das all right, podnah. Das all right. Come, Ah get you ready for de wake.'

Within an hour the news had leaped from house to house, and scores of people had gathered. There began the creaking of harness along the levee in the dark, and the hollow scraping of sleds. Across the river lights twinkled on one by one, outlining the shore. Someone hailed the pilot boat to notify Pilot Town. Two old women whom nobody seemed to know appeared and covered the mirrors, stopped the clock, scrubbed the floors and dripped a large pail of coffee.

As the night passed the crowd became too large for the house. The men lounged about the woodshed, the front porch or on the levee, sitting against Mocco's sign in the moonlight; but the women stayed in the room where Grampaw lay half-covered with orange blossoms. The women sat around the walls in borrowed chairs. They engaged in much low talk and discreet laughter. When a new visitor arrived and walked self-consciously to the center of the room, all the faces watched him stand looking down at Grampaw, and the eyes would follow him to the next room, where he shook hands with Tony sitting in his corner with his hat off. Tony would shake his head and sigh. 'Who would have thought I would have lived to bury him?' he said, if the visitor was Slavonian. 'A few hours ago he was singing in red health.' Tony had quite collapsed, but he remained sitting up. His bed was full of children.

Sister had fled from the house that was now packed with milling condolers. She prowled in the warm moonlight where she might weep alone. Among the trees her tears flowed with a bitter sort of relief. She continued to wander. She stopped at the packing-shed and sat on the step a little while, within sound of Bonus's voice talking to Mocco. Soon she got up and went off through the tender webs of moonlight. The rich silver beams seemed palpable enough to trickle off one's fingers, and through the lacy branches she glimpsed the grave and watchful chief of the sky, red Mars, high and stern above the wrinkled groves, burning as rosily after Grampaw's death as it would after hers. She felt the roots beneath her feet groping for nourishment, unaware that a man had died. Even her own vitals were pinching her after an all-day fast. She sat against a familiar tree and her fingers found the earth. How quick and cool, home of the slumbering trillions, the dead! Grampaw had always warned her to see things whole. She felt behind the east the glorious onrush of dawn, and cattle obedient to their milkers' hands — the soundless crumbling of embers on cooling hearths, the shuffle of feet through the cobbled alleys of unknown lands, the beat of rain in the deep ravines of the earth, the seething of lonely seas . . .

Her eyelids closed out the witchery of the woven moonlight and she clasped her hands, but she could not pray. She could not annihilate herself and become a Voice. She was not weeping for Grampaw. Her tears were for herself. She could not think of Grampaw dead — yet. 'Another phase of life,' he had smilingly called death. Only the dead could understand the dead. Ah, it was a mockery, a mockery! Why had he been born at all — lying there unable to laugh who had laughed so long?

A man approached, searching.

'Dat you, Sister?'

'Yes, Captain George-Pete.'

'Me, I got to talk to you, Sister. You comin' inside, you?'

'Talk here, Captain.'

'It's about duh funeral. Duh pall-buryers. Yo' paw say for you to pick duh pall-buryers.'

Sister mentioned six names, six good friends of Grampaw's, most of them from his native town in Dalmatia.

'But Pretty John is colored, him,' said the man.

'He was Grampaw's friend.'

'Duh people ——'

'I'm thinking of Grampaw.'

The funeral was a great public affair, the largest funeral ever seen on the lower river. Long before the appointed hour, countless boats of all shapes and colors were tied to the landing and the willows. Sister sat in the second boat with Mocco. The first boat contained the priest and the coffin. The funeral moved slowly out until it was caught by the swift current. It was a warm sunny afternoon. The sun flashed from the numerous oar-blades. The willows had just begun to green out. The river was spotted with driftwood.

In the house, after the people had gone, Tony found himself alone. He raised himself in his chair and called to Melia on the levee. When she came in, Tony said, 'Stay wid me, woman.' Melia, who wanted to watch the funeral, went into the kitchen grumbling, 'Some folks sho' can talk English when he ax a favor.'

At the cemetery landing they bore the smartly glittering casket up the steep levee, paused for breath and descended through the ankle-deep clover. The graveyard was bordered with flowering orange trees, and clumps of false indigo and pampas grass. Pretty John, the mulatto, stood in line with the pall-bearers, his head shining ivory-bald. While Father Sam chanted in Latin, somewhere a wandering Swee-Sweet (Solitary Sandpiper) was calling busily, and some boys perched in the willows in the river were quarreling in loud whispers. Presently the chanting ceased and all eyes were raised to the dark square gullet of the family vault, with the name KALAVICH worked in iron above it like a frown. Two brickmasons piled on brick, and applied a coat of cement and smoothed it over. Then one of the masons with the point of his trowel traced a cross in the cement. Pretty John's shoulders jerked with sobs. A woman whimpered. Instantly the spectators swarmed to the vault with their flowers, some of them eagerly brushing their neighbors aside in order to reach preferred places. Father Sam stood clicking his tongne at them. When the crowd came away, the vault was completely buried by flowers of all colors.

Behind the crowd climbing the levee, Father Sam, like a worried shepherd, motioned them away before him. 'Go to your work, now,' he said. 'Go and pray for his soul, and remember Saint Vincent de Paul's Society meets at eight o'clock tonight.'

Sister and Mocco, left alone, began to pull up the grass around the vault.

Bonus was waiting behind an orange tree for Mocco. He was throwing bits of gravel at a basking fiddler crab. The crab leaned backward, fiddling frantically. Bonus was trying to remember a prayer that some old woman, probably his grandmother, had taught him long ago in Alabama. He recalled the smell of frying bacon, and a dog scratching on the floor, and a near-by steam-shovel grunting, taking iron from the earth, but he could not remember the prayer....

Two women on the levee glanced backward at Sister and Mocco.

'Look to me lak Sister she don' take it hard much.'

'Ah say them kind takes it harder than everybody. Ever you see a person ack so quiet for somebody dead, they feel it for sho.'

'Who she gon' stay wid now? Duh father, they say him he dawn want her.'

'But them is mean people, yes, them Tockos. And dat gul can work, lak you see her there.'

'Eh bien! She come back pretty for sho', Ah know dat. She can take her pick on dis river now.'

'But a mulatto pall-buryer! Don't you know she's funny lil rascal, pickin' a mullato?'

'Eh bien, duh cullud people is proud today!'

In the morning a fog settled over the land. Tony lay abed with his face to the wall. Mocco spent the entire day in the packing-shed with Bonus, sleeping, both of them.

Sister scrubbed the house, washed the curtains. Then she busied herself weeding her old garden, the staunch bits of color that were now almost choked by weeds. The day was damp and sunless. With their abundant crop of white blossoms, the orange trees seemed stark and tortured. The child was restless and peevish. He would not play in the front yard. He had never before walked on land. It seemed to frighten him, the twisted, slanting shapes of the trees, all dolorous and blurred, the sharp tufts of grass, the gaping passersby on the levee. He clutched the flesh of her legs through her skirts.

'Do you want to stay here, honey?' she asked.

'Mum-ma!' the child fretted. 'Mum-ma!'

'What, darling? You want to go home?'

'Mum-ma!'

She gathered him in and tickled him, but he would not laugh. He clawed at her hair, whimpering, digging his fist into his eyes and ears. 'You're sleepy,' she said. She hoped he was not going to be sick. 'Go inside and lie down, darling.' She watched him toddle off, crying. It was wonderful to Sister, how the child obeyed. Sometimes it almost made her apprehensive, he seemed so tractable, so devoid of rebellion or defiance ...

She went to the store, leaving the child asleep on the couch. The levee road was familiar in every detail, hardly a change visible anywhere, yet to Sister's mind the old meanings had changed or vanished. Large drops of moisture fell lazily off the willows. Through the opaque air the land seemed abandoned.

Weeds grew everywhere, masses of harsh ungainly parasites betokening sterility and neglect. In one orchard the trees were quite stifled by wild vines. Beside the levee an upturned skiff lay rotting in the very spot in which she had seen it years before. She glanced at the opposite side of the embankment and found what she expected — a plow, scarred and bitten by the rust of years. She looked at the owner's house and saw him, a barefooted Cajin asleep on the porch with his hat on his breast and a swarm of flies creeping over his feet. In the yard a woman was chopping wood.

Home again, she went to her room to be alone, to think. But where was the point of thinking? Resolutely she fought a desire to lie on the bed and brood. She would not be tempted into the mournfully indolent mood of the day!

So in the afternoon she changed clothes and went visiting. There had been a rain at noon. The road was churned into an unsightly brown paste by hoofs and wheels. Heavy clods accumulated on her rubber boots, burdening her journey, tugging at her, the sentient earth, like a dogged sadness. She stopped in to see Pretty John and his wife, and called on some of her maternal cousins, the Durots, but hurried away after being mournfully greeted by these people, who were all in deep black, lounging about indulging in a sort of holiday of grief for Grampaw. On the road, again the earth gathered on her feet, and she was sad, but hers was a living, pulsating sadness, bringing her a desire to plod on faster, to renounce inertia and death — a sadness that had rhythm, almost harmony, like a stately dirge, mournful yet profoundly meet.

In the night she sent Melia away and cooked a good supper, some of the noble dishes for which she was known along the river. In the warm kitchen she put Mocco to work scouring the pans until the walls as of old were arrayed with bright utensils. He fetched wood for her. He beat the eggs for the cake. He ran to the store, and sped breathlessly back with a glass of sherry for the oyster soup. Bonus, too, helped in the kitchen, with bulging eyes and watering mouth as he smelled the aroma of the liquored soup. The scene was dear to the hearts of Sister and Mocco — only there was no laughter tonight.

Sister went to bed tired, gratefully tired and strong, mistress of herself. . . .

Next morning she left her bed with alacrity at sunrise. She went to her window and stood contemplating the long vertebrae of varicolored houses down the reptilian levee. Already summer was somewhere in the ground and waters. The scene had the slumbrous feel of a Delta summer morning, colored by details which Sister had never before particularly observed — an aged Cajin taking his wife to church on a mule-drawn sled; shrill children throwing sand at each other; a squatting negress eating gingersnaps on a log, dipping the cakes into the river before each bite; and on the levee by Jule's store, the dapper cartridge salesman from New Orleans amusing a group of idlers by shooting at coins thrown into the air. . . .

But she was apart from these good people, all of them indolently living and letting live. Something inside her was different, something Grampaw had discovered — passed into her unsure custody to be guarded and nurtured and passed on by her. . . . She knew not how to examine her apartness, but it was there. It had always been there, had it not? Yes — always. She had never taken these people to herself. They had not taken her. They seemed half afraid of her. And among them she, herself, was afraid — wary, abrupt of tone and manner, unable quite to master their eager birdlike patois; never joining in their rhythm of life, which was as slow and hot as the sun; always vaguely impatient of their amiable cunning way of getting from their groves more in fruit than they gave in labor.

Already she was longing for Grampaw's camp, and the security engendered by the knowledge of vigorous busy workers near-by, his countrymen. And the friendly gleam of polished lamps across the canals at dusk — the infinite reaches of clean salt water — the tranquil sheen of rushes in the breeze — the vast unobstructed sweep of dramatically changeful skies. Thinking of the countless handsome books that now belonged to her, of the new sewing machine they had ordered before Grampaw's death, of the quiet evenings she would knit and dream by the fire — she was almost happy. She could not banish the feeling that Grampaw's death had been somehow fitting and proper, like the questioning pause at the end of a beautiful story....

She went to Jule's and obtained the names of several sporting-goods houses up the river, and wrote them each a letter stating the prices at which she would knit good quality nets and seines.

That day the child was baptized Raymond Bruce Kalavich.

THE DARK PILGRIM

BOOK THREE

20

MOCCO remained at home, a sulking martyr, to await his father's death. Sister hurried across to the camp. The sinews of her spirit were toughened. She found herself eager to embark upon a new life, her own mistress. The wind was lusty. Playful gusts beat her skirts at the washtub, almost jerking from her grasp the clothes she struggled to pin to the line — Grampaw's few soiled working garments, the trousers frayed at the knees and their cuffs filled with shavings. Because the place was rich in tokens of his pride in life, his love of clean disorder, his mellow humor and childish curiosity, the aura of his presence lingered for weeks, often frightening her when the night hemmed her in with darkened rooms.

She waited for orders for nets. Paddling to the post-office each afternoon, she wore the new dresses she was making, the gay mail-order fabrics Grampaw had helped her select. Little Bruce had learned to sit still in the delicately balanced pirogue, holding their raincoats, humming or muttering in his secret labial jargon — an odd, self-sufficient child, perched motionless for an hour, seeming to comprehend the danger. 'If I reach that muskrat nest in less than ten strokes,' Sister thought, 'there's a letter at the post-office.' The water was slick and dusty, with a meandering line of willow poles marking the channel. She traveled the distance to the muskrat nest in eight strokes, paddling gradually slower, cheating herself. Occasionally a huge gar would gently break apart the surface, roll over lazily, and dive with his brief gulp of air. In the big empty silent marsh, the flashing of the fat, predatory body of the gar, armored with stony scales which the Redmen of old used as arrow points, caused an icy, half-pleasing tremor to pass through Sister's flesh.

There was no mail, no orders for nets! Crushed, she walked through the knot of loungers in the store. Mateo Lucich was holding a meeting in the saloon, sitting on the pool table surrounded by stout, bony, fiercely-mustached Slavonians. Since Grampaw's death, Mateo was bossing the fishermen's association. Outside, Sister greeted the people sitting on their porches. Everywhere in the balmy evening the children screeched at play. A man in the river was scrubbing his mule with a broom. Sister walked thoughtfully. A feeling of tightness spread through her. It was almost exhilarating to be facing destitution. Her heart was aroused, pumping fatefully; her spine stiffened.

At home she spent the evening knitting crab-nets on a few wire frames stored in the loft. When in three days she had finished this, she took the nets to Mateo, who promised to display them for sale. Perhaps visiting sportsmen would buy them. She must not depend wholly on orders from town . . . She caught some mullet which she salted and dried in the sun, and smoked the roe.

Near the end of spring, from her Gulf coast summer home Loretta Dobravich wrote:

'Nick just learned through the Slavonian Society of poor Grandpa's death. Imagine no-one thinking to notify us! Nick says he understands, so I must try to. He was horribly shocked, looking ghastly for days, yet he didn't consider it strange he wasn't notified. What strange people! Do you need me? Why not come live with us — or have you a prospective husband, or some other means of subsisting in a world that is cruel to poor unmarried mothers?'

There was a long description, partly lyrical, of Pass Christian, Mississippi, and its sylvan environs.

Mocco delivered this letter. Sister saw he was tipsy. 'What does Loretta say?' he asked over her shoulder. His face gaped inanely, like a livid matrix of vice. 'Let's see the letter, Sis.'

'Mocco, you look like a pig. A *pig!* Go wash! Go!'

'Does she want to help you? If she does, take the money, Sis! Take it! *I'll* take it. I can't buy any more milk for Papa. I had to sell one of the window sashes yesterday to a man build-ing a houseboat, and cover the window with palmettoes. Three dollars! I plowed an arpent two weeks ago to make some cucumbers and the alligator grass is growing over it already. Sure I'll take Loretta's money!'

Sister was slack-shouldered and pale. Mocco was so flabby and weak-looking. He seemed to be a living weight upon her — a burden pulling at her, straining at her breast, rather than borne upon her back. She leaned in the back doorway staring with white curled lips at Loretta's tinted and perfumed page. Far down below her the naked sun, vanishing in a dull red stillness, was tilted seemingly near enough for its twirling proper-ties to be discerned. The child on the floor rustled a page in his book. An unseen water-bird piped afar, and the dislodged thatching on Loretta's camp flapped as softly as crippled wings.

'Papa got a jug last night,' Mocco droned. 'He lectured me. He blames you for all this. *You!* And me for not controlling you, keeping you from living alone like an outcast. Some peo-ple say you are chewing tobacco. I took your part. I know you're all right, Nicolene, and I'm going to hell with you. All of us together. The Kalavich gang going to hell together with the family name. Not even Nigger Bonus wants us any more. Now *he's* gone to Lacroix to work in the rice. Papa will last about a month.'

In the girl's mind each sound fell inertly through the echo of the last; then the first silence, the silence of the prairie, vast and all-embracing, flowed in again and lay about her, more benignly than before, yet somehow confused, as if with conflicting mandates soundlessly voiced. The chaotic emptiness! The silence without peace! The humorless and crazy network of events! The waiting shapes of the ashen past trooping in once more!

'I'm not interested in all this,' she told Mocco.

'In what?'

'Any of it. I've got my own life to live, my own self to feed. Sit down. Don't get angry and leave. . . . And you think Papa will die?'

'Any day. He *wants* to die, Sis. Last night——'

'Why don't he die, then!' she cried in an outraged tone and strode away, wringing her hands. Before Grampaw's saddle and the terrestrial globe she stopped distractedly, like a cornered animal seeking refuge, any refuge, the smallest hole.

'Any day,' said Mocco.

Sister picked up her child and sat with him, brooding, stroking his buttocks. She rubbed her cheek dreamily over the child's curls and looked at Mocco with a gleam in her eyes. 'You think it will be soon?' she asked, almost whispering. 'Any day, Sis.' They stared at each other alertly, like plotters in a lawless deed. Mocco looked away then, suddenly guilty, and Sister stared ahead. The tinted letter on the table was moved a few inches by the breeze. Sister watched it hang precariously, then flutter down, with its dire hints.

'Are you worried about my future, Mocco?'

'I don't know. You'll marry Mitch, I guess. Unga'll be back to keep you company as soon as — as something happens to Papa. Unga left her husband, you know. She's working out.'

'You know her address?'

'The niggers won't tell on the river. Unga's still afraid Papa'll go to town and kill her.'

The next day brought two orders from New Orleans firms, one for a cast-net and one for a small trawl. Sister worked day and night knitting these, and earned enough to keep them for a month.

She answered Loretta's letter: 'I am very sorry, but I cannot accept your help. You are not my friend. You cannot keep your mind on anyone or anything. I wish you would please stop trying to make me picture myself as a poor unmarried mother, scorned by the world. I will not play such a part. I have a child because I did a thing that pleased me. I have been scorned very little by the world. I believe I can look out for myself.'

In a month, all the net money was spent. She spent the last penny for a sack of rice. Sister and Bruce subsisted for some days on fish and rice. She could not bring herself to ask Mrs. Lucich for credit. She would have bought some vegetables on credit, but no peddlers crossed the river that spring. Aphids and caterpillars, now breeding fast in the unusually warm spring, had destroyed the remains of the winter truck on the Margin. There was not even coffee in the camp — no sugar, flour, or meal. Little Bruce did not mind. Sister found some cinnamon on a shelf, a vestige of the days of tasty desserts. She borrowed a quart of molasses from a neighbor. The child devoured with relish, night after night, the outlandish but wholesome mixture of rice, molasses, and cinnamon.

Grampaw had left a large quantity of wine, some Tokay (szmarod and maslas) and some Dalmatian. This provided good nourishment, although even taken with bread it awakened slumbering lusts and hatreds and caused her one night to stagger to bed sobbing with self-pity.

The world and its life took on a new aspect to Sister. She ignored the shapes and hues of nature. No caroling bird enticed her from her daily bent. No gorgeous cloud-mass gave her pause. Literature and music were no longer indispensable to her life. Often, however, missing a meal or two, she felt strangely light-headed, spiritual, apart from life, almost physically purified. Through the telescope she saw smoke pouring from her father's chimney on Grass Margin. Under the royal blue heavens, among the towering thunderheads, there plied the busy masts of fishing boats dotting the sunlit waters. From near-by came the ring of hammers building a new camp. A dark trapper close by the camp, waist-deep in the oyster-grass, stopped to club some captured beast. The gruff cannon at the distant forts boomed all day, shooting at a target in the river. People everywhere were nourishing themselves through work, working through nourishment. Sister longed for a thick slice of fresh white bread. She imagined she was growing thinner every hour, that her hip-bones in front projected out farther than her belly.

She visited Paul Cristovich, a bearded old friend of Grampaw's, and asked him to sail her to Grampaw's oyster beds. She must have a change of diet, and the child, too, needed different food. Cristovich was very courteous behind his masses of uncut hair and untrimmed beard.

'You want oysters?' he asked, puzzled. 'Oysters no much good now. No fat. Empty like bladders this time year.'

'I want to try them,' Sister answered.

'You wan' try tsome from my beds?'

'No. Grampaw's beds.'

So the old man took her to Grampaw's beds, far out in Bay Saint Francis. They sailed in Paul's lugger, the *Big Dipper*. Sister wanted to fish oysters. It was hard work. The old man watched her with twinkling eyes. Plying the great tongs was like handling a seven-foot nutcracker, bringing into action the muscles of the shoulders, biceps, and breast. It occurred to her that a man's breasts were not the useless appendages she had considered them. They were strong levers enabling a man to crush or to embrace. Between the man and woman, they fished several bushels, and returning to Grampaw's camp they dumped the oysters into the canal, whence Sister might take them as needed.

Sister taught herself to open oysters as she had seen her mother do, smashing the sharp bills with a culling hatchet to get a purchase for the knife. And they ate oysters for two weeks, in every style — raw, fried, souped, roasted, minced with rice, baked in the shell.

She attained some proficiency with Grampaw's gun, and wore his hip boots on her forays through the ooze. Once she brought in a dozen plump marsh hens. How delicious they were after a long diet of fish — roasted in the pot, steamed in their own sweet fat!

In the year that followed, Sister grew to be somewhat of a legend. No one could quite understand how she lived, for she never begged. Aside from selling an occasional net, she was known to have no definite calling (she never encouraged men to visit her), and yet her chimney smoked each day, and at night her lamp shone as brightly as any. People became accustomed to encountering her in out-of-the-way places, always courteous, always clean, always in a hurry, with her great dark eyes roving and her skirts twinkling briskly, and a freshly washed meal-sack slung across her shoulder; carrying home strange berries, wild salads, a pair of frogs, mushrooms — such morsels as lie hidden in the odd cracks of the earth everywhere, ignored by the well-fed, but searched out by the sharp eyes of the poor. And she and her child were not long in learning to relish many kinds of food generally tabu, but much esteemed by those who dwell close to the earth and waters — sea-gull eggs, thistle hearts, chicken-hawk meat, alligator tail, muskrat legs. Three or four times a week she fared forth on such mysterious journeys, searching for nothing in particular, in boat or afoot, and returned at dusk with her magic bag, to find little Bruce, left alone for several hours, waiting for her with his grave face pressed against the porch railing. And together they would open the bag.

'Turtle eggs! Wild onions! Lotus nuts!' Sister exclaimed, and they joined hands and whirled madly. Or if she had sold a net in Dutch Scenery or a string of mudfish that day, they would have cake, perhaps a gill of olive oil. There was no reading or playing the phonograph in the night. After working heavy-lidded among the cloudy white folds of a net for an hour, Sister was ready to bathe and retire. In her virginal bed she lay thinking. During these days this was the only period she gave to the luxury of sheer reflection:

'These stars must shine on lovely heads and over cities bright, a blue electric light at every street, with bugs spinning around it. The docks are dark. In town people are going to night-school now. The truth shall set them free. Why do they want to be free? Free for what? Free to be different and get more. More food? Do they want to eat more? Going to night-school to get fat? No, they want mostly to know more, enjoy comforts and a better standard. Civics says so. Do I want the truth? I want Mitch Holt. Admit it! You can't fool me. A woman must wait. To hell with that! Receptacle! Receptacle! Empty on the shelf. Oh God of the knowing smile, give me someone to lie with me and cool the fires and take away the worry about food tomorrow! Admit it! A woman must wait. She does not go. The man comes. Pinching his mustache, a spade in his hand or pockets full of little pieces of paper. To hell with that! That is not true. Some women set cozy traps. Then she can wait! Food and shelter at the bottom of it all, for the babies. Nobody knows.

'I will never, never, *never* not care for pride and fun. Keep busy! Keep busy! What shall we eat tomorrow?

'Mitch would play jokes on the prison guards. Perhaps he has led a mutiny. Poor fellow, he is my friend. How can he stand discipline — so self-willed and impatient and gay?

'The loveless gather faggots in the dusk.'

Profane as vultures, some of her thoughts left her abashed. And more and more she relapsed into her old Grass Margin habit of cursing, swearing at the snakes that sprung her traps, at the fickle tides and weather, at the egg-yolk congealed on a saucer edge, or the flapping palmettoes on Loretta's abandoned camp. In fall, just as the ducks begin arriving from the north, a bastard eagle — also called duck hawk or great-footed falcon — took up its abode near the camp. Sister, who had been practicing shooting with as many shells as she could afford to buy, went one gray morning to the near-by marsh pond to hunt. This pond was overgrown with wild celery and water peppers, an ideal spot for ducks. She made her blind and lay there in the wind. In a little while, there came a flock of hundreds of blue-winged teal, followed by several scores of pintails. Sister's breath came faster, and her mouth almost watered. Before the flocks could light, from some place just behind her the bastard eagle leaped into the air, climbed so rapidly that the ducks had little time to check their momentum; then selected the leader of the pintails, swooped down upon him and struck him a loudly thudding blow and sent him tumbling downward, and quickly plunged to recover the prey before it struck the water.

Sister was almost in tears. 'Bastard! Bastard!' she screeched, unknowingly addressing the marauder by its Creole name, brandishing her gun and stamping her boots. And all the way home she swore, cursing the balky pirogue, the wind, the troublesome water hyacinths. The pond, which she had come to regard as her private preserve, would perhaps never be visited by ducks again. Eating her dinner of fish and rice, she had to smile back at a picture of herself in the throes of rage.

During the night there was a blow of wind, the first nor'-wester of the season. Sister awoke at dawn, leaped from her bed in one of her gay and dangerous moods, rapturously conscious of the change of seasons — restive northern wind; ominous murkiness of sky; dark brief passage of blown fragments of migrating flocks. And, 'To these,' she thought of the ragged bunches of birds sweeping by, '*we* are now the North, gray and inhospitable, shut in upon ourselves. And south they turn, flying over the Gulf to food and love. But handsome Mr. Duck Hawk! To *him* we are the South. Warmth and ease and many juicy banquets! Suppose, Bruce,' she said to the child, 'we give him a taste of death!'

A chill coursed down her flesh.

She went to the pond again. She wanted to conquer the hawk! It was ideal duck weather — waters roughened to a salty sheen by the wind; wild millet and sawgrass tossing brightly under a lonely mackerel sky. But she wanted the hawk, to conquer him in the only way that lay open, by ending his insolent career. And if she could not kill him, then she must *see* him!

As she approached the pond, the cold metal of the gun focused her faculties in her avenging fingers. Almost she secretly felt she would never approach within striking distance. She knew a hawk! Yet she must! She must!

Suddenly, between the swaying stalks of a clump of cattails she saw him! There he stood, the dread bandit of the skies, not fifty feet away, as debonair and unperturbed as an abler foe benignly granting truce and parley in the dawn, perched motionless and grave upon an old gray post, watching her quizzically. Sister's nostrils paled, to see so closely for the first time in her life the soft, the incredibly soft, insinuative gleam of slate-blue plumage. His eyes held her fixedly, unblinking, with that level, cruel yet nobly guiltless look she had noted on even the most rapacious of wild creatures. But she was challenged! His black mustaches glittered at her, emitting a kind of dull sparks, it seemed, when brushed by the wind. The grave impeccable power! Her eagerness was kindled.

So she moved. Soft, breathless, slow, as if caution might avail, she drew closer. She took half a dozen tender, fateful steps — but the falcon's gaze remained upon her, burning, smoldering, very innocent and sly, urgent as a charm. The sky behind her vivid target was bright steely gray, the bleak and shoreless north. And all around her a chilly silence now ensued, frigid and strange, emptying the heavens of all winged life, as though the fowls of the shore had stayed their morning functions to await the falcon's flight or fall. Two more thrilling steps she drew nearer the delicately poised quarry. He moved no quill or sinew! Exultantly her heart bounded! Now she could examine the great fang-like talons, sharper than thorns, murderously black and curved ... Softly, softly, with infinite tenderness and care she advanced leg after leg, all the time bringing the gun nearer her shoulder, and fingering the fatal trigger with her trembling hand, into which had gathered all of her quivering young impatience and rage.

Now the hawk moved. With the gun close to the sighting position, she saw him very deliberately turn his head away and look across the pond, as though no longer aware of her presence — as though her queer conduct no longer interested him.

Sister drew the trigger. The hawk fell softly, a heap of struggling feathers.

Then in every direction about her here and there birds leaped from the thick grasses and whirred frantically away. Buffleheads and yellow-throats and blue-headed vireos and myrtle warblers. She went to the spot where he had fallen and saw the hawk standing at the foot of the rotted post, very much alive and composed, except that one wing hung limply. His sharp eyes examined her curiously, as if to learn whether she too had been shot. Small beads of blood were sliding down the disabled wing.

There was an old broken pushing-pole on the ground near-by. Sister picked it up, and with it gently prodded the hawk. The bird opened his beak and vented a singular whining sound, low and plaintive. Then he began to creep up the pole toward her. Sister was startled, frightened, and would have dropped the pole, but the bird still held her with its glistening, audacious, appealing look, and continued so delicately, so gently, to mount the pole. When the falcon reached her he rested, with one foot upon the back of her hand that held the pole, the murderous talons encircling without hurting her fingers. So! Sister cocked her head humorously. Then, as if matters were entirely settled, the falcon looked to his wounded wing, smoothing down his feathers with his beak. Sister hesitantly stroked the hawk's back.

She brought him on the pole to her pirogue and paddled home with him. All along the canal, doors opened and open-mouthed faces followed her progress. The wing did not appear to be seriously damaged. No bones were broken.

The hawk steadfastly refused fish, but readily ate a muskrat's flesh, and the entrails of the ducks Sister brought in from her pond. She was learning to shoot with some skill; and the pond had become a feeding-ground for many flocks. The hawk, his wing healed, cut a dashing figure perched in the sun on the porch rail. He would return from hunting and remain for hours, preening himself, dreaming in the sun like a subdued demon, like Poe's Raven, about to utter prophecies at any time. As Sister moved about at work, the hawk's eyes followed her with that strange, half-alluring gaze. Often he went into the camp, and once he perched on a chair-back for hours while she sat knitting a net. 'Now,' she thought with a smile, 'I need only to start digging herbs to become a village witch.' As the weeks passed and game became more plentiful, the hawk spent more time around the camp. Sister grew so attached to him that she would await his return, or feel anxious if he remained away too long.

Presently he came to be a real household pet, and he lost his wild, innocent look. He was falling into objectionable habits, growing officious and over-bold. When very busy or in a cranky mood Sister would scold him roundly, put him outdoors. And he was getting sluggish, eating and drowsing more and more, and appeared to be fatter.

Then one day little Bruce in play was throwing some balls of moss at the hawk, who sat drowsily on a stool. Suddenly with flashing eyes the vexed bird cried out and flew to within a foot of the child's face. Sister screamed and snatched a broom. She dealt the hawk a blow that sent him spinning into a corner. 'Get out!' she cried. 'Get out and stay!'

As he soared through the window, she swung the broom again, and knocked the hawk into the mangroves below. He rose and beat a frenzied retreat. Sister watched him soaring off until he was but a speck in the blue. She sighed. Doubtless he would never return.

'Good riddance to the sassy loafer,' she thought. 'He never even tried to catch a mouse. Anyhow, he was getting to smell like one of those old men who come down the river all the way from Minnesota in a canoe.'

21

SISTER was reading the wise and pithy verses of 'The Rape of Lucrece.' And it was spring. Another spring! Warming her, urging her, hurting her, more than the last. She had learned to pray again, but no longer on her knees. She had sent to Mitch Holt in the Atlanta prison some handkerchiefs worked for his birthday. 'Another birthday,' she wrote to him, 'another rattle on your tail. If you're not allowed to use these, save them. They will be elegant to wear when you come back and become the leader of your people. I am mad with you today. I'll never speak to you again. I'm almost sure.' The working of the hand-kerchiefs had coincided with the noisy and pompous advent of spring: the coming of spring had occurred during the reading of Lucrece. These cunningly made phrases seeped through her mind as a sweet brook nourishes the searching roots of a vine.

Now she was receiving quite a few orders for nets. One supply house in New Orleans had asked for a small trawl fashioned along the same lines as the trawls used by shrimp fishermen. For this she had received fifteen dollars; and though it was an arduous undertaking, she had finished it in two weeks, cursing it while it grew, but sending it off with regret, wondering whose hands would haul in its heavy catch. The room had been filled, draped all over, with the folds of its gauzy meshes, and once assured of how to proceed she had worked quickly, swearing or singing. Little Bruce loved to walk among these devious hanging folds and out again, and in and out, while Sister sang him a nursery rhyme. Or he would sit on the floor with his lap full of lead sinkers, watching Sister's twinkling fingers toss the good stitches, quickly stab through the loops, and draw the knots with a deft, illusory motion that Bruce thought most wonderful.

One morning Mocco came. He was closely shaven, clear-eyed, and Sister noticed his fingernails had been trimmed. His hands were thin, pale, as though from long fasting. He wore a black suit. Sister felt herself blanch. She thought her father was dead.

'What's wrong?' she asked. She had never seen him so self-possessed and thoughtful. He seemed to have acquired a strange equanimity and poise, as from a vital shock.

'Loretta's in Lacroix,' he said briskly, 'if you call that something wrong.'

'Loretta Dobravich?'

'Yes. She'll be here tomorrow evening.' Mocco removed his coat and rolled his sleeves.

'Here!'

'There!' he answered, pointing over to the empty camp. 'Isn't she wanted?'

'Her camp wants her. It's coming loose.'

'Oh, no, it's not! I'll tend to that roof. Have you got a trowel, Sis? I've got a lot to do. The artist is with her, Mr. Davidson. He's been living with us on the Margin for three days. He's going to teach me to paint!'

'A fine painter you'll make — color-blind!'

'Never mind! He says it might make my pictures better. Did you know that some music composers are deaf?'

Sister could not realize . . . Mocco's words intruding upon the peace of spring sounded like a dim familiar knell heard over vague horizons.

She pictured the shabby, well-mannered artist Loretta had told her about, sitting at his easel unmindful of her, living in the future — ahead of his time. And she was aware of colors vibrating about her. Bruce's hair had tawny glittering outer locks the sun had fiercely touched. A distant clothesline was a red and yellow checkered festoon. Tall clouds bent hugely over a ragged pool of sepia, and over the boundless marshes bearing all the streaked and whorled and mottled greens of new grasses springing out of the matted blur of rich decay.

'I've got a skiff-load of pansies for Loretta's flower troughs,' said Mocco. 'Haven't you got a trowel?'

'Pansies! But——'

'From Miss Pretty John. Lend us a trowel, Sis! The furniture's coming out on the boat this evening with the champagne and groceries and nigger cooker. I've got a lot to do. She's got guests with her. They're going to fish.'

'What's he like, well? The artist? What sort of person?'

'Small as you. Smaller, up and down. And quiet.'

'You surely describe him well! I can see him now.'

'You'll see him.'

'Is Nikolai along?'

'No. Seven people and the cooker.'

Loretta and her guests remained at the camp three days. There were four women and three men. Sister the first day occasionally saw the people across the way. A handsome woman would lean on Loretta's railing and gaze across the wide secret marshes and breathe deeply, throw a cigarette into the canal, or idly note the passage of a bird. Or a couple, man and woman, would sit in rockers on the porch, having nothing to do. There would be laughter at the card tables inside. And Sister heard the crisply animated sounds of dinner, faint clinks and clatters under the gay talk of the well fed. These folk were not different from her, she decided. They had their times for gazing over the earth. They guessed at a swift bird's errand. They grew merry while feeding. Surely they ogled themselves in mirrors too truthful, obeyed their chubby priests, and wept for the dead. And rapture slept in their hidden nipples. And if *she* knew not strange pavements, they knew not years of silence; and if she had never slept with silk, they had never slept with hunger.

Loretta came to see Sister the first night. She brought with her a short, dark woman called Mrs. Charbonnet-Boatner, and René Davidson. 'A most remarkable girl, Sister is,' Loretta told her companions while crossing the canal, 'considering her background. There's good blood in her somewhere. Notice especially her carriage.'

They found Sister sitting before her net, her hair gathered into thick black coils over her ears, which accentuated the fine structure of her skull — though the slope of her shoulder was somewhat angular at this time. Waiting on the porch for the women to come up, the artist saw her first. His gaze traveled swiftly over Sister's person, measuring. He knew at once that her members were well co-ordinated, and also that she had the faculty of losing herself in the doing of physical tasks. And her serene, unselfconscious demeanor caused him at once to feel oddly at a disadvantage — almost antagonistic . . .

'Sister!' Loretta called. 'It's so good to see you!'

Sister smoothed her apron and rose. 'Good evening,' she said primly, with her eyes on the artist.

After introducing her friends, Loretta peered into the bedroom. 'Where's Bruce?' she asked.

'Asleep.'

Loretta's smile died. 'I — I brought you an aspic and some wine,' she said absently.

'You shouldn't have troubled. Have a chair, won't you, Mr. Davidson?'

'You're thin, my dear,' said Loretta. 'Not ill, I hope.'

'I'm well, thanks.'

Sister returned to her knitting, composed, her heart throbbing dependably, eagerly abetting her serenity. Loretta's face was wan. Sister could feel Loretta trying to appear more wan. But her hair was lusterless, almost ashen, her skin dull and unwholesome; her green eyes had grown baggy. Loretta did not know what to say.

Mrs. Charbonnet-Boatner yawned. She was very attractive, with fine small features, sleek hips, delicate feet accustomed to strange pavements. But this was no pavement. She made the camp seem small and crude. It was not her fault.

René Davidson was ill at ease in the silence. 'May I see the dolls your grandfather carved?' he asked.

'Why, certainly!' Sister responded, and quickly tripped into the bedroom and brought out the box. She resumed her knitting without glancing at the others.

'Ah!' the artist exclaimed. 'Wonderful!' Now he was at home.

'You're working hard,' said Loretta to Sister.

'Yes.'

Mrs. Charbonnet-Boatner yawned again. Sister, plying her needle, glanced again and again at René Davidson. He sat under Grampaw's oiled saddle. He looked like a young boy with the incongruous hard-carved lips of a grim student. He had gone without many things in life. Discipline showed like a benign irritant through his measured and worldly composure. He held one of the dolls at arm's length and smiled, then gazed at Sister with his fine, dark, tortured eyes ... Had all the beautiful things he had studied made him suffer? Sister wondered. She looked up and found him regarding her face with a sort of lingering reluctance, and heard him saying to her: 'This is my country. This will be my country.' Then he fell into a kind of palpitant pensiveness, as though to capture and reweigh his decision, or to cope with some dark deterrent. (He felt that Sister emanated a certain unconscious power, and this seemed strangely to achieve expression through her manner of knitting the net.)

Loretta cleared her throat. 'I've been telling my friends about your famous cooking, darling,' she said to Sister. 'I'm afraid their mouths are watering for some of your noted dishes. We're all such gluttons in this salt air.'

Sister vented a low laugh, without answering or looking up. Loretta was using an odd, affected tone, because of the presence of the other woman. She had never spoken like this to Sister alone ... Mrs. Charbonnet-Boatner left her chair, strolled casually toward the door, and stood looking out. She wanted to go.

René Davidson began to tell Sister about some dolls he had seen in Milan, the ancient Italian bambinos. Now Sister stopped her knitting, and during the telling examined the man well. He was indeed smaller than Sister, curly-haired, dark, rather thin. Sister could think of many dishes that would fatten him. He was most unassuming, and yet in his presence the others were nothing, mere gown-shop customers or ceramic collectors, or searchers after quaint scenes that might be viewed in comfort. Pretty Mrs. Charbonnet-Boatner had become a nullity, a blank-faced attendant of another's whims and ventures.

'Shall we go?' she asked when René finished talking.

Loretta asked Sister, 'Are you going to try the aspic, dear?'

'I'll try it,' Sister answered, pulling her needle.

René Davidson did not notice the constraint of the women's meeting, or he perceived it and ignored it. While Sister knitted, he examined the bookshelves: Heine in German, Blake, Martial, Catullus, Aristophanes, Moschus, Huxley in Russian, Swift, Thoreau.

Loretta got up and walked over to Sister. 'Will you honor us by cooking a supper, dear?' she asked. 'Arthur's dying for court-bouillon that your mother had from her mother. And panned oysters in wine, eh, for lunch? Shall we say tomorrow evening for the dinner? I'm anxious to hear what you'll say about my kitchen.'

'I can't,' said Sister, working on.

'Why?' Loretta asked, pale as death.

'Because.'

'But, darling! Do you mean you'd rather not?'

'That's right,' said Sister. She bent her head and bit apart one of the knots in the knitting. 'I'd rather not.'

Loretta turned away.

'Will you come and see us, then? Bring Bruce and meet my friends?'

'I don't think so.' Sister smiled across at Loretta.

'You really don't care to come over?'

'No.'

The other woman walked out. Davidson was reading a book.

Loretta approached Sister. 'Then this is the end of our friendship?' she whispered. Her voice was breaking.

'What friendship?'

'Our friendship.'

'I think so.'

Sister went to the porch with Loretta. The third woman waited in the boat below. The stars were spattered prodigally, and far south the rigid beams of a lighthouse swept round and round.

Loretta did not know how to leave. She said: 'I left some pecan trees for you on the Margin. Everyone on the Mississippi coast is planting them. They don't freeze like oranges sometimes do ——'

'Thank you. I'll notify Pretty John, because Mocco won't plant them.'

'—— or rot like peaches. They taste of the sun — pecans.'

'Yes.'

'Of the sun.' Loretta put a note of desolation in her voice.

'There are really *two* suns here — one in heaven and another in the water. That one burns the water-women to the thighs.' She uttered a light, hysterical laugh. 'So our friendship is — over.'

'I think so.'

'I hardly blame you. I dropped you. I came to pick you up again. That's the way it is. I drop things. I get tired of things — weary — weary. But about *people*, perhaps I can't help it. I have a soft heart, and you know I have been used. Used, and used, and used. For years.'

'Whose fault is it?' Sister asked.

'My fault. Good-night.'

'Good-night.'

Inside, Sister found René standing before the terrestrial globe, idly turning it. Alone with Sister, he became self-conscious, wearing a rather stiff smile.

'She's gone,' said Sister. 'Have you had supper?'

'Yes.'

Sister smelled the aspic Loretta had brought, and began to eat it. It was very good.

'What's the matter with Loretta?' she asked René.

'She's a victim of things. Too many things. And she lives by a fiction. She's neurotic. She dramatizes herself as The Barren Woman, or sometimes as The Poor Rich Girl.'

Sister laughed, spreading her legs apart, digging her fists into her lap. 'What is neurotic?' she asked. 'Are you neurotic?'

'Yes.'

She looked at him curiously, her head on the side, her face flushed from the wine. René was in front of the lamp. His transparent ear glowed rich as a ruby — no other color about him but that, his soft intent visage somewhat blurred out. She turned to pour him wine, and he observed the fine white scar that clove the tissue of her upper lip and rather coarsened her

mouth. It's shape fascinated him ... René was puzzled. He
had never loved a woman before.

Mocco was hired to guide the men out fishing for two days.
They caught no appreciable number of fish. Mocco told them
they were not taking the fish seriously. They were always wanting to eat. They took food out with them — napkins, silver-
ware, little well-seasoned delicacies in jars. While fishing they
nibbled the food and drank the iced bottled beer. They asked
innumerable questions about the country and the 'natives.'
How much money did a river pilot make? Where were the
beautiful octoroons when they were not octorooning? Who
owned the marshes? How did oysters get around for mating?

There were two men, both partly bald. They wore the same
kind of clothing, and said the same kind of things. On the second day they were very tired of fishing. On the way home they
grew facetious. The dearth of fish that day made them humorous. Their jokes turned on the country, implying that they had
been victims of a huge prank. Mocco wanted to oblige Loretta.
He humored them and tried to divert them. He showed them
the pelicans diving for fish.

'Could a fisherman rent one of the pelicans?' asked one.

'Those aren't pelicans,' the other answered, 'those are mosquitoes. The mosquitoes are not bad this time of year.'

'They're not bad. They're not harming anyone, Arthur.'

'See them dive? Hey! Got a trout that time!'

'Eat all the fish! Ha! Ha!'

'We have white pelicans and brown ones,' said Mocco. 'The
white ——'

'Oh, Arthur, was that a brown one bit you last night while
you were looking for an octoroon?'

'All the octoroons are in town.'

'Sold up the river, eh, Arthur?'

'Sold to Lulu Black in town. Ten mirrors, ten women.'

'I want some soda. Is soda good for sunburn, Arthur?'
'Clouds are good for sunburn! Ha! Ha!'

René Davidson did no fishing. He lounged around Sister's camp all day, sketching, talking to Sister. Sister enjoyed that. René told her he would be back soon, and live in Loretta's camp.

22

SOME days later Mocco and René Davidson walked the levee in Grass Margin. They both carried paints and paper. The girls of the Margin peered at the artist from between the orange trees, or they bathed and changed clothing to visit the post-office on arrival of the mail boat. Mocco felt very important. The stranger now being discussed from Fort Jackson to Spanish Pass was his guest.

To René, Mocco belittled the Margin people. He wanted it understood that his residence here was only temporary. He told René the people practically subsisted on stews filled with spa-ghetti or rice, and that many of them were tuberculous from malnourishment. They placed a necklace of shark bones around the neck of teething infants. They thought the will-o'-the-wisps seen in the rear prairie were the souls of babies who had died unbaptized. He told René about Ole Moe, a withered black octogenarian and witch doctor who performed strange rites with ailing women.

René was overwhelmed with excitement. He could not be-lieve his ears. He also doubted his eyes. The river was incredi-ble — rolling past in fleet tawny coils, spotted with whirling patches of driftwood, and giving out a sound like an unseen multitude laughing or applauding afar. And the water's smell today was the oddest he had ever encountered. He kept try-ing to recall a certain fruit or flower he had smelled long ago in some deep dim ravine, it seemed; or a warm, half-bitter brew he had sipped after a bracing tramp somewhere among cold unpeopled crags . . .

His brushes rattled briskly in the box; his tubes were filled with good paint. He was trying not to be impatient about painting: the impact of the country must first be dispelled. He must fall into the languid, pliant tempo of the region, doing only one water-color a day for the present . . . The willows in the river wore long hairy growths sagging about their bases, like brown vigorous beards. The complex filigree of the May-Pop flowers resembled the work of a cunning jeweler. 'The people are neither of the land nor the sea, but partake of the elements of both,' he thought. 'Tony Kalavich has probably quit using his lungs and lies there breathing the fog through a pair of gills. I should like to help this big brute Mocco. He is at the other end of the pole from Sister. She is a lovely vision, he a fleshy fact. Yet they are so alike, both at war with something. What are they struggling against? . . . Are the trappers brutalized by continually beating animals to death? Do these people's thoughts ever turn southward? Do they always flow toward the iron North, against the current? Why do most of the men hate the soil, and the women love it? What can these women hope for but marriage to a pilot? These gorgeous Easter lilies, and the misty orange blossoms, yearly girlhood of the tree!'

'Shall we paint here?' he asked Mocco.

Soon a crowd assembled to watch them. Mocco glared at the barefooted idlers. René did not mind them. Their French was incomprehensible; it was rather agreeable to be hemmed in by their warm dark eyes.

'How do you like mine?' Mocco asked after they had painted an hour.

René screwed up his mouth, and glanced briefly at Mocco's work. 'It is too well done,' he decreed.

'It's almost exactly like the real boat,' Mocco said.

'Precisely. You must keep trying to make it exactly like Mocco Kalavich. A real boat is not an important thing, you know.'

After two weeks with René, Mocco cherished no illusions about becoming an artist, but he was enjoying himself. He had never before done anything too well.

'You must have something to say, you know,' said René.

'I'll tell you what I like best, René. I've been thinking. The human figure. Will I paint with you when you get a model?'

'We'll see.'

René intended employing a model for a day when he had enough money. Mocco hoped it would be a woman nude, a yellow girl he knew. He felt he would have lots to say about the girl's figure.

'Perhaps we'll induce Sister to pose,' said René.

'Jeezam! Do you mean naked?'

'Not necessarily.'

'She wouldn't pose anyhow.'

René thought, 'I could not paint her if she should. Perhaps some day . . .'

René took long brisk walks to Fort Jackson, among the rear forest swamps and canebrakes, and down to the head of the Passes where the Delta forked out. He went to the Port Eads lighthouse depot and painted the curiously shaped bell-buoys. In three weeks he made twenty-five water-colors. Then he found an old mulatto woman who was willing to sit for him, a barefooted and ragged hag of seventy named Tante Aurélie.

They worked in the packing shed behind the Kalavich home, the room where the negro Bonus had lived. The place was just as Bonus had left it, strewn with assorted objects the negro had acquired from various sources. On a shelf was a tin fog-horn and a huge conch shell. René placed the naked crone on an orangewood stool just under the shelf. Her little great-grandson, a fat black boy whom she insisted upon keeping with her, sat on the floor holding her hand. It was fine study, and René was excited. He forgot Mocco sitting beside him. Mocco was amazed at the queer shape and texture of the old woman's body, the large, deep creased navel, and the breasts hanging like long parchment flaps. The woman's rheumy old eyes watched René with a dull, passive, yet dignified look.

In a little while Tony Kalavich came hobbling from the house, leaning on a stout cane. His bleached face looked like white naked bone with deep holes in the temples and cheeks. He wore a greenish overcoat fastened at the neck with a large safety-pin. 'What is going on here?' he thought. 'Everything so quiet.' He was too weak to walk farther than the fig tree near the packing shed. He sank into a sitting posture against the tree and began to call Mocco. He could hardly hear his own voice. He picked up a stick of wood, and with a great effort threw it against the closed door. Mocco soon came out.

'What is going on in there?' Tony asked in Slavonian.

'René is painting Tante Aurélie's picture.'

'A negress! Painting a negress here! Help me over there!'

'Go inside, Father. You are too sick to be out.'

'Help me to that window, I say! Do you want me to get angry, a dying man?'

Mocco assisted him to the window, and he stood looking in. When he saw the stark nude woman, his eyes bulged. His nostrils lifted, trembling outward. He walked in the door and raising his stick, brought it down on the woman's bare shoulder. René said, 'Listen here!' in a stupefied tone. The old woman touched her shoulder, but made no protest, only stared at Tony with her expressionless face. He struck her again in the same place. She winced, then continued watching Tony without a word. 'Get out!' he shouted. 'You!' he turned on René, 'go! No paint nigger here! My house! No wunt you here, paint nigger! My house! Go out! No come back!'

René gathered up his paints. The naked negress sat quietly,

holding her great-grandson's hand. René handed her a dollar bill and told her he was through with her. She did not move. The little black boy did not move. René followed Tony to the big house. He went upstairs to the room he was occupying, Sister's room. He walked from window to window. Below him outside, the neglected orchard was a soft mass of thick, impenetrable, rather beautiful vines covering the tree tops. Tante Aurélie, now wearing her clothing, was lingering down on the levee with the little black boy, looking at the house in a bewildered manner. Soon the dusk began to fall and cast musty shadows inside. The room was full of mosquitoes flocking in at the windows; the only refuge was the netting on the bed. René went downstairs. Mocco was at the stove boiling a salted duck.

'Does your father really want me to leave here?' René asked softly. He cast a pained glance toward Tony hunched up in his corner. Tony had stirred the artist's compassion. He had never felt more pity for anyone.

'Don't mind him,' said Mocco.

'No like you here,' Tony mumbled. 'You go! You un'stand?'

'We don't hear what he says,' said Mocco. 'Hush up, Pa! He's got the fever, don't know what he's doing.'

'At least, then, I'll stay the night,' said René. 'I've no idea where to sleep, you know.' He bowed his curly head and smiled courteously at Tony.

Tony glared. 'No like you here,' he muttered.

'Very well, I'll leave promptly in the morning.'

René sat looking through the window at the moon with a melancholy stare. He was sorry for these people. He disliked them intensely. Mocco would never achieve anything as a painter, beyond a certain facility in copying what he saw. René was not lonely. He loved the country. Or did he love it? He had wearied of the meager, badly cooked meals; the growling of frogs at night; the bellowing of lonely cattle over the river; the moths, ants, crickets, roaches, gnats, mosquitoes, and lizards infesting the house. But his pulses quickened at thought of the vast regions not yet visited — primeval groves full of damp unearthly light; the saurian hush of primordial bogs; floating islands drifting a few inches an hour; wind-bowed trees waiting on lonely shores. How stimulating after two years of New Orleans and the anemic dilettantes who lounged in Loretta's living room! Was he romanticizing it all? Good! Excellent! He thought of Sister Kalavich, his lips puckering curiously and the scholarly frown leaving his face. He meant to see her again, to be her friend, to be near her, let her feed him. They would explore each other's minds. She would tell him of her life, her affair with the itinerant boatman. Yes, he was ready to see her now. He had mistrusted his first feelings. Now he felt he could see her with more detachment, a saner perspective . . .

He went out to see a steamboat pass, the crisp curl of the first swells rapidly advancing, catching the moonlight and scattering it with a hoarse roar among the gnarled willow roots. When he returned to the house he saw old Tante Aurélie, still sitting on the grass with the boy.

'Did you want anything, Aunt Aurélie?'

The old mulatto drew closer to René, a waddling bulk of flesh. 'Ah been wantin' to tell you — dey got a bad so' troat goin' aroun' de levee now.'

'Sore throat?'

'Yassa. Plenty peoples got it. Look lak lil raid pamples down in de side of de troat. Mr. Paul Step-Fred taken it today. You wants to be caffle.'

'And you were waiting to tell me that?'

'Yassa. Be caffle. Nice man lak you better be caffle down de river. Don't stay heah too long. I been heah 'bout fifty year, seen an' smelt an' heard everything. Don't you langer too long.'

'All right,' said René softly, looking at the low brassy moon. A noiseless great-winged insect flew past his cheek. 'I'll be careful. Where do you live? Do you have a little shack? When will you eat supper? Is it far, your home? Can you see in the moonlight?' The thick chill fragrance of orange blossoms was almost intoxicating. Far up the levee in the saloon a gathering of soldiers was singing.

'What do you do at night, Aunt Aurélie?'

'Ah sets home.'

'Are you lonely?'

'Nawsa. Ah waits fo' my son.'

'On the porch?' he asked in a rather eager voice.

'In de rockin'-cha'.'

They talked almost in whispers, like intrigants against the night's emphatic forms — sly stars just emerging, and devious winds, strong waters, pushing seaward with a mighty churning, and the tall sentient willows gathering the salty darkness to themselves.

'How old are you, Aunt Aurélie?'

'Don' knowsa. Ah buried two husbands an' fo' chirren. Ah seen the Yankee bus' de line an' sail up to take New Awlins.'

'The what?'

'The Yankee chain across de river at de foats. Ah mus' be ovah ninety. I belonged to Doctah Fall at Hug-Me Bend, waitin' on his table, an' was too pretty, an' his wife taken me out de big house an' put me in de fiel! Too pretty dat time. I seen de mine-boat was pickin' up mines from de river an' blow up an' my husband fin' a man's elbow on de back shaid. Jes a black elbow. Ah seen de Irishmen wid dey wheelborrows built this levee. Dey live in tents an' cook in buckets an' chunk knots at de chirren. Yassa. Wudden but two houses heah. Irishmen put big logs an' dry-goods boxes in de levee. Right where you standin'. Big pile o' trash in de mud, ef your wants to know why de levee leakin' tonight.'

'Who is the handsomest colored woman here, one I could paint?'

'Unga January, but she in town. She be back soon, when Mistah Tony die. She scaid o' Mistah Tony, Unga.'

A bird overhead cried, 'Quock! Quock!'

'Don' you langer heah too long. Not down dis rivah.'

'What do you mean?' René demanded. Tante Aurélie was moving off, waddling, dragging the black boy by the hand. René started after her. 'Don't you langer too long!' came her voice from the shadows. René stood peering after her. The strange bird's cry sounded again, out over the turbulent river . . .

Next day René went to live in Loretta's camp across from Sister Kalavich.

23

EARLY an April morning, Sister and René were in Grampaw's camp. Little Bruce was asleep. There was a thin fog. Sister stood at her round copper dishpan with wet deft arms, humming a song. A yellow-and-brown shawl hung in a point over her shoulders. René studied the foggy glare playing over the polished stove, the globe and saddle, the crisp humps of the freshly baked bread. Though she had knitted until a late hour the previous night, Sister was in high spirits, with plenty to do that day, and an admirer sitting near-by watching her ankles or something, and the comical little pan-man out in the canal shouting his wares in a nettled tone, growing more and more angry as he paddled, because no one came out to buy.

Humming her tune, Sister thought: 'René and Mitch are somewhat alike. Both do as they damn please, only the things they do are different. Both are quick and nervous, both active and alive, both attractive to a woman. How sweet it feels to be nice to René! How sweet it feels to fight Mitch! René thinks his thoughts, Mitch does his. It would be nice to have them both here now. Mitch would tease me. René would sit gloomily thinking, thinking. What thoughts run through his mind? Is he forgetting things now? Why did he say it is a sweet privilege to forget? This is called a generalization. Grampaw used to say them. They are very fine. I don't like them. If this good-looking man should say it is a sweet privilege to kiss, it would not be a generalization. What is he thinking of? He needs a haircut badly, and it is attractive. I wish he would eat large meals. Poor fellow looks neglected. Is he really shy, or only proud?'

René in the window was thinking: 'The bright smudge of marshy greens through the mist... Their green has another meaning, a vibrant quality associated elsewhere only with red. I will make this country mine, my point of departure, my destined background, my nameless goal, fitting my nature and clothing my dream. Wild geese feeding roar like a tempest trapped among frozen firs. In the blue-green deeps and shallows, sinuous presences vanish and appear, subtly gliding, weaving, phosphorescent, turning, shrinking, swelling... The waterspout is a mad blue protest against gravity. Oysters lie in a plump dream, served by nourishing currents, inertia triumphant. Alligators copulating at night scream like tortured panthers and thrash the earth into a slushy pulp... This woman knows she is loved. She feels it through her pores. This moment is a duel of thoughts, with her the aggressor, washing her dishes, so skillful in her own domain that I am reduced to the muteness of an impersonal audience. But she would be stronger than I. She would moan through her wet white teeth. God! how to woo her? The usual maudlin dramatics? The petty gestures and attentions? The drab garments of propinquity? No! She must come to me. She must feel the power of my mind and come to me.'

He turned to Sister and asked, 'Where did you get the saddle?'

'From Grampaw. Do you like it?'

'Very much.'

René was pale, despising Grampaw who was dead. Sister went and dusted off the saddle, tenderly. She took the dishcloth out and hung it. The pan-man below called to her in French. She smiled and gesticulated to him, showing empty hands.

'What shall we do today?' René asked her.

'Bruce will be waking up soon,' she answered. 'Let's see your pictures, eh?'

René blushed, and his heart leapt. He had known her three weeks, but she had never before asked to see his work. He went over in the skiff and brought a folio of water-colors, and placed a chair as an easel on which to show them. He had long since arranged them in the order in which he wanted them viewed by her.

One by one he began placing them.

'What is that?' she asked when he came to a view made in an old New Orleans cemetery.

'An abstraction, of course,' said René, somewhat crestfallen. 'The subject doesn't matter. It's a lot of old masonry with scrawled crevices, and an urn. Do you like it?'

'Not — very much.' Sister did not understand why the subject did not matter. She put her head on the side and frowned at the picture, concentrating intently. She was disappointed in René's work. Sister had never seen any art, except Grampaw's few reproductions of old painters. She vividly remembered Franz Hals.

'Is it because you've never seen anything like this?' René asked.

'I don't know. Perhaps that's it.'

He showed her a picture of a handsome lady-bug the size of her hand, resting on a huge violet fully eighteen inches wide. The drawing was skillful, the colors bright and strange. It did not resemble the other pictures in any way.

'I like that!' she said.

René's heart sank. He did not want her to prefer that one. 'Why?' he asked.

'I can't say. It doesn't seem important to say why.'

'But it is, Sister!'

'Well, I can't say. The artist should know why I like it, eh?'

René frowned, at a loss for words. Sister was very sorry for him then. She had never before seen him so perturbed. 'I just want to — to —— you see, it's tremendously important that you like the picture for the right reason, if you don't mind.'

'My! the painter has a lot to worry about! He must paint the picture, see that people like it, and that they like it for the right reason!'

'It is a language,' said René. 'A visual language. He wants to be understood.'

'I understand *you*. Even if I didn't, I would still like you.'

René smiled, flushing all over. 'The picture is me,' he said.

'But no!'

'Yes. It *must* be me.'

'No.' Sister took up the picture. 'I could use it for kindling,' she said. 'And look! There's nothing on the other side!'

'It is me.' René had never loved her more. He could feel beneath her surface a hundred new charming selves waiting to take growth.

'No,' Sister insisted, laughing.

'You must say why you like it before we proceed.'

'Very well! I like it *because!*'

This woman-word charmed and baffled him. This was the first time that René had ever permitted levity to enter any discussion of his work.

After breakfast the three, Sister, Bruce, and René, went to sail around Bay Saint Francis. The morning was cool and clear, the earth all aglitter, the kind of morning which usually hurt Sister in some obscure way, but which today lifted her senses up and up, like a sudden gay song. Bruce sat in his favorite position in the bow, a manly little figure with his hair tossing furiously and his plump brown fingers gripping the combing. Bruce was growing apart from her these days, a separate being at last, a will apart; so that, seeing him impersonally, Sister could love him, as it were, for his own sake. The child seemed not at all impressed by the outer poise and fine manners of the stranger from far away. René, who seemed rather removed from the world of human birth and death, hardly noticed Bruce; always took him for granted, and if he did not fondle or play with the child, neither did he patronize him. Sister was not sure the two liked each other at all. For this she was almost grateful: the association might therefore leave a clearer impression on the child.

René was learning to sail. In a fair wind, the lesson did not prevent him from talking. He lacked manual dexterity, but Sister marveled at his instant grasp of the theory of physical effort. To his prehensile mind, the grasping and the assimilation of things visual was one and the same act. He seemed never to examine anything twice: to glance at a thing was to make it his.

He talked about art — form and color. His function as a painter was to change mankind's conception of the visual world. To interpret the intellectually significant forms that exist amid the mass of dull and tawdry objects with which nature, with her predilection for the obvious, has cluttered up the world. His pictures appeared flat because the paper was flat. He did not strive for the depth and roundness of the sculptor, or the perspective of the architect, which in painting were illusory spatial encroachments. Anyone trying to evaluate his work must remember it was like nothing ever seen before — ahead of its time. No worth-while work could be otherwise.

This talk was unimportant to Sister. She was poorly equipped to affirm or deny. To her it was rather like tearing apart a lovely flower, or prying into the entrails of a handsome bird. But she was most attentive because she knew how important it was to René, and saw how rosy his ears were when excited. And whether it were true or not, she was pleased to know that René assumed that each crisp wave about them, each brave light or cunning shadow, each distant growth or shred of cloud, meant the same to her that it did to him.

'Are we going anywhere?' René asked once.

'Yes, we are hunting a place to eat,' Sister answered.

'I hunger!' Bruce complained, pouting.

'And I thirst,' added the mother. 'Steer for that orange-colored shack by the pelicans, and tell us about Italy.'

'Which Italy?'

'The hills. Once I dreamed my first lover was a blond Italian singing to his oxen.' Sister laughed at the picture. René watched her ripe gay mouth, the willful, filly-like toss of her head, the strong young body that achieved expression almost solely through physical toil, yet moved like music, without dissonance. He loved the manner in which her reflexes obeyed her sensations, which seemed some rare physical quality residing in an exceptionally strong and articulate spine. The spine! The seat of impulse, without which she might have been but a handsome plant. He kept thinking of that, until he could visualize beneath her flesh and clothing its transparent bones ruddy with sun, its tough silken fibers delving outward, and the fluid charged with youth and heat.

They reached the orange-colored dwelling set precariously on stilts leaning crookedly from a recent hurricane. The property belonged to one Nick Popich, a countryman and friend of Grampaw's. The owner was out. Sister darted up the stairs to hunt food, while René pulled off a little way in a skiff and vigorously sketched the place.

Sister found some boiled snails, a box of salted anchovies, a rich Ethiopian cheese, hardtack, and good wine. She tonged up some oysters from the water, and opened them. On the knife she bore the whole weight of her upper body, prying. Each time she grasped a pried oyster to sever the muscle, her fingers worked so close to the shell's wickedly keen edges that René winced.

But he relished the oysters, the creamy living flesh, rich and salty, gulped from the half shell. Little Bruce ate fully a dozen, tilting his head and wrinkling his nose to devour the succulent mouthfuls.

They ate this meal on the sunny porch. Below them in the dark waters they could discern the patient jackfish cruising round and round the fenced-in oyster beds, slow and phosphorescent, searching with their grim primordial doggedness. On the porch of another camp near-by, two girls were threshing rice, strong young women, each with a large mallet pounding into the hollowed-out top of a stout log. One of them was singing a doleful Dalmatian ballad, and their thudding mallets describing alternate circles kept time with the tune. These were Sister's people, René reflected. He was not yet able to associate her with the River and the groves and gardens of Grass Margin, but could think of her only as a creature of lonely reefs, fiery heavens, long silent horizon-vigils, sudden alarms of the fickle elements — dwelling on a perch, in a world above a world, needing no fruitful bush or assuring tree, but only the mercurial ebb and wash of potent waters, and the infinite curve of the sky. He learned she did not like the superficial intimacies that women cultivate with each other. Indeed, she did not like to approach people at all.

'I'd like to sketch the larger of those two girls,' he said. 'I suppose they're friends of yours.'

'I have no friends here,' she answered, 'but we'll ask her to pose for you, although I'm afraid she'll giggle.'

'And you have no friends?'

'No. Why should I?'

'Oh, I'm rather like that myself, but — but *you!* I should think——'

'You may find other things to draw over there,' said Sister.

They pulled over. The two girls stopped their work to watch

the approaching boat, and René saw, then, that neither the face nor body of the girl in question interested him.

'But where do they grow rice?' René asked.

'Out on the mud flats.' Sister explained how rice was grown on the muddy formations around the mouths of the river; how the rich waters covered the plants and prevented weed growth. No cultivation was required. One merely sowed the crop and waited for the ripening of the grain.

'We could raise a crop on any of the flats,' said Sister.

'Eh?'

'You and I.'

René was silent for a time, his very soul throbbing with excitement. He had never put a seed into the ground in his life, nor remembered having seen it done. Sister saw his reddened face, the deeply flushed ears. The childish pleasure shining from his eyes hurt her. Her breast seemed to melt toward him.

'It would be a lark,' said René.

'Not all a lark, but it might be some fun. And we'd make some money if there's no storm.'

So it was agreed. They would buy and sow the seed at once.

In the warm, comfortable kitchen that night, René sat cross-legged. While Sister cooked, he talked about Leonardo studying the flight of the tamed swallow. Sister, always an ardent listener, through René's talks felt herself beginning to penetrate the far fringes of the outer world, and to develop a sense of the past more vivid than that acquired by years of greedy reading. On the previous night he had told her about a modern factory. She had kept him until midnight answering her questions concerning the manner of life of the workers, and had gone to bed with senses in a whirl of conjecture and horror and awe. With his rich, deliberate words, René had done his best to make her feel an industrial center, and how the individual was lost in the vast rigid pattern. And the pattern was always static, for

all its motion and bustle — angular and rigid, with nothing fluid or plastic save the swift current of material gulped in the raw state by one door and, with a name and price attached, scornfully spewed forth by another. He pictured the people themselves as great herds of automatically controlled puppets, especially since mass production was beginning to spread.

Sister could not see it so. She felt the many component parts of the pattern as human beings who bit their fingernails and overslept mornings and barked their shins and saved the icing on their cakes until last. But after René's telling, she could not help feeling that in the world outside, toil was exploited and cleverness extolled, and the vision was ever obscured by the thing.

After the meal, when the child was asleep, René asked Sister to pose for a pencil sketch. 'Crouched,' he said, 'as you are when you put wood in the stove. I want the bare back, the curve of the spine.' He really wanted her entirely nude, but could not bring himself to request it — yet. Sister came out of her room in a wrap, and knelt beside the stove, exposing her curved white back, burning with shame, but determined to appear casual. René's swift pencil broke the silence with its faint resonant scraping, and the child in the next room breathed loudly. Sister wondered how her back looked. She felt sure it was beautiful, as though all the youth and vitality had rushed from the other parts of her outraged body and settled in the cool, exposed back. She wanted the drawing to be satisfactory to René. She wanted this part of her body to become articulate to him, to answer the eloquence of his words.

But the result was not what René wanted — an experience completely new to him. Somehow he felt foolish. All the evening, the thought kept recurring that this hour had been a critical one in his life.

A week later on such an evening, stubbornly he asked Sister to take the pose again.

When the drawing was half finished, René suddenly and vehemently clutched the paper and crushed it into a ball. Sister was startled out of her wits. René covered his pad and threw it on a chair, and lit his pipe. Sister said nothing. She left the room, gathering her gown about her, feeling very foolish, like a chastised animal slinking off. In her room she fought an approaching fit of giggling. She could hardly dress herself. She sat on the bed. The paroxysm returned, shaking her all over. She was sorry for René. This seemed to increase the uncontrollable laughter that welled up and all but escaped. She regained control, but, thinking of how René had frightened her, the giggling began all over, worse than before. She buried her face in her pillow. The whole bed shook. The imperative need of returning to her visitor quickly brought back her self-control, but when she was partly dressed, back came the picture of the foolish fright in the kitchen, and with it another surge of giggling. Until at last she heard the front door open and shut. René's footsteps came to her, going down the stairs outside, slowly, one after the other.

René did not come near her for a week. He was short of funds, but managed to be invited to many meals by various Dalmatian fishermen thereabouts.

At first Sister was relieved. Then, as the days went by and the interminable evenings, she was lonely. The quality of bare green isolation lying over her domicile, never before unduly emphatic, heavily oppressed her now. She had many orders for nets that steadily engaged her, yet the rhythm of the needle no longer induced the out calm webs of thought. Seeing René one morning awkwardly paddling out the canal, she answered his salute indifferently and watched with some contempt the working of his frail shoulders; but she took up the telescope and followed him until he stopped and erected his easel far out against the empty horizon. That day she scoured and dusted the camp to its last crevice, and vigorously attacked a score of tasks deferred since René's coming.

At evening, with her grime and sweat washed off and every jaded muscle summoning her to bed, she lay relishing the feeling of her fleshfulness. The other self, the gracious and nervous one lately awakened by René, seemed already sloughed off, and with it all the quick bright stimuli aroused by everyday forms and hues, the exciting sense of the outer world, the sweet nebulous dreams and designs of searching youth. She was conscious only of a spent body and a good bed where she might roll and stretch at will. If any vision beguiled her, it was that of the morrow's refreshed awakening, the bowl of fragrant coffee, and another day of unceasing toil.

She wrote to Mitch Holt, recounting many small bits of lower River news which she knew he wanted to hear.

While she was drowsily penning this letter, René Davidson came. He gave his customary soft yet imperative knock on the screen.

'Who is it?' Sister called. Sleepily she dabbed at her hair. René entered, smiling. 'May I?' he asked with his slight flattering bow. Sister glanced at him as through a dream, murmured something, half-noted that his fine nose was peeling from the sun, and returned to her writing. René took his usual seat under Grampaw's saddle, laid his folio against the wall, and picked up a book. And there they sat for more than an hour, without a word, without a sound. Sister's left arm was bandaged. A catfish had pricked her the day before. When René came, she had been about to close her letter to Mitch; but now she was slowly, drowsily filling fresh pages one after another. René's half-real presence in some way caused her weary thoughts to flow and flow toward Mitch Holt with a dim, slow yet vital impetus, like the slumbrous wanderings of some dark subterranean current:

'Once a long time ago you were angry with me. I remember. It was a night. A row of shoes drying under the stove. You said I never asked you to do anything for me. I remember. That was the day I had promised to be your sweetheart until Sunday. I never asked you to do anything for me. You were angry. I ask you now to do something. Become the man you were born to be. I ask that. I want you to use the strength of your hands and brain for building something. I don't care. I am your friend. You are not a felon in prison. You are like being kept in after school. All of you are boys. I am tired of thinking that. Mocco too. You crazy fools. You don't need to write to me ever. But I will always write. It is nice to write. Don't you like riches? Don't you like telling plenty people what to do? You can do it here. Riches in the ground and sky and waters. Make your plans well. Come and lead your people for the fun of it. I am asking you to do something now ...'

René's voice was in the room, buzzing. It seemed to labor wearily toward her and set into life some dulled mechanism in her ears: '*I think you are dozing, Sister.*'

'Huh?'

'Dozing.'

René's legs were wrapped about each other. His body curved above the hard white square of the page, watching her in amusement without lifting his face. Sister sighed, sank back in her armchair, gazed ahead under lids that closed unmanageably again and again. The room droned in the heat of the dying stove. Sister folded her hands in her lap, throwing her thighs into outline in the lamplight. Waves beneath the camp crashed musically. René discarded the book and began talking, telling his doings of the past days. Sister came wide awake, attentive. But the muscles of her eyes would not obey. Her head fell, and she brought it back sharply. She rubbed her eyes and listened.

René, lying back with his face toward the ceiling, talked on and on — so soft, so murmurous. Once he asked her a question. No answer came. He straightened up in his chair. His full clear eyes wandered over Sister's relaxed person, the small white chin reposing on her breast, her dark hair full of vigor and the glint of her body oils, and the lonely hands locked in mutual embrace ... She had fed him well, cleansing his thoughts of the old daily scheming for food. She owned rich land, rich and generous and warm as she. She would always feed him well.

'I love you,' he said softly, wincing.

Her breathing was deep and slow. The twin swellings of her bosom rose, sank, paused a little before each lifting. René's eyes possessed her, tasting each proud and poignant curve of her sleeping flesh. 'I am a virgin,' he murmured low. 'I have prowled the darkened avenues of the earth. I have talked by candlelight in barren attics. I have gnawed a crust under a bridge. I have trodden soundless carpets and looked on lovely whores without desire. Now it is the dreadfully gorgeous quagmire, the globe and saddle. You! It is the end. I go no farther. I have reached my beginning. Why are you inaccessible to me? Why don't you come to me? Don't you know I cannot go to you? Does one meet an artist every day in the week? Don't you know what I have given you, and have yet to give?'

Embers in the stove collapsed with a gentle crash. The agitation of the waters below beat upward like pulses from a chasm more desolate than the wrinkled sea. The position of Sister's head puffed her lips into a curious pout, like a petulant child's. She looked like an overgrown girl exhausted by a day of hunting out mischief, childishly cruel, and yet soft with a dark knowledge.

'Self-sufficient,' René said.

'What?' said Sister, awakening and looking around her.

'I saw pelicans fishing today,' René replied. 'All in a circle.'

His eyes darted about the walls, burning darkly, mad with suffering. His fingers gathered a new hold on the chair arms. 'The circle closes in, I notice, driving the prey toward a central core. Then suddenly all the birds gulp their fill. The circle closes in.'

24

RENÉ and Sister found a place at the mouth of Main Pass, and planted their crop of rice. It was a mound of silt that lay under river water, tidal backwash, part of each day — very fine soil, dense yet friable and sweet. That was in April, a kindly time of year, the river bringing still the cold of northern streams. Together they would make a crop of rice, the golden grain of Carolina, each friend through and for the other looking ahead with certitude to the coming of the living stalks, and the protesting swell of golden hulls. The muttering Gulf was near.

All day they threw the seed well. The muttering Gulf was near, hidden from them by fog as they were hidden from each other, but constantly felt in its busy vastness. The man and woman paddled their pirogues back and across the flooded land. The damp white hours crept, an incredible milky blankness. The fog began imperceptibly to thin. And in the soft pallid flux of shifting vapors, the two were now lost to each other, and then magically revealed. An unseen whistling buoy outside kept sounding its deep call, a far sea-sound in the fog; and curious snipe and terns swung about to salute the two figures scattering the grain. René at last caught the trick of throwing the seed far without upsetting, and the leap of the silken handsful quickened his blood. Sister would call out cheerily. The fog enfolded her like pearly fumes. Then she reappeared, singing a German ditty of Grampaw's:

When I have money
I am happy,
When I have none
I am thirsty!
To me it is all one:
Money or none!

Again she was lost to him, as if forever — smudged out by a cunning screen of vapor. But he heard her clear unreal noise, the seed falling, then her laughter warm and wild, as though but a few feet away. Through another sudden thinning of the mist he beheld her lovely arm, strangely pale and transitory, as through the membrane of a dance-veil — one bright and fluid member of her body quickly glimpsed in the rather poignant act of casting away seed. Then the faint liquid swish of the fallen seed, and the arm was gone. He took a handful of his seed. As he cast it, the fat grains leaped through his fingers in a quick stream. Then at last the tender sibilant kiss of the seeds plunging home.

After the fog the pirogues went homeward. They stayed side by side for a time, while the occupants talked. Yet the talk was desultory, half-conscious. The task was done. The seed was sown. But René was desperately tired. He feared he would never paddle the miles home. Sister could paddle now like a man. Her companion was growing physically sick of the heady odor of river water, and of watching the rhythmic fall and rise of Sister's paddling hand, up and down, up and down, lit by sun and gloved in shade, clenched and limber, light and dark, up and down, light and dark ... She was increasing her speed, courteously at first, but gradually more and more. She must get home. She must feed the child waiting there. The sun burned low and dull. The east was darkening. Distant chimneys smoked. Sister was having her usual moments of anxiety over the child alone.

'For the love of God!' René thought, 'how much longer!'

His clothing was soaked with sweat. Sister was drawing away from him now. He had to stop and rest, and pant, and allow his hammering heart to cool. Irritated, he watched the clean, tireless, somehow wicked flashing of the woman's paddle far ahead. Ah, how sharply it nettled him at times — her peasant coarseness, her vigorous, thoughtless, almost truculent manner of doing things!

All summer long Sister knitted, striving to keep abreast of the orders. René watched her many a night. He continued to take his meals with her, the delicious meals which, however, never fattened him. He spent with her most of his idle hours. He talked to her by the hour, and he watched her watching him talk. And in her eyes there was a dream. She was completely taken out of herself. And whether he described a Mexican bull-fight or recounted bits of life among the students in Paris, in his words there was tenderness, and power, and the thrill of thrilling. They were alone, always alone. The strange unobtrusive child did not matter to René. There was about them only the smell of the sea, the dim sheen of scrubbed wood, the sounds of the marsh that came like small silences through a larger. But they were not alone *together*, he reflected again and again. The apartness was there, always there, like a gentle hand.

'Tell me more,' Sister invariably begged.

She never asked to see his work, questioned him about his progress, inquired who bought his pictures, suggested subjects for him to paint as most people did. Indeed, he half-suspected that Sister considered there might be some things more important than his work; and, fearing this might be true, he put his finest passion, his very soul, into his talks about the vocation of painting. At least, he consoled himself, Sister's mind was not warped by the sentimental, popular notions of painting, which he called 'art-on-the-cob.' He would teach her all she need know about painting. She would learn. She would come to him, too. Ultimately, she must see his light!

Yet it irritated him beyond thought night after night to see her sitting there full of quiet power and beauty, with her faint hint of a red smile and her swift subtle needle weaving a gauzy dream.

Sometimes Sister talked at her work: 'When I was little, once Grampaw brought me home on an evening like this. We had t en to Lacroix to see the locomotive. Coming down the river I saw that same star in the willows. I had on a blue dress. I asked Grampaw why my breast hurt, and he laughed. There were blackbirds perched in a dead willow. They looked like black fruit, and the sky was a lonely color. When the pirogue bumped into the bank Grampaw had something to show me. He stooped over to tie his pirogue and his shirt slipped out of his pants, and it showed a row of round knobs of bone running up his back, and I counted them with my finger. He went to a hollow log and took out something heavy and hard. I was afraid to hold it. It was so heavy and cold! "That's a rock," he said. "You're the first little girl in Grass Margin that ever saw a rock." I was scared, or sorry, partly on account of the sky and the blackbirds like fruit. No one had made the rock round like that. Perhaps nobody's hand had ever touched it. What made it round? "Traveling about," Grampaw told me. The hollow log had drifted down from Tennessee, perhaps Minnesota. I held the rock, thinking about everything in the world coming from rock. All the way home I held it pressed against my stomach, and the rock was warm when I got there. Then it seemed a different kind of rock. Papa came home with Mitch Holt. Mitch was about eighteen then. They were drunk. Mitch had been helping smuggle in Chinamen, and made plenty money. I hugged my rock in the corner. Grampaw was angry at Papa. After supper he took me to the levee and told me all about rocks, the rock mountains in the old country, "hairy like a skin," he said. And cities were built of rock. Rocks on rocks. And the seasons grind rocks to yellow powder to color the river. He said the river was like a man and the shore like a woman — the river with its deeps and the shore its flowers. He was sober.'

'Who was Mitch Holt?' René asked.

'My beau. The man people have picked out for me to marry.'

'I don't think I know him.'

'No.'

René looked at her fixedly. Sister worked on, saying no more. Her thoughts were flowing back into the woven meshes of the net. René's mind weighed the other man's name, as though a grasp of its properties might yield some elusive substance. Mitch Holt! Probably some trapper or boatman who greased his stove with turtle fat, and owned a pet otter that rolled in the sand after its swim and then crawled into its master's bed . . .

'You don't consider marriage for yourself, do you?' he asked her.

'What makes you think that, René?'

'I'm asking you.'

'Don't look so solemn, René! What do *you* think?'

'I don't think you do — consider marriage.'

'Now, how on earth did you discover that?'

René smiled rosily. He blew a ball of smoke neat as a period. He emptied his glass of wine. Sister finished her glass, and poured more for both. They were drinking Grampaw's old Tokay.

'Marriage is a good thing for most people,' said René. 'A custom like any other, a way of attending to property rights and other social details, instituted by the people. They seem to want to keep it. Let them have it! It's none of my business.'

'You've never tried it yourself?' asked Sister in her most casual tone, feeling very worldly.

'No.'

'Not even once?'

'It's never occurred to me.'

'Tell me more.'

'There's nothing more. Marriage is all right for most.'

'But not for you?'

'Nor you.'

'How?'

'You want your loneliness. At least you would be too proud to take part in this ritual in the ordinary way?'

'What is the ordinary way?'

'Oh, getting a man with the usual tricks a woman uses to make him think he does the selecting. Wanting to own a man completely.'

'Tricks, René?'

'Surely. You've seen it. It's the special faculty of ordinary women, their sole preoccupation from birth. Every action is sexual. Their first years are devoted to getting a man, the remainder to holding him. Only the exceptional woman has time for anything else, or inclination. I think you would be impatient of tricks.'

Sister went to baste the raccoon she was roasting for their supper. She returned, and stood hugging her breasts, frowning at the floor.

'You call them tricks,' she said. 'I don't know about these things. Perhaps men have tricks. All this business seems to me like play, a nice little game, as Grampaw called it. Birds play that way, and horses I know. It is very nice, courting, playing with each other, especially in nice weather, or under the lights at an entertainment or dance. Getting mad and making up afterward is surely fun ... I had a beau. I have a beau. He is far away now. When he gets back we'll be married, I suppose. It's expected of us, I suppose.'

René's wine cooled in his veins. If it irked him to stumble over Grampaw again, it emptied his breast of all emotion to hear about this 'beau.' Sister knitted on. She loved a silence. Having had her say, she would say no more, but only worked on, silent in her reluctance to clothe instinct in reason, willful in her right to ignorance, quietly sure in her mastery of the lore of field and stream . . . Once she looked at René and saw the miserable look on his face. At once she felt happy and magnanimous. She nodded toward his folio standing in a corner. 'Did you bring me a picture?' she asked. 'I'm so glad! Let's see it.'

'It's no good,' said René.

'Therefore you thought I'd like to see it.'

'I brought it because it's in rather a new manner, as they say. I don't give much thought to what people think, one way or another. Not even you, Sister.' His voice trailed off, low and feelingly, on the last words, lingering like a faint hint or signal on her name.

Sister dropped her eyes instinctively, thinking: 'Now he's going to say something. My, I hope he doesn't!' The silence grew electric. 'He will say it beautifully, because he has been drinking good wine. Is he afraid to speak?' She stole a glance at René.

'One's work, no matter how precious, must remain apart from one's — passion,' René said with overmeasured calmness. 'Or so I judge . . . So I judge. I think my work is a product of reason, or obeys reason purely.'

Sister placed her cheek on her shoulder, all relaxed and listening.

'Passion deadens reason, happily,' said René in a voice now quavering. 'We know that.'

Sister's gaze did not leave the floor.

'It springs molten and pure from the deepest cauldron of one's being, unbidden and unashamed. I know it as wild proud music. I hear it and I am a god . . . it is dangerous for the artist, who must be hard when he must be. Of course I will be happy if you admire my work. But passion has nothing to do with reason, and reason has nothing to do with passion.'

Another long silence went by. Sister sighed, thinking: 'What the hell is he getting at? Is this passion, or is it reason?'

René was sweating. He said: 'This is what I think. I may be wrong. It is a new thing to me. I've never had much of an emotional life — before.' He was trembling in every nerve and bone. His throat was rough and rigid.

Sister saw his face. Her heart melted. 'This is a boy,' she thought. 'How he is suffering, poor fellow, so timid and fine!' Her arms wanted to hold him. Her breast felt as if it were opening to him. His clothing had grown shabby recently, his shoes were badly worn, as though from fruitless seeking.

Someone was calling Sister below. She started toward the door, and stopped back of René's chair. From behind she reached and took his face into her hands, and pressed his wild curly hair tightly against her breast, and made a little sound, low and soothing, deep in her throat ...

The visitor was clumping loudly up the stairs. Sister went out and called, 'Who is it?'

'Old Man Holt! Were you sleeping, Jolie?'

'No, sir. Come on up.'

Sister returned to her seat. Passing René she squeezed his hand.

Old Holt stood in the doorway with a sack of oranges sent by Mocco.

'Have you any news from Mitch?' Sister asked.

'Yes. Mitch expects to be out soon, maybe for Christmas. Who is this?'

'My boarder, Mr. Davidson, Mr. Holt. René lives across the way.'

'Boarder? What are you two pups doing here alone?'

'Talking about world politics. We're not alone. My son lives here.'

'Yes, another pup.'

'What else about Mitch?' Sister asked.

'Nothing else. Maybe Christmas. He asked about his pirogue, wants me to keep it soaked. I'm hungry.'

'Can you wait for supper?'

'No.'

Sister fixed the old man a cheese sandwich, and he sat uncouthly stuffing it into his burned and stubbled face. René Davidson opened a book and sat apart. The old man drank his wine and sat examining the room while Sister knitted. He sucked his teeth loudly. René thought: 'In the name of God, what am I doing here? This hog smells like bog-water, sucking his teeth!'

Sister asked, 'Is there any news from home?'

'I never see them. Mocco's raising bullfrogs, I understand. He's talking about growing Easter lilies on a big scale with niggers. Your father's better.'

'Better!'

'Sits on the levee on Monday, Wednesday, and Friday waiting for the doctor-boat to pass from Quarantine Station. They won't stop for him. When they pass he cusses the doctors out and shakes his fist and dances a jig. They quit attending to him a long time ago, because he was throwing their medicine away and using some nigger's *remèdes*. Now he's got a big doctor-flag up on the levee, a tablecloth on a pole, but the doctors won't stop for the signal. That flag's been there almost a year, all faded and torn, awaving away. Blue and white checkered cloth.'

'Mother's good linen tablecloth,' said Sister. 'The only thing left from their prosperous days. I was to have it when I marry.'

'They say your father's place is up for sale for taxes.'

Sister stopped her knitting and looked out of the window. She could see the pilot range-light on the bank at Dutch Scenery, and farther back, the light in Grass Margin. The old familiar prick of homesickness struck her heart.

Old Man Holt did not once look at René. He had heard about

the painter who was supposed to be Sister's lover, who had tried to teach color-blind Mocco how to paint. Let Sister have her fun! Mitch would soon get her ...

Sister found her purse and brought out some bills. 'Will you do something for me?' she asked. 'Give this twenty-five dollars to Pretty John on the Margin and tell him to get the notice from Papa and pay our taxes in Lacroix.'

When the old man left, Sister and René were silent for a time. René was cursing Old Man Holt for having interrupted them — the blind stupid cruelty of it! Their late mood might never return. He let his tortured eyes rest upon Sister, calmly pursuing her confounded knitting, thinking God knew what alien thoughts, of taxes and tablecloths and Holts.

'Will you look at the picture now?' he asked.

'Yes! Of course!'

'The man is Bonus, Mocco's negro friend,' said René somewhat nervously. 'He killed a man once, by the way. He sees the ghost when the sun is hot. He talks to the ghost.'

'Is he seeing a ghost now?'

'I don't know. That doesn't matter.'

'I like it!' Sister backed off, then approached the painting closely.

'It's not supposed to be smelled,' René said.

'I like it!'

'Why?'

Sister picked up a sofa pillow and threw it at the man's head. René was almost happy. 'You must try to tell me, really,' he said.

'You must tell *me* why I like it.'

'Because it's plausible. It looks real. Is that it?'

'Everything in it is *right*,' Sister ventured. 'I would like to have one like it.'

'The picture is yours, painted for you.'

'No-no-no! You must send this one to your dealer tomorrow. You need money. He will sell it quick.'

'Do you think so?'

'Yes. It is beautiful. It wants a beautiful home.'

'No. It is a bad picture.'

'Yes, I know. Painted for me.'

'I mean it is full of compromises. You are not ready for the other kind.'

'I understand. I've got to be made ready.'

'As for being beautiful, I don't know the word.'

'At last! Something you don't know!'

'Talking of beauty is like trying to talk of God.'

'H'm . . . full of compromises!'

'Yes. It will be called a genre painting of the purest kind, burdened with feeling.'

Sister tapped her foot. Must she be always fighting people, even René? The artist's face shone with sardonic elation, chilled into recklessness by a sense of the pain he had endured because of Sister, and of the past indignities of his precarious career. 'Particularly burdened with feeling,' he mused. 'Brooding and dark, perhaps. Aided by native models, the artist breathed into his work the poetry of an entire people, without sacrificing imagination and point-of-view.'

'What does that mean, René, all your fine words? I guess I ought to feel flattered, painting it for me, then explaining how bad it is for *lagniappé*.'

'You just said you like the picture.'

Sister stamped her foot. Without a warning she left her chair and blew out the lamp.

Suddenly alone, recovering from his amazement he heard her returning to her chair. 'But what are you doing?' he asked through the abysmal darkness.

No sound came but the dim sputtering of the food in the oven. The blackness was so dense that the night outside formed murky oblongs of the windows. René relaxed in his chair and waited. Many quiet minutes went by.

'I'm sorry, Sister,' René said.

His words floated about in the black depths. Then ensued another vast noiseless oblivion, interminable with listening. Once he heard below him the faint diligent sound of something gnawing on wood.

'These things must be said,' René asserted to the darkness. His words were sounding inordinately loud and strident. 'What needs saying will be said.' There was no reply. His words had lost their power. He could feel what he did not see or hear — throughout the sodden reaches of the star-dimmed prairie outside the busy nocturnal burrowing and scampering of sly amphibian swarms. There was no moon. Was Sister there, or gone? How had it all begun? What was it he had said? Was she hugging her breasts now? watching him through the dark? brushing away a tear? He felt her there, more real and compelling than he had ever seen her in color. He crossed his legs and waited. Another long interval of nothingness.

'Shall I go, then?' he asked.

There was no reply. He left his chair. His fingers scraped softly along the wall. His foot collided with a bucket. He found his folio and took it to the starry doorway, then turned, but he could see nothing behind him . . .

Before René had reached his skiff below, Sister lit the lamp. She was very hungry. She ate a large portion of the roasted 'coon with sweet potatoes, and went to bed. In the night she dreamed of a ship with sails.

Crossing the canal, René went thoughtfully, unhurried, rather pleased. It had not been an unsatisfactory evening. Sister knew how he felt toward her! His head had lain against her breast! They had achieved the intimacy of a quarrel! He had the power to hurt her! 'Full of compromises!' he said softly. Of course! The picture was a fatuous botch, as weak as cold oatmeal. The whole business of winning a woman was a matter of temporary compromises . . .

In his room, René carefully placed the picture of the half-mad negro Bonus in the proper light, and studied it while he undressed. He could not help admiring the draughtsmanship, at least. And the colors perhaps were rather nicely chosen, too — but he would have to see it again in daylight to decide that.

In the morning he painted a plausible view of some luggers with a sky — in the same manner as the Bonus picture. He put in a heavy brutal figure of a fisherman.

The completed thing certainly had its points. He would send it to his dealer with the Bonus thing — both as pot-boilers. His first pot-boilers.

'My botches are better than *their* masterpieces!' he thought.

25

THERE was a cool July, and rainy. Sister bought another cistern, one thousand gallons. The cistern-makers from New Orleans came down on the steamboat with their curious tools. The foundation was there. Grampaw had built it years ago, always expecting to add to their water supply, to indulge Sister's continuous plea for water. She would use a big deck-broom for scrubbing, and pitch bucketful after bucketful across the floors, because she liked it ... Little Bruce watched the workers with their strangely shaped tools, erecting the numbered staves into place around the disc bottom, banging down the hoops tightly. It was of cypress, finely milled, one inch thick. And in two days the rains filled it, and Sister was proud of more water. Every midday brought its sagging clouds arriving puffed to a great fullness. They opened and drenched the village, scoured the porches, polished the roofs blue, shined the wilting verdure of the marsh. Bruce wandered the porches naked, which Sister had sanded to keep splinters from his feet.

The fishermen were happy. Encouraged by the benefits of Mateo Lucich's oyster co-operative, they sailed their big luggers all summer with heaping loads of oysters for scattering in the little bays and canals where they would receive the essences of the bogs and fatten by fall. And men, women, and children sat in the skiffs all day, in the sun or the shelter of gaudy awnings, breaking apart the huge clusters of oysters, tossing them over their shoulders into the new beds. Tons of oysters would go up the Valley in the fall. The association had appointed representatives in Chicago, St. Louis, Denver. There was talk of a school on Bay Saint Francis. The broods of Dalmatian children were growing up. Full skiff-loads of them went daily to school at Dutch Scenery. There was a movement for a dance-hall out in the Bay. Camps were being enlarged and painted. One man hauled mud from the river bank and built a high island, so that his children might have a few square feet of earth to play on. Some Dalmatians were buying land across the river in Grass Margin for growing oranges in their old age.

In Grass Margin the young men were growing restless. The face of the earth was changing. The character of the river traffic was changing. Twelve new fruit ships had appeared in the river within the last year — white impatient vessels with refrigeration for the bananas. They would not stop to take a dying man to town, nor throw a bunch of bananas into the water for a pretty girl shouting from her pirogue. The itinerant Irishmen had been sent for, to build with their shovels and wheelbarrows a higher levee. More and more wagons and buggies were appearing on the levee, and in the river, gas-boats went to and fro. Everyone wanted to own a 'pot-pot.'

Someone had made up a paper to send around for the people to sign, asking the Parish authorities to dig a canal behind the Margin to drain more land for oranges and truck. None of the old people wanted to sign. Drainage would bring sickness. Drainage would heat up the Margin. Drainage would breed more mosquitoes. The young men argued excitedly. Did they want to keep the swampy woods in their back yards? Wouldn't it be nice for each family to have two more arpents of dry land? Were not schooners coming down every week in season with cash money for a load of fruit? The young men wanted drainage! They knew the word.

Grass Margin now had thirty houses scattered along two

miles of levee. Some of the new ones had tin roofs, lightning rods, phonographs. Alligators, scared by the gas-boats and steamships, were leaving the river, going down the passes to breed. Muskrats, mink, otters, were no longer caught in one's back yard. Rarely these days did anyone shoot a goose from one's front porch. The long-discussed game laws would soon be effective. Duck and goose hunters were thinking of other lines of work. Some were planning oyster camps on Bay Saint Francis. At the rate at which muskrats were being trapped and alligators fished, the day would come when a man would have to look for his living either in the land or the sea. The marsh camps and houseboats would lie rotting.

Mocco Kalavich had built a solid cypress fence around a dark pond among the trees behind his home, to keep out the snakes. Here he was raising bullfrogs. The squatting frogs peered out from among the bright blue hyacinths floating.

'Make young ones!' he whispered, smiling. 'Nothing can hurt you now! Squeeze your females, bite them, claw them until they lay a thousand eggs!'

He spent hours and hours in the shade of an aged tupelo watching them, and the sun floating over the brown pond's face lit his eyes strangely. Sometimes he waded in the pond with a little net, hunting the globular clusters of gelatinous eggs among the lily pads, transferring them to another pen. Already, he estimated he owned thirty thousand tadpoles.

'The salvation of this country!' Mocco told his father.

Tony sat on the levee watching for the Quarantine Station boat. Above his head the faded tablecloth moved its tatters in the breeze, barely trembling.

'Go mow the vines away from the oranges, you bad boy!' Tony replied from the depths of his rotting chest. 'I want milk! Milk, do you hear me?'

'Let the people watch me and do as I do,' said Mocco. 'In the fall I'm shipping a hundred dozen frogs. I'll fence six more ponds next spring. Thank God I wasn't made a pilot! I'll send you to the mountains when I make enough money, Pa. Why don't you take down that damned flag? Do you think anybody pays attention to it?'

'A sick-flag is a sick-flag!' Tony croaked. 'I will take it down when they stop their boat and attend to the dying.' He glanced down the river, the pale empty stream with its rollicking porpoises and contented gulls lying on the wind. Two small boys were waiting in a willow near-by, listening to Tony croaking in his strange language. Other boys were approaching, to be present when the quarantine boat passed and Tony went through his funny capers. After the boat passed, Tony would turn on the boys and revile them...

Mocco returned to his frog-pond and sat by the tupelo with a big stick. Since spring he had killed hundreds of moccasins and canebrake rattlers. He wondered whether snakeskins could be sold. Some of the snakes would climb near-by trees, crawl out on the limbs, lie for hours dreaming, eyeing the plump frogs below, now and then raising their head quickly and ejecting their tongue to listen... A huge blue dragon-fly sat impudently on Mocco's knee. He swiftly scooped the insect into his hand, removed its wings and threw it into the pond.

It was a cool July. René Davidson had thirteen hours of fine green daylight, and he painted diligently against the coming fall. He never lacked material. The oyster camps with their long skeletal legs provided endless new forms and groupings. The canal waters surged with fresher hues. Often at night he worked in Sister's kitchen with charcoal, sketching insects, plants, household objects, clusters of oysters. He had sketched almost every face in the settlement.

Sister stood in the doorway, all fresh and starched, glowing with summer color. 'Supper is *ready!*' she said sharply. Sometimes she spoke to him in the tone of an exasperated wife.

'I'm coming,' he said. 'Please wait a moment.'

Sister turned away. She began to serve Bruce. She had never before seen anyone work as René did — at least any man. She would not delay the meal for a boarder who paid no board. He would surely ruin his health, and he so delicate! She added another drop of oil to his salad, which he loved and always ate first. Then she herself began to eat. She had her own work to attend to.

The wholesale concern in New Orleans was sending her a greater and greater volume of orders for nets. Each mail brought two or three, with cash payment for the last. Indeed, the work was getting too heavy for her to handle alone. All of their wants were filled, yet the money accumulated, little green sheaves of it in drawers and on various shelves, everywhere one turned. One day she gathered these bits into one pile. Some time later she made another gathering. Now she had two large piles, totaling over seventy dollars. She ordered a winter suit for Mocco, but there was still fifty dollars, one gold bill and the others green. She stacked them neatly into a book with pages. She placed the golden page on top.

'Look, Bruce! A gold book!'

'Buy me! Buy me!'

'I've already bought you. Long ago I bought you.'

'Me want moozey.' He meant a harmonica.

'But you have two!'

The child watched her. His eyes were black. The long lashes threw shadow. She glanced into the mirror to see her own, the same kind of eyes, only made shrewd by living, and humorous. Bruce toddled off and brought her a harmonica. Sister played a tune. Bruce turned a sort of solemn somersault on the floor. 'Long ago,' he murmured, 'long ago.'

So each of the two camps on the canal housed a happy laborer. René wore white trousers in the heat, and a thin colored shirt. Often he dashed away from the table frowning in his thoughts of his work. The heat did not affect him. He never perspired. His body seemed to absorb the heat and use it. One day in sport Sister and René jumped into the canal fully clothed. A fisherman saw them, and word went around they had been drunk. Mothers called their recalcitrant daughters a 'Sister Kalavich.' Natasha brought the story to Sister, who was amused.

'My mother is sick,' said Natasha.

Sister thought, 'I'm glad!'

'She saw a jack o' lantern — two of them. They was fighting in the plairie. They would separate, then come together and fight. She's got a sickness like sun-pain, but cold river water don't do no good.'

'Natasha, do you want to work with me?' Sister asked.

'Sure I'll work with you, honey.'

'Take some of my orders for nets. I'm getting too many. The pay is good. Do you want any money?'

'I want plenty money, for God sake!'

'Here are two orders. Make the nets well. I'll write and tell them you are helping me. You mail them the nets. They'll send you the money.'

When Natasha went home and told her mother, the old woman said 'Humph!' and her balloon bosom jumped with the grunt. 'Dere's a treek some place,' she warned the girl. 'Vatch out for dat crazy vomans vit her treeks.'

Now Sister had more time for rest and play, as much leisure as she had had during the time of Grampaw. She made handsome kites for herself and Bruce. While day-dreaming, she wove stars and crosses with palmetto. She was teaching Bruce to swim, and they gathered shells or colored birds' eggs, the beginning of a collection for the boy. Often she made great batches of cookies or fruit pies. This she called play! But it *did* change the atmosphere of the house — the woman spattered with flour, singing pathetic songs, the child licking pots and pans, René frequently dropping in to eat his fill. One day she made stuffed crabs, one of her most tasty dishes, nicely browned with buttery crumbs and seasoned in their hot red shells. René never ceased to marvel at her cooking. She prepared food without any care, as she did other things. Gaily and carelessly she bustled about, yet so deftly that the ingredients seemed to leap together of themselves into a savory whole. René ate copiously. Yet he gained not an ounce, nor did he lose his delicate, almost feverish look.

'He lives in a fever,' Sister thought. 'I think his flesh is hot as fire. He *burns* life. Even his thoughts are fuel for a fire. But all inside. All deep down within — showing only through his eyes.'

That summer she read over and over *The Winter's Tale* and *Othello*. She read them for both the poetry and the formal dramatic values. She wanted to feel herself part of an audience in the hollow dark theater, with fretted gold twinkling dimly on the walls, and the decorous listeners banked row on row, all sunken into a common dream. She could hear a barely audible sigh here and there, the scrape of a foot or rustle of a program. And the theater was hollow and high, street noises vague and unreal. But best of all she loved to hear René read selections from the plays, his voice vibrant with passion. He told her many tales of stage life. He knew many professional actors. Once in New York he had helped do the scenes for a play.

'We must get rid of this money,' she told René. 'There are too many things I could buy. How shall we spend it?'

'Books! I have some new publishers' catalogues!'

'Books and dance-music!'

The books and phonograph records were ordered and received. René taught Sister to dance the new two-step. It was a loss of precious time for him, but he enjoyed it. Sister was a proficient dancer. They wore out the records, and sent for more, spending the remainder of Sister's 'book' of money.

One day René announced that his dealer had sold one of his pictures. It was the portrait of the negro Bonus, over which they had quarreled. The second painting, done in the same style, had been hung in a show, and the critics had praised it. Sister received the news with a noncommittal smile that René in his elation did not observe. But he asked her later: 'What have you to say? You knew the picture would sell.'

'I had no idea it would sell or not sell, René. That was only talk. I only knew I liked it.'

'Well, we have eighty dollars. How shall we spend it?'

'You must save it,' said Sister.

'Indeed not! We spent yours.'

'This is yours. You'll need it.'

'Here? What for?'

'Well ... to live on. Perhaps later. You must save it.' Sister thought, 'How funny the poor stupid does not think of helping pay for the food!'

René fell silent. He was beginning to perceive and to chafe under Sister's blithe air of protection toward him. Her vigilant solicitude for his needs had assumed proportions of a robust passion whose faintest manifestation now irritated him. He did not *want* — at least overtly — such a vulgar and unfair relationship — as much as he appreciated her laundering of his white pants, relished her habit-forming victuals, and enjoyed the lure of her evening lamplight. He turned and asserted somewhat gruffly, 'I'm accustomed to no money, to letting the future take care of itself.'

Sister blinked her widened eyes.

'Again, the critics like your new kind of work,' she said after a moment.

'Eh? Yes. But that doesn't necessarily signify it is bad. I admit it has its points. Anyway, it *is* a unique style, and may be perfected.' As a matter of fact, René had done a dozen more pictures of the kind — certain subjects he deemed ill adapted to a purely abstract treatment . . . He would ship his dealer a few tomorrow . . . 'Coincidentally,' he went on, 'this change in manner was first inspired by you — engendered, I should say.' He preferred to avoid the word 'inspired,' which savored of the occult.

Sister blushed prettily. René, too, colored.

'But it is my job alone to perfect it,' he added, frowning.

Sister was amused. The corners of her mouth twitched. 'For me?'

'For myself.'

'That sounds right,' she said. 'I'll engender and you'll perfect. And let's try to have some fun at it. Why don't you crease your eyes, René?'

René's eyes twinkled, but he did not smile.

'Crease them good!' Sister protested. 'Aren't you glad — making your first sale? Can't you be happy?'

'What do you mean — happy?'

Sister's face clouded. 'Don't you have a good time working? You seem all tightened up when working or thinking of your work — can't stay still or take a nap. When I see you dashing about I say, "There goes René, trying to stay ahead of his time." Are you always being determined to make your work good?'

'I don't know, I'm only learning,' said René softly. And Sister's heart warmed, because humility, rarely assumed, sat upon him so wistfully. 'I'm serious by nature, I suppose,' he went on. 'They call me an adolescent poseur — Loretta's French Quarter friends in New Orleans. They go about all tightened up, too, with secretly clenched fists, grimly resolved to be casual.'

The words 'adolescent poseur' suggested heraldry to Sister — a sort of formal beast or flower embossed in rows across a shield.

She would nap in the doorway with a pillow, as her mother had often done. She lay without a movement in such a position as to be awakened in an hour by a crack of sunlight. She lay with Bruce's head upon her thigh. If he refused to be still, he was cuffed like a pup. And the two slept deeply in the afternoon, and the band of sunlight crept over the floor until it lay across Sister's face.

'Story!' Bruce demanded. 'Te' me story.'

'An old trapper found an egg in the prairie. And it was half white and half green. "Whad you call dis?" he said. He took the egg home and put it under a hen, and the hen hatched the egg. But one end of the bird had a bill, and the other end had a beak. And all the people came in boats to see the bird that was half duck and half falcon. The trapper put the bird in a cage, and he fed rice to the part that was duck, and meat to the falcon, and the bird grew larger and larger. One day the falcon looked around and saw that his tail was a duck, and he chased it all day. And in the evening he caught it. The little boy standing by the cage saw that, and he ran to the woods crying, "Papa, come quick! Our bird is eating its own self!" But when they reached the house there was nothing left in the cage but a falcon's beak jumping about, snapping at the air.'

In the bar of sunlight Sister made a leaping beak with her fingers.

'And that was all that was left of the adolescent poseur,' she said, laughing a low peal of gurgles that jounced the child straddling her belly. Bruce did not laugh. Sister tickled him. He crawled off and sat apart with his big eyes wide and his plump weak mouth agape, rapt in the spell of the tale.

Sister lay on her back, the hard grain of the wood cool and solid against her flesh, her legs uncovered almost to the juncture of the rosy thighs. Today she felt like a Grass Margin Cajin throbbing with hot slow juices. The warmth and the drone of the mild air brought her a curious sense of soul-dormancy. She stretched her bare legs, passed her palms over the scrubbed flooring, inhaled an avid lungful of salty wind, rolled her eyes backward to see and whistle at a cardinal that flew by just then, drawing a brief red streak like a spurt of wine across the tented sky. Life these days had taken on the aspect of an agreeable void — on the surface. And under the surface was just enough of drama to appease the fretful soul. The drama of René Davidson was arresting, and somewhat humorous. The drama of the child, the little brown animal whom she could not realize as having sprung alive from her body — was fascinating, and humorous, too . . .

She saw René outside paddling toward Dutch Scenery. His strokes were much too labored, as though he were not pushing a light pirogue forward, but rather pushing the whole earth backward, bent upon being ahead of his time.

'Hey! Ask for my mail!' Sister shouted.

René nodded and waved. She could discern his smile, the flash of his teeth among the hard green shimmer of water, his countenance glowing with alertness and love.

In the evening he returned for his supper. They had boiled young snails, and Sister had fixed potato pancakes made with grated potatoes, onion, a little flour, and egg-yolks, poured and nicely browned in the pan.

'My dealer wrote to me,' said René after supper as they sat outside in the dark, 'the warmest letter imaginable. In his admiration for what he calls my new manner, he neglects to say a word about possible sales. From him this is most important.'

'Has he quit saying you're ahead of your time?' Sister asked.

'The best work is timeless.'

For an interval the woman was wordless. She identified herself with the grave and starless immensity of the night. The static atmosphere was growing oppressively warm, humid, heavy, rich as marrow.

'Timeless,' she murmured, regarding the night.

René leaned toward her. 'You have that quality,' he said intensely. 'You personify it. My work is achieving it largely through you.'

Sister left her chair and wandered back and forth hesitantly, like the blind. Folds of darkness, coils of darkness, eddies of darkness, surrounded her. She stopped and sat on the top step of the stairway leading down to the canal, hugging her knees. In the water below some torpid presence slapped the water lazily. A sudden feeling of depression lodged in Sister's breast. She felt nullified, lost. She did not understand it, because she was physically well ... René was talking, telling her about his early life. He told of his aunt who had raised him and insisted upon sending him through an Eastern college where he had got himself expelled by exposing the ignorance of the teachers; who had sent him to Paris to study art and, when she saw the sort of pictures he was painting, refused to support him any longer; who at this time was grudgingly mailing him a few dollars each month.

After a pause René said, 'Now I have found myself, and I owe it all to you. All to you!'

'Why do you say these things to me?' Sister asked in a shaken voice.

René did not answer.

'As if I were of any importance!' she persisted forlornly.

René's chair creaked in the silence.

'It's going to rain,' said Sister. 'That will be a change, at least. It's been too nice lately — everything. I wonder how our rice crop looks now!' They would soon be harvesting the crop by the seashore. They would have to rent a small barge to convey it to the landing at Dutch Scenery.

'You are of infinite importance,' René said. 'You've given

life to my work, replacing bloodless cerebration with the juice of life, somehow. Your warm healthy presence permeates all I am doing. No wonder Loretta always returned home filled with the joy of life!'

Sister heard him crossing the porch toward her, kneeling, groping for the hem of her skirt. 'Dear, dear Sister!' he whispered, 'don't you see how much I need you?' He was pressing the garment against his face, kissing it. Sister rested her hand on his head. Her hand seemed curiously large and heavy. Somehow, she was aware of an odd sense of *guilt*. Was it guilt? How could it be guilt? But it *was*. It brought her acutely conscious of a long train of dark and violent doings for which she then felt wholly responsible. Her mind caught a brief glimpse of the shocking scene which had caused Grampaw's death; and of her father staggering down the levee cursing Unga January; and of Mocco crouched by his father's bedside; and of Unga in New Orleans looking for a place among the hurrying throngs to sit down and rest; and of Bruce wandering about the rivers with a puzzled look in his eyes. And now René was kneeling reverently at her feet, speaking of warmth and mysterious power.

She pushed his head away. 'Don't!' she pleaded. 'Please don't ever do that. It's — an insult, or — It makes me feel ——'

'All right, Sister,' said René. 'You don't understand.' He left her and leaned against the farther railing. Sister paced the boards back and forth. She stopped beside him.

'Don't be mad,' she said. 'I owe you a lot, too, René. Since knowing you I really enjoy living. But you are so funny!'

He gave no answer, but stared into the immeasurable night where nothing existed but a single star glittering insolently.

'Always your work, your work!' Sister exclaimed.

'It's my reason for living! Here I am on the point of recognition in my own lifetime, after years of lonely toil. Remember that.'

'I know. But you see *me* only through your work, and expect me to feel honored.'

'Don't you?'

'Yes.'

René smiled in the dark.

This thought enabled Sister to lose the feeling of guilt; to see herself as a thing of growth, moving toward some definite point or goal, or many points and goals. The guilt existed, but it could not be helped.

'What about *my* work?' she asked.

'What work?'

Sister laughed. 'Let's see ... my reason for living ... making children to appreciate your pictures, would you say? I don't know. What would you say? A net-knitter? A fishwife?'

'Do you imagine you think or feel or act like a fishwife?'

'That's your fault, mostly. Grampaw's. Loretta's. A dirty trick!'

'No turning back now. You must keep growing, since the roots are there.'

'But *why*, I wonder!'

'Perhaps your work is to remain beside me forever, helping me as you have done. Suppose you think about that.'

'After years of struggle I'm going to be recognized!'

René stood against the railing with a deeply thudding heart. A heavy cold drop of rain struck his forehead, shattering. Other loud drops beat sparsely on the roof, then ceased abruptly. A short violent shower of rain pounded over the marsh somewhere close by, not touching their roof at all. Small frog voices tinkled.

'Mitch Holt,' Sister muttered.

'Your old sweetheart.'

'Yes.'

'You've outgrown him.'

'Maybe.'

'As much as you have the others around here.'
'He has a big job, too, when he gets back.'
'And he'll want you to help *him*. And you'll do it.'
'Maybe.'
'I don't think so.'
'Maybe ... maybe.'
The man raised his face to the unseen sky and smiled.

26

IN AUGUST the fevered earth throbbed. All things and hidden creatures throbbed. Many growths relinquished their juices and gladly sank back whence they grew. And the air was heavy with salt. Sister heard that in Grass Margin, ten miles from the western edge of the peninsula, salt was rising out of the earth. Men saw it between the cracks of dried ditches, frosted crusts of salt. Someone said the orange trees themselves were suffering. And the river was uncommonly low, full of Gulf salt, crabs, stingarees.

'Telescope weather,' Sister thought.

The terrestrial globe reposed in its dim corner. Sister dreamed before it. She was Venus, or she was one of the she-stars of the Pleiades. Nicolene Kalavich, care of the Pleiades, forty-nine years from Grass Margin. A slight movement of the eye carried her from the lonely tip of Cape Horn to Nova Scotia, where her maternal ancestors had lived.

She took the telescope to the porch. The earth was throbbing. The waters were burning. The telescope cleanly pierced the incandescent air. She saw the black silhouette of the tin soldier pacing the works at Fort St. Philip, and watched him a long time walking in the round frame of the lens, pretending she did not care to look at Grass Margin. But the telescope of its own accord drifted round at last and stopped amid the willows of the far Margin. The Kalavich house was gaunt and gray, a hot gray box in need of paint, palmettoes on one window from which Mocco had taken the sash to sell. On the levee the tattered tablecloth hung limply, her father's fruitless sign.

All day René sat on the porch with a fan. The heat had got him at last, smitten him into fretful inactivity. But he hardly sweated. He only lounged about, wasting the precious middle hours of the day, saying no complaint, but his face revealed an inner nervous tension. To see Sister washing or scrubbing or knitting as usual, with a dark patch of sweat between her shoulder-blades, made him feel hotter. Often during this month he did not stir for a whole day, nor visit Sister's camp, but reclined on the porch of Loretta's camp with a book until the two suns approached each other at the horizon.

'Come and eat!' Sister would call across the canal at noon.

'Nothing for me, thanks!' he answered.

'Why didn't you tell me?'

'No energy!'

He kept thinking of a little village he knew in the Adirondacks, wishing he might be there — with Sister.

Mateo Lucich came on the first of September. With him was André Laval, the constable.

'Dad rice out by Main Pazz. Is belonk to you?' asked André.

'Yes, sir.'

Mateo came forward. 'Is fine rice, Nicolene! How much you vant?'

'We don't want to sell,' Sister answered. 'I was going to ask you to rent us a small barge.'

Laval blinked his one sad eye. 'How you gone cud duh rice, you?'

Mateo said: 'Is hard to cut rice, Nicolene. Storm comit now any days and blow it down. Better you sall it quick when is ripe. Me and André buy it right now. You finish wid it. Is the month for storm.'

'We don't care to sell,' said Sister.

André Laval spat. His rubber boots were full of mud. His eye, doubly bright and puzzled, surveyed Sister benevolently but firmly.

'Your man,' he said, 'he can cud rice, him?' André's greenish beard was like a marsh growth. His tow hair resembled a bunch of sisal grass worn in a play or charade.

'Who are you talking about?' asked Sister.

'Your man.'

'*Who?*'

'Your man.'

'Yes. He can cut rice.'

'Pooh! If I'm gone believe dat, me! If he can cud rice and he is more little than you, dat picture fellow, I give you my shirt for kite-tail.'

'He is not small as you are,' Sister said.

'I can *cud* rice, lak you see me here.'

'You can't cut *our* rice, Mr. Free Will.'

'Dis is not decent, no.'

'What is not decent?'

'You wid dat picture fellow. All duh pipple dawn lak to see dat, and you grandpere was such honez' man, him. Bud we ain' god no law to stob you, and daz a shame, all duh pipple talking and you such pretty lil gul. For what he dawn get married wid you? You want to go to duh devil, you?'

'Yes.'

'What! You dawn care for duh devil when you die?'

'No.'

'Sacre nom de 'tit chien!'

André and Mateo pulled away in their skiff. André, straining at the after oars, looked up at Sister. His single eye burned and burned toward her with a lingering avidity and hopelessness. She called to him, 'Quit looking under my dress, Mr. Free Will!'

Despite herself, Sister could not dislike this man with his scandalized look and his head full of laws. And Mateo, the schemer, too, was looking up at her legs with a sly and timid hunger. This filled Sister with pleasure and pity and wonder, that men should so forget the business in hand to peep at her calves — two ordinary instruments of locomotion — with a curiosity that seemed wholly unrelated to *her*. She felt for Laval a sort of humorous compassion. Him and his laws and brains! Brains and logic and the devil! She had once heard Grampaw say André's face belonged in a picture of a mob grouped round a nude woman burning. And it was a man like André who had invented the devil-god, when a crowd of tribesmen huddled round a tree had seen the lightning select one of their number to destroy . . .

'Whad she means — Mr. Free Will?' André asked Mateo.

'She play vid you.'

'Plenty thing I dawn understand aboud dat gul, me. Dad family Kalavich. Mocco, him he raise frog now. Whad you call dad, fo' God sake? And she god de world on a table, and sing song nobody can understand. Is nod Deggo, is nod Franch, is nod English, is nod Oustrian. Whad you call dat language, hein?'

'Is no language. Tche makit vords herself, any kind vords. You no like? I *like*, by gar! Tche needit goot strong man, dat vomans — *Slavonian* man. No be afraid of her, André! No be afraid. No crazy family! Got tsense! All got tsense! Cajin valk far away to get bullfrogs, Mocco sit under tree and raise frogs in backyard. Nicolene cook fine grub, make fine babies, vork hard and tsing. Is makit me feel like cry because I got bashit vife, can't catch Nicolene for myself. But vait till Meetch come from jail! I sell him lumber schooner tcheap, he makit monet, marry Nicolene. Den pipples stop calling her Immaculate Conception. Meetch gone tame her, by gar! I like. Is nice, eh?'

On the second of September, Sister and René and Bruce sailed out to see the crop of rice. Autumn was in the earth, and the sun had swung south. 'Soon it will branch off cold,' said Sister. There was a haze in the southeast, the elements gathering for a blow. They passed camp after camp, blue, red, some gray, the color of neglect. Some of the people waved at them; others merely stared. In one camp Sister saw a woman dragging a milch goat up the steps to her porch. The tide was rising.

'There's a blow outside,' she said to René.

'Out where we're going?'

'Sure. Feel the wind.'

Their sail was taut. Sister looked to their oilskins piled in the bow. She and Bruce dodged the boom as René tacked. René could handle a boat creditably now. They passed a green island frayed with foam. A long, impassive file of pelicans passed over them, forging seaward without flapping a wing, spaced the same distance apart.

'Shall we go back?' René asked. They were leaving the land behind.

'The wind's not so fresh now!' she called.

Soon the wind almost calmed out. Sister relaxed, and sang nursery rhymes for Bruce. For three hours or so they sailed along nicely. Only the seas were growing higher. 'There's the place right ahead!' Sister called. 'I see the rice!' René saw it too, a thin band of agitated gold. 'We'll have rain and fair wind going home!' Sister said.

The sky was all gray now. Its color intensified the yolky brightness of the distant patch of rice. They were across the gaping mouth of Main Pass, where the river poured into the sea's wide maw. René was lost in wonder and reverence. The place where he and Sister had sown the seed was now covered with an incredibly thick growth of delicate green stalks, like curved brush-marks. Heaped upon this was an opulent top layer of yellow grain, as bright and lavish as boiling gold. The whole scene was as if fashioned from metals — the hard dull sky of steel, the brassy waters of the Pass somewhat tarnished by mixture with salt, and the two golds, green and yellow, of the rice-heads.

They lowered the sail and threw an anchor near the shore, but could not disembark. The tide had already half-covered the rice stalks. Their shouting roused great flocks of birds that had been feeding on the rice. The wind was blowing furiously again, lashing the waters, scourging the heavy, unwieldy heads of grain.

'We came in time to see it ruined!' Sister shouted. She smiled and spread her hands outward. 'Big gale coming! Look! We'd better run!' René was irritated by her blithe acceptance of disaster, this quality that was born in her bones. He looked at the sky, the vast gray vacuity that darkened and seemed descending slowly upon them. The wind was beginning to wrench off and scatter into infinity small clusters of the ripe grain. A bolt of lightning dropped somewhere as heavily as a fearful chunk of lead. In the boom and the long majestic roar of thunder, René saw Bruce scream and grab his mother's legs. The rain rushed upon them, drenching them all in an instant.

'We must go in the Pass and wait!' Sister yelled with an almost joyful, delirious look in her eyes.

Sailing up the Pass, they could see behind them the rice-field now almost completely trodden down by the wind. So quickly had it all occurred that René was befuddled, and stood trying to orient himself, and trying to understand why he had thus far felt no fear. He was concerned only about the rain, which was beginning to blind him, beating into his collar and coursing down between his skin and clothing. The damned child was still screaming. René glared at Sister's rain-whitened, laughing face with its glistening hint of madness — laughing among the swirling gusts of rain. And the brutal wind, growing more merciless with every gust, flaying her thin garments to search out her most secret curves and hollows, induced in her a certain wanton rapture. Each burst of unholy blue lightning gave him a magnificent vision of her in regal, briefly illumined, clothed nakedness, swaying mirthfully like some capricious sovereign of all this senseless fury. He detested Sister! He was horribly jealous of the bold wind that mocked her yet seemed at the same time to propitiate a wild, assertive, unknowable aspect of her nature.

The boat would not answer its helm, because the wind was growing denser than the water. Sister came back and took the tiller, but she could do nothing — nothing but giggle like a silly child. She ran the boat aground. They lay there a long time. The sky was almost black. One terrific blast went by that made them gasp, giving them a notion of the comparative mildness of the previous gusts, and a hint of the fury yet to come. As if enraged at having nothing else to annihilate, the wind vented its spite upon the loosened sail, which was now booming and beating itself to tatters.

Soon a shrimp trawler was blown into the Pass. It was one of the new-style trawlers, propelled by a gasoline engine. René and Sister hailed the fishermen, and so they were towed to Port Eads without mishap. All the way René sat quietly warming himself by the exhaust pipe, while Sister talked with the fishermen, holding her child close to give him the warmth of her breast. Outside all was opaque desolation. The vast prairie was completely flooded with sea-water, the sharp tips of the grasses all slanting in the same direction. Once they passed three otters crouched on a log, and near them a coiled snake — thick, relaxed, motionless. And the flattening of the marsh grass revealed the lonely mounded dwellings of muskrats scattered far.

'If it comes a real hurricane, our camp is gone,' said Sister.

Port Eads lighthouse was already half filled with people seeking refuge — Government employees from the boardwalk village, the crews of two redfish schooners, and some families of marsh people. In one of the lower rooms of the lighthouse, shawled women were making coffee on a charcoal furnace. Bedding, clothing, and cans of food were piled everywhere in this room. Two dogs roamed about, smelling all newcomers. There was no ventilation in the lighthouse, and the air was rank. There was much talk and laughter, a sort of festive air. The spiral iron stairway leading up to the light was jammed with people, waiting, dozing, talking about previous storms.

There was to be a hurricane, the keeper announced. A real hurricane was headed for Port Eads. The wind grew more violent. Huge seas from the Gulf rolled far up the river's mouth. The group of refugees oddly became more animated. Under their congeniality there was terror, a kind of delicious dread — especially the dark Cajins, the swamp people, the religious, the amphibious. They knew the hurricane. They remembered it from last time, tearing through their lives — pure, impartial, smashing unsightly buildings that nobody had energy to demolish, flattening the over-fecund grasses and weeds, dispersing the slimes and odors, reconciling stubborn enmities, reviving dormant schemes...

There happened to be among the refugees a sleek and cheerful salesman of storm insurance, and he stood upbraiding the people through a self-satisfied grin, excitedly tilting and re-tilting his green derby hat, grasping shoulders, plucking sleeves, tapping chests, shouting to make himself heard. 'You understand? I'm really *glad* you didn't take storm insurance last year. *We* don't care! *We're* ahead. How much is your house worth? Ha! Ha! Then we're ahead a hundred dollars! You've made me a present of a hundred dollars!... Ninety miles an hour! You hear that? And it'll blow a hundred and twenty before we're through!'

In the night, Sister Kalavich placed her child among the others sleeping on the bedded floor, and made her way up the twisted iron stairway to the light-room. Climbing, she could hear the wind outside flogging the tower. It sounded like streams of fine sand hurled against the outer wall. She lifted herself through the square hole and presently stood in the light compartment, where the gas flame burned fiercely and the big crystal prisms and lenses slowly revolved. The blasts of wind shrieked past this glass cage, and refracted beams from the lenses threw curious geometric designs of light round and round the glazed walls. She could hear the maddened roar of the sea, and each burst of lightning showed her the earth far below all covered by tiny waves; and farther out the rocky jetties pounded by slow gigantic seas, enveloped in twirling veils of spray.

After a while there was no more lightning and no more rain, as though the wind, growing more robust, had destroyed these minor fiends. The fearful core of the storm, its spinning heart, was near. Once the lighthouse itself trembled. Strangely, a word came to her that seemed to embody the storm. It was the word *thus*. She said it aloud: '*Thus!*'

Then ensued a long, awful, soundless lull, marvelously pure and still, a hole in the storm. She could hear the labored beat of her heart plodding through the oblivion. She stood listening. Strange and wonderful! not even the grumbling of the sea was audible, and the voices of the refugees huddled below were stilled. She turned her back to the hurricane's direction and waited, while the gas-light filled the world with a soft purring, and the guttural moan of a lost sea bird trailed briefly past, and the ungodly webbed shapes reflected by the turning prisms pursued one another across her person and round the floor and wall and ceiling.

Suddenly the wind rushed again out of the void. It bludgeoned the lighthouse so cruelly that the very stones quaked. The cylindrical room of glass was surrounded outside by a

stout iron grating; and through this network the hiss and
screech of the wind was almost deafening. And now she heard
below her the faint wailing of women and the harsh voices of
the men who tried to silence them.

René, searching for Sister, climbed the stairs and found her.
His face was white and haggard, and the prism beams sweeping over him gave him a ghastly look. He was not afraid. He
had been sickened by the crush of people down below.

'They're gone wild,' he said. 'They're afraid the lighthouse
will go. Are you quite all right?'

'Is Bruce all right down there?'

'Yes. Still sleeping.'

'René, let's go out on the gallery!' Sister said.

René smiled. 'Isn't it rather pointless and foolhardy?'

'Not on the lee side. Only pointless.'

'Aren't you dramatizing a common occurrence?'

'Yes. I love to dramatize!'

She opened the iron door. The loud roar of the storm entered.
They were well over a hundred feet in the air. 'Come on!' she
urged. René's coat was jerked forward as if by a dozen insane
hands. Together they were pressed against the cold iron rail.
The iron seemed to ring, to twang with life. The immense living
darkness, uttering defiant phrases and unearthly paeans, drew
them together in mutual frailty and fear. Above them revolved
the long slices of light whose pale inexorable sweep no wind
could mar or dim. And this also brought them together as one
— he and she alone at the hub of the wheel that had no weight,
sound, smell, no property but pure, frigid, unwavering light
scattered out and everywhere in clean noble beams. The
vibrant humming of the ironwork set up a singing in Sister's flesh.

'We have renounced the world and climbed to hell!' René
called into Sister's ear. The wind, cut in twain and swirling
round either side of the lighthouse, met and pressed the man
and woman firmly against each other.

'We have renounced *them!*' Sister shouted. 'The *people* be-low!'

She turned toward the wind, as she would face a respected adversary. It seemed to sharpen her face, to scour her beauty. It forced her eyelids closed. Her coiled hair sprang loose. It straightened out behind her like a runner's. She was nothing. She was the air. She was a thought. In the wind, or over or behind it, she heard the crash of cymbals, the ripping of strong linen, the words of a judge denouncing a felon, the thudding of books being closed in a classroom, the whisper of hot irons plunged into water. Now she and her companion were as one, locked together forever by the wind. No archaic remnant of decorum impelled them to draw apart. Their struggles would only weld them more closely. Half of Sister's body was numb and chilled. The other side, mingling with the glow of her com-panion, was alive and warm. And as the chaotic moments passed, some instinct more ancient than her will kindled a somber yet goodly heat that thawed the other half, the dead half, of her body. Her vitals droned in a kind of prolonged sleep, a lulled contentment that asked no hope of future peace and shared no burden of bygone guilt. Far below in the village, in the world renounced, she would hear dim vehement hints of ruin — sheets of metal grinding and fluttering, resonant joists and stanchions tumbling end over end along the boardwalks. Feeling a certain cunning delight, she giggled.

'Houses are breaking up!' she called.

René responded hoarsely, 'Yes!'

'The sky is falling!'

'Yes!'

'How do you like dramatizing?'

'Fine!'

Sister's flesh hummed on, seemingly for hours, vibrant as a musical string, rooted in the singing iron with the man, yet also flowing with the wind — part of the husky storm, of the neighing darkness, of the unyielding blasts of light circling above them. She felt uncommonly light and gay, eased of every woe, and she bore toward René a feeling of rich sweet comradeship. Her head drooped sideways and the cheek rested on his friendly shoulder, as softly as that of a violinist dreaming on his instrument.

Once René moved one of his hands. Unwittingly it grazed her left breast.

The spell was broken.

A thrill rushed up her throat like a prodding dirk. She was awake to the fact of flesh and of imperative nearness. She fought it. It was abhorrent in the storm. She hated her volatile flesh, the trickiness of the carnal self. She clenched her thighs. She took René's hand between her own.

'Let's go inside!' she cried, holding him in her arms.

'Why? Why?'

'Please!'

'No! Stay with me! Isn't it nice?'

She held René like a child on her bosom, and sobbed, brushing her cheek softly against his. Timbers down below were cracking apart loudly. Sister's knees were weak. She reached for the storm-door latch and opened the door. There was a great burst of yellow light, and the blinding sparkle of prisms revolving. She clutched the doorway and hauled herself in. At once she descended the iron stairway. 'Bitch!' she muttered. 'Bitch!'

The people downstairs were all praying, heads bowed and backs curved forward. At the foot of the stairs stood a reddish man, a priest or minister, holding an open book. Sister stood above him in the curve of the stairs. He looked at her. His mild eyes widened and his mouth fell open. He blinked, and his lips began to form gentle words.

'Why, what's the matter, child?' he asked. 'Are you afraid? Are you sick? Did you come to pray with us?'

In the morning the wind was gentle. Some of the houses in the boardwalk village were unharmed. Government and pilot boats took away some of the refugees. Sister and René obtained a sail for their boat. A man had given René an old Panama hat to wear, and he looked comical. He sat laughing at himself, very sunburned and boyish. He had not thought about art in almost twenty-four hours, and he seemed more genial and human than Sister had ever known him before. She loved him as her brother. They were sailing up the calm river, in sight of Main Pass.

'What are the people trying to do up there?' she asked out of a sudden whim.

'Where?'

'Up north. New Orleans. Everywhere up the river. What are they trying to do?'

'Many things.'

'But what? What do they want above all, I'm asking you?'

'That's hard to say.'

'On an average. What are they after, do you think?'

'Things, I guess. Mostly things.'

'Things that you buy, or things that you make?'

'Things that you buy.'

The roof of a house floated past them, turning round and round. Then a new wagon seat. Then a pigeon-house with many doors, nailed on a long pole.

'The women too?' Sister asked. 'The women want things?'

'Yes.'

'Tell me more, then.'

The world was good. It had a new cover on it, in places. The sky was dressed in rich colors. Momentous events waited in the air, waiting for people to happen to. The wide waters covering the prairie were smooth. On the horizon the two suns were slowly moving apart. Sister gave Bruce a large ginger-cake. She had put from her mind the events of the storm. Their lives had been spared. Now they held together a thing which none would ever lose or forget. But a dark curtain had fallen on the past; a door had closed; a song had ended.

She told René, 'If the camps are gone, your pictures are gone.'

'That might be a good thing,' René said wanly.

'Then you can start over.'

'Where?'

'Somewhere.'

'Where?'

In the afternoon they crossed Bay Saint Francis. They poled into the canal. One camp they passed had a great hole in its kitchen, as if a giant fist had gone through it up to the elbow. Big skiffs of various colors wandered in the canal. The boatmen plunged in their poles, then leaned on them, walking from bow to stern. René saw these fishermen as seagoing pedestrians, walking across shallow bays and walking back home. Another camp came into view. It was roofless. The roof had been removed and neatly deposited in the grass a little distance off, as if the giant had lifted it off to see what was inside.

Grampaw's camp was unhurt, except for one of the cisterns, which was blown off its foundations. Loretta's camp was intact, only that the palmetto thatching was gone, nowhere to be seen, and the shell island was strewn with chewed-up reeds.

Sister sped up the stairs of Grampaw's camp. She hurried to the chicken-house on the rear porch, where she had locked in a hen and sixteen chicks. The hungry chicks were cheeping. Sister made a bag of her lifted skirt and gathered them in. Bruce came toddling, whining for food.

'Now you must wait, fella,' she told him. 'You've eaten and the chickies haven't.'

Sister stood peering down at the crumbled cistern lying in the marsh. A coal-black rooster in the pen, reflecting green light all over, strutted about talking to his hens. 'Cut-cutoo-caw-took-took-took!' The chicks in Sister's dress, bundled together in the dark, had stopped cheeping. Far out in the prairie a man was poling a pirogue through the soft mud. Sister stood motionless in a queer attitude of waiting or listening. She turned her face to the back door of the camp. She watched the door vigilantly. Presently the door began slowly to open, and Mocco stood in the doorway. His eyes were swollen. He had been crying alone in the camp. Each stood waiting for the other to talk.

'Bad news about Papa,' Mocco said, smiling nervously.

Sister frowned. She smiled. Her face turned sallow. The chicks were tumbling out of her dress.

'What's the matter with Papa?' she asked softly, looking away. The chicks roamed about at her feet, cheeping forlornly.

'Well, he died yesterday before the storm,' Mocco said. 'We buried him this morning. I couldn't find you anywhere yesterday. Kraljevic saw you sailing outside. I had an awful experience all alone with him during the storm, the body. An awful experience. I thought the house would go any minute, but it didn't. Only one of the hives blew away.'

Sister stooped and began gathering the chicks.

'What did he have to say?' she asked softly. 'About me?'

'Well, he — shucks, he didn't know what he was saying.'

'Tell me.'

'Well — he said you could have nursed him back to health, like you were doing before — before ——'

Sister raised her eyes to the green day.

27

MOCCO lost interest in the bullfrog business, because he was afraid to sleep in the house where his father had died. He lived all winter with Sister in the oyster camp. Under Sister's cheerful but authoritative nagging, he worked the oysters, shipping about a hundred sacks for the season. He detested this kind of work. The oysters had not received proper cultivation since Grampaw's death. They were growing together in large clusters. They had never been broken apart and moved to richer waters. Mocco had to loosen them with a culling hatchet. Their mud-caked shells were sharp as razors. Mocco's hands were full of cuts in various stages of healing.

Sometimes, on fine calm afternoons after eating his lunch of smoked mullet roe and hardtack, he would take a sleep in the skiff, far out in Bay Saint Francis, with his cap over his eyes. Once a pair of young fishermen passed and saw him asleep. They decided to play a joke. Untying the painter of Mocco's skiff, they quietly towed him home, made fast the boat to Grampaw's landing, and left Mocco sleeping there. All the passersby laughed.

Sister soon found him. She ran down the stairs with blazing eyes. 'Mocco, you trifler! Haven't you gone to the beds yet?'

'I've been at the beds all day,' he answered, looking about him in a dazed manner. 'Somebody must have towed me home while I was taking a little nap. I was exhausted. The damned hurricane covered all the oysters with mud a foot thick. It takes three men to bring up a tongful.'

'But you slept in your bed till daylight this morning!'

'Jeezam, Sis! I'm not used to this kind of work.'

'You and your damned excuses! You're lazy, that's all!'

'All right, I'm lazy, then! Whose fault is it? Is it my fault, or God's fault, or whose? What can I do about it?'

Sister turned away, completely outdone... Their finances had reached a critical point. She had been to the post-office that day and found no mail, no orders for nets. She had not received an order that week. She could not understand it. Since she had turned over part of her work to Natasha Lucich, she had been receiving fewer orders.

Next morning she approached Mocco for a serious understanding.

'Something's got to be done, Mocco. We've got only a dollar in the house. We won't get returns on your last shipment of oysters until next week. What are we going to do?'

'I'm doing all I can, damn it! Can't you get more board out of René? He eats more than any of us.'

'I wouldn't think of asking him for more. He's paying four dollars now, and we're practically living on that. When are you going to town?'

'Do you want to be rid of me?'

'No, but I don't want to keep you here against your will. You've always been anxious to leave.'

'I'm going after the winter. Don't worry. Just wait and see.'

'Couldn't you trap until then? There's a month of trapping left.'

'Will you skin if I trap?'

'Of course I'll skin. Muskrats are worth a dollar, they say.'

Mocco did not mind trapping. In fact he liked paddling the silent bayous witnessing the interesting life led by the marsh creatures. But he abhorred the task of skinning the animals and stretching the pelts. Next day he went to Grass Margin. He found his two barrels of traps in the orchard. Vines half an inch thick had grown over the barrels. Stout tendrils had pried their way under the covers. Rain had beaten through these openings and rusted the traps so badly that they were unfit for use.

Meanwhile, Sister had received a letter from the Crescent City Angler's Supply Company:

> Referring to your several letters inquiring why we have discontinued sending you orders for nets and seines:
>
> Miss Natasha Lucich, with whom you divided your work several months ago, has made reductions in her price from time to time, and at this time she is selling us nets for 20% less than we paid you, and consequently has received as much of our business as she is able to take care of. Your workmanship is excellent, and we will be glad to send you half our orders if you will meet this reduction. Are you willing to do this?

Sister burned with anger. Evidently the two Lucich girls, and probably the mother, were now making nets.

She scrawled across the bottom of the letter the word *NO* and enveloped it for return mailing.

Mocco returned and broke the news about the traps.

'How's the orange crop?' Sister asked.

'Half a crop. We better pick it.'

'Yes. We'd better. We'll have to move over there. With the mule we can make a living on the Margin. I'll send Bruce to Tante Inez for a while. René can board with Pretty John if he wants to come along.'

'We can sell the three boats after we're finished moving.'

'Yes. We'll have to.'

Sister was highly excited now, eager to plunge into the living of a new life. She was tired of the sea. Her growth, somehow, had stopped. She wanted to feel dry land under her. She was hungry for the earth. She longed to plunge her hands into the soft rich land.

'I'll soon be leaving for town,' said Mocco.

'You'll never go, Mocco. And if you should, I'll manage. I'll have Claiborne to work.'

'I forgot to tell you, Mitch is out! He's been out for months, I heard today, working in different canning factories in Alabama and Mississippi. And Unga's back in the delta too, supposed to be living in a shanty boat somewhere below Fort Saint Philip. She's got a kid.'

'Is Mitch coming back to the Margin, I wonder?'

'In spring, they say. You ought to know that.'

Sister turned and looked at herself in the mirror. In recent years she had grown a great pile of hair, almost too much for her face. There were fine lines upon her brow. Her eyes were deep, shadowed, sea-weary. Her mouth was humorous, self-derisive.

They sold two of the boats, Grampaw's big lugger and a skiff, and moved to Grass Margin. A man whom they did not know, a new Slavonian from Dalmatia, ferried them across the river. Sister took the books, clothes, and some utensils. The furniture she left in Grampaw's camp, to be used in case of summer visits. The globe and saddle and telescope went with them to the Margin.

That same day, Tante Inez, a very stern and tidy Creole matron who knew no English, came for little Bruce. She had two small boys of her own who spoke English. Sister kissed the child good-bye, and went immediately into the house out of hearing of his pitiful crying. Tante Inez pulled away from the landing quickly, her skiff riding high against the yellow current. She lived four miles up the river.

The next day Sister scrawled a sign:

NETS AND HONEY

and stuck it into the levee in front of the house.

She began at once to break ground for a crop of early beans. Day after day the mule plodded through the rows of vine-covered orange trees with the plow. The plow had only one handle. Sister steered it as best she could. Some of the rows came so crooked that she laughed. Overalls covered her legs, flopping jauntily as she marched; but near the hips they encased her body too snugly, like tough blue skin of a darker hue. She would be sweating there. She thought: 'Land birds are fat and careful, not so free as the terns and frigate hawks that wheel around the oyster reefs. Sparrows avoid the sky. Tree lice! Road lice!' She picked up a rotted orange and threw it. 'Shoo!'

Sister was tired today, but her spirits were high. The Bar Pilots' Association was giving a dance that night at Venice down the road. She had made a new dress for the occasion. As the mule lowered his head and forged forward, Sister clutched the single handle in one hand and the cross-brace in the other. She allowed herself to be pulled bodily forward by the plow. It was late in the evening. There were no steamships passing in the river, no wagons on the road, no singing hens or romping children. Half-relaxing her spent tendons, she won a certain pleasure in being forcibly urged, as a tired child is urged homeward, through the thicket at dusk. The fat trees huddled in rows so closely that they formed a kind of single growth with many thirsty trunks. The mule snorted faintly. 'Poor fellow, you're tired,' she said. 'One more furrow, then you'll rest.'

At the end of the row she gathered the rope reins. Claiborne halted, an obedient mass of moist hair and sinews, one of his hind legs sagging limply. The woman, too, threw her weight on one hip and rested, hearing the loud pulsing of blood through her head. She could smell the night coming over the rear marshes, cold and swampy. She dreamed over the plow, thinking: 'A curtain has fallen, a song has ended, a circle has been drawn.... I will bathe first. That will make me stop being tired. Then I'll rest. Never mind supper. There will be boiled shrimp at the dance, maybe raw oysters. I wonder if Mitch Holt will be there? They say he's been home since yesterday. Who cares? If he's not there, boiled shrimp will be. I've got enough second cousins to keep me dancing all night.'

Claiborne's big head turned. His large patient eyes questioned Sister. He blew a long breath through his nostrils, shifted his weight to the opposite hind leg, jerked his head at the cloud of mosquitoes that worried him.

'Come up!' said Sister.

The harness creaked. Again the sod was springing open, brown under the plow's quiet crunching.

After plowing she stabled the mule and rubbed him down. In the dim stable she sang as she scoured the huge panting body with a burlap sack, feeling more than seeing the animal's bulging contours. When she stooped, her weariness lay upon her back like a triangular pain pointing downward into her loins. 'Meat!' she thought. 'Hot meat. Energy moulded into proper shapes and patterns of muscle, hoofs for gripping and big hams pushing at the collar. Good mule. We'll make a farm out of this place, you and I. I'll take good care of you. Plant more oranges, raise big painted peppers and squash like white pottery. New plow. New disc harrow. Woman riding on the harrow. I like things to ride on. Hay rake. Well-greased buggy and a trotter horse clopping past the post-office.'

She took a bag and a pair of clippers and hurried into the orchard. She selected a tree, tore apart the vines that covered it, and shouldered her way through. She stood as if in a cage, and sang a song of her own making:

> Courage tree, courage tree,
> Wow-while-a-wow-de-o!
> O the brails and the zails and a go-to-hell,
> McGulp my shibes in a moll and a mell,
> And a gricking and a grucking and a go-to-hell,
> Wow-while-and-a-wow-de-o!

Despite the vines, the trees this year were doing their best, bearing quite a few oranges. These were bright in the dusk, heavy and hard. The bark of the limbs, roughened by old fungus, cut deeply into the crook of her arm. She thought: 'Can Mocco help it if he's lazy? Somebody better tell me that.'

She lit the kitchen lamp, and began packing two boxes of fruit. She wrapped each orange in a square of tissue paper labeled 'Louisiana Oranges.' When finished she put a foot-tub of water on the stove for her bath.

Mocco came in from the back Bay with two baskets and a string of fish. A negro boy was with him. The negro carried a third basket full of fish. Mocco stood in the lamplight holding the cluster of glittering silver that revolved slowly on the grass string. 'How do you like these for salting down?' he asked. Sister had been eating fish for two weeks. Looking at the fish, she felt her hunger disappear, as if she had breathed it out of her — simply gone. 'Did you bring the salt too?' she asked. The eyes of the fish seemed to be watching her, saying, 'Well, well, well! Here we are back again!'

The negro deposited his basket on the back steps. 'We can dry them out, you know,' said Mocco. The negro boy lowered his head, as if he were about to butt Sister, and croaked in a voice deep as a man's, '*Yossum!* Yall kin dry um out!' Cats were coming out of the weeds from neighboring back yards, one by one, three cats, smelling the baskets. The negro lowered his head again: 'We set undah *one willa tree* all day an cotch um! We ain move out dat willa tree all day.'

'A right nice miraculous draught of fishes,' said Sister. 'But I thought you went out after meat. Deer or rabbit. Did you bring any rabbits?' She could hardly hold in her laughter.

Mocco turned fiercely upon the negro boy. 'Take the fish away! Take the three baskets on the road and sell them in the morning. Take them!'

The negro gathered the three baskets. 'Too much to tote!' he grumbled. 'God damn dat!'

'Bring me half of what you get!' Mocco called after him.

The negro staggered away.

'I'm all worn out, Sis,' said Mocco. 'My system's out of order. I've got those saw-teeth in front of my eyes right now. Colored lights dancing, shaped like saw-teeth.' He hung his hat on the handle of the coffee-grinder. 'Jeezam, I'm full of gas!'

'You need exercise,' said Sister. She turned away from the pitiable spectacle of Mocco, lifting her head, fighting black despair, fixing her thoughts on the Pilots' dance and holding them there. 'Are you going with me to the dance, Mocco? I ironed a shirt for you and cleaned your good suit.'

'I'll have to go, I guess.'

Sister was stenciling on the fruit crates the name of a New Orleans commission house.

'And you're shipping fruit?' Mocco asked. 'I thought we'd wait for a better market.'

'I need a plow. We'll need new harness soon. Claiborne has trouble pulling the disc. We need feed for him too. I — we're entirely depending on the mule until somebody buys nets or honey — entirely!'

'I know! I know!' Mocco mounted the stairs. The ceiling creaked under his walking and his mollified settling on the bed upstairs. He removed his rubber boots. They held a great quantity of water, which spilled on the floor. He took a deep drink of orange wine from a jug. He thought: 'The hairs of my chest smell. My feet smell. These damned smells that come out of me! *She* always smells sweet, yet the same father made us both. I've *got* to get away from here. Not sick enough to quit eating and too sick to work. I hope I'm going blind. Live in an institution somewhere. No more bothers. I ought to be a commission merchant in town. I know the land. I know the people. I look well in a clean shirt... If I had the money I'd go up on the packet tomorrow.' He closed his eyes tightly, but could not shut out the zigzag lights.

Sister's tired hands moved skillfully, cleaning the fish for Mocco's supper. She put seven large trout into the pot for him. She carried the two boxes of fruit to the end of the landing, and tied to the piling a bamboo pole with a white flag, for the New Orleans packet to stop in the morning. The levee road was empty and gray in the dusk. Alone on the road, she danced about, whirling. The night was like a low tune, the stars, the gnarled bare willows twisted and webbed, the river's eternal flowing, the half-visible road tracing the levee's aimless turning.

She bathed in the light of three tallow-tree candles in the packing-shed, standing in the foot-tub covered with crisp suds. The lather cloaked her like plumage. She soaped her sweaty armpits and pulled the good tepid water over her. The packing shed was still furnished with the oddities which the negro Bonus had gathered. There were a few muskrat skins stretched on a board, the result of one of Mocco's attempts to earn money for his New Orleans trip. From a near-by shelf a row of wooden decoy ducks stared at Sister's nudeness with bright dead eyes.

Mocco passed by from the stable. He called to her: 'You know I believe Claiborne's sick. I don't believe we can ride him to the dance.'

'How?' Sister shouted.

'He's lying down breathing hard, Sis!'

'He's tired. I worked him cruel today.'

Mocco went off. She heard a buggy pass on the road, full of the laughter of girls, and young men teasing — going to the dance. People from far up the road. She rubbed her breasts with the towel, thinking, 'I don't want to be first at the dance, and I don't want to be last.' At the dance the people would talk:

'You seen Sister Kalavich, you?'

'Oui. Her firs' dance for five year.'

'Sence she got duh baby, po' t'ing.'

'She did not come wid dat picture fellow, no.'

'You ever seen dem walk together on duh road?'

'Mais sho', dey walk far apart lak brother and sister.'

'Some time one behind another.'

'Ain't das a shame, makin' fun of a po' crazy gul!'

In the kitchen Mocco was eating fish. He held the fish like a mouth-organ, sliding it back and forth, spitting a stream of bones from the side of his mouth.

'Call me at seven o'clock,' Sister said.

'I think Claiborne is sick, Sis.'

'Call me. He'll be all right.'

In her room she crawled under the mosquito bar and lay in her kimona for an hour of rest. She would lie behind this hour, letting languor spread down to her toes. She enacted in her mind the scene of their going down the road to the dance, she in Claiborne's saddle and Mocco perched on the rump. Laughter thrown over her shoulder like confetti. The first thin filaments of music far ahead, and her pausing to recall the name of the piece. There would be a large bright-eyed crowd under the gasoline lights in the big orange-shed, emptied tonight of its bins and boxes, and scrubbed and waxed for the occasion. There would be merry trappers and Coast Guards and soldiers in uniform, old women and men nodding to one another, children hanging asleep across the bony laps of the old.

Sister dozed a long while, and awoke. A boat passed outside laden with boisterous couples. A creaky buggy on the road, no voices in it. This would be a single couple, or perhaps two couples, holding hands, or kissing. She jumped from the bed and dressed. Her party dress was white, misty, fragile. She handled it gently. It had come out of the earth, born of the earth, made of plants, woven by busy machines and machine-people far away. Made to be loved. Made to be loved in. The night was full of hands far away and everywhere sowing, plowing, weaving, for love. She tied a narrow black ribbon on her throat,. pinched her cheeks to make them red, danced a few steps, and her scampering shadow on the wall was a huge, frilled woman-shadow. She walked down the stairs, watching Mocco's uplifted eyes, conscious of her rounded beauty, searching Mocco's face for a sign of admiration, wonder, surprise. Stupid Mocco! Watching her with a frown and blazing eyes.

'I tell you the mule's sick,' he said. 'I think it's anthrax.'

Sister felt her face go small and white. She could not swallow. 'Anthrax!' she whispered. She bared her teeth in a crooked, quivering smile.

She hurried to the stable. Her party dress brushed past stiff weeds and leaves licked her skirt with cold dew. She could not see Claiborne.

'Hold the lantern. Do you reckon it's anthrax, Mocco?'

'Yes. At least no dance for us tonight. Guate's roan had it. It moves through the ground, they say. No dance for us.'

'Does anthrax always kill? Hold the lantern. He's got a fever, I know.' She peered at the large sick presence, the limp belly flattened outward swathed in heat, giving off a hot, almost pleasant flow of warmth. She ground her teeth. 'Listen!' Mocco whispered. A curious distant thumping came through the silence from somewhere, like the muffled beating of a ship's engine, steadily belaboring the night with profound and vital blows. 'His heart!' Mocco said. 'His heart fighting the sickness.'

Mocco ran inside for various accessories, buckets and rags and a syringe. Sister took off her party dress and donned overalls. They worked together quite a long time. 'Hi! Get up! Get up!' Mocco urged, tugging at the tail. Claiborne could only raise his head. He tried to gather his feet, then fell back in a great trembling, all his skin rippling. In a little while the great breaths came faster, and Claiborne could no longer lift his head.

'Will I go to the Fort for the horse doctor?' Sister asked. 'He'll come by in the morning. Will I?'

'No. No use. You go inside and get your rest, Sis.' It was surprising how tender Mocco had become.

Sister went into the house and folded her party dress. It was half-past eleven. She set herself mechanically to some small tasks about the house, telling herself all was well. Later she went to the levee. Her impulse was to send a keen screech of rebellion like a javelin toward the stars. The hour rankled with a need of rebellion, but there was no person or thing to cry out against. The virile wind tugged at her sleeves, wrenched her hair into disarray, urging her away from home. A swollen moon seemed to leer as it peeped over the horizon. The battered visage of a cloud crawled past it like an envoy of dread. The river's wind-bitten surface was blotched by patches of brazen light. The blasts of wind, grown raw and willful, stung her coatless back, belled her overalls and swirled under them, fingering her limbs.

She thought: 'Torments and torments, and no why, no answer, no voice. Now we have left a piece of ground, a man and a woman. I'm hungry. I've got to eat oranges tomorrow all day. Let's try to be calm, now, and see this thing straight. We have here a man and a woman and a piece of ground. The man will not work. That is a pity. Not real. None of it real. Only the hunger. . . . Why should I have to feel lonely because the wind whistles around the house, desolate because a screaming gull is blown over my head, helpless and lost because a mule dies? Why should I hunger? I want warmth and a home and safety, a full wood-box, and a pantry with meats and meal. A pantry. A man to warm me. A woman for every man. A man for every woman. Dragging logs! I don't like it. Dragging logs, pitching manure. I don't mind the plowing. I don't like it, but I don't mind it. If he were sick, yes. "You'll do it and like it!" says the Lord God. The Bon Dieu, invisible and working His wonders to perform. Walking invisible, indivisible, behind my plowing, sowing weeds. Why, hello, Mitch, when did *you* get back? Come up and have supper some day, hear? ... Mitch Holt! I've got to let him see me right away. Tomorrow! ...'

28

RENÉ enjoyed living with Pretty John and his wife. The son of a stray Jewish cosmetic peddler and a mulatto woman, John was the most intuitive human being René had ever known. His eyes were fine but saddened, as though from something he had once seen, and perhaps still saw. In a charming, sometimes startling but never offensive way, John would often appear noiselessly out of space, or disappear in the same manner. And he lived in a sure knowledge of the properties of cork and lead, the two ultimates in a fisherman's ken.

René made many sketches of John, whose enormous ears, like pectoral fins, grew low on a small bald head which bore a pointed, dorsal tuft of hair. His right cheek showed three parallel scars received during his youth in an encounter with an alligator. The scars were perfectly straight and evenly spaced, as if the alligator had somehow taken pains to achieve precision. Passing a stranger on the levee or in a boat, he would involuntarily rub his right eye to conceal the scars with his hand; and with the free eye he would appraise the passerby curiously from head to foot, as though to determine whether this queer creature might float or founder.

René and John sat on the wharf each evening after supper. John liked to go back into the past, discussing his mottled career, the big fish and the women he had pursued around the Coast in the old days. He was fond of recalling details of his childhood: 'When I waz ten-leben year old my mother she waz run away from me and taken a job cook on a show-boat. Den I waz live wid a gang of trapper. Dey was make me skin muz-rat, and pud my foot in a trap when I waz bad.'

Often they would lie on their stomachs over the roan-colored water and smoke silently, savoring the calm, until something happened along to stir up their words — a flock of ducks plunging toward new feeding grounds, or a steamer from New Orleans hurrying downstream to reach the Bar before night, groaning like a worn bassoon. Occasionally they heard Miss Pretty John inside singing a Creole ballad over her dish-washing. Miss John cherished her white blood. She ate alligator tails only in secret. To John's disgust she religiously avoided intercourse with negroes. She cultivated her white relatives, fishmongers and ruffians all, sending each a frosted fig-cake on his birthday. Sheepishly amiable with the whites, she copied their fads, aped their morals, invoked their Virgin during a storm, and constantly invented occasion to seek their company, in which she was anything but happy.

'Soon as you smell white,' John would tell her when a group of sportsmen approached looking for a guide, 'you start actin' lak you got a mullet-bone in yo' bridge-work.'

They lived on a small bit of land, a quarter-arpent. The house had been built out of planks found floating down the river — three tiny rooms of different shapes and heights. Even the furniture was diminutive. René slept on the floor of the front room, on a feather mattress. Above his head, a hole in the ceiling had been plastered over with the cover of a book of sheet music to keep out the wasps — an old-fashioned song entitled 'The Parboiled Gander.' The pot in which Miss John made her coffee was as small as a toy. Alongside the house were frugal little patches of vegetables, and here Miss John would crawl about on her knees, cultivating the small bits of soil with a teaspoon. René was fascinated! He always thought of the Johns as little gnomes.

The little woman was always touching René, placing her tiny fingers on his knee while talking; smoothing his collar; walking into his room when he was partly dressed; sitting beside him on the floor as he drank his morning coffee. 'You don't god no gul, you?' in a coy tone that was very amusing and charming, for she was old and wrinkled. 'You dawn go to see Sister no mo'? Whad's duh matter, hein? She dawn leave you sleep wid her?'

Since moving to the Margin, René had seen Sister only twice. He had decided that while living in the oyster village she had seen too much of him. Now he would give her an opportunity to *think* of him — to examine while alone the copious stream of words he had spoken. He was certain that in her thoughts and feelings she was gradually coming to depend upon him. His work, he thought, was getting better. He now worked more swiftly and surely.

The night of the Pilots' dance he came in from the marshes with Pretty John. At the post-office after supper he learned there was to be a dance. He wondered whether Sister were going. He resolved to find out, and walked the five miles to Venice, and stood looking into the big orange packing shed. Sister was not there.

He trudged homeward in the starlight. His tennis shoes made no sound on the earth. He was chewing on a piece of pilot bread, which he liked to nibble between meals. He had finished a good landscape that day in the marsh, and was still in a lyrical mood.

'A crust and a lonely road!' he thought. 'This is better than the bread in Paris. Will *she* come to Paris with me? If only I had the money now, to get her away from here! My God, the years I wasted doing pictures in the manner of that *Douche Bag and Crucifix!* Perhaps a thing of mine done in my new style will take the Independent Show prize next month.... Here's where I'll do my next big oil — that cross-shaped house with the cylindrical cistern and the tree like a verdant explosion. I'll do the fruit *most* carefully.... A tree is a creature of contrary rhythms like a man, vertical flow of sap and the planetary movement of fruit around the swollen boughs. That observation would have made a stir among my old gang.... Is she thinking of me tonight? She *shall* think of me! My will must never waver! That night in the lighthouse she was very near to submitting. Next time her head rests on my shoulder it will remain.... Lovely mouth, the trumpet of her soul! Ripe lips, drooping like fruit, heavy with songs unsung! In this place she is wiser than I, saddened by the secrets of the soil.... This inescapable network of stars! Blurred stars, blurred hedges, blurred footfalls. I am a footstep in the mist! My thoughts grope softly as quick roots fumble for the sweet secretions of the night.... Saddened by the secrets of the soil! I must tell her that! No — it is too full of hisses...'

At home in his room René took from his pocket the letter he had received at the post-office. It bore a French postmark. He had not bothered to open it before. He knew it was from Roy Titmus, member of the group of impressionist painters to which René had belonged in Paris, disciples of some new French school, who knew too much about painting to paint well. René opened the letter:

Dear Davidson:
  I just saw a seascape of yours at Lawtell's, recently painted, I take it. It is a puerile and obscene daub. Is the thing a joke? It seems to have been painted for a calendar of a marine insurance corporation. Have you sold out to the dealers? I cannot believe that of you. I saw here in Paris one or two of the first things you did around the mouth of the Mississippi, and they were grand. What is the meaning of this?

René tossed the letter aside, smiling.

The rain came before dawn, assailing the sheet-iron roof at Venice with a roaring that almost drowned the music of the negro band from New Orleans. The people heard it, and while they danced they were glad. A long dry spell had almost emptied the levee people's cisterns. Now there need be no lugging of tubs of water from the river, no searching of attics for peach-stones to settle the mud. Some of them, those who had journeyed far, wondered how they would manage the trip home in open pirogues, but still they were glad for the rain. Old people sitting around the walls with their children's children on their knees smiled at one another. Boys swung their partners more recklessly, and the girls, sensing adventure in the forthcoming journey homeward with tipsy escorts, quickened their steps and sang with the music.

Mitch Holt stood in the doorway. Fine swarms of mist floated in and glazed his coat. Near-by on the porch a bare-footed drunken trapper slept with his paddle under his arm and his corduroy cap partly concealing a face that still wore a smile. Mitch leaned on the door jamb with the heel of his hand, smoking, appraising the besotted figure on the porch with amusement. Among these people of the sun Mitch was pale in his dark clothes. He gave off a quiet, blond power, a sort of contemptuous vigor, a pale relaxed strength. When a trapper or hunter or soldier motioned him inside for a drink, Mitch joined them, but spoke very few words. When he did speak, all in his vicinity were attentive.

Presently he went back to the doorway, and stepped onto the porch to be alone. The piercing eyes beneath his hat-brim shifted restlessly about the noisy black wetness outside, and he thought: 'Now I really feel free, since the rain. I wonder if my oilskins are still in the loft.' A negro boy came and gave him a cup of coffee. He went to the prostrate trapper on the porch, who was his father, dragged him to the wall by the collar, and propped him there. Tenderly he poured the hot liquid between his father's lips. The rheumy eyes opened and gazed past Mitch.

'My son's out of jail,' mumbled the old man.

'Out to stay,' said Mitch.

'I never been to jail in my life.'

'And look what a fine man you are!'

'Go to hell,' the old man blubbered.

'Same to you, o' man,' Mitch answered, wiping his father's tears.

Mitch left his father to dance with a girl. She was a Slavonian named Kottie — quite pretty in a square, heavy way. Kottie was the best orange packer and dancer up in Poverty Bend. She was a familiar figure at all lower river dances. She barely trod on the waiting tip of each clarinet phrase. Her fingers drooped over Mitch's shoulder, clinging to the fine warm serge. Mitch's eyes gleamed. He, too, was a good dancer. People made room for them. It was like old times.

'What you been doin' since you got back, you ain't been to see us, Mitch?' the girl asked. 'Mama mad.'

'Sitting around the shack. Resting.'

'Resting! You gone rest when you get in graveyard. You skinny, Mitch!'

'Little older, too.'

'You gone bring in more Chinks soon?'

'No.'

'I'm glad you got sense, fine fella lak you.'

'No more than I'll need. I'll need a lot of sense.'

'You seen Sister?'

'No. What's she doing with herself?'

'Take-caring of Mocco. You know the fadder die? Sister didn't wear no mourning, but they paint the purple trimming off the house, Mocco did. Lucky Sister got mule to work.'

'Claiborne.'

'Yah. She plants, works trees. Everybody talking. That

Mocco! All time he's sweating in the feet, never on face. Pimp! You better look out, Mitch! Sister goes with artist fellow. He's gone beat you out. A fine man, Mitch, so well-raise and smart. What's matter you and Sister? You got 'nother steady girl? She need you.'

'I can't help her.'

'Never goes nowhere, only walking levee with Mr. René.'

'How's your mamma?'

'She's got a gall-bladder. Mitch, I swear I could shake you good! Don't you wan' listen about Sister?'

'Sure. I'll listen. Go on.'

'Don't you love her no more?'

'Sure I love her.'

The music stopped and they drank wine served by André Laval from a barrel. Kottie was claimed by another partner. Mitch peeled his shrimp in the window. He watched the milling throng, but with an ear turned toward the trees standing in the rainy darkness. The roaring deluge had passed into a calm purr, with the soft labial patter of secret waters dripping in the dark. The Fort searchlight far above was sweeping the lonely sky. The wine Mitch had drunk all night had not yet reached his brain. He thought: 'I've lost the trick of drinking, and not used to women yet. I feel like a stranger, as if I'll never feel at home here again. I'm all changed inside. I'm more careful now. Stronger. The people respect me more than they did ... I've got to have a plan. What do I want to do? Something the sheriff and Coastguard will approve. What is it? Money and prominence? No! Find a task! That's it! Don't think — step in and begin. Step in anywhere and begin! Sister is right. I am a leader, or I've got to think so. How the hell does she know that?'

The dance was over. On leaden feet the throng flowed toward the doors. Good-nights were bidden and babies wailed. Mitch Holt walked briskly, moving faster than the other cur-

rent, until he caught up with Mateo Lucich, who was carrying
a sleeping child. Mateo was expensively dressed. He was making money these days. Mitch pulled his sleeve.

'Hey, Mateo!'

'Haw! Haw! Mitch Holt! I wan' see you. Come! Take
drink wid me! Here, ole woman, take bebby! Come, Mitch.
We drink!'

Mateo's body now was built of thick ovals, oval arms, oval
legs and torse, oval fingers no longer scratched or calloused.
He ordered two best whiskies. 'I want you comit over my place
for dinner Sunday. Bring your gul. Bring Sister. I gone fixit
nice turkey dinner myself and spaghetti lak you always lak it.
I got somethings to show you. Listen, you wan' buy nice boat?
Nice lumber schooner? Joost the boat you need, Mitch. I
make it cheap.'

'I'm broke.'

'Broke!'

'Broke and through hauling Chinks. Finished. I want work.
I want a job in one of your oyster sheds, Mateo.'

'You joke? You gone shuck oysters? It must be you drunk,
boy.'

'Try me. I want work.'

'Jes' Christ! I can't catch you no job but shucking. All da
foremans is my brudder-laws.' Mateo's smile was growing less
intimate. He considered it bad business, hiring one's friends.
And Mitch would want to do things his own way ...

'Put me to work shucking, then,' said Mitch.

Mateo drained his glass. His wife was calling him. 'If you
wan' try dat, sure! Come see me. Dat's gone be hard vork,
by goh.'

Mateo left without saying anything more about the dinner
invitation. He shook Mitch's hand negligently. Mitch felt a
smile spreading under his face.

'Some day he'll be working for me,' he thought.

Mocco could not sleep. The presence of death! Big familiar
Claiborne was stiffening downstairs in the dark. So big and
friendly and alive the mule had been, with ways of his own,
neighing impatiently for feed, stamping with thudding blows on
mosquito nights . . . The searchlight from the fort kept crossing
the sky, reflecting into his room its pale unearthly glow. He
left the door open between his and Sister's rooms. Her nearness comforted him. But after the rain she sank into her young
animal sleep, leaving him alone with the dim liquid utterances
of the river and grove. There were some jugs of orange wine
under his bed; and at last he sought comfort from one of them,
gulping the amber liquid until his stomach was full, and warm
oblivion swayed near. He carefully brushed his teeth, knelt
by the bed, and began his prayers:

> Oh, my God! I am heartily sorry for having offended Thee!
> I detest my sins because I dread the loss of Heaven and the
> pains of hell. Turn, then, most gracious advocate . . .

In the morning he awoke on the floor, with the grain of the
wood imprinted on his cheek, and his clothes wrinkled. Outside in the cold sunlight he heard birds quarreling among the
trees. He heard voices. He looked from the window. Sister
stood outside, barefooted, deep in green dew, talking to a man.
Mocco blinked, uncertain. He could not see well. His eyes
seemed to obstruct his vision. He saw there was a boat tied
to the river willows. It was the *Vicer Verser*, which belonged to
Sam Gruden, owner of a small tallow works down the river.
Gruden had come for Claiborne's remains.

'But no one knew!' Mocco thought. 'How did he find out
so soon?' There were no buzzards in the sky. 'How did Old
Buzzard Trailer know?'

Mocco went below and stood in the doorway, belching.
Sister and the tallow man faced each other, motionless. Mocco
sensed that one of them had just made a proposal and was now

waiting for the other to accept or reject. Three hens crossed
the grass and passed between the man and woman, searching.
One hen returned and plucked a bug from a weed between
Gruden's feet, then passed on. Gruden cocked his face backward and squinted at Mocco, grinning, aiming his long pro-
jecting teeth at Mocco and snickering.

'He was a right good mule, Claiborne,' Gruden said. 'A
good cotton mule, light but willin'. Huh? But he's gone now,
nothin' but a chunk of meat full of charbon. Now two six bits
is a good enough buy, but it's a better sell. Huh? I don't want
a thang he's got exceptin' that mess of tallow from his insides.
But yet I takes the hull mule! Gettin' him out yo' way and
payin' you for lettin' me do it. Huh? Mocco! Just thank!
Just thank! You'd have to burn him up! You dasn't leave
him on the road, and you dasn't chunk him in the river to the
sheriff deputy's knowledge — not with that-there anthrax-
sickness in him. You'd tote him in the canes and burn him.
And nobody'd lend you e'er horse nor pony to git him drug
out. Not with that-there charbon-sickness. Just thank! Huh?
I've got my overhead. Make it two-seventy-five!'

Sister spoke without moving her face, without taking her
eyes from the filthy visage with its oblique teeth. 'A while ago
you said you'd lose money at two-fifty,' she said. She picked
up a hoe and turned away, chopping the ground around her
roses. The roses were burdened with glassy dew. Mocco
slumped on the sill and held his head in his hands, shivering.
Gruden took off one of his shoes and knocked it upon his hand
to remove a fragment of clamshell. He was not impatient.
Neither was Sister. Mocco rubbed his numb scalp, thinking,
'How did he know Claiborne was dead?'

Gruden walked to the levee and remained there a while.
He returned and stood near Sister, thoughtfully swaying from
toes to heels. The sun was growing hot. Insects sparkled past.
Sister's hoe rose and fell, crunching. Gruden began monoto-

nously to tell off the various items of his factory overhead, checking off each item on a claw-like finger.

Sister thought: 'Three dollars will buy good shoes and stockings. After dinner I'll walk past the Holt shack. My ankles are attractive in white. The wind is good. It will keep my clothes pressed around my legs. Almost any girl looks nice to a man when she walks against the wind.'

A breeze from the region of the stable washed warmly over their three faces. Gruden's brow wrinkled alertly as his nostrils picked up the delicate smell of decaying flesh. He scrutinized Sister closely. Presently he saw her eyes straying toward the stable.

'Now you can see,' he went on, 'two seventy-five's a better sell than a buy. Huh? Huh?'

'Three dollars,' Sister said.

'Better leave me cawl my niggers and carry off that mess, git that mess out yo' way. Manure's heating it up, now. How 'bout it, Mocco? Cawl 'em? Cawl 'em?'

'Three dollars,' said Sister. She went to work in the rose bed nearer the river, where the rose-smell fought the mule-smell. Her face was white around her compressed lips. Another gust of wind brought the smell to Mocco, who spat, thinking, 'Maybe he passed here yesterday and smelled Claiborne getting sick.'

Gruden smiled and rubbed his hands, squinted at Sister and resumed his soft, unhurried discussion. For half an hour, while the stable odor grew ranker, he drawled on. Now he was deeply engrossed in his operating expenses. He spoke of fuel, labor, license, chemicals, freight. And each item engendered its detailed analysis, or a timely anecdote.

The earth began to reel under Sister. She set her teeth and tried to imprison her breathing.

'So I reckon two six bits'll break me even, Miss Nicolene,' Gruden drawled. 'What say? What say?'

'Three dollars.'

'Two eighty-five!'

'Three dollars.'

Gruden removed his hat and scratched his rhubarb-colored hair. Above his lifted eyebrows the skin puckered into waving lines which Sister compared with the shape of a postal cancellation mark.

'Throw in a bushel oranges!' Gruden cried impatiently. 'Them-there navel oranges, seedless.'

'Good!' said Sister. 'And you do the gathering.'

'And I pick out the tree!'

'And you furnish the sack!'

Gruden executed a low bow, placing his hat on his breast.

Sister hurried away, down the levee as fast as she could walk. Gruden abruptly raised his hand. Instantly, simultaneously, three ragged negroes sprang from among the levee willows, jumped in unison down the levee, and ran one behind another toward the stable, without a word or glance for the others, bare feet thudding eagerly.

Sister went to the store for the shoes and stockings. There were two crooked ruts in the muddy road. She walked in one of them, balancing herself with her arms. She saw a squirrel slide up the trunk of a hackberry. A frightened mocking-bird made a sound like a loud kiss. Sister climbed the revetment and sat in a mossy retreat to examine the new shoes. The smell of leather was pleasant, the dye and chemicals of newness. Children passed on the levee with ribbon in their combed hair, holding hands. There was a group of white ones, and behind them a melon-headed negro boy. They were going to church. Today Father Sam was conducting the yearly ritual of blessing the children's throats. 'Your noses will need blessing when you pass my house,' she thought. A wagon with one of its wheels wobbly passed. It stopped and the white children climbed in. The negro stood watching them with his big melon head resting on his spine. He had a flower in his fist, a large chrysanthemum.

'Rodney!' Sister called.

The negro boy came toward her bushes, searching.

'Rodney, do you want to work for me? Work half a day, and I'll teach you to read. You want to learn to read English?'

'Yossum. Ah kin read. Ah reads fum de readah. Ah can't read so much.'

Sister giggled. 'Come tomorrow, Rodney, hear? I want three boys. Listen, ask your brother Black and some other boy, hear? Early tomorrow morning. Setting lettuce and carrying out trash.'

'Yossum! I tell my maw.'

Rodney walked off, then came back and stood looking at the ground.

'White boys is gon' hit us wid shells,' he said.

'No!' said Sister. 'I won't let them. You be sure to come. Nobody's going to bother you. Don't forget, now.'

'Yossum.'

Sister put on the stockings and new shoes. She threw the old ones into the river, and went home. It was cloudy, but far ahead of her the world was bright with sun, bluish roofs, bright horses grazing, willows and hackberries misted over with pale green buds. So that the part of her which could travel far ahead was happy.

At home a man was waiting for her. He followed her into the house, put aside his pirogue paddle, and opened a little package. It was a lump of dental wax. The man had bitten into it, to make an impression.

'Nicolene, I god to send this wack to duh dentiz in town. Das a toot'-wack for making my new plate.'

'Yes, Romain. You want me to mail it back for you?'

'Ef I want you to mail it? Oui, I want you to write duh letter. How mudge you gone charge me?'

'Twenty cents.'

He gave her twenty cents, and she wrote the letter to the dentist.

After Romain left, Sister put another cardboard sign on the levee:

LETTERS WRITTEN   20¢ A PAGE

29

SISTER went down the road. Everything was settled. She was going to force herself back into Mitch Holt's life. 'This is free will,' she whispered, thinking of Grampaw, and his books, and René's illogical logic and Grampaw's search for the forces that make us what we are. She felt a strange kinship with a sodden log she saw floating far out in the river, as slowly as she herself moved, painfully revolving in the grasp of some capricious eddy, drawn beneath the waves at intervals by a perverse minor current. The afternoon had gone clouded and grave. There was no voice, no face, no footstep, no movement in leaf or blade. Nothing, nothing but the frowning clouds massed over the trembling river. How doggedly the drifting log kept its course toward the annihilating sea!

Now she passed the little cemetery snuggled in a curve of the levee, where her dead people lay. She recalled an All Saint's Day night long ago, when the tombs were lit by rows of candles. She and Mitch had met there. The cemetery had been filled with dark figures moving among the glowing white-washed tombs, or standing in little groups gossiping and laughing among the dead. Grampaw had brought her there. His big pockets had been stuffed with candles, and they had placed them around the top of the tomb. Mitch had come, looking for her, to bring her a funny paper. They had wandered to the rear and sat on an old untended grave, and seen the Scorpion in the sky. And he had led her behind another forgotten tomb. Among the dead, she had trembled deliciously. Mitch had taken her bony girl wrists and brought them behind her back, and kissed her, pressing her with his strange man-force against the tomb until she felt the cold masonry through her hair.

'You hurt!' she had whispered.

'Don't you like to be hurt?'

'Yes.'

'I like to hurt you.'

'Yes.'

'Can't you say anything but yes?'

'Someone is coming.'

'Let them come. Ain't you mine?'

'Yes.'

What was he like now? What had they done to him? She had often thought about prisons. 'What are they like, these strange houses? What do prisoners say to each other? When a new one comes in, are they glad to see him? Do they ask him, "What did *you* do?" Yes, that's what they ask him.'

Now she was within half a mile of the Holt shack. A gaunt negress on a porch was sweeping cobwebs. When she saw Sister her long black jaw dropped. She plodded out to the levee. 'Miss Nicolene! Well, Miss Nicolene!' She laughed affectionately, mounting the levee with her broom a blue-goose wing on a pole. They stood talking for a time. Sister resumed her journey, her step more buoyant and her face held higher. The negress had admired her starched white sunbonnet, and told her she resembled her mother when her mother was young. And she walked more lightly also because the sun had returned, gilding the slim willows, mottling the orchards with light. The levee was rounded softly green, with a rambling crown of pounded buff silt, and it wound away unhurriedly behind her, so familiar and yet so strange. Her solitary companion, the drifting log, was far down the river. She could barely see it bobbing seaward, winking faintly.

Presently a pirogue far ahead moved slowly out. Someone ashore had seen the drifting log. The pirogue's occupant was paddling with all his strength; the distant strokes flashed swiftly. Reaching another opening in the willows, Sister saw there were two pirogues going after the log, racing. The first man to reach the log would own it. Firewood had been scarce that winter. There had been little driftwood the previous spring.

She could see the Holt shanty ahead, built on tall poles on the river side of the levee. Men there were shouting encouragement to the two boatmen. She gained another clearing in the trees, and saw that one of the pirogues was manned by Mitch Holt himself. Her memory leapt backward across the years and recalled his paddling — the deep, long effortless strokes, with the paddle held the wrong way, too obliquely. A rush of hot panic ran through her. The thick-set shoulders above the spare waist! The shock of yellow hair! The defiant chin thrust out! The vital white speck battling grimly through the waves, all white with distance, gave off a sharp sparkle of energy. Mitch Holt! But he seemed to be struggling several yards behind his adversary.

Sister reached the Holt shack. The spectators, mostly ragged and barefooted mulattoes, were grouped at the water's edge. Old man Holt was under the shack chipping a log with an adze, hewing out a pirogue. There was a blue serge suit, newly pressed, and some of Mitch's underwear hanging on a line. The old man smiled at her and invited her down. He seemed to have expected her. He had been thinking this morning of Sister, wondering if she and Mitch had seen each other yet. She was the one for Mitch! She would keep him plump and tame. Heh! Heh! Her breasts were firm and generous. She was a deep one, deep as the river with its queer moods and its shady past. She would breed men with thick wrists and authoritative laughter.... A wise move, her taking the first step toward Mitch. Taking the first step, yes, but she'd make Mitch pay. Heh! Heh! Mitch would pay for that, the damned fool!

'Sit down and drink with me, Jolie!' he commanded.

The whiskey stung Sister's gullet pleasantly, and quickly soothed her blood. Out in the yellow river, Mitch's opponent had reached the log and was driving in the spike for towing. Mitch was farther downstream, resting, partly obscured by distance, no longer gleaming white, but drifting. She could feel how he loathed defeat. The old man plied his adze, talking between his careful muted strokes, and Sister sat quietly in the strong cypress fragrance, with her back to the scene on the river and her hands in her lap. The curly chips sailed about in red curves, falling about her feet like dropping embers. Through the trees the sun once found her dreaming face, touched it awhile, and passed on. Now for the first time since leaving Grampaw's camp she felt she had been transported to another world, so remote from the realm of books and ideas and decorous talk, that the other might never have existed.

'Thirty-nine year I've waited for this old sucker to get big-around enough for a good pirogue!' said the old man. 'You remember him, growing right over there where you see the stump. You remember. Since before Mitchell was born I've had my eye on him. As pretty a grain and mellow a smell as you'd want. That wood's got body. You smell it? Lots of body. Here's Mitch now. Git on a jacket, Mitch, you're sweating bullets. Who won the race? Did you git the log?'

'Sure, I got it,' Mitch answered.

'Was it cypress? Here's a lady I want you to meet. Come here.'

'Why hello, Sister!' Mitch said under his breath. She saw a fire leap into his eyes.

'Hey, Mitch!' she greeted him softly.

He walked past her. He sat on another log, breathing heavily. He kicked at the ground, then examined the palms of his hands. 'What are you doing 'way down here, Sister?' he asked, but did not wait for her to answer. 'Yes, o' man, it was cypress. Better piece than you've got there. Stouter.'

'Better my tail!' said the old man. 'They don't grow no better. Where is it? Did you get it?'

'Yes. I got it taken away from me. I see where I've got to learn to paddle again. Got any coffee made? Some coffee, Sister? No! No liquor for me o' man, I'd rather coffee. I'm tired and I don't want to feel good.'

'Too bad about you. Well, there's no coffee.'

'Sister'll make us some. I'm going to look after the pirogue. There's a fruiter coming, throwing swells high as a horse.'

Later Sister and Mitch sat facing each other up in the shack. Sister's arms formed a pensive triangle with the table, her chin resting on the point. Mitch sipped his coffee from a saucer. He gazed through the window, hard and unseeing, while he balanced the saucer delicately on his fingers. She could see part of the hard strange face reflected in the saucer, because the dying sun illumined the face into a mask of copper, sweat-polished. She could not determine wherein the face was strange. The lines falling downward from the nostrils were deeper, the eyes had a cloudless blue quality of infinity, bitter unguessed infinity. The mouth ... ah, what had they done to him? She kept swallowing back the tears. The hair by his ears was ashen, a lower tooth was gone. But it was not these little alterations that wrought the nameless change. It was something beyond. Before prison, Mitch had always a joke. They had spent much time teasing each other. It was not that he was indifferent to her. He seemed indifferent to everything else, and yet to be stubbornly husbanding some secret unutterable aim which alone kept him moving, talking, vital.

'I could tell you a lot,' he said again, with a new kind of crooked smile.

Seeing his eyes, she knew he would not. What did he want? What did he need? Should she urge him to tell?

'So you've got a baby,' he said.

'Yes. A son.'

'What about that?'

'About the baby?'

'Sure. The baby and the fellow and . . . who he happens to be, maybe.'

'I don't know much about him, Mitch. There's no use in talking about that.'

'Suit yourself. Why not? We're pretty good friends.'

Sister was getting cold. Swallowing her bit of liquor she poured more. The old man below had quit his hacking, and gone up the levee to leave them alone.

'I thought we'd forget what happened to us and start over, Mitchell. I'm grown up now, and . . .'

'Start what over?'

'Well . . . living, I suppose.'

'I've been living right along. Haven't you? How do you mean start over? Get married, you mean?'

'Well . . .'

'Hell no! Not now.'

'Not yet?'

'Well, not yet. You women take the cake. Think a minute. Here I am. What have I got that you could want? Name me one thing. One measly damned thing you'd want. I've been here five days. I can't paddle a pirogue yet. Haven't even looked in my gear locker.' He tossed her a handkerchief, and she wiped her cheeks, holding her peace.

Pride, love, contempt, the need to survive — all had merged in a vague whirl in her brain. The man spat through the window and tugged at his belt. Mitch Holt. Mitch Holt, the thing he was called, it hissed and barked across one's tongue like a sneered epithet. And she had thought it wonderful to have him back again, his home so close to hers! To hear him calling his dogs, to pass his shack on cold nights and smell his venison broiling!

The immaculate white fruit liner passed, cleaving the silence, close to shore, dazzlingly unreal with its empty decks, like a piece of property sliding by in a play. In a moment its breakers were falling upon the shore with a deafening growl.

'This other fellow. Did he offer to marry?' Mitch asked.

Sister would not answer.

'Who was he, then?'

'A stranger, I told you. Beached for a night. He went back, somewhere in the mountains, he and his lugger.'

'So he owned a lugger! Go ahead. How did it happen? I'm curious. I never got you myself, and I'd like to take my hat off to him. What kind of medicine or presents did he use?'

Sister murmured, 'Words.'

Sister told the story. She did not once look at Mitch. With a pencil she drew on the margin of a newspaper random figures, squares, triangles, circles, and blacked them in. She and Mitch watched the moving pencil, giving as much attention to the irrevocable darkening of the figures as to the tale's calm flow. Mitch noticed Sister's hands were roughened, man-shaped — not particularly large but cast in a masculine mold, fingers somewhat blunt, wrist thickened, and at the base of the thumb a rounded pad of muscle from grasping handles or wielding tools. Her voice had changed to fit the grown body, and it was quiet, controlled, with hardly any Slavonic accent.

Finishing her story, she waited, all alert, covertly scanning his face for some sign, some token of emotion or concern. Mitch stared idly at the figures on the newspaper, as if his mind had branched off into another path. Behind her mask Sister was beginning to rage, to loathe this man's insufferable power of infuriating her without lifting a finger. It was utterly beyond conception. The man seemed to have grown wooden, inhuman. He turned and looked at her briefly, his face a graven matrix in the gloom, diffusing on the side nearest the window a hard sheen, deeply bitten by the stony hollows of restraint. His eyes were alive with glittering savagery and amusement.

'I'll walk up and have supper with you,' he said shortly, and stood up.

'There's nothing to eat,' she said.

'I'll get something at the store. Let's get out of here. I'm hungry as a shark.'

They walked up the crooked road, past many old familiar spots the lapsing seasons had not marred.

'So you're in a fix,' said Mitch. 'Nothing to eat, eh?'

'Never mind about that.'

'We've got to talk about something.'

'Just as you say, then. Yes, I'm in a fix, and that's why I came.'

'That's the way to talk!' Mitch held out his hand. 'Put it here!' They shook hands. Sister was smiling now.

'It's nice to be back!' Mitch said. He took her hand and swung it. Sister was shaking all over with sobs. She allowed him to put his arm around her and squeeze her breast. 'Don't cry,' he said. 'Everything will be all right.' He looked behind them to see if anyone was on the road, and crushed her to him, kissing her mouth.

'What do you — think of it all, Mitch?' she asked. 'You haven't said a word.'

'What's the good of words now?'

'Aren't you interested at all in that?'

'Sure. A nice story. You've learned how to talk, Jolie. Who gave you all those words?'

'You don't think I'm — corrupt?'

'That's against the rules, asking me that. Do you feel corrupt? You sure don't look it. What do I care if they say the kid's mine? I don't expect any more from you than I can give you. I'll take care of the kid, and damned well, when the time comes. We'll get married when the time comes. No hurry. You can always add salt to the soup, but you can't take it out. You had a chance once. If you had married me I would have been more careful and not got caught. It's your fault, in a way. Now you'll have to wait, like I've got to. It might be worth your while. I've been studying, and I'm going to see about this country needing a leader as you say. You've got to wait. Let's clear away all the fancy words and look at this thing straight. The way I see it, you need someone to look after you, and I need someone. There's no one else here for you to marry, and there's no one else for me. You haven't been sleeping with this artist they talk about?'

Sister shook her head.

'Fair enough! Well, you need a husband and I need a wife and we both need a home. Right?'

'Right.'

A man was coming down the road toward them.

'Wait,' said Mitch. 'I want to talk to Cooney on business.' The other man was a minor politician. He carried an armful of political posters which he was attaching to buildings and trees. While the two men talked, Sister walked on and sat on a stump. She watched Mitch standing in the gathering dusk engrossed in alien talk, obviously all unmindful of her. She saw the deferential manner in which Cooney behaved toward Mitch. Who was this stranger, Mitch Holt? Stranger, a broken man, and yet somehow more whole?

She waited, completely ignored by both men, for at least twenty minutes. It was getting dark.

'Mitch, I'm going!' she called.

'Wait!' he answered. 'I'll be right along.'

'Never mind!' she shouted. Mitch put his hands on his hips and glared at her, then turned his back to her. Sister started toward the store in a half run. In a little while she looked back. Mitch had not moved. She continued up the road, all her fighting blood aroused.

She stopped in the store and bought a pound of rice and some sugar, with which to make supper.

Next day she borrowed an ox from one of her cousins, and plowed in the orchard. Over and over during the day she recalled Mitch's words of the day before. Her pride was hurt, but there was something inspiriting about his frank, clean-cut, masculine summing up of the situation. She was filled with courage and a sort of gay and carefree resignation. It was gratifying, too, to know that her encouraging letters to Mitch in prison had worked a change in him.

Mocco came home in the evening with an armful of groceries. He announced that he had a job planting grass on the new levee in Venice. The work would last a week.

René Davidson called that night, and the three sat about the fire. Sister had received an order for a net, and she knitted the whole evening, sunk into herself, only occasionally talking to René. Mocco was reading a magazine with a sombreroed horseman on its cover. René opened a letter.

'My dealer writes to say one of my colors has become the rage in New York,' he said. 'It seems a dress designer saw the color of the dried marsh grass in a picture of mine and matched it in dye and called it Marsh Yellow. He used the color in one of his creations, and it took the fancy of the public.'

'How wonderful!' Sister exclaimed.

René sat on a deerskin on the floor and lit his pipe. The smoke ascended like a blue blossom swaying on a stem.

'Are you going to visit New York soon?' Sister asked.

'Not just yet. I've found Unga January. I'm doing a portrait of her. I think she's remarkably handsome.'

'I haven't seen her for some years. I wish you'd tell her I'll pull up to see her soon.'

'She told me to tell you that same thing.'

'I saw Mitch Holt today, Sis,' said Mocco.

'I saw him too,' Sister answered. She pulled a knot and threw another stitch. René watched her narrowly. Love and animosity flared together in his heart. The woman seemed unduly tranquil tonight, throwing her quick, accurate stitches, poised so neatly in her chair. Observing her closely, René thought he detected in her a change, both in person and manner.

'I should like to meet your friend Holt,' he said.

Sister seemed to be rather startled. She looked at René with lifted eyebrows. 'Would you, René? You'll meet him soon. But I don't think you'll like him.'

'Why not? Why shouldn't I?'

'Just so.'

'But *why?* Granting I *want* to like him, why shouldn't I? *You* like him.'

'But I know him well. And I'm a woman.'

René bit his lip and glowered at the fire. He wished they were back in the oyster village, back in the solitude of the marshes. This damnable change in Sister! And so many people always about. Why didn't Mocco leave them alone? On his last visit, too, there had been a visitor, some stupid woman. And the river outside, so big and sluggish in its power, never still, never quiet.

30

AFTER Mocco's job expired the Kalaviches lived a lean month. Sister was very thin. Occasionally she made a few dimes writing letters for illiterate people, or mending a net— enough to buy cornmeal and rice; and oranges were plentiful. She ate the oranges, but a fare of beans and rice sickened her, and sometimes she would not eat them. She had not seen or heard from Mitch Holt since the day she had gone to see him. Mitch was working hard in the cannery over the river, everyone said. He was living there. Sometimes she searched for him along the opposite levee with the telescope. She did not mind waiting. She was slowly gaining some headway in her own work. Half of the orange grove was clear of weeds and creepers, the trees hoed for the first time in years.

Mocco had fallen into utter degradation. He borrowed money of anyone who would lend, and paid visits to distant relatives during meal time. He came in late at night, after Sister was abed, and left his room furtively in early morning, while she was afield. He had grown too fat for his clothes, and frequently suffered digestive disturbances and dreadful headaches.

Once while watching the soldiers drilling at Fort Saint Philip, Mocco was seized with a sudden feeling of hunger and faintness. The colored lights shaped like saw-teeth began to form in the corners of his eyes. They were a brilliant blue and gold, dancing. Mocco left the parade ground and hurried down the levee toward Dutch Scenery. He would go to Unga January's houseboat, where he would doubtless find food to stay his dreadful weakness.

Unga lived in a stranded houseboat halfway between Dutch Scenery and the Fort. She was earning a livelihood by selling pounded red brick, which fishermen used to clean their lugger decks, and housewives bought for sprinkling on their doorsteps on holidays. There was an old ammunition magazine near-by, abandoned by the Government and now inhabited only by snakes and owls. With her bare hands Unga had clawed great ragged holes in the moist red walls of the crumbling structure, carrying away the bricks day by day.

Mocco traced a devious path through the dense tangle of creepers surrounding the houseboat. A drowsy hound under a tree beat the sand with his tail. Mocco leaned against the cistern, listening, noting the plugged-up holes in the cistern where Unga had once sent a charge of buckshot after a night intruder, and let out all the water.

Mocco smelled roasting pork.

'She's expecting company,' he thought. 'The plankwalk is scrubbed cleaner than I've ever seen it before.' He looked toward the driftwood pig-sty. It was empty. Unga was cooking her pig! Mocco remembered Agnes, the little sow, a compact, spotted cylinder of wandering fat, armored in dried mud, forever grunting along the levee, through the ditches, under houses and out again, with her blunt snout to the ground, a mass of stubborn gluttony so densely packed with fat that one imagined a pin pricking her hide would cause a fearful explosion. Once, some boys had wounded a rattlesnake in the road; and Mocco had seen Agnes pry her way through the legs of the bystanders, knocking two children down, seize the reptile and squirm off, squealing under the sticks that belabored her, but doggedly holding the snake, whose fangs were now buried in her jowl.

Peering into the brown crypt that was Unga's kitchen, Mocco saw the outline of the woman's lithe, rather angular body stooped at her charcoal furnace over the golden coals she loved to kindle. For a moment he watched the strong gathered hunch of female back and shoulders, the diaphanous sleeve holding a large fork of pork over the embers. But on the table lay one of the animal's joints. It was crisp and brown, varnished over with a glistening coat of coagulated juices. At the end of the bone, heavy beads of amber marrow had congealed. Mocco's hunger coiled more tightly about his vitals. In his mouth the saliva stirred, and a frown of suffering appeared on his face. He was famished to the point of quaking, and a dull feeling of dissolution possessed him. He felt he must have a piece of the meat; but he could not accept it from a negress. He had hoped Unga would be away.

He crept into the trees and selected a long stick of wood. With this he stole to the bedroom window. Unga's baby lay asleep in a cantaloupe crate. The child was always zealously guarded from the sun. It was bluish white, lying naked with fists clenched over its enormous head, bluish vulva gaping extraordinarily large, legs drawn up like a swimming frog's. Mocco raised the stick and was about to lean into the window when he saw René Davidson sitting crosslegged on the kitchen floor making a picture of Unga at the furnace. Mocco twisted his fat body out of sight, and sought protection behind a fig tree. The sensation of dissolution, the light and airy feeling of befuddlement, completely unmanned him. He did not know how long he sat beneath the tree. Once he heard footsteps approaching. René Davidson passed close by him without seeing him, carrying an empty bottle, going to the store for wine. Mocco roused himself and took hold of the stick.

At the bedroom window he reached in and viciously prodded the baby in the armpit. He was back at the kitchen door when

the awakened baby began to yell. Hearing Unga's bare feet
thump into the adjoining room, Mocco entered the kitchen
tiptoe. As he was reaching for the joint of meat on the table,
he heard the hound in the doorway growl softly. He jerked his
hand back and sat casually in a chair. The dog, watching him
with its mournful eyes, stopped growling and signaled friendship with its tail. Unga was standing in the bedroom door,
motionless, with one foot behind her, deep eyes filmed with
fear, the baby audibly gulping her tawny breast.

'I never hear you come in,' she said.

'That straw on the levee is ankle deep,' Mocco said.

'Oui. Dey was spread it yistiddy. Fanny's Noel, him, he
is sick negs door. How Sister is?'

'Fine. What's the matter with you two? You haven't seen
each other yet?'

'I dawn knaw. I dawn knaw whad's duh matter.'

'She says that too.' Mocco felt at the moment that everybody in the world hated everybody else. 'You know Mitch
Holt is back?'

Mocco's eyes would return to the meat on the table. With
something of a timid caress his gaze prowled about the conical
shape of the roasted limb, realizing each gleaming ridge and
hollow of its surface, dwelling long on each shred of scorched
tissue. He was unbearably conscious of the strong odor of
crisped meat.

'Midge Holt is fine man,' said Unga. 'All duh white guls
wants him. Whad mo' a woman can ax? Me, I hopes dey ged
married.'

'They will, if she doesn't marry René.'

A sharp light sprang into Unga's eyes, and the blood dyed
her face a darker hue. She dropped her gaze, touched the
baby's hair. 'So she wants René!' Mocco thought.

Unga asked, 'He loves her, Mr. René?'

'He wants her — been wanting her. I don't understand it.

He does nothing about it. He told me long time ago anybody chases women will never chase anything worth while.'

Unga gave a mirthless laugh. 'Look!' she said. 'He makes my pitcha. It is gone go to New York, my pitcha.' After a pause Unga said, 'Dey say you still talk aboud going to New Orlean'.'

'The river went up another foot last night,' Mocco said.

'Whad you doing for living?' Unga asked.

'Living on my interest.'

Unga shrugged. A look of contempt crossed her features.

'You asked me that Sunday,' said Mocco.

'*Pardon!* I dawn mean ——'

'Everybody seems worried about me.' Mocco left his chair and went to the door. Unga's baby was sleeping. She turned toward the bedroom.

'Come back again, Mocco,' she said, and disappeared.

Mocco grasped the joint of pork from the platter. He rubbed its wet under-surface across the white tablecloth, to make it appear the cat had dragged it off. He called a gruff farewell and left with the meat. He went toward Dutch Scenery. He walked in the trees, where René would not be encountered. He sat and devoured a portion of the pork, and wrapping the remainder in Spanish moss, set out for the village.

The whiskey drummer was buying drinks in Mateo Lucich's place for a gathering of young fishermen. Mocco joined them, and had half a dozen drinks. He produced the joint of pork, and someone bought some crackers. They all had a jolly time eating and drinking. Mocco drank wine. After a while their talk drifted to the inevitable topic, teasing Mocco about going to the city.

'How you lak city last wik, Mocco?' asked one.

'None of your business!'

'Did he went to town laz wik?' asked a Cajin.

'Sure! Eh, Mocco? Tell us about putty city.'

'Yah! Tell us! You see putty gels?'

'You quit beeg job in city, Mocco?'

'No! He vork hard, come home for vacation.'

Mocco left the place in a storm of laughter. The whole world was against him. He was still furiously angered at Unga January because he had stolen her meat. He walked down the levee for a long time, muttering and working himself into a drunken frenzy, raising his fists as his father used to do. It seemed that everywhere he looked in the village, there was a laughing face. He wept. He laughed. He cursed.

As he left behind him the peaceful village and staggered on farther, the earth ahead flattened out into an endless stretch of bright green marsh. The grandeur of the piled clouds frightened him. He cursed the marsh. To him it signified the end. It was waiting to receive his body, to suck him down and down into oblivion. Yet he dared not retrace his steps. He lifted his bloated face toward the majestic heavens. He raised his hands and beat them against his head.

Someone was coming. Mocco sat on the grass, dried his eyes on his sleeve, and with his body swaying from side to side watched in a dull haze the approaching figure, which was that of a small boy. The child had a sunny face, shining like an apparition, round and rosy with small, dark, innocent eyes, and carried a little net on his shoulder. He wore goatskin breeches of white and brown, and his bare legs were clean and lightly powdered with glittering river silt. And as Mocco looked at him swaying forward, he appeared surrounded by a large frame or halo of brightly tinted, zigzagging colors.

'Where are you going, little boy?' Mocco asked.

'Nowhere,' the child answered, backing away a respectful distance.

'I'm not going to hurt you. Do you know me?'

'No, sir.'

'Well, I'm the last of the Kalavich's. Can you remember that? I'm a victim of myself. Are you an altar-boy? Do you go to church?'

'No, sir.' The boy stood very erectly with bare feet firmly planted, and a manly, upright look in his face.

'Where do you live?'

'With my folks in the houseboat yonder.' He raised his arm and pointed. This gesture seemed very stern and irrevocable to Mocco. The dark, knowing gaze of the boy never once turned from Mocco's face. The tears suddenly poured down Mocco's face. The boy stood like an image, gazing downward, unblinking.

'Do you want some root-beer?' he suddenly asked Mocco.

Mocco was sobbing horribly. He raised his woeful, blood-shot eyes to the boy. 'What?'

'Root-beer. My mother makes root-beer. She'll give you some.' The boy again pointed the irrevocable finger. Mocco looked down the river and saw the houseboat. After regaining composure, he took the child's hand, and together they proceeded down the path, Mocco staggering and dragging the child from side to side.

'What's your name?' Mocco asked.

'Charles Millings.'

'I'll call you Charlsey. Mine's Mocco. I'm a contractor.'

'Did somebody hurt you?' the boy asked.

'Yes. Somebody hurt me.'

They reached the houseboat, both staggering. A woman opened the door. She was quite beautiful. 'Charles!' she called. 'Come in here right away! What's the matter?'

The boy took his hand out of Mocco's, and went up to the woman in the doorway. 'What are you doing, bringing a dirty tramp around here?' the woman asked. The two went inside. The door closed.

Mocco turned away, back toward Dutch Scenery. Once

he stopped, swaying. He looked back at the houseboat. The boy's face was in the window, watching him gravely. He stumbled on, and began to weep again.

When he returned to Mateo's saloon, the young fishermen were waiting for him. They were all drunk. They plied Mocco with more whiskey. They did not tease him, but spoke kindly to him, winking at one another behind his back. Mocco drank until his head fell upon his crossed arms.

When he was completely unconscious, they carried him out to the wharf, where a smoking towboat was tied up, which had come to the landing to tow a barge to New Orleans. The jokesters bore Mocco over the tug's deck and into the barge. The captain of the tug leaned from his pilothouse and laughed loudly. The fishermen placed Mocco on a bed of old sacks and gleefully ran ashore.

'Get him a good job!' someone called to the tug captain.

The tug cast off and steamed up the river toward New Orleans with the barge.

When Mateo Lucich heard about the prank he was angry. He chased the drunken fishermen away, and sent a man over the river in a skiff to tell Sister Mocco had decided to go to New Orleans.

31

THE ox was tractable and slow. For a yoke Sister used Claiborne's collar turned upside down. The new cultivator gave a feeling of newness to her toil. A three-day rainstorm stopped her field work, but she used this time indoors making three nets to display on the end of the wharf, two deep shrimp nets and a crab-net. She crossed the poles of the shrimp nets and nailed them, and hung the round crab-net in the center of the cross. She put a price sign on the wharf, large enough to be seen by passing boatmen. In good weather this was her night work, making nets — alone or with René sitting near, talking or reading to her. Or he would watch her teaching the little negroes to read by the fire.

From time to time Pretty John brought her news of Mitch Holt, who was now foreman of the oyster shuckers of Mateo Lucich. Mitch was said to be interested in his job, the most competent workman on the lower river. Sister did not mind waiting. Waiting was part of her forthcoming marriage. Occasionally, when she had money, she would fix up a particularly tempting meal and send it over to him, carrying it at the right time to the cook of the New Orleans packet, who would keep it warm on his range until the boat reached Dutch Scenery.

René frequently passed by to see her during the day. There was a false spring. The orange trees bloomed out a few flowers. The redbirds sang the songs of courting. René would walk down into the orchard where Sister was cultivating her lettuce between the trees. A schooner, the *Hail Mary*, was tied up at Sister's Landing, as it was now known. René carried himself erect, and his eyes shone with suppressed excitement. 'He has done another picture that pleases him.' Sister thought. René hailed her, then lounged against a tree, watching her work, admiring the huge ox. René was learning how to relax. Very often these days he spent half an hour in idleness, strolling the water's edge, or watching some levee-menders at work.

He went and leaned against the warm dome of Sister's clay bread-oven, passing his hand over and over its smoothness. In the packing shed, three little negroes were packing oranges to be shipped on the waiting schooner. Hearing René cough, they appeared in the doorway holding partly wrapped fruit, and watched him out of their dark bright eyes. It was so quiet that René could hear plainly the gnashing of dice aboard the schooner in the river, and the voices of the gamesters naming their points. He turned and studied the heavy effortless movements of the ox. He was always attracted by animals, and his mind searched for the secret of their grave dignity. He seldom passed a horse or dog without visualizing the skeleton beneath. 'Woman and ox,' he thought. 'Ox and girl.' Once Sister stopped near him to mend with her hands a part of a row where the cultivator had unearthed some lettuce roots.

'You are a good farmer,' he said.

'Yes, thanks. These will be ready for shipment soon, if we don't get any heavy frost. Money, René, money! The late oranges are bringing three dollars now.'

'What about Mocco?'

'Oh, I had a letter yesterday. He's been working for a commission merchant on the wharf. He's going in the office next week.'

René loved the peace of Sister's orchard. The lettuce was indeed beginning to hide its cool white hearts, shrinking into itself, rank after rank of pale brave buds, unharmed by frosts. It was tender, yet deeply rooted and brave with Sister's care, her knowledge and her toil. The strong cunning woman body was bowed in tough compact curves near his feet. The brown soily fingers kneading the earth found a frightened worm, and prodded it back home among the roots.

'You like this work, don't you?' he asked.

'I'd rather be inside making green curtains, and hearing my guavas boiling, and powdering my baby's legs, if he were a baby again.'

René frowned when she mentioned the baby. 'But this work — don't you like it?'

'Oh, yes!'

Suddenly his heart sank, to see her contented like a peasant, imitating the selfless rhythms of the ox, thinking of babies. . . . At the orchard's margin a redbird fluttered from the thyme. . . . The evening was unbearably sad. Back came his old animosity toward Sister, her body melting from rhythm to rhythm with unconscious grace. 'Her's and Unga's bodies are as different as water and stone,' he thought. 'Unga's body fairly paints itself.' He saw Sister smiling at him. She knew he was analyzing again. She could always detect it in his face.

'Why do you like this work?' he asked.

'Please don't begin to "why" me now, René. I don't care to think. You'll get me in the habit of taking myself apart again, and it's so hard to put myself back together. Well — I'm satisfied, I think. Since there's no more Mocco to depend on, I can better manage to get food. I've got a shrimp trap in the river and lots of cornmeal to bait it with. I've saved the beehives from the ants. There's plenty of fruit and *kostric* for salad. And I've found a redfish hole in the back Bay. And it's better — working with the ox.'

René thought: 'What is changing her? This accursed quiescence! Does it come from working with the ox?'

On the schooner a bell struck several times. Coffee was ready. The little negroes burst from the packing shed and scampered up and over the levee. Sister loosened the ox and led it to a patch of grass. René followed her to the schooner, thinking: 'The ox looks neither backward nor ahead. He moves, irresistibly stationary, pushing the rows behind him, as soft and cruel as the seasons. Lonely. He disdains the mandate to beget. What does he care about bawling calves or plump cows waiting in heat?'

On the schooner they had coffee and crisp oaten cakes with old Captain George-Pete. The little negroes had their coffee in the galley.

'Suppose ef I see Mocco in town?' asked the old captain. 'Whad I mus' tell him, Sister?'

'Tell him what you saw here. I am well and getting along. Tell him to see a good doctor about his stomach.'

'Stomach! But he ain't sick, dat boy! I see him every trip on duh wharf and he look busy and happy, him. Me, I don't blame him from not farming duh ground. I was a farmer, too. Fighting duh frost and duh drainage, and duh Bon Dieu, Him, he's follow duh plow and sow weeds behind you. Das a shame to see you out dere making bean. When you gone get married, you and Midge? Big Mateo give him foreman. Is what you call a *man*, dat Midge Holt. Everybody on duh river from duh Old Jump to Home Place ax dat question from me — when you get married.'

'We don't know,' Sister answered. 'We don't know when. They know as much as we do. Tell them we're waiting for the proper season.'

'Duh proper sizzon?'

'Yes.'

The captain blinked, sucking his pipe. Sister laughed, and reached over to tickle the coils of his fat belly. Sister did not look at René's face but the captain did. He saw the color sink out of it. He said nothing. He was an old man. For thirty years he had been taking the Kalavich fruit to market. He could remember when the place had been a bustling, well-kept home managed by old Wolfgang's wife while Wolfgang was fishing oysters on his beds over the river. The captain remembered when Sister as a brown tot had taken coffee and cakes in this same cabin, sitting large-eyed and dark beneath this same old engraving of a startled roebuck, listening to the exchange of river gossip, or a discussion of young Mitch Holt's latest escapade.

Sister finished her last cake dreamily, nibbling the brittle edge and discarding the middle. Sitting with her back to René, she did not know he had left the cabin until he called her outside. They sat on a tobacco hogshead near the dice-game. Captain George-Pete dozed in his chair inside. The three little negroes had not yet returned to work. They were playing on the levee, throwing dust over one another. Sister clapped her hands loudly at them. They turned startled black faces toward her, laughed, and ran back to their work. Sister smiled.

'I've got important news,' said René.

'You're going to New York!'

'No. I've sold — my dealer sold six of my pictures.'

'René! Six!' She clutched his arm impulsively. René could not share her joy. He was dreadfully embarrassed. 'Which ones?' she asked.

'The canal in the canebrakes ——'

'Oh, I *knew* you'd sell it!'

'A negro head, two portraits of Unga, the cannery roofs, the boat in the willows.'

'But *six!* I'm so proud! Who bought them?'

'Oh ... some collector. I don't know.'

'Well I'll be damned! Imagine your not caring!'

'That's meaningless. He paid two hundred each for five of them, three hundred for the canal thing.'

'The one you did after the storm, after you forgot about art for a whole day.'

'I've got thirteen hundred dollars. Look!' He brought out the money, as proud as a boy, now. But it looked so strange, the money in the grasp of his delicate, nervous fingers.

'It's all messed up,' said Sister. '*Unrumple* it, René!'

The dice players stared incredulously. Sister herself had never seen a hundred-dollar bill before. It was like magic, that a piece of paper representing so many potential things should be carried about.

She must trip wildly in and awaken the old captain. 'Wake up, sleepy-head! Look! Thirteen hundred dollars! René is rich! Hooray! All hands on deck! René sold six pictures! Six Davidsons! Speculators! Davidsons! Hundred dollar bills! Fame and fortune!'

The captain opened a bottle of fine Irish whiskey, and they all drank to the event, even the roustabouts crowding round with their tin cups. Sister ran into the house to get a folio of René's stray watercolors for the captain to see. The pictures puzzled and fascinated the old man, the scenes of shores and buoys and driftwood. Among these was a picture, an abstraction, filled with daring splotches and distortions, painted long ago before he had evolved his present manner. René's attention was arrested by this one suddenly appearing among the others. The contrast thrilled him. Was it merely the contrast? He did not know. He reached out and took the picture. He wanted to study it later, alone.

'That's an old one,' Sister told the captain. 'Not as good as the others, eh, René?'

René rolled the picture into a tube. 'I'm not sure of that,' he said, with a confused look. 'It may be the best picture of all. I want to take it with me.' He stood by thoughtfully.

He told them he must leave. He had an important letter to write before the mailboat went up.

'Be sure to come back for supper!' Sister insisted.

He walked homeward with slow, jerky steps, frowning, biting his lip. The little fiddler crabs swarmed on the levee like busy vermin, thick as a carpet splitting in two before his approach. He kicked at them petulantly. Fleeing through the grass, they produced a loud dry rustle.

Sister had vexed him again. Her enthusiasm about the sale of his pictures, the thought of her radiant abandon, the lovely selflessness of her joy, caused an icy thread of hostility to dart through his breast. He had known it would be so. He had known that when he told her the news, she would give way to pure animal delight. He remembered her working with the ox, the unstudied gracefulness of her forging legs and grasping hands. He remembered her laughing in the lightning on the boat during the storm. And these memories, hateful and yet cherished, added to the inexplicable chill of animosity which possessed him. He thought, 'The primordial mists and slimes! The loathsome twisted roots! The calcined dunes of bleaching shells! She is in league with the ancient Gulf, the four-clawed delta, the fabulous Spanish Main!'

A stout, handsome woman wearing sharkskin shoes and balancing on her head a big basket of wild salad leaves passed him. Behind her were seven children. He made way and allowed them all to pass. Then he turned and looked behind. They were all standing there looking back at him, their dark, velvety eyes fixed upon him with friendly curiosity. He had to smile at their soft, dark tranquility. And for a moment his nerves were soothed. At the village store, some trappers were playing, throwing their skinning-knives at a target. Their laughter was thrown into the sky — a sudden lifting of the rows of bright gold teeth.

How placid **was** the evening — the orange trees smelling faintly of citrus oils; tall, unruffled threads of smoke issuing from every chimney; the jaws of the recumbent levee cattle revolving in a suave, unhurried rhythm! René stopped once to watch some cedar waxwings perched in a row upon a hackberry branch, breaking off clusters of the berries and passing them down the line, each bird delicately detaching a berry before passing the cluster on.

His nerves were soothed. The thorn in his heart was forgotten.

At home in his room, he unrolled the impressionistic picture he had taken from the others on the schooner. He tacked it to the wall in his room. He examined it from many angles — with his shade drawn, partly drawn, fully raised. Then he lay on his feather mattress on the floor with his hands behind his head and studied the picture for a long time, trying to recapture or to remember the mood in which the picture had been created ..

Later, he returned to the Kalavich house. He had resolved to defer the return until next day. But his love, or hatred, or some perverse craving for self-torture, drove him back against his will. It was a rare, sweetly pastoral evening, soft with color and smells, slow bended figures working far off in the truck fields, and a thin, motionless blue mist drawn over the river's waveless surface. Sister's fruit had been boxed and loaded on the schooner. There was no wind for sailing. The schooner's crew, harnessed to ropes fastened to the masts, and their thick bodies laboring obliquely along the shore, were slowly dragging the craft upstream, singing a doleful negro song as they marched.

René walked up to Sister on the wharf. She had finished her cultivating, and changed her overalls for a starched white house dress with red figures. Her lovely unpaintable presence glorified the dying day, lent a feeling of timeless poignancy to the row of dark figures lugging the schooner upstream, to the brooding sky washed with saffron, and the immense mistiness of the river. She stood waving her hand to Captain George-Pete at the tiller of the distant schooner.

'Do you wish you were going with them?' René asked, standing at her back.

He saw her shoulders slightly fall. 'What good is it — wishing?'

'Do you feel like traveling?'

He heard her catch her breath, saw her raise her face. 'What?' she asked in a queer unnatural tone — not turning to face him, but with her face still lifted, as though straining to hear a distant call.

'Traveling,' he repeated. 'I say would you like to travel?'

'Travel?' she echoed in the same low, remote voice. 'Travel?'

'Yes.'

'Where — travel? Where?'

'Anywhere. North. Tomorrow.'

Still she kept her back to him, her face toward the receding schooner, the savage wail of the roustabouts' song. 'What do you mean — north? Where — north?' It was the north that she was facing. She turned her face this way and that, but a sort of needle in the wavering compass of her mind remained pointing ahead. So her eyes strayed back ahead and were still. Half her body was reddened by the low sun. She strained her eyes on the horizon many miles north, where the river veered aside, and a solid gray band of distance lay like a hurdle inviting her nimble fancy. René was speaking, but he seemed not to be there at all, as though his words were coming from *her* mind.

'Anywhere you say,' said René, speaking jerkily over her shoulder, his lips and cheeks pale and violently trembling. 'Traveling. Anywhere. The places we've talked about. The galleries — cathedrals — bazaars — snowy valleys and all the rest, crossing the sea first. Look! All this flat land is really a prison. You are imprisoned here.'

'René——'

'I love you, dear Sister! Don't you see? Look at me! Don't

you love me? Couldn't you love me? Of course you could! Haven't I been kind and tender? Haven't we been brought close to each other by my work? Among the fjords and vine- yards you will — forget.'

Sister took René by the hand, and they went to the house. 'Go in and wait,' she said. René went in and sat by the fire. Presently Sister came in with some things from the clothesline. She was still in a daze. She sat by a large net she was knitting. René put out his hand.

'Please!' he begged. 'Don't! Don't take the damned net now!'

Sister raised her eyes and smiled enigmatically. She slipped in the stick and began to unwind the twine from her needle. René said no more, but sat watching her strong and plastic hands curve in and out. Each adroit jab of the needle pierced his very soul, and yet he could not tear his fascinated gaze away. He clenched his hands until the knuckles whitened, and looked at her long brown throat. A shudder passed through him. He could not keep his fingers still.

But Sister stopped her work, then, and turned to him. She hugged her breasts and looked at him with her head cocked sideways. It was one of her most winsome mannerisms.

'You mean so much to me, René,' she said, groping deeply into her mind for the warmest words. 'It's been wonderful — discovering — things with you. I was wishing the other day I were a different kind of person, so we could ramble off together and live as you've always lived — like the birds, finding little bits to eat here and there. But do I love you? That's the ques- tion. Do I love you? ... We never touch each other, play with each other. It didn't begin that way with us. It grew into something else. You understand?'

'Perfectly.'

'You see, I would want marriage, to protect myself. I want to go through all the motions, as you would say — wreath and veil, home and kids. Marriage to me is like a big rugged tree. The other is like a pretty bush, and the blossoms die when frost comes.'

'I know. I know. You are right, Sister.' He seemed anxious to convince her that he was wrong.

She turned to her knitting. René reached for his hat.

'You're not going!' she said.

'Yes. Good-night.' He would not look at her. He opened the door quickly and was gone.

After René left, Sister went to the levee and watched him until he turned the bend. She went to the end of the landing and sat looking into the north in a puzzled manner. A little breeze of wind had sprung up. The *Hail Mary*, far upstream, was white with sail. . . .

René walked home quickly. His steps were light. His spirits were light, elated, as though he had shed an irksome burden. He walked into Pretty John's whistling a gay tune, and at supper he was unduly talkative. After the meal he strolled the levee alone. The stars seemed uncommonly bright, the massed willows and hackberries darker and more vital than ever before. He threw back his head and breathed the cool and heady night air in long, eager breaths. The brutal laughter issuing from a negro cabin, the creaking of oars on a passing skiff, the baying of a hound far away, were like strange savage music to his ears.

Before bed, he burned all of the paintings on hand which he had done while under Sister's influence. He made a large crushed ball of the pictures. They burned swiftly on the river bank, springing into a tall yellow jubilant fire.

He went to bed and slept more soundly than he had slept in many months.

NETS AND HONEY

BOOK FOUR

32

IN THE little orchards the blurred fruit glowed all day, like embers in the smudge of trees. Tentative fungi quivered up through the mould. Fat drops continuously spattered down into the ferns. The frigid river was cloaked in fog. They on the moist and tepid shore could feel but not see it — the river's flow, burrowing its cold nervous course far beneath a silken mist that hovered like a soft and pallid oblivion.

Sister, tubbing her clothes, thought, 'How do the people in London dry their wash?' Hearing the crunching of unseen wheels, she called her boy: 'Bruce! Stay off the road, now!'

From the levee space was the bellowing of a distant bull, or the tired query of an anchored bell or fog-horn. There was much laughter in the ships that lay along Grass Margin, unseen. Sister groped among her roses with eyes wide and ears alert for a visitor.

René lived with Unga January in her stranded houseboat. He painted in the kitchen while Unga hoed the polebeans. He wrote innumerable letters, roamed about sketching foggy objects with a gray scarf on his throat. He had found peace. He had learned to idle. The sun could only be *felt*, a warm thwarted presence wallowing somewhere overhead.

The fog begot music. On Mitch Holt's side of the river, accordions hummed in the Slavonian shanties. On Sister's side, there was singing even in daytime, bowed gleaners bearing shrill tunes back and forth. In the warm sodden rear marshes when the sun chanced through, the vapors prowled in slow blue or golden shapes, half concealing an occasional nimble phantom looting the kitchen gardens and leaving cloven marks, like Pan's.

Sister found the deep fine hoof-holes. They appeared in the cabbage rows. There were circular chunks chewed from the cabbage heads. She loaded Grampaw's gun with buckshot. She wanted venison, too. She would quit hoeing and lift her face, listening. She had never killed a deer. She flirted a glance behind her, thrilled by some noise of the field. Nothing appeared. There came only the faint hoofbeats retreating, or even circling about her in mockery — a delicate musical thumping or strumming behind the mist. She laughed, thinking, 'You go to hell!' She would grasp the hoe, relieved. She was now hoeing as she had seen the negroes do it, gathering the slow strokes in with a tireless rhythm that every muscle shared. The handle rested against and slid across the tough bulge of the pelvic cushion. The lifted hoe was merely released. Gravity buried the whispering blade deep. Thus she could work between darkness and darkness without sweating, stepping inch by inch along the cabbage rows toward the toothache trees on the back canal bank.

She felt the big marsh beginning to ferment now. Alligators were awakening to sun their icy eyeballs. Hyacinths were peeping through the muck. She leaned on the hoe and brought her eyes north, to rest them in dreaming. She thought, 'Spring! Yesterday it came, tomorrow gone, leaving tracks of red and blue. Spring walks north, against the current, right behind the finches and the teal.'

Now she was sending all his meals to Mitch Holt. A negro boy brought them over for a nickel a day. Mitch paid him that. Once she was sick for three days. She told the negro not to inform Mitch of her sickness. She wanted to see what would happen. Mitch on the second day sent a note:

> Dear friend:
>   If you've got no money let me know right away. I'll send you some
>   Love from,
>
>   Mitch

In the office of the Southern Produce Exchange, Mocco was paid to compile 'returns.' A 'return' is a piece of paper mailed to the farmer who has consigned produce to a commission merchant. It tells the farmer how much money was realized on his produce. The farmer may show this paper to his grocer, as evidence of ability to pay. When the commission merchant's check later arrives, the farmer has only to endorse it over to the grocer.

Mocco's office was huge and warm, feebly lit by the pale light of the wholesale district — a dreary retreat where snowy cauliflower and succulent pears were never seen. Mocco sat with a dozen other clerks behind an ornamental railing of thick proportions. The space in front of the railing contained only a single chair and a trick cuspidor fashioned into a bronze turtle whose fiercely protruding head when stepped on raised the turtle's shell and revealed the cuspidor within.

Mocco rather liked working for a middle-man. While the quiet afternoon slowly died, the other clerks never stopped working; never glanced at him or each other; never said a word. Perhaps a phrase suddenly uttered at three o'clock would have startled them all. The gray, emaciated chief clerk, dreaming over his figures atop his elevated platform like some model somnambulist, paid them no heed at all. He only drew in at intervals a shrill sniffle, which might once have signified that authority was hovering near, but which now connoted only a disgruntled nose capturing a bit of stale air.

Thus free from supervision, Mocco frequently discarded his pen and dreamed his dreams. He spent much time dreaming of promotion. He aspired to the position called Incoming Man. The words were magic to his ears. Each time he heard an official telling a caller, 'You gotta talk to our *Incoming* Man,' his heart leapt. The Incoming Man's duties were to supervise the reception of produce, arriving mainly on boats from the great trucking regions below the city. He had an office on the docks, nestling among the familiar river smells and the lusty cries of longshoremen and vendors of hot pies. This office was the lounging place of river men, most of them acquaintances of Mocco. Spending most of his lunch hour each day in this office, Mocco, with the aid of the present incumbent, old Vincent Grafagnini, was acquiring a fair knowledge of the Incoming Man's duties. Grafagnini was getting feeble, and also the officials had learned he was going to church again. The tacit understanding was that some day the position would be Mocco's. Mr. Gussy, the vice-president, was naturally expected to award the job to someone who knew people and conditions on the lower river.

Mocco's dream was interrupted by the office-boy, who threw a folded paper at him. Mocco opened the note:

'Darling, am waiting in store-room by the filberts.'

Mocco glanced at the chief clerk, took a paper, and left the office. The filberts were stored on the third floor. The two flights of steps were poorly lit, but Mocco knew the way. He had gone up there to meet Violet, the boss's stenographer, many times. He found her sitting on a sack of filberts, weeping. 'Mocksie!' she exclaimed, as he embraced her corseted waist.

'Shh! What's the matter, honey?'

'We got to get our marriage blessed right away, dolling!'

'All right! All right! Did your people find out?'

'No, but — oh, I feel funny. I'm scared.'

'Scared of what? Now, now! I'm here with you, honey!'

Mocco thought, 'It can't be anything *wrong!* We've only been married a month!'

'Oh, Mocksie!' whispered the girl. 'I feel like a Protestant! Don't you know we're living in sin, married by a judge? Today's the first Friday of the month. Everybody at home went to Communion, and I never missed it before in my life. Mama looked at me so queer. Bernadotte too, kept looking. I had to turn my back. Do I look funny?'

'Honey, you're crazy! Get back to your work, it's late. Do you want to ruin my career?'

'Yes, dolling. But I keep thinking, suppose something would happen to one of us. You're always hanging around that wharf. We'd go straight to hell, Mocksie. And the *other* one — the one who wouldn't be dead. Imagine how it would feel. Let's go see Father Gelpi tonight, dolling. We can have a quiet wedding.'

'Anything you want, honey. I'd rather wait until I'm Incoming Man, but ——'

'Oh, dolling, let's don't wait. We want the world to know it! Papa'll quit his job Incoming Man, and you'll get the job, and we'll live at home. I already ordered my new bedroom suite, anyhow. Father Gelpi said he'll marry us like as if we'd never been to Gretna.'

'Father Gelpi! You went to see him?'

'Shh! Yes. Are you mad? Don't be mad, dolling. Remember, he's my confessor.'

'What did he say?'

'Whenever we're ready he is.'

'Well, I've got to think.' Mocco thought, 'Where is the wedding money coming from?'

'You always look mad when you think,' said Violet.

'I'll see what we can do. Maybe a little later ——'

'But papa won't quit the job until we marry!'

'He'll quit when we set a date.'

'After all my plans...'

'Aw, honey!'

'If you cared for me ——'

'Shh! Don't start crying again. Violet! Honey! What's the matter, really the matter today with you?'

'I'm si — sick — I mean I'm *not* sick — I think — can't you understand? Don't look at me like that! It's not my fault. I could kill myself!'

'I've got to think, honey,' Mocco consoled. 'Don't worry. There's nothing to kill yourself about. You've *got* to live, now.'

'And you're glad, Mocksie? I mean if it's true.'

'Sure I'm glad! Only, I've got to think. We'll go see Gelpi. Leave everything to me, honey. Everything!'

Mocco slipped out of the building and hurried to the Incoming Man's office. Old Vincent was alone with his Genoa newspaper.

'Hello, keed!'

'Dad, I've got something to tell you,' Mocco stammered.

'Awright! Looka! I got sickus head broccoli for supper. You gunna take supper with us tonight?'

'Sure. Dad, I've decided there's no use me and Violet waiting any longer. She promised me to marry next week. Sure! Is it all right? Can I have your girl? I'll be good to her, Dad!'

The old man's eyes were misty. He held out his hand, as if in consolation. His face was shaped like an ancient ram's. He kept swallowing, blinking at the negroes carrying celery outside. 'I gunna tella you — you gotta my good luck forever. Take her! Neckus week? You beega bum! Sure, das awright. I gunna fickus you wanna gooda weddinga present — eh? I givva you dissa job! *But!* Don't you takka too mucha graft, you begga bum!'

'That's what I want to see about, Dad. We want — we'd like you to give notice tonight to Mr. Gussy.'

'Eh?'

'Tonight Dad. Violet wants it! Her heart's set on it. We'll get everything over today.'

Old Vincent hesitated, but finally promised to resign that night.

Mocco hurried back to the office and crept in unnoticed.

He searched his desk until he found a 'return' covering a shipment of lettuce received three weeks previously from his sister in Grass Margin. He wondered whether Sister needed the money. He hoped not. The thing could be simply done . . .

He took the 'return' to the cashier, and explained that his Sister had asked him to send the money at once. The Cashier, after speaking to Mr. Gussy, drew a check and gave it to Mocco. When his day's work was over, Mocco affixed Sister's signature to the check, then endorsed it himself. A near-by saloonkeeper cashed the check.

On his way to the Grafagnini home, Mocco stopped in to see Father Gelpi, and arranged to marry Violet the following week. No one would ever know they had already participated in a civil wedding.

When Mocco asked for Violet, her mother said she was not well. What! Not well? No, Violet could not be seen that evening. She was lying down in her room. Overjoyed, Mocco ate three plates of spaghetti.

Next morning, the chief clerk combed his hair, cleared his desk of all papers, and sat for a long time with folded arms, sniffling and scrutinizing all his clerks. Then he sent the office-boy ten feet across the way to call Mocco.

'Sit down, Kalavich,' he said. 'How long have you been with us?'

Mocco told him.

'Do you feel you have made a mistake?' the chief clerk asked.

'If I have, it was not on purpose.' Mocco was uneasy about Sister's check.

'Kalavich, you've been an exemplary employee,' the other began in a tone just loud enough to be heard by a new man sitting near-by. 'This concern needs men of integrity. We've only begun to expand. I've called you here to tell you that you have been watched, and watched closely.' The chief clerk paused, while Mocco broke out in a cold sweat. 'I have heard about your visits to the Incoming office in your spare time, Kalavich. A noteworthy sacrifice, a banking up of diligence for the future. It is unfortunate for us that *certain of our men* don't see fit to prepare themselves in this way.... Kalavich, our Mr. Grafagnini has resigned!'

'Resigned!' Mocco felt like weeping for joy.

'Yes. His successor has been chosen. You are our choice. I hope you will not thank me — in words. Beginning today, you are the Southern Produce Exchange's Incoming Man, at a salary of seventy dollars a month.'

'Mr. Norton, really ——'

'Tut! Tut! No thanks, mind. You've a heavy responsibility. When I received my present appointment — but we'll discuss that later. Even now, we're wasting time. You will report to Mr. Grafagnini at once. If you happen to have my own sort of feeling about symbols, you may take your pen and penwiper with you. And ——'

Just then a buzzer sounded — a long and a short. The chief clerk quickly rose and, brushing Mocco rudely aside, dashed for the vice-president's office. He stood by Mr. Gussy's desk rubbing his dry hands. Mr. Gussy threw a paper at him. 'Handle!' said Mr. Gussy. Mr. Norton mumbled and treading softly, turned to leave.

'Did you tell that fellow Kalavich I said to get out on the wharf?' Mr. Gussy barked.

'Oh, hours ago, sir! Nothing else?'

Mr. Gussy did not answer.

After the wedding, Mocco spent three weeks of bliss. Violet, in a crisp kimona, each morning brought coffee to the bed. Living in the attic of the huge, ancient building on Decatur Street in which the Grafagninis dwelt, they gave themselves to each other with abandon undisturbed, spending their week-long honeymoon at home in bed, or lounging among the palms and myrtles of Jackson Square.

Violet immediately prevailed on Mocco to see a stomach specialist. The doctor asserted that Mocco was considerably overweight, and digging his grave with his teeth. Mocco's most frequent symptoms now were a desire to doze after meals, followed by fiery claws gouging his right ribs. He was given a diet, and told to walk to and from work. In a little while he lost weight rapidly. He grew cheerful, energetic, while Violet altered his shirts and dosed him with soda to fight the fiery claws. He found himself thinking more clearly, and less inclined to forgetfulness and irritation. He wrote Sister a letter once, and sent her a Carnival paper.

The Grafagninis were a big noisy Italian family, innumerable children and grandchildren living in the same building. This house was built with a kind of anatomical intricacy, long intestinal stairways winding through great hollow cavities divided by membranous curtains of gauze. And little joys and panics and sorrows like nerve impulses traversed it all day. On the third floor, where one of the family operated a miniature cigar factory, a machine throbbed all day like a heart. Mrs. Grafagnini was of an old Italian family. The building was hers, and no one paid rent. On Sundays the entire family, twenty-six in all, gathered in the old lady's rooms for a dinner meticulously cooked, and flavored right. All morning the women busied themselves in the kitchen, while the men gathered under the front balcony honeysuckle to discuss fruit and produce, and compare the contours of the women passing from Mass, and the children played within smelling distance of the pots. On that day Mocco waived his diet, with Violet's permission, and gorged to his heart's content.

Violet was very good to Mocco. She permitted him to do practically anything he wanted.

Mocco received a letter from Sister:

Dear Mocco:

I am happy to know you like your position. We are in a long fog. Hardly walk on the road. I want to take Bruce to town for Carnival if the boats offer good rates. But I may wait another year for that after all. Cloe Ravine, who worked for Jule at the store, committed suicide yesterday. Filled her apron with bricks, jumped into the river and held her apron closed until she drowned. They floated candles on the water to locate the body, but the candles did not stop at any particular spot. The current was too strong. They floated down the river, all the people watching them. Your friend Bonus is back on the Margin, staying with some colored people. He asked me to tell you he is well, and may see you in town soon. Mitch Holt is practically in charge of Mateo's canning factory now.

Mocco was homesick for a whole day.

33

IN APRIL the fog remained, unwanted. Summer could not break through. On the Margin, fruit still glowed in every milky orchard but Sister's: prices had been good, and her neighbors needed no immediate money. They would wine the remainder of their oranges, or let them rot. Would not the rotted fruit fall and make more fruit? No one complained. The river would soon come warm and swollen, bearing next year's firewood, or maybe a few nice pieces of furniture — if some up-river towns should flood out.

A big empty coal-barge drifted down from New Orleans. A shout went through Grass Margin. A party was quickly organized. Fourteen men in fourteen skiffs rowed out. Each man drove a spike in the side of the black hulk, and to this spike tied his line. Ashore, people ran to their wharves and made a commotion shouting to one another and to the fourteen rowers, who sang 'Duh Ole Hen Flewed in duh Garden' as they laboriously pulled the barge in . . . Thus, many families often won some fine pitchy firewood, or planks for repairing houses or wharves.

Sister heard the commotion. She ran in from the field. She took the telescope upstairs and scanned the levee over at Dutch Scenery. There was a long line of men watching the salvaging of the barge, but Mitch Holt was not among them . . .

Another day, the Fort gunners were shooting at a target in

the river. This drew all the people to the levees on both sides. Again Sister focused her telescope on the onlookers in Dutch Scenery, but Mitch did not appear. He was too busy, she supposed. She made a wrinkled nose at Dutch Scenery, and went back to work thankful that Mitch was following the advice she had written him in prison...

Trappers and trawlers were back home with money. Some brought hot appetites. The seasonal mail-order trinkets were arriving. In the levee fog, the brown homecomers bared their throats and emptied their full chests of laughter.

There was a death. A mulatto woman called Tupelo Ramsey fell into a ditch with her five-year-old child, cracking her spine. The mist rose, fell, brooded, accursed of the pilots. Sister contributed twenty-five cents to help send Tupelo's child to its father in Biloxi. She knitted all day now. Or she paced from window to window, waiting for a visitor, or some fell summons to purge her blood of the mockery of spring. She could not understand why René had dropped out of her life so suddenly, before the fog. She was beginning to resent Mitch Holt's giving himself so completely to his work. In pain and confusion she saw the serried treetops in blossom, the dazzling clusters of flowers etched across the fog. Their humid fragrance was inescapable. It oozed through every crevice in every wall, lingered in dark corners, possessed her garments and bedding with its vagrant touch, clung subtly to the very food on her plate.

She was making money with her cabbages, and the cucumbers were swelling on the vines — almost ready for picking and shipping. With part of the lettuce money she had bought a bony horse. She grassed him each day on the levee, which bore a fine crop of wire-grass. She rode him to the post-office, astraddle, dressed in overalls.

Passenger ships from New York and from tropical ports passed close to shore in the high river, throwing noisy swells among the willows and hackberries, which sent the squirrels leaping into the tops of the trees. Passengers leaned along the ships' rails, dreaming with faces saddened by distance, or they waved handkerchiefs at the brown children shouting for bananas. Sister studied the clothes of the women passengers.

Once Bruce killed a garter snake in the thyme. Sister made a silk dress, using the handsome brown, green, and buff coloring of the snake, selected from a color chart in the mail-order catalogue. The day it was finished, she wore it in the living room all evening, sitting alone with a book.

'Do' wunna go to bed!' Bruce whined that evening. 'Somebodday comin'!'

'Nobody's coming, Fella!' said Sister. 'Look! Cross heart!'

'Somebodday comin'!'

'Because I'm dressed up?'

'Somebodday comin'!'

She finally persuaded the child to bed; but later, lying awake, he called her.

'Mama!' he whispered. 'You dressed up for God?'

'That's it, Fella! Or perhaps the devil!'

Under the warm tight silk, a little thrill passed through her.

René Davidson was painting a picture on the river bank near the green shanty that was Mitch Holt's office. Each day he visited the spot, and worked until foggy dusk. Finishing, he would trudge home alone, tracing the river's foggy sheen to Unga's houseboat. As soon as he arrived Unga would make him a tea, which she called a 'blood-drink.' 'Drink, cher,' she said tenderly. 'You knaw dat come from good ground, dat tea. From behind duh Foat, where duh deers feeds in summer.' He gave it to his dry throat quickly, and stood looking into the empty cup until his stomach took the smooth dark impact; then he smiled at Unga, or touched the baby's hair.

Their twilights would melt in peace. René had screened the

houseboat. There was the sad whine of mosquitoes, or the beating of moths on the screens. Tall slow lights steamed past in the river, or a ship's bell spoke. Unga rarely talked, except in the language of her swift eyes. When the rain brought idleness, or sometimes at night, sitting naked in the lamplight, Unga would ask René to recite. She had learned the ways of pleasing a man.

Mitch Holt's office was bare of all but desk, chairs, and papers. Three or four times a day he would stop his labors and lie on the bare floor and sleep for half an hour with his coat for a pillow. In the evening he took soap and towel to the river for a bath and swim. Then he would eat the supper which Sister sent.

Once at dawn as he sat on a pier reading a State Fisheries report, the orange blossom smell drifting over the river surrounded him so completely that his eyes left the page and stared into the fog. His mind was instantly lost among a babel of bright insistent memories. It was as if the bleak and stony battlements of his purpose were left momentarily unguarded, admitting a host of radiant besiegers. He had not seen spring for years. There was no spring on this side the river, only sawgrass and the dun rabble of muttering mangroves. Alone in the fragrant mist, Mitch remembered forgotten dawns, snug rooms brimming with rosy wives' jargon, soft afternoons rich in wine, still nights glistening with jeopardy, warm rains tinkling down the bayou of his birth. And women waiting. Lamplit girls humming in windows over the river, all lamplit and alert, with knowing bosoms and knowing tunes ...

A ship anchored near-by gave a deafening whistle-blast, and Mitch discovered himself on the pier with the urgent report, and behind him the brittle clatter of oyster shuckers, and behind them the sun struggling up through the mist. He gained his feet swiftly and walked off. Presently he was looking through a window in Mateo's house, into the kitchen where Lucich was at breakfast.

'I want four men quick!' he said to Mateo, 'and six rolls of fencing. Drumfish are eating oysters in Pen Number Twelve.'

'Today Sunday,' Mateo answered.

'Christ! Again!'

'Better vait tomorrow,' Mateo advised, chewing his hard-tack.

Mitch went to the river and launched a pirogue. He would go and see Sister Kalavich. But in the middle of the foggy river he met the mail-boy coming over with the mail. He took the bag from the boy, and found in it an important letter. He turned and paddled back to Dutch Scenery...

One day, as suddenly as a wall collapses, the fog broke for good, and summer was in. Sister was following two little negro boys hauling an orchard-cart of cabbages to the levee. As she reached the embankment the fog blew away, and she saw René Davidson coming down the road with Unga January.

Unga wore new clothes of fine material, and a fur coat — the first that Sister, dwelling in the country's richest fur region, had ever seen. A fur coat! Sister stared in amazement, at how the other woman was transformed. She might have been a passenger from some ship.

Unga smiled and nodded formally to her friend, then continued talking to René. René turned and nodded, called 'Good-morning!' and passed on. His tone was perfunctory; his eyes did not seek Sister, but roved alertly about the yard and grove. The two rounded the curve, leaving the road empty.

On the levee Sister stood alone, carved in the warm sky with the isolated puzzled look of a figure on a column, holding folded arms. Down the empty levee the rank overhanging growths stood forth as emphatically as a frame from which the picture had been torn.

Sister recalled in detail her examination of Unga's raiment. She had never before seen a negress wear new shoes without limping. The fur coat... she could not identify the pelts. They were very thick, and wonderfully sensitive to light and wind, taken from some strange beast, a gray marauder whose color suggested gloomy forests or the lead-colored rocks of a fabled clime.

Just then little Bruce came behind her and touched her hand. Sister gave a low cry, and her heart seemed to leap into her throat.

'You — you *frightened* me!' she cried.

She was cold all over.

The child was frightened too. He began to cry and ran behind his mother, who was crossing the yard, staring into space...

René and Unga walked toward the post-office, where a night rain had dyed the road a deeper buff. In every house they passed, curtains parted. The last time Unga had been seen on the Margin road, years ago, she had walked barefooted with a basket of terrapin on her head. Near the post-office a knot of trappers stood. All of them were turned toward the approaching man and woman, watching.

'Why you dawn stop and talk wid her?' Unga asked René.

The man did not answer. He was watching a bird.

'How come you dawn stop for Sister?' Unga asked.

'I've got nothing to talk to her about.'

'You wan' stop there on duh way back, cher?'

'What do you mean? Why stop there?'

'Bicause I hates duh sight of her!'

'What has Sister to do with you, Unga?'

She pinched his arm: 'Why you got to say her name?'

'See here! Must you pinch me for that?'

'I hates her! Ain' dat right, cher?'

'For the right reason? Why not, if it amuses you?' René was rubbing his arm where Unga had pinched him.

'I hates her bicause she dawn care ef *you* love her or not!'

'That's a child's reason.'

'But *do* she, cher? Do she care? She would *not* care ef you love her or not, dat woman.'

'Shh! If you enjoy hating her, let it be because she is the enemy of all I represent — not because she's white, or was the cause of your being driven away from home.'

'All right, cher.' Unga sighed and brought René's arm tightly against her ribs.

The trappers glared, the white ones. They did not care about René, but sneered at Unga because by walking with René she was insulting *their* women.

Sister's name lay fixed below Unga January's thoughts — the name! — to be associated in an insufferably uncertain way with each of René's comings and goings, and each of his flexuous moods. Unga would torture herself recalling, denying, loathing, the several winsome attributes of Sister's which she had once admired. If only René would have *talked* about Sister, about his and Sister's life together in the oyster camp, confirm or deny the gossip which Unga had heard! But René had never mentioned Sister's name, except to state that she was the enemy of all he represented, and that she had almost ruined him by causing him to paint bad pictures. Unga did not understand the reference to bad pictures. The wholly abstract things he was painting now seemed bad enough. But she knew what an *enemy* was. She knew that one might bitterly love an enemy. She herself often felt that she loved Sister.

René worked a long time on the picture near Mitch Holt's office. He had discarded the small canvas for a larger one, doing a second picture of the same scene. He had ridden his work of all trace of conventional associations; his distortions were bolder than they had ever been before. Seated crosslegged among the frenzied sand flies, surrounded by a group of idlers who came and left and came, René was happy, oblivious of the bystanders' speculations as to what the picture was meant to represent, or the bitter smell of their sweat. He scarcely heard the dim jangle of oyster openers behind the levee, or the occasional rude bang of the screen door under the sign:

MITCHELL HOLT, SUPT.

One day just as he had begun to paint, two men came on the levee above him. One was recognized as Mateo Lucich. The other man René had never seen before. And it was he, the way he walked, that compelled René's attention. It was not only that the man's body was admirably proportioned. The movement of the arms and shoulders with the brief upward thrust of leg after leg through the wind, gave René a sense of unstudied alertness and power — a curious unassuming boldness. The blond man began to speak, and his words, uttered in a low penetrating voice, fell upon René's ears like polished missiles:

'Help me?' he was saying to Mateo. 'You can help me by letting me alone. You get an account of all I do. Every plan goes first to you. You approve my plans. Why can't I carry them out in my way? Here you've been hanging around me all day interfering. We can't do this shrimp trawling scheme in your way. It's my idea. Have you got a better one? If you have, let's talk. Now listen, Mateo, I'm building up your business. You're getting the money. That's all right. I don't give a damn about the money. I'm interested in the job...'

Mateo interposed a remark, and the other man's listening face turned toward the river, the eyes gazed at the opposite shore, then fell and rested briefly on René. When the painter felt the full bold gaze and saw the face — the blond compact head, the pale hard brow, the lean unyielding jaws, he named the man in his mind. Mitch Holt.

It was incredible to René that he had never seen or met Mitch Holt before. He compared the clean and decisive poise of the man atop the levee with the thick-bodied, swaggering local misfit he had pictured Mitch Holt to be, and was puzzled at how faulty his visualization had been.

He turned to a Cajin fisherman lying near him and asked, 'Who is that man, Paul — the smaller one?'

'Dad's Midge Holt.'

'Where did he come from?'

'Him? From ride here — born on duh Margin.'

'His people have been here a long time, then?'

'His paw is English or Canada or something, come off a English bark sunk long time ago by Pazz a Loutre, and he went to work on duh jetties, when Eads waz building duh jetties. Midge is good, bud he works too hard, him. He's god to catch up on himself, account of raising some hell and dis and dat when he waz yong.'

'He's gone build up dis plaze, yes,' said another bystander. 'He done already put a hundred new mens to work almost. You see dat offize up there? Go 'cross duh river twelve o'clock to-night, you gon see duh light burning. Dey say duh pilots use it for range light, them.'

Another day, René went to see Mitch Holt. He walked up to the office boldly, because he was timid. He found Mitch staring from the rear window, unheedful of the creak of the opening screen door. 'Well?' Mitch asked without moving. René went in with his folio under his arm.

'I'm René Davidson, the painter,' he said. 'I hope——' They shook hands in the gloom. 'Mitch Holt,' said the other. 'I've heard of you. Take a chair. I'll be with you.'

'Am I intruding?' René asked.

Mitch did not reply. He was writing a letter. He consulted a notebook. The laboring pen scratched at the silence. Except for a shelf of books on steam boilers, shell fish, and the distribution of foodstuffs, the place was barren as a lair, and it smelled of whiskey. The refined aroma of spirits, the slow gray dusk gathering in the corners, the lights appearing one after one in the cozy shanties beyond where shrill children romped and jovial families gathered for feeding — imparted to the figure at the desk an aspect of grim unasking loneliness. 'Is he still in prison?' René asked himself.

'We're going to dig another canal,' said Mitch, licking the envelope.

'I'd like to hear about your work here,' said René.

'My work?'

'Yes. The work you've done and plan to do. You won't mind my dropping in occasionally.'

'I knock off pretty late. What would you like to know?'

'To tell the truth, Mr. Holt, I'm rather cut off from conversation down here. I'm staying in a houseboat up the river a way. Would you come up and have dinner with me tonight? I'll walk back with you. I can tell you all about the tuna fish industry in the Northwest.'

'I've got to be here at eight o'clock,' said Mitch. 'Let's eat at the boarding-house. Fish dinner tonight for a change . . . My work — it's, well, I've started it. I'm only beginning here.'

They ate fish and drank wine in the boarding-house by Little Big Canal. Afterwards they climbed the levee and sat talking. Mitch revealed his plans. He hoped some day to have his own factory. He hoped to turn the profits into new factories. There was much to be done. Mitch spoke quietly. This was the first time he had revealed his plans. He had no idea where the money would come from to make a beginning. He would find out about that in due time. He would get the money.

When Mitch excused himself, René was disappointed. He

wanted to spend the whole evening with his new friend. Would they be friends? Mitch was self-sufficient — not superior, but living in and for himself. The night-shift whistle blew, with no echo from the smooth infinite marshes. René descended the levee at Mitch's heels. Below in the canal, tightly cargoed luggers lay like squat black beetles. The fluid onyx of the canal stirred gently under the lenient tidal heave.

'I suppose I'll go,' said René hesitantly.

'Come back again. Bring that book you were talking about.'

'Oh! The *Novum Organum.* Yes. It will interest you.'

René walked homeward quickly. He thought, 'His idea about a big industry here is sound, but who would lend money to an ex-convict?'

When he reached the houseboat he found the door locked.

'Quel que la?' Unga called in answer to his knocking.

'René and mosquitoes! Open the door, dear!'

An oaken bar was removed, a heavy chair dragged away. Unga balanced the lamp over her head and passed out a reed mosquito brush. René flailed it in swishing circles and darted in. Unga did not ask where he had been, but climbed back into her bunk, naked. He had never come so late before, nor failed to explain any delay.

René did not take any food. He sat by the lamp with a book. In a little while Unga saw that he was not reading, but staring absently at the page.

'You dawn wunt no nice crawfish bisque, cher?' she asked.

'No, thanks, dear. I had a good supper.'

Unga swiftly left her bunk and sat on René's lap, with her hot breast against his ear, as if to send him the aroused, drum-like marching of the heart within. But he stroked her leg with cool, remote fingers, not showing his eyes. She stole back to the bunk. 'Good-night, cher.'

'Good-night, dear. Will the light annoy you?'

'Non, ma cher.'

Toward morning, René lay in the dark thinking of Mitch Holt as an insolent boy scampering among the rivermen, as a smuggler piloting cargoes of trembling Chinamen through the patrol, as a young convict sitting with barred sunlight in his hair. 'Lonely strength!' he thought. 'What is his goal, in this land of no ruins and no echoes? I must find a way to help him. Perhaps at last I have found a friend, a manly friendship! I must avoid talking about art to him, encourage him to speak on his topics. This is what I need. A friend.' For the hundredth time he changed his position in the bed. Out of the dark sounded the low warm caress of Unga's voice, tentatively, to learn if he were still awake:

'You sleeping, cher?'

'No. What's wrong, dear?'

'You feel bad, my sweetheart?'

'No, thanks. Just thinking.'

'Tch! Tch!' There was the clicking tongue, and the long pull of a sigh.

'You lef' your paints and pitcha there,' said Unga suddenly.

'Left them where? Oh, he'll look after them.'

'Who?'

'Mitch Holt. I was with him.'

Unga's clenched hands went slack. She smiled in the dark. But Mitch's name would set her thinking of Sister Kalavich, who cooked good suppers.

One evening René went to the boarding-house at Dutch Scenery with the book he had promised to lend Mitch, *Novum Organum*. Mitch ate four large meals each day. Two hours after eating the meal sent by Sister, he would have another supper at the boarding-house.

During the meal Mitch talked to René in his warm yet impersonal way, about a new project. René gathered the man was possessed by no desire other than that of filling his life with activity. Through his talk one perceived no sign of personal ideal or profit. Afterwards they sauntered toward the oyster cannery, and stopped in the doorway just as the whistle set the night hands into motion. The place was whitely illuminated by the hard glint of tin cans stacked in tall blunt peaks, the air moist with sea-food vapors. Mitch walked to an endless belt near the doorway which had been just installed, and began picking at random from the cans moving past, examining each one selected. The girls were eyeing René. They were mostly large Slavonians. To protect their legs from mosquitoes, they had wrapped them in newspapers with large headlines, or colored comic supplements. Bugs danced madly about the lights. René was ill at ease. Clearly Mitch had forgotten him.

'By the way, I'm going to New York in two weeks,' René said. 'I'd like to take some of your figures with me.'

'How?' Mitch asked. 'What figures?'

'Your figures. I believe I can interest a cousin of mine in your new factory.'

Holt's face jerked around so abruptly that René flushed.

'What cousin?' Mitch asked. 'Who——'

'My cousin Tim Davidson. He's a banker. I believe we can interest him in putting some of his money to work down here. He's rather romantic, too, about the function of big money.'

'He must be. Hell! I can see him backing a man he don't know from Adam!'

'I think I can convince him, Holt. Tim and I don't agree in many ways, but he respects my intuition. He's tried two or three tips of mine.'

'Let's step outside.'

'I can't see how you could fail, Holt. You've got——'

'Hell! If you knew! If you knew what we've got!'

'Inexhaustible stores of sea food free for the taking; cheap land for raising fur animals as they are doing elsewhere——'

'Rich soil and a climate for raising canning vegetables the year round. Transportation close by.'

'Plenty of labor. Don't you see, Holt? Everything an investor could ask for.'

'Get him down here!' Mitch said. 'Get him ... It ferments! Can you smell it — the land over there? The cream of the whole valley skimmed off by floods and laid down here. Listen to it late some night. Christ, you can *hear* it fermenting, for want of being worked. Get your cousin down.'

'Unless I'm mistaken, he'll drop everything and come down. He has ideas like yours, creating employment and so forth. They've all been money-grubbers, the whole family. Tim's the best of the lot. At least he's had some fun with his investments.'

'I reckon you'll want to invest in this proposition,' Mitch said.

René smiled. 'I don't think so. I've got none of their money, and I want none.'

Before leaving for New York, René went to see Mitch and bid him good-bye. Mitch went aboard the New Orleans packet with the artist. He gave René a sheaf of papers, the outline of his scheme. His figures on soil, fur, and fisheries were substantiated by Government bulletins.

'There's something I don't understand, Davidson,' Mitch said. 'Tell me, where do *you* come in?'

'I like the country and I like you, Mitch. I've got faith in you.'

'I thought maybe ——'

'What did you think?'

'You might be doing this through friendship for Sister Kalavich.'

'No,' said René. He looked away. His face was pale.

'Not that it would matter to me.'

'I tell you I'm doing it through friendship for you.'

'Fair enough!'

34

IT WAS Mardi Gras in New Orleans. Mocco and Violet went masking with a group of young friends. Everywhere, the Carnival King's colors fluttered gaily. The narrow streets of the old French Quarter from the river to the cemetery rang with cries of delight as clowns tumbled, Indian warriors whooped, devils swung their stuffed tails, Colonial dames danced with toreadors, and throngs of tinsel-slippered feet wandered shuffling in unison to the strains of plucked music.

Mocco was supremely happy today. He was costumed as a dashing pirate of old. With a roguish false mustache, a long wicked dagger in his sash and a painted frown that terrified all the children, he cut a bold and gorgeous figure swaggering at the head of a long procession of brown monkeys, dainty ballet dancers, knights in real armor, and one circus ringmaster who cracked his whip while a big lion with a pasteboard head danced a waltz. Violet was garbed as a little page-boy in silken tights and a flowing cloak of crimson velvet.

'Oh, dolling!' she exclaimed. 'My big handsome boy! I get funny little shivers every time I look at you! I'm almost scared you'll carry me off! I adore that terrible frown. Can't you try to grow a real one? It makes you look so bossy.'

All morning their crowd wandered, visiting and serenading friends and relatives, wending their frolicsome way afoot, unimpeded save by an occasional bespangled carriage drawn by a jovial horse. Occasionally they met another group of maskers traveling in the opposite direction. Then the two groups would mingle and dance together. When a boy masker met a girl masker, he tried to guess her name. If he succeeded, he was rewarded with a kiss.

At noon, at the height of the festivities, Mocco's group went to the Grafagnini home for the customary coffee and dough-nuts. Violet followed Mocco into the kitchen, where they remained a while alone, making love.

'Let's go upstairs, I feel wild!' Mocco urged. He was admiring his wife's thighs, which he had never seen before. He wanted to feel them.

'Now, dolling, I'm going to get mad!' Violet pouted. 'You quit acting nasty, now!'

Just then her father, old Vincent, walked into the kitchen. He seemed much excited. Mr. Gussy at the Southern Produce Exchange had sent a messenger-boy for Mocco an hour previously. Mocco must report to the office at once. Probably a shipment of produce had arrived unexpectedly, with no one to receive it.

'You takka my horse and buggy outside, queek, run!' commanded Vincent. 'Here, Violet, you go widda him — see your olda boss — show him how sweeta you look. I makka da boys and gels wait till you getta back.'

Mocco and Violet drove at once to the Southern Produce Exchange a few streets away. People along the route, the maskers and the out-of-town visitors who sat on the curbings, smiled admiringly at them. Mocco waved at everybody. He had his big dagger between his teeth, and occasionally he would scowl to frighten some child.

Reaching their destination, they mounted the stairs and stood hand in hand in Mr. Gussy's office doorway. Mr. Gussy was the size of a half-grown boy, with purple skin under the light, a great belly, and no neck. He was eating a Carnival doughnut. He sucked the sugar from his fingers, threw his bulging eyes upward, and asked, 'What is it?' without looking at the couple in the door.

'You wanted to see me, Chief?' asked Mocco, nudging Violet and winking at her.

Hearing the false hoarse voice, Mr. Gussy turned and saw the big fierce man with the dagger. And he saw the legs of the page-boy, who wore a lace-trimmed mask and uttered a somewhat familiar giggle.

'Who are you?' asked Mr. Gussy, smiling indulgently at Violet's thighs.

The pirate fingered his mustache and smiled. 'I am Mocco Kalavich.'

'And this,' giggled the other, 'is his wife!'

A momentary shade of displeasure crossed Mr. Gussy's face, as though something foreign in the doughnut had reached his taste; then it was gone, and he was smiling as he chewed. 'Oh, yes! Sit down, Violet,' he said. Then, to Mocco, 'Come here, my boy.'

Mocco crossed the office. Something in Mr. Gussy's voice vaguely disturbed him. It was very quiet there. No sound was heard but the faint strains of music from Poydras Street, where bands of revelers were gathering for the awarding of prizes given by the commission merchants for the most attractive costumes. Mr. Gussy wore a badge, signifying that he was chairman of the prize committee.

Mr. Gussy's fingers drew a letter from a special delivery envelope and handed it carelessly to Mocco. Mocco read the letter, which was postmarked 'Grass Margin, La.,' and addressed to Mr. Gussy:

> Some time ago I sent you a shipment of lettuce on the schooner *Hail Mary*. The captain says you received it. No 'return' or check has been received. Kindly send this money immediately. I will ship you some cucumbers soon.
>
> Nicolene Kalavich

Mr. Gussy bit into another doughnut, and turned and inspected Violet's hips. 'How's papa?' he asked her. Mocco put the letter on the desk. His face was a peculiar greenish color under the paint. Mr. Gussy, chewing loudly, picked up a canceled check and passed it to Mocco. It was Sister's check, which the saloonkeeper had cashed. It was tinted a gay sky-blue. The saloonkeeper's name on the back stood forth in a black pugnacious scrawl: H. H. Funk. In the lustrous oilcloth boots, Mocco's legs grew weak. As yet, Violet across the room did not know anything was wrong, because of the bold frown painted on Mocco's face that towered above the little vice-president.

'You cashed that check?' Mr. Gussy asked Mocco, cordially.

'Yes, sir. Sister owed me the money. I can't understand this, Chief. Captain Henny promised to tell Sister I was taking the money she owed me. I sent her word by him, but I guess he forgot. I'll——'

'Yeah, he forgot,' said Mr. Gussy very gently. He might have been deprecating the messenger's carelessness. And he chewed slowly, inexorably, and his gaze lingered around the delicately sagging curve of Violet's thigh.

'Sure!' said Mocco, more confidently. 'But I'll sure fix it up right away. Tonight I'll write her a letter . . . I see you're on the prize committee, eh, Chief?'

'What's that?' Mr. Gussy now glared at Mocco — his mouth open and one side of his face full of doughnut.

'I say I'll write her a letter tonight.'

'That's right. Because tomorrow you'll want to be hunting a job, since you got a wife to support. Although she's gunna be a good little manager, ain't you, Violet? . . . Yeah. You better find something to do right away. Maybe Bick & Foley will take you on. They don't draw much water around here, but they won't ask for no recommendation. As far as we're concerned, you done learned too fast. You really ought to be a produce man yourself. . . . Well, it's a pity, in a way. I was just telling Norton Monday to raise you five dollars. Then another thing, figure *our* position. You wunt me to tell you what's gunna happen? Your little Sister's going out on the levee and talk about the crooks she shipped her stuff to. And that talk's gunna travel. You know how it is, down in that forty-mile row of houses where they got nothing else to talk about. Yeah! Calling *me* the crook!'

Mr. Gussy rose, gulped the remainder of his doughnut, and reached for his hat. 'Folks, I got to be going,' he said. 'You-all gunna try for the maskers' prize?'

'You mean you're going to let *me* go, Mr. Gussy?' asked the fierce pirate in a boyish whine.

'I've done let you go, my boy,' Mr. Gussy answered softly, almost kindly.

'After all the lunch hours I've sacrificed, slaving ——'

'You don't look like you missed the lunch. Listen, can the Southern Produce Exchange afford to have men like you holding important ——'

Violet left her chair in a rush, and stood furiously before Mr. Gussy. 'Here!' she blurted. 'Don't you dare call him a thief! You been stealing your own self for ——'

'I ain't calling him no thief, honey,' said Mr. Gussy in a soft, wounded tone. 'I'm only showing him the writing on that check. I never mentioned the penitentiary. In fact I mailed his Sister another check today. But I can't talk no more, honey. I got to be going.'

Mocco turned away in disgust. 'Come on!' he snapped. 'Let the old son-of-a-bitch keep his old job. He'll regret it, by God, he'll live to regret it! You want me to tell *you* what's going to happen? Well, I've learned your business, now, and I'm going down on that forty-mile row of houses and form one of these co-operative associations, like our oyster men have. And I'm going to be vice-president, if God spares me. And we're going to sell our produce to the consumer. And to hell with the middle-man!'

'Take him away, honey, before I send him to jail,' Mr. Gussy warned Violet.

'To hell with the middle-man!' Violet yelled, and took Mocco away.

'Dolling, you were grand!' she whispered at the head of the stairs. 'Now let's forget about it and have a good time!' Suddenly she ran back and hurled into Mr. Gussy's office a stream of scorching Italian profanity. Mocco reached into the main office, picked up something, and slipped it into his shirt bosom.

'Fix your mustache, dolling,' said Violet going down the stairs. 'What have you got in your shirt?'

'I took the turtle cuspidor. We'll have fun with it.'

'Dolling, you didn't take the spittoon part!'

'No. Just the turtle.'

They returned the horse and buggy, but did not rejoin their party of maskers. They would spend the remainder of the Mardi Gras alone, on Canal Street, where the crowds were densest and most jolly.

Mocco used his turtle to frighten the girls, the ones who roamed about unescorted, in laughing bevies. He would plump the turtle up suddenly before them, and they would scream, amusing the crowd. In the surging crush of humanity, occasionally a young or old man would slyly pinch Violet's pretty leg as she passed, or touch other parts of her person, until she began viciously to slash at them with the long switch she carried, of the sort sold to girls for repelling the overbold . . . They ate peanuts. They played 'pop-the-whip' with total strangers. They fell in with a tipsy sailor from the battleship in port. Violet wore his uniform cap and he wore her plumed headgear. They paraded around arm-in-arm with the sailor until he was separated from them by a boisterous crush of college students, and Violet lost her hat, and worried about the poor sailor losing his.

In the night, they were far up St. Charles Avenue when the last great pageant passed, the climax of Carnival. Now came the prancing line of mounted police, followed by a mass of dazzling green flares. Through the acrid smoke sounded the piercing blare of trumpets, the pulsing of strong drums, and the masterful grunting of tubas. Violet beat time with the music, audaciously wagged her head, squeezed Mocco's hand. 'Oh, dolling!' she whispered, 'isn't it wonderful to be starting out new tomorrow?' The flares lit up trees and houses with an unreal light, and poured a lavish trail of sparks behind them. The tableaux were coming, the vividly tinted floats towering above the delighted crowds, moving in tinseled majesty through the clouds of vapor emitted by the colored flares. Each float moved through a din of applause, evoking a brief vision of some gaudy legendary epoch.

After the parade, Mocco and Violet walked homeward down the avenue, accompanied by hordes of weary homegoers. For a little while Violet was silent, still under the spell of the pageant.

'I'm going to make a novena,' she said to Mocco presently. 'I want *you* to be the leader that your country down the river has been waiting for.'

'Yeah,' said Mocco.

The long streamers of electric light were going out. The street was filled with the rubbish of Mardi Gras — peanut shells, discarded cartons, fragments of what had been humorous placards worn by cavorting masqueraders, candy wrappers that clung to one's shoes. There was no light, now, but the pale bluish glow of intersection lamps. In this sort of light the costumes of the erstwhile revelers looked somewhat tawdry. Mocco and Violet sat on a curb to rest. She leaned her head on his shoulder. Mocco had lost the gay bandanna head-wrap from his head. The turtle was grown cumbersome to carry around. A solitary clown passed by, limping. Behind him was a Roman soldier, with the handle of his spear dragging the ground. A man went by carrying two sleeping children and growling at his wife for walking so slowly.

'We might as well go home and tell Papa,' said Violet.

'It's all Sister's fault!' Mocco cried. 'Why couldn't she write *me* that letter!'

'She must be a terrible person, dolling.'

'What the hell do you mean?'

'Well, don't scream at me. Didn't you say it was her fault?'

'Don't *you* start backbiting her. She's not terrible. She's a fine person, and I'm not worth a setting of buzzard eggs.'

'You are!'

'I'm not. I took the check for wedding money.'

'Why didn't you come to me? Did you think I had nothing saved?'

'What have you got saved?'

'I'll not tell you.'

The next day Violet told him. It was Ash Wednesday. Church bells were ringing. Throngs of penitents with sore feet and rebellious livers were limping to church through the cold rain. Mocco and Violet were still in bed. Mocco was worried. He would not make love. To cheer him up, Violet told him she had a thousand dollars' worth of homestead stock in a local building and loan.

For a long time they rejoiced under the covers. Then Mocco told Violet he knew of a wonderful way to invest their money. He had thought up an invention, a device that would be cheap to make, and was sorely needed in all cities. It was a little signaling apparatus to let street-car patrons know when a car was approaching. As you came walking down the street toward the street-car stop, if you saw a yellow light, it signified that no car was coming and you need not hurry. But if the light turned red, the car was coming; you must run.

Violet thought he was joking. 'Crazy!' she laughed. 'We're going to go down the river and start that association like you said. We'll need that money to fix up your house. Papa will send you up to work a while for Uncle Nookie in Tangipahoa Parish. They've got a strawberry growers' association up there, doing fine. You'll learn the business. Then we'll go down the river to your place . . . or rather *her* and your place . . . I wonder if I'm going to like Sister.'

35

OLD Father Sam paddled up and down the river, visiting his parishioners. It was May, the month of the Blessed Mother. Father Sam often worried about the soul of Sister Kalavich. He had seen a Voltaire on her levee bench. He knew of her association with René Davidson, whom he regarded as a particularly dangerous sort of unbeliever, of the kind who are honest, tolerant, aloof from religious wrangling.

Sister drew the priest a glass of wine and produced fresh hardtack to dip in it. Little Bruce grunted on the floor with a metal store toy. The priest chewed thoughtfully, and examined Sister peeling figs by the window. His fine old eyes, canopied by frosty brows, burned to lay hold of the secret of her good or evil charm.

'I never see you on the levee, Sister.'

'I go to the store at night, Father.'

'Your work keeps you out of things — away from the neighbors.'

'I haven't wanted to go anywhere since you blessed the trawl-boats. I took Bruce to see that.'

'Mama, look the big drudge-boat, Mama!' Bruce cried.

'I found it strange you were not at Marie Pugas's wedding,' said the priest. 'Those people like you, Sister.'

'Marie understands. The others don't matter. She brought me a piece of the wedding-cake.'

'And you slept on it.'

'And dreamed of being married to you!' Sister's eyes brimmed with mischief. She sat on the arm of his chair and stroked his unshaven cheek. 'You were young again, and so handsome! We ——'

'Enough of that!' He pushed her away. Bruce clapped delightedly.

'Judge Pugas performed the ceremony!' said Sister. 'A secret wedding. The Bishop ——'

'Enough, I say, you little witch! You know why I'm here?'

'To see why I don't go to Communion.'

'Exactly. Did Our Lord say the Church must come to you? Pour me some more wine and tell me all about it. Begin with the big sins at the bottom of the list.'

'Yesterday I worshiped the sun.'

'I am not surprised ... This heathen artist's influence, and that luxury-loving doctor's wife from town! Your grandfather too — as much as I loved him. They have destroyed your faith, and I have stood by in silence. And what have they given you to replace it? They have made you undergo all the doubts and torments of the faithless. Educated above your neighbors and therefore alone. Nobody to turn to but God, in Whom you probably don't believe.'

'He doesn't believe in me, Father.'

The priest chuckled. Then he glanced at her shrewdly. 'I want to know,' he said with a sober look, 'what on earth is your conception of God?'

'I have thought of Him as a sort of great Loneliness, living out where it's always cold. I'm telling you what you asked. I pity Him. I have hated Him.'

The priest's florid face paled. He looked at her in fascination. 'Go on.'

'I hate Him when I suffer hunger. I mean stomach hunger,

days of it at a time. There's no excuse for hunger. It's the worst insult *I* ever knew.'

'Go on.'

'You remember putting up a lightning rod on the steeple, Father? I was a little girl. That was the place I had planned to run to, if the levee should break or a hurricane come. When you put up the lightning rod I was miserable all day, to think there was no safe place in the world.'

'And that would make you pity God ...'

'Yes, Father.'

Father Sam searched for a word. 'Arrogance,' he said. 'What else?'

'Sometimes I pity everything.'

'That's all right.'

'It's a feeling. Yesterday I walked on the levee. It was dusk, one star out and everything quiet. I passed a cabin. A woman was moaning. I heard it through the boards. Moaning. I felt sorry for her. I pitied everything.'

'The woman was suffering *then*, my child. Another time she will laugh.'

'She was not in pain. She was making love with a man, Father.'

The priest frowned out of the window. Out there a bright green lizard was creeping over a board, searching for sun.

Sister said: 'When I was little, every evening I heard little Chauncey Guate next door being whipped. His mother would dress him and sit him in a wicker chair on the levee. She told him not to move from the chair. As soon as she left he would climb down and begin playing in the dust, messing up his clothes. Every day he was whipped for that. His mother called him stubborn. She beat him with willow switches, for his own good. One day she decided to give the wicker chair a coat of paint. She borrowed a brush from us. I went and watched her. She found nests and nests of bedbugs in the cracks of the wicker chair. Mrs. Guate burst out crying. I was angry at God.'

Father Sam smiled. 'I see. I see.' Sister's brooding female indefiniteness moved him. Her overalled legs were held widely apart, as a man sits to think, with her elbows on her knees and her knuckles supporting her temples. 'She has lost her God,' he thought. But watching her devoutly, probing for the soul, the soul within that was his passion and his charge, he glimpsed no token of corruption or pride; and this left his mind, long smoothened by the simple wants of his flock, weary and confused.

'Mama, look, the drudge-boat!' said Bruce.

'Yes, Fella.'

'Big-big drudge-boat! Look out the way! Big drudge-boat shoveling up the levee all night long. Mama, when's the drudge-boat comin' back, Mama? Mama, what does a schooner do, huh?'

'Skoons, I suppose.'

'Yeah! She skoons up the river tell she gets little-little.'

The priest thought, 'The child is the image of the mother, as if she had conceived him alone.' He turned to Sister, 'I will come again and see you, Sister. I wouldn't think too much about God, too deeply. There are clearer waters nearer the surface. You like your Mass, eh?'

'Oh yes! Who doesn't like the old Latin music, oil and ashes, fire and water, chimes and flowers, and the incense smelling like God's breath? I love it all but the sermon.'

'I am no preacher ... No preacher. I have a long way to paddle, and I'm tired. God bless you. Try not to feel angry at God, or sorry for Him.'

Leaving, Father Sam glanced uneasily into the sitting-room, refurbished now with green deck paint — a bookcase and polished center table, a newly caned lounge draped with a spotted deer hide ...

Immersed in some wide crystal dream in the doorway, Bruce studied the departing priest with eyes limpid and sightless.

Father Sam lumbered away through alternate zones of jagged sun and shade, preceded by a brown mass of scared fiddler crabs. His careful knees revolved stiffly from years of prayer. He turned and sent toward the house and the kneeling bushes a tired gesture that was half benison and half salute. He slung his meal sack to his shoulder and plodded up and over the levee's pounded bulge. Some rain hurried by. It pocked the river's frowning face, but the sun tarried and seeped hotly through the willows. Bruce's wide eyes stayed fixed on the empty levee; the toy dangled forgotten; his lips moved, framing a secret phrase.

'He's got some white skin on him, Father Sam,' he said aloud without rippling his glassy dream. 'White skin on his forehead, Mama.' But his mother's quiet answer did not come. Sister was busy elsewhere. Her singing became part of Bruce's reverie. He opened his fingers. The toy clattered down, shattering the dream. He hopped across the yard with the sun over his hair like a gold turban in a picture-book.

Mr. Tim Davidson from New York came up the levee. He was boarding with the justice of the peace. Everybody knew him, having seen him going about the country in boat or hip-boots, interviewing trappers and fishermen, inspecting groves or patches of spring truck... Mr. Tim was making haste. Everybody talked about Mr. Tim for that. 'Dat man sho' make hase when he pazz by, him!' Bruce himself had secretly learned how to make haste. He would run around and around the cistern. He would feel the yards of cool beaten haste unroll behind him.

'Hello, Bubber!' said Mr. Tim, and kept on walking past Bruce, and called, without looking back, 'you want to be my little boy?' and disappeared behind the house. Bruce thought: 'There wasn't any Mr. Tim come up the levee. The levee imagined that.' But he heard Mr. Tim inside talking to Sister. Bruce was a frog. He leapt toward the house. Near the front door, he was a tree that hears everything. A fiddler hole was there. It fitted his big toe. He put in his toe and listened to the voices inside:

'*Bruce is a remarkable child, Sister, and I mean what I said. I'd like to put him through some good schools.*'

'*That's splendid, but he wouldn't leave me now.*'

'*Later, then.*'

'*If we are still fixed as we are now.*'

'*You will be if you stay in this place.*'

'*We won't be, if you help Mitch with his factory.*'

'*Look here, why can't I help you now? There are so many things I could do.*'

'*All right. Peel these peaches thin.*'

'*Will you remember, I am only waiting for you to say the word?*'

'*Is this a proposal?*'

'*I wish to God it were! If my wife were not an invalid . . .*'

Inside Sister turned a big orangewood spoon in a bowl. 'Stay on your side the table, Tim. I'll be asking for that in black and white. What are you all doing about the factory?'

'We've abandoned the original scheme for another. I'm thinking it over. Mateo Lucich got wind of my being here and fired Mitch Holt.'

'You men! Like Bruce with his colored blocks, only Bruce's play has meaning. Where is Mitch? The boy who carried his supper over every evening says he's gone.'

'Out looking over muskrat lands for us. I'll probably invest over there or place Holt elsewhere. Good man, keen and strong. It's funny about René, though. He hardly paints any more, thinking about this factory project. What can he see in a man like Holt? And there's René and this octoroon. I'm told the people are rather bitter against her. Strange animal, René, living in that ramshackle houseboat. He's always preferred squalor to comfort, or says he does. He won't take a penny from me. Insults my friends right and left. Yet I like him.'

Bruce outside was no longer listening. He worked his toe in the fiddle hole, making a pleasantly nasty noise. His other mind had retained and now fondled a few of Mr. Tim's words — 'abandoned' and 'project' and 'ramshackle.' A hot buzzing in the trees mixed with Mr. Tim's voice, deer flies. Bruce felt his hateful afternoon nap coming on. Sounds made his head tingle. He was a bull-wolf. He went to the levee on all fours. A negro boy approached, kicking up twin geysers of hot slush, and stopped and stood blackly robed in sun, gazing down mournfully.

'Bruce, do me favah?' he asked.

'Can't you see I'm busy?' Bruce answered, stuffing twigs in a fiddler hole. 'Ain't got time to bless myself.'

'Do me favah, Bruce. Ax yo' maw she got some work today?'

'Is this a proposal?'

'G'on, white boy. Tell Mama Alfred say ef she got some work.'

But the negro was already leaving, walking backwards, printing negro tracks in the road that slowly filled with creamy water. 'White bastid,' he said sadly.

'Black bastid.'

'White bastid.'

'You don't show dirt. That's why you never wash.'

Mr. Tim was coming. He stooped and caught Bruce back of the neck with his great soft fingers. 'What's that? What did you call that boy?' Bruce rubbed his ear against Mr. Tim's shoulder. 'That's a bad word, Bubber.'

'When you goin' back to Noo York, Mr. Big-Tim?'

'Right now, if you say bad words. You don't care if I go.'

'Say me some big words.'

'Mogilalia. Gesundheit.'

'*Big*' ones!'

'Plenipotentiary. Excommunicate. Disestablishmentarianism.'

Mr. Tim was already twenty yards away, making haste. Bruce looked after him with his mouth wide open.

After dinner, Bruce lay on the sweetly scoured floor. Sister was at the table listing her fall seeds. Bruce passed his fingernail over the pink skin of her heel. He could see through the trees a plump cloud creeping east.

'Time for your nap, Bruce.'

'I'm taking my nap.'

'Not on the floor.'

'Don't a man nap on the floor?'

'Not this man.'

'I'll go without today. Can I? I got so much to do.'

A lizard trickled down the wall in bright twitching leaps toward a fly under the table. None of the fly's thousand eyes saw the lizard. After each leap the lizard raised its smiling face, gauging the distance. It leapt again. The cat lay near Bruce. He was watching through the fine gleaming slits in his head. He quietly clawed a hold on the floor. The slits became ovals. The lizard saw. He flattened himself, turning a paler green. Slowly he crept toward the fly, with his eyes on the cat. Bruce uttered a faint sleepy 'Shoo!' The lizard darted for the fly, and the cat sprang . . .

Trotting casually through the back door, the cat stopped once and looked back at Bruce. The lizard between his teeth was turning gray. The fly had settled exactly in his former spot. The doorway was empty. Across the river a whistle blew, the ice-boat from Lacroix. 'Whoever wants ice hurry up! Something's the matter with Mama, since Father Sam came . . . Mama likes Mr. Tim, always making haste, never carries a sack in case he finds a turtle on the road . . . bananas . . . sorry for God . . .'

Sister turned the pages, searching for tomatoes, thinking: 'The church points to the hereafter, and we want the present.

Let's consider my wedding as being in the present. The past is full of regret and the future sometimes makes you afraid. Poor Christ limp on the Cross. When the sermon begins we all become greedy hypocrites again. I will live a beautiful and interesting life without trying to obey any Commandments but my own. Poor Tim would promise anything now. The slanting look of a man for a woman! To make a woman moan in her bed. *"All right, Tim. Send Bruce to school!"* He'll come back tall and elegant, ready for women and work and the harsh capers of manhood, larger colored blocks. No. Let's make him a pilot, blowing the whistle for me every trip. Drinking with foreign skippers. Winding through life on the polished bridge. Worshiped by the river boys and sought by women. Carrying in his mind a secret picture of the hills and valleys on the river bottom.'

One day the New Orleans packet blew for Sister's Landing. In low river she could see only the texas and the stacks. She heard the croak of the old piling as the nose bumped, and a roustabout jogged over the levee. But why had they stopped the engines? Sister leaned through the vines. She wondered if Bruce in play had put a flag on the wharf.

'No freight here for you!' she called.

'Got a mess o' stuff for y'all, lady! Two passengers comin'. Dey got off at de pos'-office. Dis a lettah for you from Mr. Mitch Holt.' Sister looked at the sweating negro, all befuddled.

'Two passengers? What passengers?'

'Man an' lady from N'Awlins.'

'Coming to this house?'

'Yossum. Where we go' put de freight, lady?'

Sister's eyes skimmed the ticket. Tree spray . . . plows . . . G. oak bedroom suite . . . paint . . . roofing . . . The goods were consigned to Mocco Kalavich.

'Put it in the yard.'

She tore open the letter and read Mitch's signature. She hardly dared discover what came before. A burst of light from the levee blinded her — the sun reflected from a mirror being borne to the house. The light was insolently intrusive. She looked at the letter again to discover its last word — the word 'love.' Her face hardened into a smile.

'Dear Sister,' she read. 'I can send news now. I've learned all there is to know of this business. Able to start in my own way and have fun at it. We soon begin building our first factory. Tim Davidson's going to invest. It's like a fairy-tale. We will pay good wages to all. Imagine a rich man bothering about all? We will put Lucich out of business with better and cheaper products, later. When the factory is finished we will get married, if you still feel the same about our proposition. I will make a house either on this side the river or on yours, as you say. I won't promise you more than a good home. I'll be over to see you soon. I've been working too hard to think of you very much. Try to understand. With love. Mitch.'

Someone was coming down the pathway. She bosomed her letter. The arrivals were Mocco and wife. Sister was disconcerted, greeting Mocco, who looked very handsome in city clothes. Mocco kissed her. Her head was buzzing with confusion. What did it all mean? Mocco was telling her that the well-dressed, pug-nosed but rather pretty young woman was his wife — Violet. Sister murmured a welcome and passed her hand through her hair.

Mocco saw to the freight. The women exchanged small pleasantries. Sister concealed her surprise, not wanting the other to know Mocco had never announced his marriage. It galled her, this thought. But what did it matter, this or any other of Mocco's doings? He was a selfish child, a child, with his fancy vest and his Violet.

'They treated us nice on the boat!' Violet said. 'The Captain's a personal friend of Papa's, and the river's so clean down by the Gulf, and I haven't felt a mosquito yet.'

'There's one on your chin,' Sister said. 'I hope Mocco brought screen wire; they torture strangers. Try not to scratch the bites. If you want to change, I'll make coffee. My room's upstairs to the left.'

'I hope we're not putting you out of your room. This stairs is a real ship's gangway.'

'They found it floating down.'

'I'll be right down to help. I want to help with everything. How do you get the floors so white? It's going to be fun. Mocco wants me to put on weight like the Slavonian type. They like them fat. That came from the Turks. I want to get strong as you are — lifting that suitcase like you did. Is this wild iris? Just imagine!'

Violet's smile was bright and friendly. She gave the impression of energetic, demonstrative warmth of nature. Who was she? Mocco was outside with his thumbs in his belt, telling the roustabouts a funny story. Presently he came in. 'Where's Violet?' he asked.

'Upstairs.'

'Jeezam! Is your room fixed up?'

'Yes, the decorators just left.'

'How you like my little surprise? Did you know me at first? Better times are coming, Sis. Look in the yard. You know what that means? Drainage out back, fences, spray dope for the sick trees. I've got to get me three niggers right away. We're going to make a home here. I've got to go down the road on business. We're going to form our own shipping and marketing association and pro rate the expense. To hell with the middleman! Horray for the off-ox!' He dragged her to the door.

'Steady there!' she said.

'Look, Sis! All the things we needed! A home for us all!' He gathered her into a great hug, enkindling her sisterly warmth.

'It's time you confided in me,' she fussed. 'And how did you buy the supplies?'

'I was paid for my services, I think. And Violet had some money in banks and stocks. She's a business woman. That girl was the brains of the Southern Produce Exchange, like you see her there.'

'Did she have charge of mailing checks?'

'Oh, let *me* pour Violet's coffee. I know how much cream to put.'

'I suppose you brought the cream.'

Little Bruce was chased to the store for canned cream. Just as he returned, Violet came down, all fresh and happy. Mocco leaped from his chair and assisted her, pulled up a chair for her, poured her coffee, snatching the pot from Sister.

'Isn't he a cute little dolling!' Violet exclaimed on seeing the child. 'And who is *he?* Who are you, honey?'

Mocco looked at Bruce as if for the first time in his life.

'Come tell me who you are, honey,' Violet pleaded.

'That's your new Aunt, Fella,' Sister said. 'Tell Aunt Violet who you are.'

'Drink the coffee, Violet,' Mocco said.

'He's shy,' said Violet.

'He's forgotten whose boy he is,' Sister smiled.

But the child stood watching Violet gravely, round-eyed and confused by the vivid color of her clothes, troubled by something felt under Sister's smile, aware of Mocco's discomfiture — perhaps suspecting some trick. He flung an agonized glance at Sister.

'Aren't you my boy, Fella?'

'Yeah.'

Violet took Bruce's hand and turned brightly to Mocco.

'Why, you didn't even tell me Sister was married!'

'Sugar, please,' Sister said, 'and a cookie for Bruce. Take your cookie, Bruce.'

Violet sipped her coffee pensively, no longer noticing the boy, nor looking at Mocco. When Sister was clearing the table, Violet put out her hand impulsively. 'Can't I help?' she begged. 'I can wash dishes.'

'Later,' said Sister. 'I can't let you spoil your pretty waist. You won't find any like it down here.'

Violet glanced through the window at four dresses airing on the line. '*You* sure have some lovely clothes. Mocco told me there's no place to go, down here.'

'Crawfishing and Mass are the only places I know,' Mocco said. 'Some of them dress up to wave at the pilots.'

Violet gazed outside at the trees. She loved trees. They made her think of picnics, cute cakes and sandwiches, snakes and spiders that made one screech delightedly.

After supper Mocco and Violet walked down to the store. Violet wanted to meet the storekeeper and his family, and others about whom her husband had talked. As Mr. Gussy's stenographer she had written letters to many of them. She knew a lot of gossip to tell them about the horrible Mr. Gussy, who had looked into her bosom one day. She wanted to like the people down here. She had spent many an amusing hour finding mistakes in the letters they had written Mr. Gussy, but now she would overlook their ignorance, because Mocco would need their good-will.

Mocco was received in Grass Margin with a good deal of warmth. All agreed this man's transformation was wonderful. He went about with a new briskness and aggressiveness. He meant business. He inspired confidence. He revealed to the people they were living in poverty. He explained they lacked modern conveniences they could not do without. He showed them pictures of grading and packing of fruit as practiced elsewhere. He reminded them that over the River, Dutch Scenery was building up — new houses erected, more Slavonians arriving, a big new cannery planned. He hinted that he, too, had a plan up his sleeve.

Sister answered Mitch's letter: 'The boat brought your letter. Your remarks about the work are interesting. I understand clearly that your work comes first, and that you are doing what I wanted you to. Pay me a visit when you have time, but don't bother. You will see enough of me later on. I feel the same way about our marriage, or our bargain. If you change your mind, you must let me know. If you are going to make a house for us, I would prefer this side the river.'

She walked to the post office to mail it. She smelled figs. In every yard, figs were fermenting. There were too many for the birds, and people were tired of them. Their leaves rubbed together like sandpaper. The Fort searchlights moved over the sky, as if trying to scour away the stars. Back home again, Sister brought inside a sack of tallow-tree berries she had saved a long time. She heated a pot of water for melting the wax off the berries. Until midnight she was busy skimming off the wax, pouring it into a cane with cord in the center. She stacked the warm candles in a box. She took one of them up to her room, the room next to her old one. The other was larger. Mocco and Violet used it.

They were talking. They seemed to be quarreling. Sister undressed and blew out her candle. She lay face downward on the bed. In the adjoining room she heard Violet softly giggling, and the sound of flesh being slapped. The window overlooking the moonlit river was screened, now. The wind swished through, smelling of rain. After a while the wind stopped, and there was the shy whisper of fine vertical rain, so quiet that Sister heard through the wall the sound of moaning.

36

IN THE hot weather the river fell the depth of a man. Then it was clear and calm. The smallest child could run a winning race on the levee against a drifting log. Dark recumbent shapes peopled the shadows of the Grass Margin porches. Babies whined unheeded. Fiddler crabs wandered the parched ditch bottoms, clawing for moisture. The verdant marshes shivered with the Fort guns.

In August Sister dug her lily bulbs, several hundred bright gold ones, each of which had borne a stalk of eight to fifteen Easter lilies. She shipped them to New Orleans in September, and they netted her ten cents each.

Sister waited. Things were happening, activities she did not understand concerning the factory project over the river. Two surveyors had been seen in the marshes over there. Tim Davidson had gone to New York, returned to the Margin, gone back to New York. Nobody knew just where Mitch Holt was. Sister once met his father. The old man stated Mitch had gone somewhere on business.

Through the salty heat of the day Sister waited while she worked. There were days when the bright heat was like a sweet potion to her soul. Groping, she sensed behind the dry whir of insects a lavish silence, immeasurable, profound, as from the slumbering ages of ooze. In the lenient hush, strong torpid rhythms somehow pulsed. The beat of such timeless cadences fed while it lulled the nameless quest of her life.

The soldiers at the Forts were undergoing elaborate maneuvers. When not target-practicing, the new soldiers from the north walked the levees, looking for girls, flapping white handkerchiefs at the mosquitoes. The report of their cannon sounded like the sudden closing of a large book. Their target was a raft in Cowan Bay on the east side behind Bay St. Francis. All day, a fleet gray parabola kept cleaving the sky above Unga January's houseboat, followed by a dim contented grunt far back in Cowan Bay.

'Them cannons,' Unga muttered.

Or when a smaller projectile sped past, screeching like a drunken girl, Unga clenched her teeth and shivered, while the tissues of her stomach gathered in protest. She could not endure the screams.

René painted the parabola. He made it purple as blood. He put a shivering tree into the picture. The tree was placed on a hill. Unga stopped pounding her bricks and looked at the picture, and said, 'Bud dey got no hills here, cher!'

René scowled. 'I brought my own hills here.'

'Whad you mean, ma cher?'

'In my head! Hills in my head! I am not only here. I am everywhere I have been, everywhere I can imagine myself being.'

Unga's orangewood mallet beat the log-end, pounding the moist red brick. She shook her head. 'Je ne ——'

'Close your eyes and think of the ward in the Maternity Hospital where you worked in New Orleans,' René said. 'Can you see it? Then you are in New Orleans. Now remember a certain patient who was always chasing you after a bed-pan. Or think of one who died. When you do that, you are bringing that patient here, as I bring my hills.' He looked at Unga. She was staring into space. She had forgotten him. Her mallet dangled in her hand.

'I'd like some coffee, please,' said René.

An eventful day came to Unga. First a ship broke down.

It anchored opposite her front door. All day it lay there huge and rusty. It emanated an odd rich odor, and flew the colors of an unknown race. A machine in the ship kept throbbing, throbbing — repeating a soft curious word. A ship close by, and not speeding past, was a glamorously ugly thing to see, with its black skin peeling as from some alien malady, and the holes in the side trickling red fluid like blood. Voices in the ship were saying words Unga did not understand. Then a chorus of young laughter. She understood that.

René told her about the ship. 'She came from Italy, the place I told you about, where they live between the ruins.' Unga gazed darkly at the colossal hull, unkempt and bulging with freight, all bruised by foreign suns and waters. René said, 'She's loaded with animal bones.' René stepped from the bushes and talked to an officer on the bridge. The two exchanged comments in Italian. A row of dark faces gathered at the ship's rail. 'They stopped on account of engine trouble,' René told Unga. The officer on the ship saw Unga. He cupped his hands and called something to René.

'They invited us on the ship,' said René.

'You wan us to go on duh ship, ma cher? You can take your pitchas to show.'

'Of course not! It is not my business to take my work to people. They must come to me. Get my breakfast, please. I've got to see Mitch Holt in his prairie camp.' He turned to the houseboat. 'I will probably be gone all day — perhaps all night.'

All night! Unga's languid eyes snapped open. She swayed on the brink of abysmal nothingness. The surrounding colors sprang into violence — thick quivering greens, white shells underfoot, blobs of yellow roses, the vicious blue October sky. But she followed him meekly.

'Bud cher, ain't you gone finish duh pitcha?'

'Unga, I've got other business, I say.'

Following him, she slashed at the bushes with her hand, thinking: 'Jesus, Mary and Joseph! Another night alone! Hell! Let him go to Sister Kalavich! Let him take himself and his crazy pictures out of my sight forever! This is too terrible, too terrible to stand! Why do I do things for him when he will not use me, cook nice dishes when he eats like a child, show him my body when he does not see? I will never understand his talk like *she* does. Ah, the weather is so pretty! Mama has a shady house down the river among our people, and I am as pretty today as a long time ago when a white man gave my name to his schooner.'

After breakfast René said, 'I think we ought to move the houseboat to Dutch Scenery.'

Unga had no words. She stared at her plate.

'I'll have many pictures to paint around there. I'd like to be nearer Mitch. Tim's returning from New York soon, and I suppose he'll live there. We're rather far from things and people here.'

'One time you like dat.'

'But I never intended to rot in peace here in the bushes.'

'*You* can go live there,' said Unga. 'An' stay, too.'

René raised his eyes and frowned like a puzzled child. 'But I have no place to stay just now. That's why I would need the houseboat. And who do you think would feed me?'

Unga sighed. 'You ain' satisfy here no mo'.'

'No. The walk from here to the canal is no longer amusing.'

He stooped to kiss her. She smoothed his forehead, framed by whorls of damp hair. A strange light lurked in her face. 'Why you lak Midge Holt so much, cher?' came her low voice, secretly. 'Tell Unga.'

René faltered in the doorway with his cap. He was some inches shorter than Unga. Her fingers, long and pliant as a pickpocket's, plucked a beggarweed seed from his sleeve, and slid down for his hand.

'I can't explain to a woman the manly friendship of men. I don't know why I like Mitch. I never thought of asking myself why. Perhaps it's because he's different from me, or the things he's experienced, or his white strength. Someone must help him make a beginning in his work.'

René walked before her to the levee, saying no more. To Unga his talk about Mitch meant little, only that she believed it false, all false. As if a man would walk so far and often to see another man! On the levee crown she asked him with a searching look, 'When is Sister gone marry Mitch, ma cher?'

René swung about, thin-lipped and vexed. 'I know nothing about that!' he said.

'You dawn lak to see dat happen, my sweetheart?'

'Will you let go my arm?'

'*She* got plenny white strank too, my sweetheart. Nice white strank to hol' a white man tight, my sweetheart.'

'Will you stop pinching me? I've had enough of this savage jealousy.'

'Oui, ma cher. I be raddy when you come back. I wait fo' you on my back.'

René walked to Dutch Scenery without glancing backward. He saw nothing of the stark beauty of the morning marshes. Once, out of nowhere came the sound of a faint disturbance, like wind pressing through trees, or distant waters breaking over rocks. The sound, growing louder until it became a very real and definite roaring, caused a chill to pass through the man, because it had no direction. Now it sounded like an approaching storm. He looked over his head and saw the source of the noise — a great flock of pelicans flying low, sailing on rigid wings ...

'He love dat woman, yes,' Unga thought, curiously without heat. There was no fury inside her, only the rather sad knowledge that she must get rid of Sister Kalavich. She returned to the houseboat through the warm shine of dew, stepping daintily, lost in a quaint regal solace — mistress of the maimed yearning, true to the marching heart. Inside she took from its hiding-place under the rug a sheet of drawing-paper. She had found it months ago, rolled into a ball in René's coat pocket. It was a drawing of Sister Kalavich crouched beside a stove, a white naked back, and the familiar piled hair on the bowed head. . . .

In the afternoon she prepared a batch of anise cakes poisoned with the juice of a deadly herb.

She ovened them with a last lingering touch. They came out pale and fragrant. She put them into a paper bag, and took her baby and left it with Fanny in the next-door houseboat.

The vast blond river burned, hardly stirring. The sun in the water flashed upward, gilding her throat. Her gaily colored Sunday pirogue moved as softly as a swan. The roofs of Grass Margin drew closer. She remembered her early years as a single long day, burning with soundless colors. She and Sister had played on the bank, apart from the others, hunting curious objects washed up by the stream. And Sister's father had beaten Sister in public for playing with Unga. And one day Sister and Unga had secretly pricked their fingers with a Spanish dagger thorn to compare the white and the negro blood. The tiny beads had sprung out and hung trembling fresh and rich, like surprised blossoms. And the friends had trembled with gladness that the bloods were alike. . . .

Would Sister eat the cakes?

Would René eat them, if he were there?

Many people died of indigestion before the arrival of a doctor. But the doctor would find out. *'What did she eat?'*

The news would zigzag. From village to village hers and Sister's names would be called across frogponds and bayous and velvet thickets of okra.

'Sister Kalavich is dead wid poison, her.'

'Now you know! Sister Kalavich dead and tomorrow buried.'

'Was it took or given, well?'

'Unga January did it, fo' God sake, and runned away.'

'Now what for, Unga did dat?'

'She monkeyed wid her man, they say.'

'Eh bien! She monkeyed wid her man, po' thing.'

The Kalavich house was changed. It was painted sternly white, with green shutters closed like lips withholding secrets. Unga paddled closer. The sick trees had grown strong and bright, as if painted too. The wharf was repaired. In its shade a lanky white-eyed negro lounged. The Kalavich house looked as if something secret were going on inside. White people make love in daylight. There was no sound but the other muted pulsing somewhere — in the sun, or the Gulf beyond, or from the depths of the earth. Unga moved closer. She drifted to the wharf. The lanky negro peered at her over the wharf edge, his red-figured shirt flaming in the sky.

'Is Miss Sister home?' Unga asked.

'Yassam, she inside.'

'She all by herself?'

'Nome. She wid de cullud gals packin' cukes fo' de boat. An' Miss Violet. Dat's Mistah Mocco wife. Mistah Mocco he haid man. Ah'm de outside man.'

'Oui. My bag.'

'Yass, *mam!*'

But suddenly Bonus recognized something in Unga's facial expression. His eyes kindled with gratification. They burned down into hers from a great height, probing eagerly, waiting for a flicker of recognition. The sun was behind him. He bulked like a cool dark cloud, sheltering her, taking the sun upon his shoulders to protect her thin white blood. Her eyes flashed, and so did his.

'What's yo' name, sweetness?' came his deep suave voice.

'Unga. Leave me pazz, you.'

Bonus owned her wrist. His fingers were strong kind captors of her wrist and her purpose. 'Ah looks in yo' eyes,' he drawled. 'Thank you. Thank you. Ah looks in yo' eyes an' Ah sees what Ah wants. An' why you come up heah so pale, an' scaid, an' mean, on such a pretty day, an' nobody got nothin' to worry 'bout? Is you hongry? Is you lookin' fo' work? Doan come up heah talkin' French wid me, sweetness, an' tryin' to pass fo' white wid me. Ah bin aroun' de country.'

'Leave me pazz.'

Bonus laughed with his stomach, deep and terrible. She strode out of his shadow. But the other shadow of his black laughter followed her breasting the quick sunny billows of color through the front yard garden. The ranks of color submerged her to the swinging thighs, brushing her like wisps of tinted spray. She took the vague curve of an earthen path to the rear with nostrils lifted and eyes again alive and dark, the bearer of good death.

Her steps slowed. She saw Sister in the packing-shed doorway with bright dark hair coiled, a smile on her tilted face, her hands holding a piled green triangle of fall cucumbers.

'Unga! My, it's good to see you!'

'How you feel, cher?' came the old question.

'Fine! Sit here in the cool.'

Sister went on helping the packers. She talked about the forthcoming co-operative association. Unga sat stiffly with the paper bag. Sister's rounded phrases, the new courteous tone, so like René's manner of speech, stirred Unga's hatred. This was the way Sister and René talked to each other. It was terrible. The negro Bonus slouched past the doorway and smiled in at Unga. His grin told her nothing was worth bothering about, and caused her to remember certain lazy innocent days of her animal childhood, groups of soft fat bushes on a lane-edge, rain too sweet to get out of, and the coolness of sandy paths beaten through the trees. And under Unga's hatred lay the more bitter feeling of affection she had once borne toward Sister.

'Have a cuke, won't you, Unga?' Sister said. 'There's a bowl of salt somewhere.'

Unga took the cucumber, but did not eat. She watched the packing, how Sister's strong fingers rummaged the fruit into its logical pattern in the barrel. She was bewildered by all the changes she saw in Sister, which made it impossible for them ever to be real friends again. She heard Bonus laughing with someone in the trees.

'Have you seen Mocco's wife?' Sister asked. 'She does most of the housework now.'

'How you lak his wife, you?' Unga asked.

Sister wrinkled her nose over her shoulder. 'She's all right, Unga. A cute little bride. She's made a man of Mocco without lifting a finger, only her eyebrows. She watches his diet and his accounts. Mocco has changed.'

'I'm glad for dat, me.'

'I suppose so. He's busy as Grampaw was when they started the oyster association out in the Bay.'

Unga thought of René and Sister living in the oyster settlement. Sister was more attractive than she. Unga's hands had grown large and bony, her shoulders were square. She thought, 'Give her the cakes! Now is the time.' The moment had come. The other girls had gone out. When they went into the house she would have to offer some to Mocco's wife, Sister's child. Unga's hand closed on the paper bag.

'These are Southern Wonders,' Sister said. 'Plenty juice, and brittle meat.' She bent over the barrel. She seemed waiting for Unga to act. Unga's fingers would not work. The laughter in the orchard, the sweet and fearful belly laughter kept calming her fears, telling her she need not bother about anything . . .

In the big house, Unga looked around for signs of René. She saw none. She felt a pang of regret . . .

The kitchen was orderly and gleaming, with a different kind of orderliness than Sister's had been. There were colored curtains, a cute oilcloth floor mat, spotless areas of bright paint, a cute tinted kerosene stove. No polished utensils were visible. The fat kegs of pickled game were gone. A space under the stairs that had been a mellow brown recess was now a cabinet with cute colored paper on the doors, imitating stained glass.

Unga was about to take Sister's hand and tell her how good it was to see her, when Violet tripped downstairs. 'Sister!' Violet called. 'Where's that Poline? Did you see Poline anywhere? Did Mocco get back? It's four o'clock. Where's Poline?'

'I sent her out back to break some corn.'

'I had her dusting books. She never finished her dusting.'

'Come here and meet Unga January, Violet. My old friend. Here's Mocco's wife, Unga.'

Unga smiled and bowed. 'I look a sight,' Violet said. She turned to Sister. 'The books that girl dusted are crummy. Absolutely crummy. What are we paying her for? We ought to get a girl from town. Sister, do you really want that big dictionary? I'll try to make covers for it. Miss January's a real Creole type, isn't she? I adore black eyes. Is Mocco back? He promised to bring lard. I want to talk to you about that Poline. I've been wondering why she's so lazy. Sister I believe she's a nigger. I really do.'

The clock ticked, and a fig leaf floated lazily into the room. The cannons at the Forts were cracking gently, vibrating the window panes. 'She's got that scared look, like all white niggers get,' said Violet. 'And did you ever notice how she smells?'

'Violet, please ——'

'Well, I don't know. You can't tell down here, except by the smell.'

Unga put her glass of wine down and walked out of the house. Bonus had been standing under the trees listening. When he heard Unga coming down the steps, he walked quickly to the wharf. Sister overtook Unga under a fig tree.

'Unga, you must excuse Violet. She doesn't understand.'

'Go 'way! Mon Dieu!'

She clasped the fig tree and wept. Her fingernails made four parallel green lines along the bark, from which thick white milk began to flow. 'Please go 'way from me.' Sister plucked at her sleeve. Unga shook the hand away. Violet was watching them from the window, her knuckles between her lips, her face small and frightened. She, too, presently began to weep. Sister walked away from Unga. 'What the hell's the matter with you people?' she muttered, and returned to the packing shed . . .

Bonus was on the wharf, chuckling. His pointed shoulders were shaking in merriment. Unga went to the river. Her entire lower face was drenched in tears, and horrible sobs rippled through her. When she climbed down to her pirogue she found Bonus sitting in the stern.

'Come, Ah takes you home, sweetness,' he said.

'I dawn want you,' Unga said. She sat in the pirogue. She broke into fresh sobbing. Bonus cast off and paddled away. He headed upstream. He dipped his hat full of water for Unga to wash her face. He paddled strongly, chuckling, and the craft leaped ahead with each paddle stroke. 'Nobody's go' make you cry no mo',' he said.

They stopped at Fanny's houseboat and Unga told Bonus where to go with the pirogue. The fat baby rode home on her hip. The baby, always sheltered from the sun, had some kind of sickness — swollen knees, unable yet to walk. Bonus was sitting under a tree. He watched Unga go in with the child and come back outside with a pair of René's tennis-shoes. She sat on the steps with a table knife, and began to scrape large chunks of prairie clay from the shoes. Once she raised her face and stared at Bonus.

'Don' pay no mind to me,' he said. 'Keep on what you doin', sweetness.'

'Go 'way, I say! Nobody want you here. I'm gone tell duh constabu' on you.' The baby came out, crawling backwards down the steps, and went to its mother. Bonus chuckled. He wagged his head at the baby and made a noise with his tongue like hoofs running through mud. 'Ain't dat nice, now, how y'all fixed up heah, sweet lil house an' all. Ain't you 'shame to ack so mean? Lawd, I nevah thought I'd love a wumman any mo'. You bettah stay 'way from de white folks, dey ain' go' do you any good, sweetness.'

'Go 'way, you bad man! Whad for you come in dis plaze?'

'Down dis rivah? I kill a man, sweetness.'

The baby was trying to open Unga's dress to find a nipple. Unga lay on the grass and the baby straddled her body and sucked her breast, pinching the breast, sleepily murmuring through its nose. The men on the anchored ship had lowered a plank scaffold, and were chipping the paint off the ship with hammers. Unga's arm lay deep in the cold grass, and through the tree she watched a diminutive man working high on a mast.

'My man, he is come soon,' she said to Bonus. The negro smiled, his face all shining around the white teeth.

'Neb' mind,' he said. 'He can't do me nothin', that man o' yourn. I know who *he* is. He painted me once. Ax him. Ax him 'bout de boy dat talks to de ghost... Don't bothah yo' haid about dat, sweetness. You jis' git used to me, 'cause you go' see lots an' lots o' me. I ain' go' let nobody make you cry, nevah no mo'.'

In a little while Unga began to weep gently, and the sleeping child's puckered face, drunken with milk, lifted and sank with the heaving of her bosom. Bonus quietly got to his feet and slipped away toward Dutch Scenery.

When he returned next day, Unga went into the houseboat and locked the door. Bonus left on the doorstep a bag of sunflower seed.

On the day after that when he came back, Unga was not there. He left on the doorstep an armful of sweet corn.

Another day when he came, Unga and René were inside eating a gumbo. Bonus backed away a little distance and whistled a slow-drag song, and on a near-by stump he left a bottle of Midnight Shoe Dressing.

A week later he swam the river with his clothes on. Approaching the houseboat he saw Unga sitting on a bench by her washtub. She was weeping, holding a pair of René's trousers pressed against her face. Bonus went and put his long skinny hand on her shoulder. She leaned her head against his wet leg, and was quite overcome by grief.

Suddenly she leapt to her feet and rained a vicious tattoo of blows upon his chest, until he ducked his head under her arm. She kept beating on his hollow wet back, while Bonus giggled richly.

'Quit ticklin', sweetness! Quit ticklin'!' he laughed. 'Come on, le's quit this playin' and tawk dis thing ovah.'

Unga broke and ran. She stopped to pick up the small heavy orangewood mallet used for pounding brick. She turned and hurled it. The hammer struck Bonus in the forehead. He sank to his knees, and quickly rose again, laughing. Unga ran inside, slammed the door and shoved in the bolt. She rummaged in a drawer and brought out a blessed candle. She lit the candle. Bonus went to the window, still smiling, pleading, 'Don't you want me to heal you, sweetness? Come, lemme heal you out dat sorrow?'

'Go 'way, I say!' She stood with a little skinning-knife uplifted. Bonus pointed to the large lump on his forehead and leaned in the window. 'Sweetness, you see dis? Dis is yo' las' rock! You couldn't bus' it wid yo' hammah! Now de Lawd,

He sont me heah fo' dat puppus. 'Cause mah haid's fulla
love, an' ——

> 'Cause mah haid's fulla love, Law!
> An' love's de Rock of Ages,
> An' *shall* heal de 'bominations, Law!
> An' uh-confound de 'bominations, Law!'

While Bonus preached in his bloodcurdling shouts, waving
his long sharp elbows, Unga knelt before the blessed candle,
trembling and praying. Bonus finished his sermon, and she
heard him chuckling. Something fell with a sharp rattle on the
table beside her. She looked at it, shrinking. It was a lead
rosary — gray beads strung on fishing twine, a heavy leaden
cross.

'Ah made dat fo' you, sweetness,' Bonus drawled. 'Pick it
up in yo' han'. It's made outa buckshot.'

'Me, I'm gone tell duh constabu' you kill a man,' said Unga,
watching the beads on the table. She could not take her eyes
from them.

'Lawd, Ah done paid fo' dat, sweetness, an' got no receipt.
You ain't de only one had to bus' rocks, sweetness. Ah done
suffah an' cry lak you, too. Plenneh times Ah see myse'f layin'
undah a box-car cryin' in de night.' Unga put her knife down,
and with the tip of one finger touched the cold lead cross.
Bonus reached in swiftly and passed his warm black hand over
hers. He closed his eyes and trembled.

Unga looked up. Bonus was backing away through the
trees, and the belly laughter sounded deep and sweet. 'Man
or wumman!' he called. 'Dey ain' nobody go' make mah
baby cry!' Unga's eyes followed him. She leaned to one side
watching him in a turn of the sun-dappled pathway. Bonus
turned and smiled back. The drooping willow leaves blurred
the white flash of his teeth.

37

WHERE the grapefruit sagged so near the levee that a way-farer might pluck his fill, the sign remained, LETTERS WRITTEN.

Negroes would come to Sister to have mail orders made out, or trappers ordering winter boots.

Once a strange girl came to Sister, standing in the doorway of the packing shed where Sister was making Bruce a kite. The light showed through the girl's dress, showing the long rounded limbs. She was about eighteen, with skin the color of the river. She wanted a letter written to a man.

'I write only business or family letters,' Sister told her.

The girl dropped her eyes. She started down the steps, then returned. 'Dis is business,' she said. Her face was powdered to the jawbones. She took a paper from her bosom, bearing the name and address.

Sister wrote the letter for her. It was to Mitch Holt, care Point Moan Willow Camp, Kindness of Captain Twigtree, care Dredge Billbo.

> Dear Mr. Holt:
> When you return to the Margin I would like to see you. I have moved next to the Esparbo place. Write soon.
> JUANETTE

Sister added a line at the bottom:

> 'How's the mosquitoes? Sister.'

Sometimes Sister returned to heavy labor for a day or two, hoeing trees, breaking the remainder of the cucumbers, cultivating with the horse the plot she intended to use for winter cauliflower. On such days she felt heavy and hard and slow, like a man with a womb, only half mindful of the signs of falling sap and the pull of the tireless beast. Her plans for future hung suspended above the flow of days like an unfinished bridge. Mitch was working in the willow camp pending completion of the factory negotiations. Tim Davidson had sent down a representative to make a survey of available oyster bedding grounds.

Mitch appeared casually one night, looking for supper. Probably he had been to see the girl Juanette. Some of his casualness was transmitted to Sister, the quality of proud sureness, which still did not take things too seriously. He was capable of loud laughter once more, perhaps even of folly. He was somewhat talkative — though Violet at supper scarcely permitted anyone else to speak.

'The man owes it to the woman, don't you think, Mr. Holt, to take out insurance, and his children too? It ought to be done the first thing. Put it off, and it never gets done. Never!' she shouted at her soup. 'There's more poor widows in town than you can shake a stick at. And from what? Neglection! It's not that men are selfish. Turn that fire low, honey. It's downright neglection! Mocco, dolling, what's wrong with your baked potato?'

'I ate it all but the skin, honey.'

'Look the potato still on that skin, silly! The skin's the best part, and he won't eat it. My father throws the inside away and eats the skin. When are they going to start building your factory, Mitch?'

'We're waiting on Tim Davidson.'

'Mocco, pass him the shrimp omelet before it gets cold. There's a mosquito in this room.'

After supper Mitch explained to Sister how the two projects, his and Mocco's, would be interrelated. Mitch hoped to use in his factory the culled vegetables that should prove unfit for shipping by Mocco's people. Mocco's idea was to subject all fruit and produce to grading so rigid that a reputation would be created immediately among exclusive consumers everywhere, and the fancy prices received upon which the success of the venture depended.

Sister had lit the lamp in the packing shed and found a task, to be alone with Mitch. He was helping her break the sprouts from some potatoes. His white arms were full of sawgrass cuts. She listened to his words as she had attended the work-discussions of Grampaw and René — her old familiar rôle of listener to men. Mitch's terse vital phrases were logical and convincing, and revealed the man's capacity to harbor iron dreams. When he spoke of artificial canals for muskrat breeding, and big ships taking cargoes of canned provender for strange countries, Sister could see the prairie's virgin roundness sundered by oblique scars, and pillars of smoke climbing the lonely sky over Dutch Scenery. Mitch made no attempt to relate this work to her. This was surely proper. She wanted no part, now, in his dream — not in the iron one.

'I'll want a feather mattress,' Mitch was saying, 'a small one on a cot in a room above my office, where I can nap during the day.'

Sister smiled. It was his old habit, as it was hers, to sleep a few minutes frequently during the day. 'I have mine,' she answered. 'I'll make two small ones of it, and give you one.' Then she was lost in thought. Mitch reached over and kissed her lips. She slapped him. He kissed her averted cheek.

'I'll give you all the things you want,' he said.

'I want no things.'

'The hell you don't!'

'Remember the bargain. I want a practical marriage, and

a horse to fit Grampaw's saddle. Did you know Bruce is going to be a pilot? I'll follow the ship to Lacroix in Grampaw's saddle.'

Bruce left his play and went to his mother's side, and stood watching Mitch Holt. Bruce had not yet decided whether or not he liked Mitch. Mitch did not notice the boy, but continued breaking the sprouts from the potatoes with fingers all browned by the tar in his cigarettes. The remark about piloting reminded him that he had business at Pilottown on the morrow.

'You're going to hire all of Mateo Lucich's men?' Sister asked.

'We'll take the good ones.'

'How?'

'Because we'll need them. I made those men and I'll need them.'

'What will Mateo do without them?'

'Get new ones, for the time being. He won't be in business long after we start. He'll need only one man — in his saloon.'

'You don't like Mateo?'

'Sure. But he'll be in the way.'

'I'm thinking of his family.'

'Better let him do that. Let's play the phonograph. I'll race you to the house.'

She crossed to where he stood in the door. She wound her arms about him from behind, and passed her face over the dense cool wads of muscle in his back, and her tingling fingers spoke to him across the years. He stood unmoving, and only brushed her wrist in a brief sturdy gesture that seemed to say, 'I am here.'

She walked to the levee with Mitch. They went through the fragrant moonlight with arms about each other's waist. Suddenly a woman's figure left the shadow of a tree in the front yard, and hurriedly climbed the levee.

'Look!' Sister whispered. 'Isn't that Unga January?' She

called, 'Hey, Unga!' But the figure continued hurrying down the road. 'What was she doing, I wonder?' Sister asked.

'Making water, or looking for René,' Mitch answered. 'He tells me she's always spying on him. She probably thinks he's still in love with you. Is he?'

'No. Where is he? I haven't seen him for a long time.'

'You didn't give him the old story, did you?'

'What story?'

'About wanting to be *just friends*. About spoiling the friendship by making love.'

'Not exactly.'

'Hell! You women take the cake! Why should a man want a woman for a *friend?* Tell me one reason why? I mean a grownup man. A young man. René's staying with us. He's a fine fellow, I guess. He gets on my nerves sometimes. I don't know what it is. I never met anyone who knew so much, and he's sure good-hearted. Can't do enough for you. He gets on my nerves. He came to stay with us. Nobody asked him. Just gradually moved in. No money. Won't take any from his rich folks. The old man keeps hinting for him to leave. There's something the matter with René. What is it? He wants to be a pal and he can't ... Unga came down home a couple days ago, the day I got back. She called him outside in the dark. I heard her crying.'

Sister stood beside the man, her body a slim graven blur. She consulted the small dead moon with her eyes. 'I don't understand any of it!' she said. 'Are things more messed up as you get older? Do other people wonder about the reason for this, that and the other, like I do? ... I didn't know you were living at home again. I didn't know René had left Unga.' She was chilled by the clammy exhalations of the trees, but she did not move to Mitch for warmth. 'I suppose René's knocking at your door. That's how I think of it. He knocked at mine for a long time, looking for friendship or something ...

Things are happening lately, all sorts of things that should concern me, but I feel out of it all. Mocco came back married. I knew nothing about it. For months I've been on a separate road, branched off and going alone. I see it now.'

'He never showed me his pictures.'

'It seems like I'm going on alone now.'

'He never talks to me about his painting. I've seen them. Good Christ! what is he trying to paint?'

'On a separate road. I hate being a woman. *Hate* it!'

'Quit it, Jolie! Nobody's got time for you now. Why don't you make some fancy-work? Look after the kid. Don't get soft. You're a fine woman, polished and healthy and smart.'

'I want to be soft tonight so I can be hard tomorrow.'

But walking into the house, she felt the little core of hardness shining within her — Grampaw's core of hardness. She swung her long legs. She tossed her head in the dark. Inside she passed a mirror that gave her a fleet hint of the sudden ivory and onyx of her passing, the fluid shadowed orifices of her eyes and the plump dark lips furled about a twisted gash. Violet was playing ragtime on her piano in the living-room. The tune sounded mouldy, because the Delta air had begun to ruin the piano. Violet, angry at the climate, tried to sweeten the tune by beating harder, so that under the piano's vibration a bowl of vari-mottled osprey eggs was moving across its top. Up in her room Sister heard the crash of the bowl to the floor, and Violet's scream of horror, and her running to the kitchen for mop and water. Sister leaned out of her window, smiling. The waiting cypresses in the river swayed inanely on their buttressed moorings, and slipping past her cheeks was the bracing odor of beaten spume.

Grampaw in discussing the people around them had once shown Sister how to fabricate a human life into a whole from a sequence of little fragments. Now she groped backward, trying to achieve a detached picture of her own life. And its major events drifted closer together, like landmarks viewed by a climbing fowl, forming at last a darker or brighter cluster in the dun-colored surrounding maze...

Certain phases, most phases of the past evoked a smile of self-derision or pity. She saw Grampaw schooling her in the language of the seasons, bringing her the smooth old words of the buried giants. And René Davidson teaching the poise of disciplined senses, revealing the fleetness of beauty and the sting that ecstasy conceals; and showing her the frenzied world of the present, the tall earthen towers brooding above the tinny clatter of Things. And Loretta Dobravich showing her all the thrilling rituals of dress and conduct...

To what did all this *lead?* What was it *for?*

A frog in the river bellowed smoothly.

She watched the departing ships a long time, one by one stealing out to sea all jeweled with belts and diadems and brooches of topaz light, the Saturday passenger sailings. The night was a great lovely stage, then, where nothing happened. Grampaw's tranquil refuge, nature, was a fatuous pageant of birth and decay — greedy birds, mincing flowers, obese trees, fermenting quagmires; and his books on the shelves were filled with cold black words.

The morning brought no peace. How lonely the world was! How could they endure it, these patient ones she saw about her: a woman painfully dragging a huge chunk of driftwood; two men riding to church one behind another, so grimly that each might have been the other's prisoner; a girl in an okra patch pausing to follow with her lingering look the passage of a man on the road; a tattered Cajin staggering down the road with a dangling jug...?

'I need laughter,' she decided one afternoon when not even the flying of a kite would amuse her.

She went to Pretty John's. John was on his little front porch painting a row of decoy ducks. His colors, blue, green, gray, were dipped out of three oyster shells.

'Why you never went to duh dance laz night?' he asked her.

'Hush up! I don't know.'

'Bud dancing gone make your eyes shine, Jolie.'

'And my nose. Why don't you and Miss John come to see us? We've got ice-water every day.'

The old man saw the curl of her lips. John devoutly cursed under his breath. This woman made everybody wish they were young and discontented again.

'You lak Mocco's wife, you?' he asked. 'Duh way she fix up duh plaze?'

'I don't know.'

'Me, I remember yo' grandpère paddlin' after plank for dat houze. I lak dat houze. She got pretty paint oudside and flagpole. Bud I wonder ef de entrails pretty lak duh hide! You maw would lak dat houze. Grampaw, him, he made it for her. You paw, him, he was not drunkar' dat time. She had love. A woman got to have dat or she ain't got nothing. Eh bien!'

John's wife inside was singing and beating dried shrimp — a barefooted and wizened little crone, finished with coquetry and pain, her children reared and scattered, alone again with her man. 'Jolie!' she howled, 'I hope you dawn listen to dat crazy foo' what he tell you, no!' Her black eyes still twinkled with love. She hovered over the tiny one-hole stove with the tiny coffee-pot. The diminutive kitchen garden outside shone like a colored rug thrown carelessly out to sun.

'Dey say Mocco gone make a meetin' negs week, Jolie.'

'Yes. Everybody's invited. It will be on the batture by our house.'

'Dey say you gone make turtle soup for duh people. Heh! Heh! Everybody want some of dat soup!'

'Me make a soup? It's the first I've heard of that.'

'Me, I never didn't see a meetin'.'

'He's calling the people together to organize his association. He wants everybody to join.'

John came in. 'Dey say duh 'sociation gone ship only duh pretty fruit and truck. Who dis 'sociation gone belonk to? Whad we gone do wid duh oranges and truck dat ain't pretty? But it taste good as duh pretty ones, hein? Eh bien! We gone throw dat away — duh stuff dat ain't pretty an' taste nize as duh pretty ones?'

'I think Mitch Holt will use the culls in his factory.'

'Midge Holt! Well, dat's different, yes.'

Mocco's big meeting was held on the river bank in the sun. The wharf would not contain the crowd. The multitude sat on the sloping levee — mostly men wearing starched shirts without collars. Mocco spoke from a boat. It was a long memorized speech he and Violet had been a week preparing, large sections of it out of a farmers' journal, out of an encyclopedia.

A proud crucial day for Mocco. The people had had time to think over his idea, and some skepticism had appeared here and there. In other quarters, interest had flagged because of the exceptional warmth of the autumn weather. Mocco bellowed his words in a strange arrogant voice, frequently stabbing his finger skyward like a crazed prophet. He explained why their soil was the earth's richest. He read them a poem about a brutalized peasant who knew not his strength, and described his hearers as the uncomplaining slaves of fat overlords who sat dictating letters under a fan while the farmer fought the Johnson and alligator grass in the sun. He accused the overlords of price fixing and described other fraudulent practices he claimed to have seen. He examined the history of other successful co-operative projects coming into being elsewhere, explained the purpose of his own, refuted several false-

hoods his enemies were spreading, and in a final possessed outburst exhorted everybody to join.

There was a silence, heavy and hot. A woman told a child
to keep still. Old men stood with their hands behind their ears
and lipless mouths wide. Mitch Holt rolled a cigarette with
the tobacco sack dangling from his teeth, and his keen gaze
traveled over the crowd. Violet, standing beneath a tupelo
biting her nails, suddenly ran forward clapping her little hands.
A few people responded.

'Any questions?' Mocco's voice came through the silence.
'Any questions? Don't be bashful.'

A man with a red beard and large freckles on his arms and
neck pushed through the crowd. He was carrying a hat full
of tomatoes. He stood on the water's edge and looked around
at the crowd. 'I wants to know,' he roared at Mocco, 'how
many these tomato is good for shipping wid your 'sociation!
Me, I pick these tomato from one vine, like you see 'em.' A
low purring went through the audience. Many smiled at the
smartness of the freckled man.

Mocco raised his hand for silence, and took hold of the rope
and pulled the boat to shore. He took the tomatoes and looked
at them. The boat drifted back out. Sitting in the boat, he
sorted the fruit. He raised his hands, containing several large,
firm, well colored tomatoes. 'Here you are!' he shouted. 'And
you'll get *twice* as much for these as anything you are shipping
now.'

'Where's duh rest?' the freckled man asked.

Mocco brought up the hat. It was half full of fruit, some too
soft and some too small.

'Now whad I'm gone do wid *them?* asked the freckled man.
There was considerable laughter. Mocco raised his hand.

Mitch Holt was pushing through the crowd. He waded
through the yellow water and climbed into Mocco's boat. He
picked up the hat containing the rejected fruit. He glared at

the freckled man and in a low, clear voice said: 'Octave, you damned fool! I'm going to put these in *cans* over the river.'

There was a husky explosion of laughter at Octave's expense. Mitch waited, smiling. 'I'm going to buy these from you,' he said. 'All you've got. All your other off-grade stuff. Where have you been, Octave? Don't you know we're fixing to build a big canning factory over there? You'd better join this thing.'

'Hooray for Midge!' someone shouted. In a moment the air was filled with whirling hats, and many bulging throats screamed the cry, 'Hell wid duh middleman!' Scared babies clutched their mothers and bawled unheard. Women pummeled the surging bodies that crushed them. People pointed to the poor freckled man and roared with laughter. Mocco came ashore, smiling and still explaining in words that were drowned by the noise.

Sister stood on the edge of the crowd, wearing an apron. Near her was the big kettle of turtle soup she had made, and a table full of piled tin cups for serving. A keg of orange wine was tapped. Everybody drank to the success of the association. Every man pledged himself, each making a differently shaped cross or tracing his name on the paper. Then they drank the soup, standing around inhaling it loudly from the cups. Sister wanted to get away. The sweating horde sickened her, the brutal contact of flesh on flesh, the confusion, the harsh discordant hues of cheap raiment, the maudlin whacking of backs, shaking of hands, raucous boasting. How she could despise these people, her people! A group of men along the wooden revetment were watching a snake fight. Two snakes had been caught by boys, and someone had found a box, and the king snake and cottonmouth moccasin had been thrown into it to fight. Mitch Holt was apart from the crowd, lounging beneath a tree. René Davidson came and spoke to Mitch. He took Mitch's arm and led him away. Sister, now alone with the crowd, went toward the house. As she passed the snake fight she could smell the strong odor of the moccasin. But it was more pleasant than the odor of the crowd . . .

Bonus watched the snake fight. He was among the spectators who lay along the top of the revetment, looking down into the drygoods box containing the snakes. The snakes did not want to fight. Each lay neatly coiled, head pillowed on body in an attitude of vigilant repose. The noonday sun seemed to focus its rays in the box. The main gathering of people from the meeting soon straggled homeward.

None of the row of men and boys on the revetment made a sound or movement. Bonus was bareheaded. The hot sun penetrated his skull, making him slightly dizzy and bringing floating dots before his eyes. He had been up late for five nights, prowling about Unga January's houseboat. A boy next to him was eating plums. Frequently the boy would shoot one of the plum seeds into the box below, trying to stir the snakes into action. He would hold the seed between his fingers, and press until the seed slipped out into the air and curved down into the box. The snakes lay motionless, each coiled in its corner. They looked like two lifeless, freshly enameled ornaments cast from metal.

The line of watchers waited for the snakes to begin. All were lulled, now, into half-awareness by the soft drone of the heat, the curious medicinal smell of the moccasin, the somewhat hypnotic effect of staring into the box. Bonus blinked his eyes in the hot sun. The surface of his eyeballs seemed dry and gritty. There was not much action in a snake fight, and you had to watch closely. The initial spring of the reptiles was half the show . . . But no one complained. They merely lay there, isolated in time and space, flattened, only their eyes alive. One man was already sleeping.

Bonus frowned and blinked several times.

He was seeing a pale milky presence, six feet high, standing alongside the snake box. It was outlined in the shape of a man. It began to turn darker. He blinked and it disappeared.

It returned again, pale, wavering. He could see through it. There were hot sunny leaves and branches moving in the wind through the vaporous face. Bonus formed words with his thick soundless lips:

'Dat you, Frank?'

Instantly the presence appeared to him as the black, smiling ghost of the man he had killed, Frank St. Green, all ragged and happy.

Bonus saw the ghost's lips moving, forming words. When the lips stopped moving, Bonus felt the words coming to him, slow and soundless. 'Hello, Bonus, boy! How you feelin'?' The ghost was scratching its hip.

Bonus's lips moved, shaping the silent answer: 'I been waitin' for you to come see me, Frank.'

'What's de mattah, Bonus? Is you in a mess again?'

'Ah'm wo' out, Frank. Wo' out fo' a wumman. Been settin' in de sun, settin' in de sun every day, waitin' fo' you to come tell me what to do, Frank.'

All the spectators on the revetment jerked up their heads in unison. One of the snakes in the box had moved. The ghost had gone from Bonus's sight. The cottonmouth moccasin had moved its tail a barely perceptible trifle. The moccasin was short, thick, black, with a spade-shaped sneering head, capable of putting the hoarded vitality of a lifetime into one deadly blow. When the moccasin twitched its tail, the king snake raised its head a bit. Then the moccasin lifted its own head about half an inch, and the snakes looked upon each other as if for the first time. The king snake was a handsome, tenuous cord of black and gold. Some of the spectators slowly raised themselves to their elbows. Both snakes in the box saw these movements, and jerked their heads around and watched the people, with their delicate forked tongues twinkling in and out. The chemical smell in the air grew strong. The snakes settled their heads slowly until they rested again on the sleek bodies, and the reptiles gazed at each other in a dream. The spectators on the revetment relaxed.

The ghost was seen again by Bonus, and the lips appeared to move. 'Do dis wumman love you, Bonus?'

'She love me, but she don't know it, Frank. I can make her laugh, now. I done got dat far.'

'You gettin' into progress, Bonus. Is she hot?'

'She twirls a wicked hip, Frank.'

'Keepa makin' her laugh, Bonus, an' you won't be long makin' her cry.'

'She cryin' now, Frank. She moanin' in de night, but not fo' me.'

'I see. Dere's another mule in yo' stall, huh?'

'A white man, Frank.'

'Whoa!' The ghost was not smiling. 'Be caffle, Bonus! Be caffle. Don't you lay hands on him.'

'Would it be awright to kick him in de pants, Frank? He's a lil bitta fella, an' I think I can sca' him away — up de rivah where he belong.'

'Ah don' want nuthin' to do wid dis, Bonus. Promise me you be caffle an' don' touch dat white boy wid yo' hands. You'll kill him sho'.'

'I promise you dat, Frank. Ah jis' give him a lil kick in de pants and sca' him away.'

'Go haid den. Sca' him off ef you kin, but . . .'

The ghost disappeared from Bonus's vision. The negro lay a long time looking down at the two snakes. He would move his lips and frown, or break into a secret smile. It was very quiet. Someone yawned.

A boat passed in the river, close to shore. There were two sudden harsh blasts from its whistle. Then there was a sound like a quickly drawn sigh in the snake box.

The king snake had the moccasin, or vice versa. No one could tell which. All the watchers jumped from the revetment and surrounded the box. The two reptiles were an indistinguishable mass of writhing muscle. Jule Pujol was doing a kind of dance, rolling his shoulders and encouraging the king snake in French. The king snake, with the moccasin's head between its jaws, was now carefully taking its hold, wrapping itself around the moccasin's body. There was a muffled snap, like a twig breaking under a man's shoe. The moccasin lashed its tail a few times, then died with its dazzling white mouth open to the sun.

Bonus walked down the river bank, dodging between the trees in swift sinuous movements, with his head between his bony shoulders, chuckling ...

38

THE next day Sister was working the cauliflower patch, mulching the bluish plants. This was early in the morning. She saw little Bruce coming out from the house. The boy came near her and sat on a pile of dried grass, playing with his slingshot. He was pouting. He threw the slingshot from him and lay in the grass, digging his fists into his eyes. He drowsed. Once Sister passed by him. She saw that his face was somewhat flushed. He had been cross the day before, and put to bed earlier than usual for whining over some trifle.

Sister bent over him. 'Bruce! Are you feeling sick, Fella?'

He opened his eyes and mumbled something. The eyes were feverish.

In the house Sister laid him upstairs in the cool and bathed his face. She stayed indoors the remainder of the day. In the afternoon Bruce was still drowsy, and his face was red and hot. 'What hurts, Fella?' she asked him for the third time.

'Nothin'. I want some milk.' When the milk was brought, he refused it. She thought of a purge, but decided to flush out the bowels for quicker results. This procedure excited the child very much. He screamed and squirmed. And Sister, feeling that after a fashion it was a violation of his body, suffered as much as he. All afternoon she kept iced cloths on his head. She looked into his throat. It seemed all right, somewhat red, but perhaps from crying.

Toward night, she discovered that the abdomen and chest were marked with tiny red specks. Later, he had a chill. Sister called Violet to watch the child, and rode to Lacroix for the doctor. He came with her in his buggy. They tied her horse behind.

Bruce lay in bed strangely beautiful. Sister stood behind the doctor, fascinated by the beauty of the fevered face, the warm aura of disease hovering about him, glowing. The doctor had little to say. He felt sure the child had been ill, in the onset of the trouble, for some days. Sister tried to remember. . . . She had been very busy. Bruce had never required much attention . . . The doctor asserted he would send some medicine from the Lacroix drugstore as soon as possible. The child must have certain attentions faithfully, and must be kept quiet above all. Sister followed him to the door. 'But what's the matter with him?' she asked.

'A fever. No danger, if he's properly nursed and kept quiet. You're going to nurse him?'

'Yes. Of course.'

'Watch him closely; send for me if there's a change. Take it easy. Don't tire yourself.'

She could not understand it. His words suggested a long spell of illness. 'Let me do the worrying,' he added. 'That's what you're paying me for.' He did not look as if he were not worried . . . After he had gone, many questions occurred to her that she wanted to ask. She turned to the bed. Bruce lay in a sort of radiant stupor, the long black eyelashes continually dropping and raising. Sister remained up until three o'clock in the morning, waiting for the medicine, sitting by the lamp striving to read a book.

All day and a large portion of each night Sister kept watch. She allowed no one else to approach the child. Violet, who knew little about cooking, prepared the meals. Once in the night Bruce rose suddenly to his knees. Sister was at his side in a moment. 'What is it, Fella?' He began to clutch at the air, as if he were climbing a wall. 'I wanna go home,' he whined. He was trembling all over. By persuasion and gentle force, she got him back under the covers. She was in a panic. The child later began to murmur incoherently. Sister walked from window to window. Or she stood in a corner, shrinking, watching him out of the side of her face, as if she were locked in the room with some savage monster that might momentarily spring. Often for hours the monotonous drone of words in some curious petulant language would flow from the child's dry, twitching lips. He would doze for a moment, while his fingers or the corners of his mouth twitched; or a swift frown would appear and vanish.

Always she felt on the verge of tears. She wanted no one near her. She heard little of the now active life going on in the rooms below. The doctor was maddeningly noncommittal. Was the child better or worse? She looked into the doctor's eyes and put these words to him, the clear brave question shorn of all irrelevant considerations. Better or worse? The doctor regarded her through his thick eyeglasses that made small blue beads of his eyes. 'He's got a lot of resistance left. We mustn't worry about *him*, but about the fever we're fighting ... mighty good nurse ...'

Unga January came one afternoon. She stood in the front yard with eyes raised to Sister's window, holding her baby on her hip. She was barefooted, and wore the beautiful fur coat René Davidson had given her. It concealed the ragged clothes beneath. 'Ah brought you a fever-egg for Bruce, cher,' she said.

'Thank you, Unga. Give it to Violet and she'll bring it up.'

Sister was supposed to rub the white of the 'fever-egg' into the hair of the sick child, and allow it to remain there until the fever had gone. A 'fever-egg' was made by taking from the nest a hen about to lay, tying her feet and hanging her upside down for several hours in the dark, while prayers were said for the recovery of the patient. Then the hen was put back on the nest and permitted to expel the egg.

The sick-room shone from frequent scouring. On some days, to pass the time, Sister would clean it three or four times, winning from this labor a sort of vague stupid surcease. She could no longer read books with any degree of interest. She would stand beside the bed hour after hour, watching the child's peculiar snake-like twistings, the head thrown back to expose the soft vulnerable throat. Bruce did not seem to be in pain at all, but rather harassed by some mental torment — muttering incomprehensible protests, answering tiresome queries, voicing dark futile pleas. At times it was quite unreal, wearing the guise of an ancient drama whose point was dulled by repetition. Through the lethargic radiance of eyes filmed over by the mists of fever he would lie watching her in disdain or accusation; or he would fix his eyes upon some incongruous part of her person, and examine it indifferently — but with clashing emotions surely contending in the breast or beating throat.

Impulsively she cupped her hands quite near, almost upon his cheeks, while her whole past and present being dissolved in his fever, mingled with his contagion, bathed in the curious stench or fragrance of the malady — and she felt the great swells of horrible tenderness beating out and out to engulf him. 'I love you! I love you!' But she tore herself away abruptly, beaten back, clawed and tortured by anguish she had never known before.

Since the meeting, many visitors were coming to see Mocco. The house had become a gathering-place for those who would be the leaders of the co-operative movement. Plans were complete for the erection of a large packing-shed and warehouse on the river.

Tonight there was a large crowd of men in the living-room below. They were drinking. Their talk and laughter rose in volume until it became unbearable. Sister dashed down the stairs.

'Break this business up!' she cried. 'I've stood it long enough!' She turned to Violet. 'Haven't I begged you to keep the house quiet?'

'I'm sorry, Sister. I didn't know it was too noisy.' Violet's eyes filled with tears.

'Well, keep them quiet! You, Mocco! Don't stand gaping like a catfish! Keep this house quiet!'

'All right, all right, Sis.' Mocco followed her to the hallway. 'I'm sorry, Sis, we're — I was so excited.' Sister clutched his arm. Her lips trembled. 'The child's *very* sick, Mocco.'

Next day Mitch Holt came up the stairs and knocked. Sister opened the door, and he took her in his arms and kissed her. 'I just heard about it, Jolie.'

Sister held him. Her fingers sank into the firm knobs of strength on his shoulders. Her dammed-up emotions surged forward in great powerful scalding waves. She leaned upon his silent immovable body. It was a kind of joy to vent her grief, to weep at last past all concealing.

They went to the child's bed. 'Christ! he's a pretty little kid!' Mitch exclaimed softly. He brushed the fine dark hair back from Bruce's hot forehead. The child turned his face to the wall. Mitch whispered, 'Send for me if you need me, Jolie.' Obviously there was something on Mitch's mind. Something was amiss. Sister that morning had been vaguely aware of a feeling of excitement coming from the rooms below . . . She asked no questions. They stood by the bed a long while.

'Nothing you want, Jolie?' Mitch asked.

'Nothing, thanks.'

'Miss John gave me some kind of weed-seeds for you to boil.'
'We can take them. We don't need to use them.'

Mitch lingered at the door. 'Did you know René Davidson's missing?' he asked. 'I've got to go now, and help look for him.'

'Missing!'

'He left home yesterday morning with his paints and so forth. Nobody's seen him since.'

Sister turned pale. 'Is he in the marsh, you reckon? In these mosquitoes?'

'Nobody knows. Tim's coming back from New York in a day or so. We're all ready to go ahead with our business.'

The doctor was coming up the stairs...

That night, sitting in a chair by the lamp, Sister dreamed that René was knocking on her door. In her dream she opened the door, a large heavy affair like a cathedral door, with a border of curiously woven thorns. The morning seemed like Easter, all shining and fresh, and a rill of water seeping through the levee sounded like music. René stood in the great doorway holding a little tree. It had the shape and proportions of a large mature magnolia, but was only a few inches tall. And around René's wrist was a snake, the garter snake after whose colors she had once made a silk dress. And René was wearing epaulettes like a naval officer's, pinned to the shoulders of a dirty and ragged shirt. He was speaking to her in Slavonian. He wanted her to help him plant the tree. 'Before the flood, dear one,' he said. 'Quick! Let's plant it.' And she became aware of the trickling of water through the levee increasing in volume. The levee was crumbling, exposing all sorts of worn furniture and assorted objects that the levee-builders had mixed in the dirt. René walked over to the terrestrial globe. Thick muddy water was already in the room, washing over their knees. René took out a knife and cut a hole in the terrestrial globe, in the center of China, for the tree planting. Instantly all the windows were filled with smiling faces. Each face was that of the constable, André Laval, and upon each face was a finger pointing to the missing eye. There was scream stuck in Sister's throat. She filled her lungs and heaved and heaved. The cry would not come out. Crazy Carrie was standing in the doorway holding a child's coffin, enameled white ... The scream came out of Sister's throat and awakened her.

Her heart was struggling wildly in her throat. She ran to the bed. He was tossing and squirming, rolling to various parts of the bed. She could not quiet him. The bed seemed to burn from contact with the hot flesh. He talked incessantly, until she no longer heard the words.

Sister grew strangely calm and strong. At midnight she sent Mocco for the doctor. The house was large and silent except for the faint high-pitched whine of mosquitoes on the screens, and the occasional careful creaking of Sister's shoe. She awakened Violet to get more ice at Jule's store.

Violet jumped from her bed, eager to serve. 'Is he worse, honey?' she whispered, with tears in her eyes.

'Yes! Yes! Hurry up, please.'

'Right away!' Violet pattered about the room with her little breasts jouncing. 'If you want, I'll relieve you tomorrow and you can sleep.'

About three, Mocco returned alone. He had found the doctor away, busy on an obstetrical case in Ostrica ...

Sister sat wordless, stern and calm, holding the child's hands away from the raw, red abdomen, which was dreadfully inflamed, as if some unseen beast with great soft lips had been sucking the blood through the pores. Sister could only sit grimly through the night, holding on to something inside her that must not break. Her mind worked with strange clearness, thinking, 'We will bury him in the afternoon.' The silence was palpable. There came once a faint gurgle or rattling in the child's throat. Sister went to the bed. 'Tch! Tch!' she clicked her tongue, and grew panicky. She wondered if she should call Mocco and Violet. Bruce coughed loudly. Sister was weak with relief. It was only phlegm in his throat. Presently he sank into a kind of sleep, tossing no more. The vessels in his throat beat frantically through the skin, but he slept, with partly opened eyes. 'My boy!' she whispered secretly. 'My boy!'

She stole to the window and leaned there, praying. Far across the river against the graying sky, she saw busy lanterns crawling back and forth. She took up her telescope. A dozen or so men were wading through the marsh back of the levee with lights, searching.

Sister remembered that René Davidson was missing. She pictured him wandering through the high canebrakes somewhere, frowning thoughtfully, greatly annoyed by the softness of the ooze and the burning of sawgrass cuts. It was horrible! She could not feel sorry for René, but only shrink from the vision of his plight — even though she could remember how his boyish features would light up when he talked to her after a day of seeking out curious aspects of the marshes ... Bruce coughed again. She swiftly returned to the bed.

In the morning she awoke after a little nap. The child was muttering again. His ice pack was hot from neglect. His body, if such were possible, was burning more intensely. But his limbs lay quiet, exhausted. She quickly straightened the bed for the doctor's arrival.

Mocco came upstairs haggard and unshaven, his black hair matted down over the eyes. 'Have they found René?' Sister asked. Mocco this morning looked very much as he had appeared during his degraded years, his eyes puzzled and all his self-assurance gone, utterly undone in the face of adversity. He sat in a chair and slowly shook his head, and answered with tears in his voice, 'We found him this morning.'

Sister knew René was dead. René was dead. The heavy familiar knowledge lay upon her without meaning. For a moment she did not know where or who she was.

'Somebody killed him.'

'*Killed* him!' René was forgotten. The thing became a vision of a Deed, swift and hidden, and a Doer whose name must be dragged forth and shown.

'It seems René was painting. There was a red buoy, an old rusty buoy lying slantways on the top of the levee. Spanish family used to live there behind the levee. By the buoy was a cedar log. They left it there years ago. I don't know. They left the log because they didn't believe in burning cedar, on account of Christ's cross being made out of that wood. René — somebody came up to him. The tracks come from the log, behind the log. It looks like this man stood by René, then walked away, then came back and hit him with something, or else kicked him in the — end of the backbone. He was painting the buoy and the log, one of these funny-looking pictures he used to paint at first, a pure abstraction, he called them. When he was kicked or hit, it looks like he went through the picture. We found it around his neck. A terrible lick he got. I think his neck's dislocated.'

Sister turned her face away, sickened. Mitch Holt came in. His face was covered with a fine white stubble, and he wore a hard bright smile, like a demon's. There was liquor on his breath. 'René's relaxed at last,' he said to Sister.

'Did you get to Lacroix?' Mocco asked.

'Yes. I telephoned Tim Davidson. Found him at the hotel in New Orleans. Send the body to town, he says. We'll take it to Lacroix for the train. How's the kid?' He took Sister's hand. His own was cool, electric with strength. 'Our factory business is busted up, I reckon,' he told her, smiling.

'What do you mean?' Mocco asked. 'Your business *can't* be busted up now. It would mean busting our association too! Don't let people hear you talk that way.'

'Tim won't come down now,' said Mitch. 'Doesn't want to see the place again. Not even interested in finding the murderer. Hell with him! Hell with all of them, I say. This is the doings of your God. Smashing us, wanting us to beg! Can't you see it? René's relaxed! All over a nigger winch!'

Sister sighed and clicked her tongue. She hugged her breasts.

'Never mind,' Mitch said to her sternly. 'You're with me still. Pledged. Pledged. Where can I get a horse or a throat-latch? My horse's throat-latch is busted. Keep moving, I say.'

'Take ours,' said Mocco. 'Keep the people from knowing on this side the river.'

'Keep moving, I say! Your God and your Savior! Your artists and books! Wait, Jolie! I know you've got your troubles. Only watch those dreams and book-reading, I say. Don't be ruled by dreams while others tackle the jobs of civilization. We'll do it. We'll drain the god-damned bogs and wipe the sunny smiles off the face of the contemptible stinking god-damned marshes. Drain them. This or another job we'll do. A throat-latch.'

'I'd say stick to this job,' said Mocco, spitting in the fire.

'This or another job. Mitch Holt abhors a vacuum!'

'Shh! The people expect——'

'What do you know about it, boy? Hell with the people! Who's worrying about the people? A throat-latch! A horse or a throat-latch!'

'Take hers in the cob-barrel.'

Sister pushed Mocco toward the door. 'Go! You're disturbing the boy now. Go outside with your latches and your king-doms for a horse!'

They went together down the stairs, and their descending voices trailed off, '. . . fix up . . . long distance telephone . . .'

In the daytime she would see passersby on the levee road. They turned the upper half of their bodies and raised their chins, looking up at her window. Or they stopped and argued, or talked to each other in low guarded tones. They seemed to possess some secret of which she knew nothing. 'Go away!' she called to two old women who stopped and whispered with bobbing heads and pointing fingers. They were the two old traditional church-scrubbers and washers of the dead. The sky seemed to grow darker behind them. 'Go talk down the road!' They looked up at her, biting their gums, then shuffled off.

Once she heard Mocco and Violet down below arguing. Their voices, the high and the heavy, came up through the bounteous tangle of clustered oranges.

'... you let Mitch Holt be the whole cheese!'

'What can we do without him, honey? Got to have a place to sell the off-grade stuff. We'll lose our members.'

'Members! You haven't got started yet! Not started! No warehouse, no representatives in the big towns! No association yet! The whole cheese! Just because *his* factory fell through...'

All day the boy on the bed murmured. Zealously Sister renewed the ice packs, the cloths dipped in a freezing bowl. She was deadened to the general sights and noises. Her eyes felt dry and hot. She lost count of time. Her tongue was furry, her mouth seemed foul.

One day, hearing a commotion outside, she went to the window.

André Laval had the negro Bonus. A long procession walked up the levee road. Bonus was in the lead. His hands were tied behind him with the end of a long rope. Laval, holding the other end, was following the negro. Behind them was a group of men and one woman, and a few children skipping to keep up. But they were all smiling. Laval and Bonus were apparently joking with each other as they marched. Bonus's jeans from the knees downward were in tatters, his legs full of cuts. He wore no hat, and his white shirt was blotched all over with the juice of crushed grass.

Laval looked up at the window and raised his hat to Sister in a pompous fashion. Bonus, too, looked up. He was smiling, but the look in his blood-webbed eyes chilled her. 'Das awright, Miss Sistah!' he called cheerfully. 'Ah swears befo' Gawd Ah didn't lay a hand on dat boy!' Then he looked straight ahead and bellowed: *'Frank! Frank St. Green!'* Laval gave a sort of playful jerk to the rope. Just then a half brick thrown by someone in the rear curved through the air and thudded softly against the negro's shoulder blade. Bonus bent over double and stamped his feet, roaring with laughter, and all the other laughing faces were turned up to Sister. Far up the road the procession wound until out of sight. Bonus could be heard still bellowing.

'Frank! Oh-h-h-h, Frank!'

Two days later Bruce's delirium cooled away, and his fever dropped a bit. He lay all day quietly. Occasionally he would be sunk under a healing wave of natural sleep. His fever rose in the evening, but he no longer thrashed about nor muttered. He was very low and weak. Sister had reached the point of utter exhaustion. Violet watched over Bruce after midnight, but Sister could not sleep more than an hour.

The next day, suddenly the child talked, in a weak but rational tone: 'Where you been, Mama?'

'Here with you, Fella. How do you feel?'

'Tired right here . . .' He pointed to his stomach.

'Mother get you some milk?'

'Don't want milk. I want you to lay by me.'

She gave him orange juice, which he loved, and did not know he had been taking for many days. She lay alongside him and soon fell into a deep sleep.

'We must be more careful from now on,' the doctor said next day.

'Is he going to get well, doctor?'

'Oh yes. He's quite a boy. He's got you to thank, too.'

Sister was almost sick with relief. She stood with all the sinews of her limbs quaking. She felt like leaning on little Bruce for support. But presently, her soul was buoyant and she seethed with vitality — a strange energetic fever of her own. She was almost glad for her past anguish. Its impact had renewed her like some potent bitter draught, evoking a quiet inner smile, or seething of the spirit. She recalled this feeling. This was the way she had felt following certain crucial happenings of the past, such as the time she had betrayed Bruce's father with her listening, and the death of Grampaw, and the night of the hurricane ...

So the convalescence was a curious hushed adventure, with Sister devising many quiet touches of humor to reassure and toughen the spirits of the child who lay so wan and tired. She brought in Grampaw's saddle. Bruce was soon to have it for himself. She lay beside him and her mouth was a well, a magic singing well. And her tongue was a wagging hairless gnome who dwelt in its depths. And the peeping gnome disappeared into the well and sang another tune, then returned for a bow. And deeper in the well were a dancing elf called Laughter, and a wrinkled old dwarf named Coughter ... She put corn on the window sill, and the jays and redbirds enlivened the tops of the oranges.

Often Violet and Mocco came up, wanting to be near Sister. Mocco was discouraged. Mocco would always be discouraged. In some way it was eminently fitting to the scene. Violet was talking about going back to town. People had entirely lost interest in the association. The trapping season was in full swing. Pelts were fetching nice money. A new settler from the north named Mr. Birchel, of German extraction, with tall strong-featured sons and daughters, had opened a little store. He was careful, humorous, kindly, his eldest son a brawny dreamer full of mellow songs, and eyes shining with love for creatures and things. Mr. Birchel was planting new varieties of citrus fruits, experimenting with Easter lilies in the field. And he leaned on his counter and told the people the time was not yet ripe for organization. He had organized labor unions, and he knew. 'Go slow!' he cautioned. 'Let's find out what is best to grow in our wonder-ful soil. Later, organize — ten years, fifteen years. Good drainage comes first, another canal. Go slow! Experiment!'

Mitch Holt came every evening now. Sister was cooking the meals again.

She loved him. She loved him. With a quaint feeling of peace and confidence she held him near. He never complained about the failure of his factory scheme and other cherished projects . . .

'Get out of my way!' he would be heard shouting on his way upstairs. Little Bruce would raise himself in bed and glance at his mother, a faint grave smile on his lips, his big eyes shining. He was so thin that Sister fancied his flesh was opaque as marble. Mitch strode noisily into the room. 'Get out of my way!' And he went to the bed and put out his hand. 'How are you today, Bruce? That damned Sanny Claus keeps following me around.'

Sister leaned on Mitch's shoulder, still warm from the sun. Mitch now seemed scarcely aware of her existence. In some way this was pleasant. It irked her, and was pleasant. Outside the flushed heavens were darkening, the cows trudging past to milking, each with its puny boy; and horses eating their way homeward.

'Mitch, I can sit up tomorrow,' Bruce said solemnly.

'Damned Sanny Claus. Look at him! What do you want, Sanny? He wants a cigarette. Always grubbing cigarettes . . .'

Now it was orange-picking time. Sister helped break off the fruit. It was a noble crop. Even the inner parts of the trees were laden. Sister worked on a slim ladder, all drenched in sun; and the treetops level with her eyes were pale verdant waves high above the earth, seldom beheld. Passionately she wondered where each fruit ultimately would go. Would *this* one be carried in the lunch-box of an overalled workman far away? She saw the man sitting in a boiler-room, which would be dark or dimly lit, spitting out the seeds, gulping the cold raw pulp.

A man came to see Mocco, to get his money back. He had contributed his ten dollars to the association fund, and had heard they were giving the money back to the people.

'Two more refunds to make,' Mocco told Sister. 'I reckon we'll be leaving you alone next week. Well ... at least you've got a nicer place to live in.'

'And I've got a little money stashed away. What are you going to do in town?'

'I'll drive a wagon, just so Violet's satisfied.'

'She looks dreadfully worn down.'

'I'll drive a wagon. I'll shovel dirt. We're young. There's opportunity up there. I've got an idea for an orange-squeezer. They tell me both the soda fountains in town serve juice.'

'Try to find me one of these sprays for killing mosquitoes.'

'I could get a patent. You throw the oranges in, and it peels and squeezes, the way I've thought it out.'

'Go and God bless you, then. I don't understand ...'

'I'll drive a garbage wagon at first, if necessary ...'

The house attic was full of yellow-jackets. On warm afternoons they crawled out and circled the gables madly. The trees would be aswarm, and Sister picked the fruit gingerly, expecting at any time to be stung on the wrist or arm. She liked the danger. The presence of the wasps seemed related to the possibility of her being very poor soon again. She sang one of her crazy songs. Mocco lingered beneath the tree, pecking at the bark with his knife.

'What — how do *you* intend making a living, Sis?' he asked. 'I'll manage.'

'Because Mitch says he's got no idea what *he's* going to do. He thinks he'll get his factory sooner or later, but...'

Sister gritted her teeth. A cold fear hovered round her. She beat it back — the dark cloud of remembered hunger. The rain was a purple shadow over Dutch Scenery. Wild geese, the first of the season, floated past the clouds, crying mirthfully.

When the fruit was shipped and the money divided, they sprayed the trees white. Bruce came downstairs to play in the cold sun. Violet and Mocco were packed up, waiting for the old *Hail Mary*, due any day. Sister picked out a frosty night to set rat traps in the orchard. The trees were so thick the moonlight hardly showed; but in the opening left by a missing tree, the ploughed sod was tinseled with dew. There would be a thick frost to kill the Johnson grass... She stopped and lay a trap on the edge of the bright spot. She heard a twig crack in the dark, near the house.

'Mitch?' she called.

'Yes, it's me,' came the frosty answer. 'What the hell are you doing out there?'

'Watch out for the traps. Come over this way. Isn't it beautiful?'

'What's beautiful?'

'Everything.'

'Where are you?'

'Did you get your supper on the stove?'

'Yes. Where are you? Sounds like you are in three places, Jolie. Where are you?'

There was no reply. Mitch stood in the silence. The slow wash of the river sighed through the trees.

'Jolie! Quit the humbug. I've got something to tell you.'

Mitch looked behind a grapefruit tree. The white fantastic

shapes of the sprayed trees were woven into a long dim empty arbor.

'Something important, do you hear me?'

From a little distance behind him, he could not tell where, he heard a loud whisper: 'Tell me, then!'

'I'm going. Leaving. Going trapping tomorrow.' He groped forward in search of the voice. 'Come here, you little snapperwhipper!' He stepped on one of the rat traps. It snapped and hurt his toes. He heard in another part of the grove a hiss of laughter escaping through Sister's nose. 'You go to hell!' he shouted, and groped out of the orchard.

'He! He!' The tinkling giggle seemed to issue from the top of a near-by tree. Mitch sat on the back steps and removed his shoe, cursing, rubbing the toes in the moonlight.

'I came here to talk!' he called into the orchard.

'Not to eat?' came Sister's voice.

'This is business. There's a time for play!' He put on the shoe and limped out of the yard to the levee. He went down the road. He passed the Guate's and took the bend. From behind some bushes just ahead, Sister jumped out into the moonlight. She came up to him. He did not embrace her, and said no tender words. The moonlight glinted from his eyes. His hand wandered over her hip and thigh, trembling. 'I'm ready to carry out our bargain,' he said, 'if you want a trapper for the present.' He touched her breast and she jerked away.

'Must we be animals so soon?' she asked. 'Look the stars!'

'It's my way.'

'Showing off.'

'It's all sport with me, honey. You tease me and lead me on, then——'

'I know. Let's go back.' She took his hand and brought it around her waist. The deep dust received their footsteps gently. 'God damn it, Mitch!' she exclaimed. 'The moonlight's beautiful! It's so nice and hellish to swear, and tease

you, and have my body felt! Hellish and sweet! It has nothing
to do with the bargain, the marriage. Nothing!'

'Right you are.'

'If only we could be lovers instead!'

'Not for me!' Mitch protested. 'You're not that way. You're
built to be a wife, Jolie. Of course, there'll be hardships. Marriage is a big thing, serious and hard.'

'So it is. My business is to keep you by my fire and my
table and bed.'

'Hell! I'm foolish about you, in my way. There won't be
time for me to run around.'

'Hardships are not bad. Nothing can hurt me but hunger.'

'How about the moon?'

Sister threw a clamshell at a black cat crossing the road.

Mitch made a trip in the marshes, trapping. He went after
only mink and otter, but caught a few muskrats too. He returned in three weeks with five hundred dollars. Sister had
everything ready. Mocco and Violet had waited for the wedding. Father Sam married them in the morning. The church
was filled with people and green light, and there were tongues
of ruby fire glowing in glass containers. Candles burned on a
triangular stand of brass, each offered by some pious woman
for a secret intention. The wind had blown two of them out.
On the wall was a sign, COLORED NOVENA FRIDAY.

In the evening they gave a big feast, a shrimp boil and deer
roast under the trees in the orchard. The guests danced and
sang until a late hour, and somebody tied a cowbell under
Sister's bedspring.

Next day Bruce was sent off for a week with Tante Inez, and
Sister and Mitch went over to Grampaw's oyster camp for a
little honeymoon. All day long, they hunted and fished together. It was pretty weather, and they ate and drank well; but
after a week of idleness they were both glad to get back home.

The Wife

BOOK FIVE

39

IN DECEMBER, only the evenings were wintry. Bruce remained with his aunt for two weeks. During the bright short days and the firelit nights Sister and Mitch were alone for another week of sport and talk and quarreling. They would always quarrel. Sister knew that. Nothing would ever keep them wholly one. Even the fruit of their union, if fruit there should be, perhaps would be divided against itself.

But when united in love, their canceled selves merged to achieve a torrid harmony. Sister at this time was nobly formed and tempered. Greedily her flesh drank the sunlight, and she slept like the drunken. In the mornings she felt capable of rising to her toes and hurling some wild and wordless song across the horizon. Often without any reason she suddenly felt a flame of pure being run through her. When she so much as thought of her husband, heaviness and warmth stole over her. She closed her eyes. The eyeballs lifted, while a pang scorched her throat. Mitch chanced to pass near her. The sputtering blond warmth of him, which would always, always be new and strange, came nudging her drowsy senses, and her fibers twanged like a taut string plucked. Mitch, too, was finely formed in the prime of manhood — slim-boned, alert, intelligent, and provocative with his touch of cynical carelessness. And because he was always quick and seldom irresolute, he made many mistakes, each promptly forgotten.

Their quarrels were devastating to Sister. Each misunderstanding was like a betrayal. It was not that she had expected a tranquil relationship. What rankled her was the discovery that Mitch was taking each quarrel as a matter of course, a thing of no importance, perhaps not without a certain ruminative amusement. His handsome blond head seemed to harbor some gleaming and grinning secret foreknowledge that all would be well again. The woman resented this cut-and-dried ordering of the future — as though matters were entirely subject to *his* omnipotent manipulation! So there was antagonism from the first.

Their first conjugal joust came one day when she induced him to hear her read some of Shakespeare's sonnets.

'Do you like it?' she asked after two sonnets.

'It's all right, Sugar.'

What did he think of poetry? she demanded. Well — he believed poetry was somewhat foolish. Not harmful; merely pretty and foolish. That was his own private belief. He himself liked many foolish things, but not *that* kind. He usually ignored the poem and thought of the poet. Like this Shakespeare, for example — sitting down alone writing poetry to some woman. It was indecent! Why not tell the woman with his mouth what he wanted, instead of working himself up by writing? It was nothing but a secret vice.

Sister lost her sense of humor. She defended the poets a little too emphatically. The thing that irritated her was that Mitch was so willing that she should please herself in her reading. If poetry was foolishness, why did Mitch condone, almost insist upon, her reading it? She contrived a tacit breach between them for the rest of the day. Not until she lay awake that night did she decide their temperamental differences were robust and good. And the thought that they were fundamentally so unlike each other thrilled her strangely. And she enjoyed her poetry the more.

Three days later they quarreled again.

Mitch had bought out Mocco's share in the property and had it fixed in Sister's name. He did not care to own land. He said he owned enough already — all the marshes to the seashore. It was vaguely understood that some day they would thin out the overplanted front orchard, filling it in with smaller trees, kumquats or limes.

Sister had paddled over to see Unga January, and when she returned she found that Mitch during the day had cut out twenty large oranges. The horse was dragging the last tree over the levee when she arrived. The orchard was dotted with horrible white-fanged stumps. Sister stood petrified, with the wind popping her skirts. Mitch said, 'Hey!' and went on with the horse. He had really planned this as a pleasant surprise.

'Hey!' she answered him. She hesitated a moment, because it was so good to see him after an absence. He came to her and she passed her cheek over the crisp golden stubble on his face, and nuzzled his sweaty shoulder.

'How does it look?' he asked.

'All right. Is this the right time to do that?'

'Of course! That's going to put more wood on your trees in the spring flush. I'll have the stumps out before I leave for trapping.'

'Trapping?'

'Sure. Don't you like the orchard thinned? Smile!'

'Surely I like it, darling. It's just rather sudden.'

'Sudden!'

'I'll have to get used to it. It's just kind of sudden.'

'Well, you know me, honey. Especially when it's a matter of doing a job for my gal!' He gave her a kiss and a little spank. Sister sighed, puzzled. For *her?* Why was he saying this was for her? She craned her neck to see down the row of trees. What had been a solid stretch of dim shade ever since her childhood was now filled with hard bright open holes. The feeling of the old grove was gone. She had an impressive yet disturbing sense of the destruction a nimble man could wreak.

She looked at Mitch and smiled. She said, 'A woman would have taken *one* tree out, to see how it would look.'

'A woman, my tail,' Mitch said, looking away.

'I mean ——'

'A *man* would say the trees are gone and talk can't put 'em back. Two years from now we'll be glad, with the increased fruit.'

'Damn the increased fruit. You're too quick to get mad.'

'If you don't like the job, keep quiet and let's eat.'

'I know you worked hard, darling.'

'Sure. I know. There's nobody mad.'

'If as you say it was done for *me*, then I have some right ——'

'I'd thank you to say no more, honey. I've been hungry since three o'clock. It's fixing to blow a gale of wind. Let's eat and make us a fire. We'll be a day older soon.'

Sister jumped on his back. He carried her to the house, passing under some low branches to tease her face. 'Are you mad?' he asked.

'I love you.'

Going through the door he passed her his rifle. She hung it on the pegs over the door-frame. He went to wash. Sister looked from the window. The orchard was darkening, but the torn stumps were brighter.

After supper they sat by the fire. The flames pervaded the room with a feeling of goodly weariness and peace. While the man sat cross-legged whittling a decoy duck, Sister folded her hands and dreamed over the swollen coals. Mitch had bought a barrel of coal from a packet boat, the first ever burned in that fireplace. Sister loved the play of the fire, the fine jets of gas spurting out here and there, the soft crumbling apart of the tarry lumps when touched with the poker. A feel-

ing of curious animal security filled her. Their home was
like a wilderness cave, warm and safe from the crisp wintry
agitation of trees and water. Time was slow, relishing the
appeasing hours before the final sleep. Passion drowsed, their
two passions. She glanced at Mitch, his hard half-smiling face
intent in the work, his curved back narrowing down to the fine
pliant hips in which the man seemed to take a secret delight.
Her vitals burned. She closed her eyes. Her fingers trembled.

But, gazing back at the fire, the seething core of their home,
soon her lust was quelled. Or it became a larger lust touched
by the quiet colors of the room and a sense of the grossly
timbered floors and walls, the fecund fruit trees outside, the
winding community planted along the river's margin. The
man beside her was her superior, her inferior, her equal. His
body was like hers, and unlike hers. He was strong in places
where she was weak, and this was good. Her body was strong
and rich in places where his was only strong, and this was good.

She was dependent upon this man who could wreak such
whimsical destruction. She felt frightened. All her people
had gone and left her alone with this man, whose arched
legs carried him wherever the whim pointed. His fingers and
knuckles — how scarred! His hips were narrow and tough,
a spring-like hinge between the arched legs and the quick
torso. His chin was roundly blunted, as if by a single deft
wiping motion of the creative hand, to give him the look of
tender pride or courage. His eyes were at once wary and
reckless, twin points of unfathomable light, given to changing
suddenly from bitterness to glee. Unknown — how unknown
he was to her! She could have cried out in pride at having
won him. . . .

She brought a net to the fire, and went to knitting slowly.
For a time they sat together, neither speaking. Mitch finished
his carving. He was skilled with a knife, as Grampaw had
been. He had been a trapper many seasons, spending long

hours alone with a skinning knife.... He stood looking into the fire awhile. He went to the window and felt the glass to test the weather outdoors. He was restless. The woman became alert to that, and looked at him no more. Mitch picked up a comic supplement some pilot had thrown ashore for him. Presently he threw it aside, and came and stood behind her. 'You throw your stitches well,' he murmured. He sauntered off and got his coat and hat. He came and kissed her neck from behind. 'Is there wood in for the morning?' he asked.

'Plenty. You cut enough yesterday for three days.'

She watched him walk to the back door, the sinewy oscillation of his shoulders and his fluid catlike way of avoiding a chair. The door slammed. The wind outside was growing stronger. The deep chill mumbling of the river came to her, the crash of waves collapsing slowly. Mitch passed through the light of the window, his hatbrim jerked low in the wind. She heard him dragging his pirogue from under the house.

Sister waited, knitting. Panes rattled, and the flames climbed the sooty bricks like capering spaniels. There was a vaguely comforting quality about Mitch's having gone and left her knitting. Somehow it made her feel richly part of the countless nocturnal functions occurring on the Margin at this moment — mothers rocking their infants; cows rasping the corners of feed boxes with their rough tongues; the doctor plodding somewhere through the dark wind; cistern faucets leaking musically; letters waiting in the post-office for their claimants; old men rubbing their anointed knees; and the silent discarded dead in the graveyard waiting with folded hands.

She stopped knitting and put out the light, and there was only the fire expelling its hoarded sunshine. She saw the sky was clearing. Tall pointed clouds marched past the moon like cowled friars pacing. She waited until near midnight for Mitch to return. He always went to bed late and rose early.

He came in and lit the kitchen lamp. She heard the soft thud of an animal's body fall upon the table, and went to see.

'I thought you were asleep,' Mitch said. His face was bright and wind-ruddied. He had trapped a rabbit among the wild indigoes over the river, and had stopped for a game of dice, losing forty dollars to a Slavonian with a big golden mustache. He skinned the rabbit at once, and Sister fired the range. She was hungry herself. Love seemed to demand extra amounts of food. . . .

'Your clothes are *cold!*' she shivered, passing her hands down his back to the fine hips. She wanted to hide the man inside herself.

'It will milden by day,' he answered. 'I'll warm you till then, Jolie. Do you want to be warmed good?'

'Yes.'

'Curled against your back?'

'Yes.'

'Or you curled against mine?'

'Each and each.'

They took their plates of fried rabbit to the fire. They drank enough wine to rouse them from the heavy contentment. Now Sister was the restless one. She wanted talk, or dancing, or a pleasant little quarrel, before giving herself for the night. For a moment she wished for some of René Davidson's smooth eloquent discourse of books and places.

'What kind of trees do you want planted in the places I cut out?' Mitch asked.

'I don't know, honey. Suit yourself. Kumquats, eh?'

'You're the boss.'

'I don't want that. Why should I be the boss? The land's yours too.'

Mitch smiled and scratched his head. 'I guess I won't have any real estate, Mam. It doesn't agree with me.'

'I don't understand.'

'It's yours, Jolie. Don't you love the land? Plant your lilies and flowers and trees? Now listen, you don't want to plant me too, do you?'

Sister said nothing.

'You ought to be proud you can run all this rich mud,' Mitch said.

'Stop playing, Mitch. We're in this together, aren't we?'

'Not so's you could notice it.'

'I surely understood it that way.'

'Not the real estate business. Hell, I'll have enough to do keeping us supplied with meat, and that's my work, with my gun and traps and lines. How about that? Do you want your husband stay home and fish crabs like old man Guate next door? Raise flowers? I'll bust your middles and do the little heavy plowing and help you tote out the fruit. Other times I'll have a man's work to do, Jolie!'

'A man's work! What's a man's work? You're going to live in the Gulf and marsh? Is that what you mean? How about the factory business? I'm only trying to understand you. Have you given up that idea?'

'I think so.'

'How?'

'I'm happy now, and all this leadership business seems tommyrot. I was damned dissatisfied working across the river, and didn't know it, I'd been so accustomed to the jail-house. I'm no leader. The leader has too many people to follow. It's nicer to work alone and do as you please.'

'I'm not sorry about that. I was the fool who put it in your head. But I don't see ——'

'You don't see why I hate to peck around like a hen on a piece of mud no bigger than a Baptist hymn-book? I told you I'll bust the middles. I'll crumb out your ditches and look after the wharf and firewood. You can do all the she-work around here in two hours a day, Jolie. Or hire you a nigger to fight the alligator grass, if you want to peddle nets or read poetry. I'm not putting you in the field. Don't you figure on teaching your little niggers?'

'Yes.'

'And writing people's letters?'

'Yes.'

'I'm craving to see you dress yourself up more, too, Jolie. You haven't got enough clothes to wad a shotgun.'

Mitch went into the kitchen for a match, whistling. Then he walked to the front room.

She called to him: 'We've each got all we bargained for, and don't forget we're only giving it a trial. After all, we'd better not see too much of each other.' She went to the front. 'Are you coming up, darling, or shall I leave the light?' she asked in the darkness. Mitch did not reply. He was on the sofa asleep.

She could hardly bring herself to waken him, to touch him. Sleeping without pillow or covering, his legs sprawled, he looked like a functional brute, a means of begetting young. Prowling the swamps and returning at dark with chunks of meat.

Yet in his way, she knew, he was as fine as she. He had a shy proud fineness, expressed in his manner of vaulting a fence, of talking to little Bruce, of getting off a horse. She reached down and touched his chest. He awoke like a steel spring, smiling, ready to stay awake the rest of the night.

The tension of their small tilt remained for some days. Sister had many words to say. She kept them. This might be considered a keen taut game, not without its thrills and pitfalls...

So it went. They loved and quarreled. Their quarrels often progressed to the verge of physical encounter. But in the brief dark fusion of love they lost their enmity and pride. They became denizens of a deep region of swirling heat where all was given without quibble and all received without thanks. And they were one.

And in the throes of daily work they were one — lost now in the doing of their separate tasks, divided physically by the distance of an acre or more, yet blindly leagued in the creation of growth and order. Mitch remained at home until the late fruit was sold. He planted the kumquat trees, cleaned the ditches, felled three arpents of tupelos and cypresses in the rear, and generally did more around the place than he had led Sister to suspect he would do. Though he was forever professing to dislike a household, he was ever willing to assist in the improvement of the property.

40

IN JANUARY their money gave out. Mitch took his last ten dollars to the gambling house in Lacroix. The soldiers had had a payday. Mitch won over two hundred dollars, gambling all night. But after a nap in a friend's charcoal schooner, he returned to the gambling at dawn and lost every penny. He returned home singing in his pirogue.

'I'll get some groceries on credit from Jule,' he told Sister, 'and go get a couple of deer tonight. I'll have to get back on my trapping grounds next week, Jolie.'

Sister looked at him. She was raking the fire from her clay oven outdoors, preparing to put in a batch of bread. She said nothing. Mitch was casual as always, but a faint frown was on his face. 'I've got to leave you, Jolie, and make us some money.' Sister stooped and peered into her oven, and raked the remaining coals. She pictured herself alone with Bruce every night. It might be pleasant for a change. She and Mitch were back where they had been the night of the tree-quarrel. He had a man's work to do. He-work. 'If you've got to go, you've got to, honey,' she said. She was carrying their first child then. Her face was peaceful.

The next day a schooner stopped on the Margin to buy oranges. The owner was a French Market trader from New Orleans, a tough Italian with two companions who also looked like hard characters. They came into the yard.

'What are you doing in here?' Mitch asked at once.

'You gotta da fruit for sale?'

'We've got ten trees of Creole sweets. We've been holding them for the good prices. When you come in here, you want to knock. We've got a goat that bites.'

They went to the rear. Sister came to the back door and watched. Unga January was with her. Unga was barefooted, and wore her fur coat. She had been weeping on Sister's shoulder. The Negro Bonus had been committed to the insane asylum. Unga had made a vow to wear no shoes until Bonus were released through the intercession of the Virgin Mary.

'I knaw dat man, me,' she said. 'He's come from duh Franch Mokkit. He is bad man, like you see him, dat Deggo.'

Mitch showed the trees to the Italians. The leader looked up at the good fruit and made a wry face. He walked along, making a wry face at every tree. His companions walked around the trees, talking in Italian. One of them broke off an orange. 'Dissa smalla fruit,' he said, gulping the juice.

'Put the peeling in your pocket,' said Mitch. 'Talk business.'

'Seventy dollars,' said the leader.

Mitch called to Sister, asking how many bushels were on the trees. Sister answered, 'About a hundred.'

Mitch turned to the schooner captain. 'A hundred dollars. You clip and wash.'

'Eighty-five!'

Mitch walked away. 'Take the other path out,' he said over his shoulder. He went into the house. The Italians walked to the back door. The captain handed Sister five twenty-dollar bills, and they went to the schooner and returned with sacks and ladders. Mitch leaned out the side window as they passed. 'No grapefruit!' he told the captain.

'Hey, boys! No takka da g'apefruit!'

Mitch went into the kitchen. Unga was gone. Sister had two buckets of water and a deck broom, preparing to scrub.

Mitch sat on a chair to watch her. Sister very gravely took a cup of water and went toward her husband. He saw her coming, and hid his head in his arms. She poured the water down his back. They had a water fight. They splashed each other until they and the walls were dripping.

Afterwards, Sister was shivering. Mitch carried her upstairs to rub her warm. Then she rubbed him. The big rough towel reddened his skin. They lay watching two lizards playing on a timber up in the corner. Mitch gathered the ends of Sister's hair into a brush, which he passed over and over her ribs. Sister tried not to giggle. Once they heard the distant roar of water, and children shouting down the road.

'Something big is coming,' said Mitch.

'But, my God! Listen the noise! The swells are going over the levee!' She peered from the window. She got a breath-taking glimpse of it — a huge battleship. All along the levee people were shouting, children standing on the green dike to be splashed. Sister and Mitch wriggled into clothing and leaned from the window as the gray monster steamed past. All along the decks, sailors in white lounged, waving. Two dogs in the bow were barking at the Grass Margin dogs yelping up the road. The murderous guns pointing in all directions, the searchlights glittering like wicked eyes, the huge gaudy flag dancing insolently, the sound of the swells thundering over the levee's crown — frightened Sister. She turned away from the sight of the gray engine of destruction and its ugly flag. She straightened the pictures on the wall which the vibration of the propellers had jounced out of place. The land they lived on was thin. She could still feel the earth slightly trembling. Laughing-gulls followed the dreadnaught and created a crazy din with their chuckling. Sister fought a sense of dread creeping over her until she found some work and her thoughts flowed again in a wholesome stream.

Mitch came in from the orchard. 'Those damned robbers!'

he exclaimed. 'They took a tree of grapefruit. Where are my slippers?'

She brought out his sharkskin slippers. 'What are you going to do?'

He removed his heavy boots and donned the moccasins. He told her, 'They're over the river now. I'm going to get paid for the grapefruit and take a punch at the captain.'

'Must you do that? Must you punch?'

He tightened his belt and kissed her.

She took hold of both his biceps. The tissues twitched and burned impatiently. 'Steady!' she said. His eyes were fixed on hers. It was a battle, very thrilling. Mitch smiled, indulging her ignorance. She heard him downstairs dragging out his pirogue. Her fingers remembered the hot quivering of his arm-flesh. It was a sultry feeling of the will made flesh. Its warmth hinted of the strong meals she had served the man.

Upstairs she took up the telescope. She focused it on Mitch paddling, a tiny weak creature, barely making headway over the ponderous river. The river was gorgeous. The battleship was far, far upstream. Its screws seemed to have stirred up from the depths all sorts of hues never seen before by human eyes. There was a splash of coppery green midstream as broad as a city, flecked with unearthly touches of raw cobalt. The opposite shore was a thin, haunting smudge of vague purple; and in a certain spot far up where the river swung round a shaggy green point, the woven streaks of blues and yellows were like thick oily dye.

Mitch was at the schooner, climbing a small Jacob's ladder over the side. She saw him talking to the brutal captain on the poop. He stood with his hands behind him, as though concealing some lethal weapon. Sister's lips curled in contempt. It was very strange. She was hoping Mitch would be beaten. It was a passion, almost bursting out in a shout, and it was curiously part of her love. There he stood, thinner than the captain, oddly pathetic in the distance and the river's tinted vacancy. She could see the sneering features of the captain, the brutal lips pursed under the unkempt mustache. She could in her fancy smell the garlic on his breath. He was taking a wallet from his pocket now, putting a bill into Mitch's hand.

Then the hand that took the money swung in a fleet arc and struck the Italian's face. The man toppled slowly, as if the strings that held him had become undone, and sat on the deck. Mitch jumped to the lower deck and slouched toward the bulwark, rubbing his knuckles on his pants. Before he reached the ladder, another man hurried toward him. Mitch turned and struck him once with each fist. A third man appeared, a short, rather jolly-looking little gnome with a naked torso. He swung with both hands rapidly and danced with great glee. Mitch now went into action with a ferocity that frightened Sister and queerly roused her hostility toward him. The larger of the men went down, but the gnome was enjoying himself beating Mitch's skull from behind. Sister was glad to see that. While she wept for his safety, she smiled every time he was struck. Teach him a lesson! Hit him again! She saw Mitch go down and come up swinging wildly. The larger man went down and remained. The captain was coming down to rejoin the fray. Sister shouted with all her wild love-hatred, until she discovered that the telescope was gone. She had hurled it into space toward the boat across the river. She could see nothing more, only the minute shape of the schooner far against the opposite bank. Weeping, she ran downstairs and recovered the instrument from the ground and placed it to her eye. Mitch was seen climbing over the side. She sat on the levee and watched him paddling toward her. His face was bruised. His shirt was gone. He continually leaned over the water, spitting blood. Sister's warm salt tears blinded her.

Mitch pulled his pirogue ashore. He stooped, a lonely figure crouched where the dike's declension met the water, a lonely figure she would never understand. He scooped water to rinse his bruises. He left the pirogue where it was and climbed the revetment. Sister gathered the maimed face to her with sick tenderness. He was trembling violently, looking around in a stupor. 'You fool!' she hissed, stroking his head. 'You damned fool! Smart aleck! Bully! Aren't you proud, beaten up?' Mitch disengaged himself. People were gathering. 'Go in, Jolie,' Mitch told her. He was smiling, but the smile was ruined forever. He limped in ahead of her. His fine proud hips seemed out of order now. Once she giggled.

Mitch changed his clothes and left without a word. Little Bruce ran after him a way. 'Papa! Papa!' Mitch turned on the road and waved.

Mitch returned late that night, banging on the door. 'It's open!' Sister called.

He stood over her bed in the moonlight. His face was badly discolored. He kissed her. She drew him close. He smelled of a peculiar odor. The entire room was vaguely permeated with it. It was a half-chemical fragrance, like nothing in nature or fancy, very faint and yet intrusive, disturbing. Mitch fell asleep at once. His nostrils were clogged with blood. His breathing soughed off his swollen lips. Sister shrank to her edge of the bed. The moon was big and heavy. Sister kept inhaling, trying again to pick up the alien fragrance. She was very lonely.

Soon Mitch set out for his trapping ground far out Pass à Loutre. Little Bruce begged to go with him. Mitch held the boy close, caressing his hair with a hand on which the knuckles were still swollen and bruised. 'Stay here with your mother, kid. Take care of your sweet mother.' He winked at Sister.

'I wanna go with my father! Mama! I wanna!'

'I want you to help your mother plant. Be sure to plant the

onions next to the potatoes. They'll make the potatoes' eyes water if a drought comes.'

Mitch pulled off in a skiff loaded with gear and supplies. Sister stood in the wind, waving. Bruce rolled on the dusty levee, in a temper, bawling hoarsely. Sister went inside and left him. He stopped crying and lay on his stomach in the dust. He had in his hand a holy picture. It was Jesus with the children on his lap and at his knees. Sister had once read the text to Bruce: *Suffer little children to come unto Me.*' Bruce studied the picture, wondering why none of the children appeared to be suffering. He looked at the skiff moving far downstream. He lay on his back, determined to stay there and suffer until dark.

Sister watched Bruce from the window. She loved him. She would not pet or coddle him. Let him have his fits of temper, alone. She gloried in that. Let him learn defiance! Let him learn to comply — unbeaten. To beat the earth was good. To curse the sky was good. She was proud of his first outburst, because she had always feared the child had no spirit.

Mitch was gone, his first leave-taking. Where had he been last night? Had anyone consoled him, smoothed his hurts? She wept slow defiant tears. Scrubbing the back kitchen steps she bore on the oaken planks, and her tears dropped into the frothy soap. Her gaze wandered up the steps to the doorway, to the dimness of the hollow interior, the heavy ceiling timbers, the roses on the mantel, the fireplace.

She walked in the gold-spangled orchard, already full of fall migrants. The soil was sweet and hollow-sounding from the velvet beans plowed under. Sister held her thoughts at bay. No more thinking on this Mitch Holt matter! No more indulging in the old frantic soul-searching. The wind brought a sea-smell mingled with the odor of citrus oils. She picked a curled turnip leaf, balled it in her hand and chewed it. She walked about, hunting a task. Her restless feet struck the earth firmly.

She broke an orange and devoured it. Already she was feeling the strengths and hungers of gestation.

All afternoon she worked in the orchard with tools, doctoring the few remaining sick trees. Some of the trunks had split in the crotch; or there was a rotted hole where a storm had jerked away a big limb. She was learning how to use the tools, to do the heavy gouging well, cleaning out the cavities, filling the holes with cement to sweeten the wounds. The trees would help her, growing whorls of new tissue over the doctored places.

At night she read by the fire, first for Bruce then for herself. Spring was rapidly drawing close. Geese swept northward.

Sister remained still detached from the community's life, meeting the folk only casually. She had several visits from the woman next below their place, Mrs. Guate, but she returned the call only once.

Mrs. Guate was a thin brown nervous wreck, neat and sharp-looking, with an uncommonly long neck and a chirping inflection in her talk. It was her habit to stand for hours on the levee, looking first up the road, then down, and stopping all passers-by for a chat. Though there was a comfortable bench near-by, she always remained on her feet, which gave her the appearance of having only just stepped outdoors for a moment. 'The poor soul is lonely,' Sister thought. 'But who is doing her work?'

Mrs. Guate's husband rarely appeared. Some of the children on the Margin had never seen him. Some people asserted he was crazy. Sister as a child had once crept upon him through the little woods that lay between the properties as one approaches a shy wild animal. He was a roundish little man, all gray and stooped from spending his days over the hoe or fishing crabs back in Yellow Cotton Bay. His wife ruled him well.

If he dared visit a saloon, she would have hysterics. She kept him working in the truck all week, and on Sundays allowed him one gallon of claret which he sipped slowly through the day. On that evening he would go tipsily to bed. And in order to prevent his slipping away while in the field, Mrs. Guate made him trousers of mattress ticking. He looked like a convict in them.

Sister dreaded to go to the store, lest she be stopped by Mrs. Guate. So she continued her custom of going to the store at night, with Bruce. The boy dearly loved these jaunts. So did Sister. Often they would sing along the way, or she would invent a story. Returning home, Bruce would be tired and linger far behind, dragging his feet. As she approached the house, Sister would watch for its gables glowing among the stars. She felt a singular exaltation of spirit, as though the structure were endowed with a spirit of welcome. And she suddenly felt it as a house without fear.

41

WHAT was the exact nature of their relationship? Sister did not know. She felt she had taken up Mitch for some obscure but good reason. But did she possess him? A man was a strange being. Sometimes when he seemed to be caught he was not made fast at all, only pretending the bonds were secure out of respect for the rules. A man like Mitch Holt — it was fascinating to guess some of the things he would be capable of doing to shatter their union at a stroke. She had experienced already his capacity for sudden profound changes.

Yet he was adaptable, too. Looking back, Sister could not understand how such a man had managed to remain cooped up in the little 'fish-office' across the river, as she called it. The pilots had used his midnight lamp as a range-light, a handy marker in their steering. He had been so absorbed that he would not climb the levee to watch so important an event as the salvaging of a drifting barge. Now he was in the marsh, all the grand ambitions forgotten — no bitterness, no regrets. Even his years in prison had been forgotten. At least no outward scars remained.

What made him want to be alone — one speck of human life surrounded by endless vistas of sodden verdure? Would he go to New Orleans to do his own fur-selling, and fling most of the money away? She did not think so. Recently he had a contempt for city people. He said they dodged into a doorway when a drizzle fell. They were always thinking — walking the streets in thought, waiting on corners in thought, riding trolley cars in thought. That was his picture of city people — dodging the rain and thinking. After having been with many city sportsmen hunting in the Delta, Mitch said that they complained when hungry. How could a man get hungry when there was nothing around to eat?

All the time he was gone, in her visions she held him near. She remembered him most vividly walking the road of a Sunday dressed up like a cock oriole at mating, so untrammeled and humorous and alert. A typical male, she sniffed. Yet there was something feminine under it all. The fancy vest he had worn years ago, the hat which appeared to be very carelessly worn yet was nicely calculated. Perhaps the hat had been adjusted at a mirror, like a woman's. Other very masculine men she knew, such as the Tocko fishermen, did not know how or did not trouble to look attractive. They were very naïve with women. It was easy to make sport of them. Their heavy strong masculinity made them vulnerable to a woman's secret designs. Their desire was very obvious — the deep clumsy need to give some woman their slow strength, to work hard for her with their square hands in exchange for food and peace and babies. Part of Sister's nature seemed to be attracted to this kind of man. Though Mitch himself had this instinct, he also flaunted these other almost womanly attributes of wit and grace that Sister had encountered nowhere else but in literature, in the feline matadors in Grampaw's reproductions of Goya, and in certain cunning and fiery Italian troupers or carefree Austrian officers.

So her husband, previously associated chiefly with her escape from past hunger, was now part of this picture fabricated out of solid Tocko instincts, matadors and foreign officers. It was a very wide vision in which her mind could flow to alien climes. When the wide vision dispersed, she was alone again. She was nothing again. Was it only with the man that she became something? Must she bend without breaking, conform to the outline of his will by yielding in places and in others holding stiff? The deeper went her thoughts, the greater the confusion. There was no such thing as detachment. She was one with the past and one with herself.

The few days preceding Mitch's return were for her a curious period. In the daytime, life was too near and bright for reality. It came to her as a forest clearing must appear to an owl at noon. There was barely a trace of depth or roundness. Passers-by moved in a sort of static rhythm, coming from no place and seeking no destination. Bruce brought her an orange leaf on which lay a caterpillar shaped and colored exactly like the excretion of a bird — the 'orange dog.' She looked at it, fixing it in the present, dilating her pupils to make the creature appear real. She heard herself explaining to the child. An amusing joke of nature's on the birds. Protective coloring. Polar bears. Grass snakes. But it was not real. Until that night by the fire, looked back upon. All that week in daytime her mind was a kind of mere muscular agent, wanting no reality. Only the vision — formed not alone with the mind but with the aid also of every pore and tendon — was real. The fluid fabric. And this was evoked most clearly by nocturnal coals. . . .

Mitch returned with his boat freighted with good meat, two deer and a huge pile of geese killed the day before. His gear and pelts were loaded in a second skiff towed. Sister rolled up her sleeves, her heart pumping furiously. She helped carry in the game. Bruce staggered under a single goose so large he could hardly walk. The gutting-holes of all the fowl were brimming with yellow fat. There was a pair of beautiful wood-ducks for her! Neighbors came running to receive a goose apiece. Mitch had crept upon a flock of thousands while they fed in the moonlight, crawling through the bogs on his belly. The larger deer weighed as much as a man. Sister potted a goose at once for breakfast. Mitch skinned and butchered the deer. They spent all day and half the night picking the geese to be salted down for summer. With Mitch close by, the feel of the ripped feathers went through Sister's senses thrillingly. His beard was reddish gold. The sun gilded him all over, and later the lantern light glittered from his laughing teeth. He was proud of their first meat, proud as a boy. 'Save a goose for Pretty John,' he said. 'He will want some of our first meat.' Sister raised her face and laughed. There was an odd lack of passion in this meeting. They were like children from separate villages meeting the first day of vacation, a little shy. When Sister scratched her nose, a bit of down remained there, tickling her into sneezing. Her hair and clothing were touched all over with the downy wisps. Mitch rubbed a handful of feathers into her hair.

'Don't!' she said, suddenly hoarse with passion. He knelt beside her and they embraced, and all her being dissolved into a deep eddy of rapture. The brackish odor of the marsh lay upon him still. A certain elemental part of her loved it.

After the work she sacked the feathers and hung the geese on the wire clothesline. She filled the kettle and walked to the front with the lamp. Roosters were blaring on both sides the river. Long ago Sister had heard a passing ship strike eight bells for midnight. Mitch was on the front sofa.

'Darling!' She passed her hand over his brow and across the softly stubbled jaws. He awoke, staring and blinking.

'Bedtime!' said Sister. 'Allons!'

'All right.' He settled more comfortably, breathing deeply.

'Darling!' She looked down at him, smiling. She pulled at his hand. She loved his helpless, inert exhaustion. He sat up and swung round, but his head dropped. Sister took his arm.

Up the stairs he half leaned on her. When he spoke his tongue was heavy. 'I never — I want ——' Sister giggled, unlacing his shoes. 'I — said — I ——' She took off his shirt and pushed him into the bed, then removed his trousers. He rolled over and lay still, with one arm twisted in a grotesque attitude.

Sister brushed her hair. She went into the next room softly and tucked Bruce's covers. Before getting into bed, she straightened Mitch's garments on the chairback. She lay beside her husband and eased him into her arms. She sighed and closed her eyes, forming her own darkness, shutting out the other. She was aware of the child suspended in her swelling womb. The man sleeping in her arms grew heavy.

Grass Margin now lay between two levees, one on the river and another in the rear to keep out sea tides. Mitch worked for some months clearing their last area of woods in the rear and hauling off the firewood. It was a job he loved. When a tree fell he gave a great shout. He worked with his upper body bared. His skin burned a cherry red and grew coils of supple muscle, different from the marsh-sinews. Sister labored near him in the adjoining field, cultivating her tomatoes, beans, okra, and sweet corn. She always managed to spell her animal on the edge of Mitch's piece, so the three could rest together. The man and woman lay talking, or they rested with eyes wandering over the land in a kind of dumb, uncomprehending way — the gray rows furled and sprouting green peaks, or the aged thicket that Mitch was reducing to a flat stretch of stumps and brush piles.

In the late summer the trees were felled. A large vacant place remained in the sky. Sister, finishing up out there, worked inside jarring her vegetables. Mitch and his Negro helper worked until the fall, grubbing out the stumps, for there was another jungle under the ground as tenacious as the first had been. He was planting little newly grafted oranges on that piece when she had her baby. The child came without mishap. She wanted to get into her kitchen next day. Mitch threatened to lock her in her room. He hired a Negress and Sister spent five full days convalescing, reading, dozing, feeling light as a girl with her burden gone, and very conscious that the child was wholly hers no more.

The baby was a boy. The life of the household changed like a road veering slightly toward a new destination. Mitch was highly amused. He would weigh the baby, or examine its strangely wrinkled soles. He remained home nights for more than a week.

Little Bruce could not understand it all. He leaned his back against his mother, shrinking from the new baby; yet his dark eyes remained on the little crib. He would lie on the levee waiting for people to pass, to tell them the news.

When Sister came downstairs, she went out to see the new little oranges. She had grafted these trees herself in the nursery, Creole Sweets budded on sour stock, each stained at the base by a little of the water Mitch had sledded down from the river. They too were babies, small and tender, wet with dew, each casting its tiny frowning shadow. And whichever way one looked the rows were straight. Some day she would climb into the boughs of these inchlings. They would never be neglected as the house was sometimes, or as the older trees had been. Nothing but flood, storm, or freeze would ever hurt them. The cleared area with its freshly plowed sod and rows of new trees conveyed a sense of finality and rightness. It was like a document sworn and subscribed to, or a hard problem in mathematics solved once and forever.

A rooster from next door jumped the ditch. Three waddling hens followed. The cock walked among the little trees, and stopped by one of them to scratch. 'Shoo!' Sister cried. 'That damned rooster again!'

'Guate's Brown Island Rock,' said Mitch.

The rooster walked to the front with his hens. He was among Sister's Easter lilies, which were just coming up, and she saw him scratch at a row. She chased the fowls with a stick, and, swinging it, caught the rooster a glancing blow on the leg. 'Foul ball!' Mitch called. She jumped the ditch and went through the orchard to where old Mr. Guate was working his onions. He stood looking like a kind donkey in the rain. The sky seemed to turn gray behind him. Sister complained to Mr. Guate. 'If you don't mind,' said Sister. 'My lily bulbs are already sold to a New Orleans florist.'

Mr. Guate was very conscious of his pants. 'Philomene her what she went and done, she went and open duh pen to make duh chicken catch bug,' he said. He looked toward his house and spoke in a low tone. 'Her she want duh hen to lay egg. They dawn lay no egg. Is not right to eat your Heaster lily and pick your mud. Dat Philomene!' He threw his hoe at the hens.

'Will you please keep them off our place, Mr. Guate?'

'Who, me?' He looked toward his house, then smiled at Sister. The fingers of his dangling hands were curved in the shape of the hoe-handle. He retrieved the hoe and stood thinking. 'Me, I got nothing to do with them chicken, Miss Sister. You batter talk to Philomene, hein?'

'All right, sir,' Sister answered. But she forgot the incident.

One day a couple of weeks later Sister found the rooster and his hens had made several large holes in the black fine earth of her best row of lilies. They wallowed in the dust, and looked at her angrily.

Sister said to Mitch, 'I've got an idea! Do you think you can catch that rooster?'

'Sure I can catch him!'

Enticed into the packing-shed with corn, the rooster was caught and brought in to Sister. Mitch in the doorway with the rooster let out a roar of laughter.

Sister was making a little pair of pants out of mattress ticking.

Mitch held the fowl and Sister adjusted the pants and tied them on. They took him into the orchard, creeping over near the Guate place.

'Turn him loose!' Mitch whispered.

'Poor Mr. Guate! I hate to do it!'

'Turn him loose! Give him here!'

The rooster ran home, whirling in circles, and leaping in the air.

In the evening Sister and Mitch went swimming in the river. Mitch had put up a new springboard. Sister's new bathing-suit, with a skirt cut to the thighs, was a scandalous thing to wear on Grass Margin. It caused her a pleasurable embarrassment.

Mr. Guate came running out of his house, chasing the old rooster up the road. His pants were like the rooster's. Presently his wife appeared, holding a broomstick. 'Kedge him! Kedge him! Chaze him back! Hurry up!' she was yelling.

Mr. Guate turned, shouting, 'Bud I can't kedge him, Philo-mene! Daunt you see he is gone?'

'Chaze him I tell you!' shouted the wife. 'Hurry up! Daunt you come back to dis houze tell you head him off!'

Mr. Guate chased the fowl until his breath was gone, then came walking back. At Sister's wharf he lingered. Far out on the landing Sister was diving just then. Guate stood with mouth open. Sister came up the ladder, and stood with all her black curves traced in sunlight, laughing.

'*Lucien!*' Mrs. Guate called.

Guate turned and looked at his wife. He did not answer. He walked closer to the wharf and sat down to watch Sister dive again. His eyes lit up and his face was creased in smiles. Sister swam to the ladder and pulled herself up. Guate remained on the wharf for half an hour, happy as a child. He looked up the road once. The rooster was returning, strutting, looking from side to side. Guate turned and watched Sister sitting on her ankle with a big white towel over her shoulders. Mitch and Sister went inside the house. Guate went off thoughtfully. His wife advanced to meet him with her stick. He looked at her, then walked past her pensively, without a word.

'Are you gone ged dat rooster?' the woman screamed, following her husband in.

'Daunt bother me.' He was standing by the window, thinking.

After a silence he turned and fixed her with his mild stare. She was breathing hard, as she did when about to have hysterics. 'What you got for supper, Philomene?' he asked calmly. He sat on the chair and removed the ticking pants. Mrs. Guate ran to the front room and began distractedly pacing, screaming, 'Mon Dieu! Mon Dieu! He is gone get dronk! Mon Dieu!' Guate shambled about, looking for a change of pants. He found a pair. He quit work for the day. He sat on the levee smoking, waiting for his supper.

The rooster never again bothered Sister's lilies. Old man Guate never again wore the ticking pants. He paid no attention to his wife's hysterics, only gazed at her with a gray fatherly look.

One day several months later Sister and Mitch heard a loud disturbance in the Guates' below. Mrs. Guate was having hysterics. Her husband could be heard in the yard, the noise of his buck-saw cutting a log. Mrs. Guate ran into the yard and raised her voice loudly: 'I knaw why you lak to go up duh road every evening, you! You want to *pazz her house* negs door!' Mr. Guate answered her only with the patient snoring of his saw. Sister was at the washtub. Mitch lay under a near-by tree with the baby. For the past week he had been in a state of mild discontent and lethargy — lazying off, he called it. He would soon be going alligator hunting.

'You god to pazz her house, you!' Mrs. Guate screamed.

'Mon Dieu! An old man! Sacré nom de nom de nom!' Sister and Mitch smiled at one another. 'Duh Immaculate Conception!' the hysterical woman cried. 'Duh dirty trash! Duh dirty trash negs door! Dirty trash! She kill her papa! She kill her grandpère! She got bastar' from nobody! Immaculate Conception!' Sister wrung a diaper. She plunged a shirt into a tub of blue water. 'Immaculate Conception!' came the shrill voice, mixed with the patient wood-sawing. 'Water-waster! Papa-killer! Raised wid niggers! Ain't got no husband now! Everybody knaw dat! Call dat a husband? He's goin' wid other women right now! Ax anybody! Everybody knaw her husband goin' wid other woman! He's goin' wid Sabina Leboeuf right now! Sabina Leboeuf! I tell duh whole world! Sabina Leboeuf!'

'Our sins have found us out,' Sister said. Her face was averted. Mitch said nothing. Sister went on washing. She dumped a bucketful of diapers into the tub. She was smiling. Her sweat burned the corner of one of her eyes. Mitch sat up and sighed.

'Is it true, Mitch?' she asked.

'Hell, I haven't seen the woman in a month!'

'Because you can tell me, you know. You can tell me, Mitch.'

'I've cut it out, Jolie.'

'I've got a good home and lots to eat, you know.'

'Hell, stop that kind of talk! I'm daffy about you, Jolie! This other business ... I don't know ...' His back was to her.

Sister clenched her jaws. Her red mouth was a straight line. She lugged a tub of water from the bench and set it on the ground. Sister was rather wide-hipped at this time. Her back and thighs had been undergoing a filling-out, and she felt taller. She would have another child, she reckoned, in seven months. It was easy, having children now. She looked at Mitch. His body had not changed. In his stalwart back there was the same deep depression for the spinal ridge. His body was beloved, in the same old way. Or it was loved as the creator of the children beginning to pass through her. The children were like uttered words. Her heart was beating words, too. She gave a hard chuckle.

'You can't help it, Mitch?' she asked. Her stomach burned. It felt sour or salty.

'It's the truth, Jolie! Look at me! I don't know what it is. Something stronger than I am wants me to trifle with women.' Mitch grew angry. He walked over to her, his fists clenched, as if denouncing her. 'What is it? What is it?' He turned away. 'It doesn't seem to harm anybody. Not at the time. But it's a wrong against you, Jolie. I won't do it again, honey. It's not right!'

His strange contrition was like a bright flag hauled down. She had never seen him so bewildered, striving for the first time in his life to take apart and examine the clockwork of the past. He looked at her once with bright wide eyes as though a solution or a discovery had occurred. Then he gazed at his feet and said nothing. She fancied she could understand how he felt: probably the way she herself had felt as a child trying to understand how clouds could hold such heavy showers without any skin on them or why smallpox germs had been saved from the Flood by Noah.

'Will you let it pass this time, Jolie?' he asked. 'And not file it away in one of those holes in your head and take it out when you need it?'

She hugged her breasts. She looked at him, her jaws clenching hard. Mitch was all blurred and shining. 'I don't know, honey,' she said, without much breath left. 'How do I know?'

'Hell! You know you can forgive.'

'I never tried that before.'

'What?'

'Forgiving anybody. And I hate to see you there begging pardon. Go away. Go out back.'

He walked off. 'I know it's serious. I know.'

'And yet if you don't beg pardon it's worse. It can't...'
She was no longer talking to her husband. He was moving
toward the young orchard in the rear, pulling a weed to stick
between his teeth. She dried her eyes and told herself he was
forgiven. Remember, now, he is forgiven. It's not hard to do.
But he would have to stay forgiven. This forgiveness clung to
her afterward like some rough strong garment. It smelled of
soapy water. Little Bruce yanked her skirts.

'Tell Poline to use this soap-water to bug the roses,' she said.
'Did you have a good time at Warren's?'

'No. I'm hungry, please,' said the child. His hair shone
gloriously. His body was hard, compact, rounded with health.

Sister frowned at him, her mouth curling. 'Tell Poline give
you a bowl of crawfish, Fella.'

Sister was proud of something. She was disdainful of something. Her mind went far into the future. She was remembering this day, recalling Mitch's puzzled face, the wash on the
line, the Negress singing in the kitchen, the puddle of soapy
drippings around her feet — all the harsh acrid sounds and
odors of a summer morning in a busy back yard. She looked
back on Sabina Leboeuf, a certain sweet girl who had worked
in the store in Lacroix. A winsome girl, scornful of the Margin
boys. There had been nobody for her to marry. She was too
proud to wave at the passing pilots, but naturally she had
needed a man sometime. A sweet generous girl.. .The daylight was red. The soapy water was crimson. Sister wrung a
bedspread with a powerful twist, until her husky forearms
quivered.

'Daunt mind him,' said Unga January.

Sister turned. Unga had been sitting under a fig tree all the
while. She was holding a dead humming-bird. 'Look!' Unga
cried. 'For your new hat, cher! Me, I caught him in my garden for your new hat!'

'Thank you. They've been out of style, though.'

'Give him to duh cat or Bruce for a funeral.'

Unga had long ago lost her lugubrious attitude, because she had learned that nothing is worth bothering about. Big skinny Bonus had never possessed her, but he had left her the great truth of his race. After his departure for the insane asylum, this truth had grown in Unga from his deeply planted seed, like a conception. Bonus knew more than anybody. He didn't sleep with no stocking on his head to straighten down the hair. Nothing was worth bothering about.

'Dat's a *man*, your husband!' said Unga. 'Nothing different, cher.'

Sister saw that Unga's fur coat was almost gone. The skin showed in places. Unga looked peaceful. Her bare toes had grown quite far apart, with no shoes.

'A better man than a husband, Unga.'

'Daunt you worry 'bout Mitch. Listen to Unga. You got him. Such pretty baby you have all duh time! Maybe next is a little girl, hein? Nobody can cook lak you, cher! Midge knaw dat. He knaw you a good woman. But in duh night-time,' Unga whispered, 'daunt you be *too* good, cher.'

'How?'

'Neb' mind! Listen to Unga. Daunt be too good. Is different from duh daytime. Is duh time to make duh man injoy himself. All duh chirren sleeping, you can ack lak bad womans! Is duh time for playing. You give him good time, he daunt go to 'nother houze for good time.' Unga smiled her beautiful smile, which was no longer rare.

'Being good all day would make you tired at night, Unga.'

'Oui, dat's true. Dem bad womans is sleeping all day, duh dirty hog! And duh good womans picks okra and knock down cow-webs.'

'How would a person act like a bad woman?' Sister asked. 'What is a bad woman? How do you know she's bad?'

Unga giggled and blushed. 'You got to smell sweet, and

you got to think up trick! All kind of crazy trick, and laugh and make duh man feel good. Dat's ef he's a *real* man! You got 'magination, because you tell nize story all duh time. I tell you we got to put these bad girl out of business! A woman got to breathe in a man's ear, and thing lak dat, and make him chase you aroun'. You got to make him daunt worry 'bout nothing all duh time.'

'Is that what you call being bad, Unga?'

'Is what all duh womans calls it dat's shame to go nekkid for duh po' man and have some fun. Some womans here is lak dat. You understand?'

Sister sat looking among the trees laden with half-grown fruit. She thought of André Laval's sad eye peeping at Crazy Carrie dancing in the barge. The furtive glances of a man at a woman's guarded parts always touched her heart with pathos. She had once found Mocco looking into the packing-shed window to see his wife bathing. It had been very funny, but also a sad thing to see, which she would never forget.

In the afternoon a wanderer walked into the yard, a wild-looking young Irish levee worker with the first pair of violet eyes Sister had ever seen, bluer than Mitch's. His arms reached almost to his knees. His beard was as happy as a work of art, a great bush of a chestnut shade.

'God bless those in this house,' he greeted Sister. 'Sure from behind I didn't think you was a geddle, with your wearin' the pants of a lad. And is himself at home?' The eyes in the woebegone face were deep and merry.

'Which himself?' Sister answered the queer question. 'You sound like you're looking for the Lord.'

'And the Lord would serve my purpose, but He's not wanting to meet the likes of me, so it's a word that I'll have with your father or husband, if you have any at all. It ties the tongue of me always to beg a favor of a handsome geddle like yourself.'

'Well — I'm his private secretary. What is the nature of your business?'

'Sure it's business I'm wanting, since I lost mine Wednesday was a week. I lost me job from drinking from a jug down the road. I've abstained six days and fasted two, and I can trudge no further from this spot.'

Sister brought him coffee and a bowl of crawfish. Before eating, he raised his eyes and said solemnly, 'Perhaps you'll want me to spit on the lad's knee-cap where he's been bruised before I break me fast, though mine's no volunt'ry fasting and the spittle might not help.'

'Thank you, it's only brush from the trees. Do you eat the shells of the crawfish?'

'Ah, the sweet little creatures have such tender shells!'

Mitch returned from fishing in the rear Bay at evening, and Sister made a noble court bullion with a sheepshead, and fried the trout. Mitch and the wayfarer were great friends at once with their blue eyes and their bright laughter gurgling out from the appeased stomachs. The Irishman after feeding led Sister a merry spell with his raillery and open flirtation, and she enjoyed whetting wits with him.

As the night passed, the house fairly shook with the laughter of the men and their tipsy banter. Sister observed Mitch, never before having seen him in such close proximity with his kind. There was in this meeting of the two men an instant recognition and respect. Each implied to the other, 'I know all about you, my lad. Of course we'll not dream of trying to fool each other — though if necessary we must fool this worthy woman here, for her own good and peace of mind.' Their appearance betokened a common quality, a certain glittering gallantry which to Sister was provocative and yet rather poignant. She watched them together, fascinated, disturbed. She perceived they were brothers in their lusty gaiety, their very tough and serviceable hips, their assumption of perilous aptitudes held in leash, and that vivid blue glitter that lit their eyes, hinting of some secretly cherished, hard-won knowledge acquired from long acquaintance with endless vistas and lonely skies. The other man's coming thus revealed her husband to her; yet it made her also aware of her freighted womb, and of all the soft and circumscribed arts of wifehood. . . .

The stranger remained another day, and he wormed the hound and mended the leak which had been trickling through the levee for years. Before he left, Sister persuaded him to plant a tree in honor of the visit, a small mandarin — though it was not certain a summer planting would take hold.

When the visitor left, suddenly a deep quiet lay over the house. Where was Mitch keeping himself all day? Out in the new orchard watering the little trees, or doing trifling tasks around the ditch banks, far from the house. He had grown reserved, taciturn. Evenings he took Bruce for a walk, or fished shrimp with the boy off the wharf, while Sister near-by amused the baby in the levee grass — Stephen, the blond baby boy.

It was a peaceful domestic scene each evening, the trees and waters all suffused by the soft nebulous shades of the day's ending. Sister watched her husband, all her intuitive faculties alert, quivering outward like sensitive tendrils. A peaceful domestic scene . . . For three days Mitch had been comporting himself like a dependable husband, showing his wife certain agreeable attentions, rather humble and tender with contrition. But he hardly laughed or played at all. Where was his debonair carelessness? He reminded Sister of the stony-faced man who had returned from prison. She found herself feeling somehow sorry for him. Was his spirit breaking? No! No! That must not be! She would rather they parted. Her heart went out to him as the days went by.

But he was not so attractive to her as he had been. She felt cheated. She grew impatient at him and at herself. To hell with it! To hell with it! Let it work itself out!

42

IN THE late summer a drought cracked the thin land. The peninsula, though skirted on either side by vast waters and cloven by the cool river, lay baking, withering in the blinding quiet. And several mocking waterspouts were seen to the east or west. The glittering black devil-horses multiplied, crawling over the drooping vegetation but a few inches an hour. And they threw queer shadows on the pale ground, their bristling leg-spines fantastically exaggerated.

Sister now was teaching six little Negroes. She lined them up in a row. 'Now you all know how to read,' she said. 'I'm going to teach you to write and spell. One hour a day. To pay for your lessons you will come at half-past five each morning while it's cool and get rid of all the devil-horses you see on the place. Bring a box with you to put the grasshoppers in. Maybe you can sell them to the catfishermen. Spend one hour in the morning. Come back in the evening after sun for another hour. Clean them up!'

Thunder mumbled. Clouds assembled each day as if to confer, and they turned an angry purple, but the rain could not fall. Slower and slower the shadows crawled. People hid from the sun. Only the alligator hunters ventured abroad for long. Most of these were dark wiry men, immune to swamp contagions, accustomed to drinking from any stagnant pool. They were neither weak nor strong, but resilient like reeds in the elements. And they possessed the faculty of assuming while among the steaming bogs a sort of plant-like dormancy. They did not waste vitality cursing the heat or yearning for a change of wind. They shook the sweat from their chins and sniffed the air for alligator musk.

Sister had a letter once from Mocco. Violet's first baby was a girl, about whom Mocco said very little. He said he was in the dumps. Sister wondered exactly what this meant. She vaguely supposed Mocco was exhausted by the prodigious exertion involved in doing nothing. They were living with Violet's family. Mocco was now earning a precarious living selling jumbo (five-cent-a-quart soda pop) at a certain baseball green on Sundays; and he was peddling a locally advertised preparation for removing stains from clothing. This was only temporary. Mocco had a wonderful scheme in his head. He planned to sell to the curio stores little vials of Mississippi River water for the winter tourists to buy and take home. There was a saying, disseminated by the tourist guides, that anyone visiting New Orleans and drinking the water would some day return for more. Something in the water would make them return. Mocco needed only a little capital, twenty-five dollars for bottles and tags. There was plenty of free river-water . . .

The road was being fixed from New Orleans to Grass Margin. Within a couple of years, people from the city would be driving cars down the Margin levee road. Was Mitch going to buy an automobile? Soon he would be able to drive his family to town in a couple of hours . . .

Mitch was hunting alligators around Bayou Tante Phine, a good wild region spotted with ponds and tall canes whose bristling interstices broke down every sound into a dry whisper. The long leaves gushed upward and curved down fountain-like; but in the heat this foliage was as stiffly fixed as tarnished brass lying flat against the annealed sky. Mitch burned very red. The sun never tanned him. He whistled loudly, keeping himself company. Mitch was happy, making big money to dress up his wife and to gamble. The weather was ideal for alligators. He had found the day before the tracks of a big male that had so far led him to the dens of six females, none of which were too large or too small, none over ten feet or under six. The Old Man was bringing down plenty of water this season. Last reports from Memphis, relayed out to the hunters, stated the water was only beginning to drop up there. Then it would not drop in the Delta for quite a while. Forests in the North were being denuded rapidly. Fewer and fewer trees every year to drink up the valley waters. More water for the alligators.

Mitch stopped at a large hole in the prairie, an oblique cave slanting downward. There was water in the hole. Mitch leaned over and smelled. He crawled into the hole.

'Kyoonk! Kyoonk! Kyoonk!' Imitating the cry of a young alligator. He waited awhile. 'Kyoonk-kyoonk! Kyoonk!' The water level lifted and sank two or three times. Gently the man felt around under water. In the dark depths his spread fingers groped, the cool water sliding between them. Presently one of his thumbs encountered the scaly blunt end of a large alligator's snout. Carefully with both hands he grasped the snout, holding the jaws shut, and slowly hauled the heavy body toward him. Now he held the snout with one hand, and with the other he slipped his hatchet from his belt. Now the eyes of the creature were out of the water. The alligator began slowly to move his feet, clawing for a hold. Mitch swiftly brought the hatchet down on a spot at the base of the head. The alligator relaxed without a tremor.

He dragged the carcass out. He severed the spinal marrow with his knife. Heavy drops of sweat popped out all over him, because the ground, the layered alluvium and peat he was kneeling on, was hotter than the sky. The earth was hotter than the sun. The bitter heat made him feel good while resting. Many alligators would be out in this weather to be cooked. They loved it. The 'gator before him was of a tidy length, eight and a half feet. Five dollars earned. A wild house-cat peeped at Mitch through the canes. He looked up and the cat was gone. He fell to his knees and began to skin. The 'gator was a nice kill, fattened by a steady fare of rabbits stunned by a flip of its tail, and nests of birds slapped out of the myrtles. The cold belly was clabbery and full, quivering all over when he thumped it. The reptile was a cow. Forty-seven eggs. Mitch smiled at the eggs. Cow-eggs. She'd never bite a hunk out of another male's foreleg.

Well, he would be through for the day. He smelled sour. He took the skin to his shack, paddling with all the skins taken that day. Mitch had regained all his skill at paddling. It was said on the Margin that Mitch Holt could paddle a load of sinker-lead over a heavy fall of dew. At his shack there were two barrels full of skins he had taken, all rolled in salt from head to tail with the legs folded in. Three or three hundred and fifty dollars. Three weeks' easy work. Mitch always hunted alone. The other boys on the Margin were afraid to work without a partner. The empty marsh was a lonely place. Suppose a man should catch a blood-poison from a saw-grass cut, or get sick from a moccasin bite? Suppose a 'gator should slap a man crooked, or break his face?

Mitch bathed in the bayou and shaved. He ate a quart of Sister's put-up figs with hardtack. He wished Sister here. Sister's fried muskrat legs and stuffed peppers, with a nice snap-bean salad right off the ice! Mitch laid his head on the table and slept at once.

He awoke in mid-afternoon, refreshed, restless. Someone had been shouting near-by. Mitch went out and shot a few blackbirds for baiting 'gator lines that night. He returned, and skimmed through a humorous magazine Sister had packed with his things, and for a while he read from his *Novum Organum*. He went to the window and looked out. A blue heron sailed past, and afterward he saw three empty shotgun shells floating down. Earlier in the day Mitch had seen, a long way up Tante Phine, a strange camp-boat painted gray. His curiosity had been aroused. He decided to visit the boat for company. Mitch could talk Canary Spanish and French — gumbo or the real.

A deep narrow fissure clove the canebrakes along the stream a way, floored with trampled canes. The brakes were high green walls leading up to the incandescent sky, forming a kind of canyon. Far above the man's head the cane leaves stirred. There was wind, but none of it reached him. His sweat did not cool him. Just because he was dressed up, he felt the heat, though the clothes were lighter than the swamp-duds.

A figure was moving toward him far up the trail. A woman? Mitch was oddly startled. This feeling gave way to one of antagonism which he always felt toward a young woman. He blinked at her through the quaking heat. Some hunter's wife or daughter gallivanting. Her walking body was animated by blue and green stripes continually falling over her form, sliding away and reappearing. At first she might have been a big bittern making itself invisible by simulating in its walk the wavering motion of shadowy grass blades, as these creatures do. But the head was golden. A woman, by God! No hat. Golden. Young. She saw him. Her gait did not change. What the hell did she mean, dressed in faded green? Where was there for her to go? The trail ended at *his* camp.

He knew her. He had met her at the Pilot Town dances. No hat. The steward's daughter. Fortinwood. Fortinberry.

'Hey!' he called, 'you looking for the show-boat?'

The face floated toward him, the shadow stripes washing over it. Mitch stopped with his thumb hooked in his pocket. The girl was saying hoarse words. Her chin was trembling. She came close. 'Cooking soda?' she was asking. 'Have you any cooking soda? I'm — I've got a colic pain.' She was pale as daybreak, grayish.

'I've got laudanum. What've you been eating, Elmira?'

'Hog.'

The girl smelled of alligator musk. Or there was a very old and ambitious 'gator prowling near. The sun was very small and spiteful, as though focussed through a glass. The girl dented her stomach, pressing it here and there, trying to smile.

'Summer hog!' Mitch exclaimed. 'I reckon your brother chased it to kill. No wonder you're cramped. What do you expect, Elmira honey?'

'I expect cooking soda, damn it!'

That answer reminded Mitch of his wife, the words stabbing the heat with the swiftness of a bounced ball. He said: 'Come on. I've got one remedy, and that's laudanum. We'll try a few drops. Why don't you ram your finger down your throat?'

The girl lay in Mitch's bunk. She studied the picture of Jim Jeffries printed on pink paper, a big handsome fighting man. She said, 'I don't know how to pay you back for doctoring out that-there cramps. I must have looked a sight.'

'You looked like old cocoanut layer-cake on the train.'

'What are you frying?'

The girl made Mitch think of Sister back home. She was not so attractive, but she was beginning to provoke him, now that she was well. He wanted to aggravate her. Later he would have to think up a trick to play on her.

'What's that you're frying smells so good?' she asked.

'Fawn livers. Won't you eat?'

'I better not.'

'This stuff will pet your belly-nerves and cradle your bile, my friend. You'll forget you ever tasted chased boar-jowl.'

'Well, I still feel messed up in there. I better not, Mitch.'

She sat at the table and began to eat with him. She ate two plates of the livers and some preserves.

The next day he saw her again. He was working in the bayou, searching for alligator holes in the side of the bank. Up to his waist in water, he had hold of a mangrove tree, and with his feet was feeling around under the water for alligator holes. Through the leaves he saw her crossing a stretch of floating land. It was thin land. At each footstep of hers the land sank deeply under her, and rose behind the lifted foot. Mitch's eyes were about level with the land's surface; and as he watched the girl, with the big empty sky and prairie behind her, she seemed unusually large, with the whole world rocking. He yelled and she came looking for him in the trees, and the oblique earthen waves rolled away behind her. Her body lifted and sank through the sunny void like a sort of gold-bannered argosy big with sail. He would tell Sister about that.

She stood on the bank awhile and they talked. The girl was an informative listener: she caused him to inform himself of many things he had never known before. A big 'gator shot out of the hole while they were talking and slipped away through Mitch's legs. He excused himself and took to his pirogue, and followed the alligator's bubbles down the stream.

Every day while her brother was away, the girl came to Mitch's camp at his breakfast time. She loved to hear him talk about the North, the big mountains, the tributaries of the river all bringing their floods to the Old Man. They made good meals of summer ducks. Elmira helped pick and cook the ducks, and washed the dishes. Mitch was proud of himself, because thus far he had conducted himself like a faithful husband. It was in a way exciting to refrain from improper overtures toward this girl, who was so vulnerable and attentive. It gave him a feeling of another kind of power — the power of having a strong force secured by the thongs of his will. Decency might after all be just as exhilarating as devilment.

Then, for no apparent reason, Elmira stayed away from Mitch's camp. Her brother had perhaps found out. It was all right. Forget it. She might be back. If not, what was the difference?

Four days passed. Mitch called on Elmira's brother, whom he had not seen in a long time. He hoped the girl would not be there. She was rather a dull person, anyway. He had been about to avoid her when she discontinued her visits, he told himself. Her brother Mike sat by the lantern soaking his arms in Epsom salts. Mike had some ugly saw-grass cuts around the wrists. Where was the girl?

'You all alone out here, Mike?'

'Elmira's with me on one-third share. She's gone up the trail to see Gramaw Poirier.'

'Gramaw Poirier! Why, I haven't seen her in years!'

'Neither me. I don't want to see her. She's still bug-house.'

Mitch went up the trail to see Gramaw Poirier. Come to think of it, he wanted to see Elmira too, in the presence of a third person, so that he could enjoy teasing her. No harm in that.

He met Elmira on the trail coming home. The moonlight was hot, almost as warm as sun. Mitch hid and roared like a bull alligator whipping a she-one. Elmira was not scared. She said, 'Hey, Mitch!' and walked on past him. In a while she looked back once. Mitch kept walking to Gramaw Poirier's.

Elmira called from far, 'Mitch! Are you going to the Pilot's Dance tomorrow night?'

'Maybe!' he answered.

At midnight when Mitch started back home the moon was bowed down, all warped like a goblet of sweet yellow spirits. The cane leaves moved past it like delicate talons clawing. Mitch heard the faint nasal squealing of muskrats everywhere behind the heat, mating for the third seasonal brood. Mitch was quite excited, on his way to play a prank on Elmira Fortinberry. Approaching the Fortinberry houseboat he crept noiselessly. He loved the still darkness glistening with danger. The houseboat sank slightly as he stepped aboard.

Elmira's room was aft. Her door was open wide. His heart thumped, and he smiled. He went in. He could discern the blurred paleness of her limbs sprawled at strange angles. He was sorely tempted to tickle her ribs and ruin his joke. . . . He lifted one side of her mosquito-bar and pinned it up with a twig. This room was full of mosquitoes. He stole from the place, brushing the insects from his face and neck as he eased himself ashore.

Next day Elmira came to his camp. Mitch said, 'You've got heavy paddling to do if you're going to the dance, Jolie.'

The girl sat on a chair. She did not answer. Her face was ruined for the dance, covered with mosquito bites — cheeks, ears, nose, eyelids, all marred with little purple dots. 'What's the matter with your face?' Mitch asked. 'Measles? What you been eating this time?'

The girl looked at him with tears in her eyes. 'You dirty thing!' she said, attempting to smile. 'You dirty thing!' She went to him and grabbed two handfuls of his hair. She yanked his head backward. Mitch was indignant. 'What's eating you, Elmira honey? Let go! Let go!' He reached back and caught her by the neck, bringing her face next to his. Her body went slack. She lay in his arms. Mitch looked down into the purple face. The livid color made her eyes look like fanned embers. Elmira dabbed his perspiring face with her handkerchief. He let her go without even kissing her. It was not right. He thought of Sister at home. Elmira in the doorway arranged her dress. 'You've got a gall, Mitch Holt,' she said.

He walked with Elmira toward her houseboat. Once he saw a trace of alligator bubbles fizzling up in the water. He slid into the bayou and felt for a hole in the bank. The alligator got away, grazing Mitch's boot.

'That's the second 'gator you've made me lose, Jolie,' he said. He was looking up at her teasingly, smiling with his white teeth. The tender warm conflict in her face fed some famished thing inside him now. Elmira was sitting on the bank, brooding, biting a fingernail. The finger was trembling. Nothing was visible on the bare landscape here but the girl — no canes, only green flatness and the high sky. 'I dare you to get in the bayou!' Mitch teased. 'I dare you!' The reddish eyes in the purple face studied Mitch, uncertain.

'You'd better get to work, instead of playing around,' said Elmira, removing her shoes and gravely spreading her stockings on the bank. She wriggled her toes, leaned back on the heels of her hands, looking at the sky.

'I dare you! I dare you to jump in!'

'You think you're smart,' she said, and slid solemnly into the bayou. 'Now!' she said, not looking at Mitch, bobbing up and down with slow, grave buoyancy. She fished around for his hand. 'You dare to let me slip in the deep part and I'll scream!'

'I didn't think you'd do it, Jolie!' Mitch held her two hands. The hot slow current was edging her against him, shoving her irresistibly with its hot bulky thrusts. Her feet pawed backwards, and met nothing but the icy slush on the bottom. Mitch laughed nervously, and made a show of splashing the lavender face playfully. Elmira grabbed his arms in a trembling death-grip, and then stooped to push down her ballooned skirts. 'I'm getting out,' she said. 'You dared me! It was your fault. You dared me. Let me get out, Mitch.' But she was not trying to get out. Mitch's hand was around her waist and she was holding it there.

'Mitch! Your wife!'

'Do you love me? Do you?' This would be the last time he would ever trifle on his wife. He would enjoy the escapade well. The last time. All married up, now! It would have to stop.

'Do you love me?'

'Mitch! Oh, yes, Mitch! I do! I do! But your wife! This is wrong! Stop it! Ain't it? Ain't it wrong? Don't you love Sister?'

'Kiss me! What's the harm? My God, out in the wilds! What's the harm just once? Who'll know it? Don't be crazy, honey!'

'It's wrong! When will I ever see you again, and Sister working hard at home this minute, and your little baby! Oh, Mitch, Mitch! I wish . . .'

The pale water was heavy upon them, sliding through the aged bogs to the sea with the smoothness of tawny oil. It caused a weighty sadness in Elmira's breast. It was a sense of the flow that burdened her, the thick, urgent, pollen-colored press of water, the heavy, meaningless exodus toward the desolate nowhere of the Gulf. She pressed herself along Mitch and offered her lips. He arched her backward across the peaty slope and fed upon her mouth.

When the willows drew a russet mist between the house and the river, the autumn was near, and the Holt family began to fold in around itself. Under Sister's vigilant hoe, the front yard camphor tree had swelled to the bigness of a verdant cloud, concealing all but the doorway, and casting cold black shade for children's playing. All day the house was noisy with Sister's preserving, the happy clinking of her jars, the upward gushing of heady smells and vapors. One by one the containers were stacked by Bruce in the pantry's dimness, the garnered riches of a fat summer hoarded against the cold months, when there would be ample game to meat them. The crunch of levee footsteps was dim as banished memories. And between the russet mist and the plundered meadows there sounded the vital yelping of Mitch's saw, building a new packing-shed and a storeroom of logs for Sister's Easter lily bulbs.

Sister knitted at night until weary; and at these moments she felt the vague contentment of pregnancy. At these moments she would have denied any remembrance of the mottled past — any knowledge that she had ever gone hungry — had ever sung weirdly to relieve her seething breast — hissed her badgered defiance at the craven stars — gazed outward enthralled at the fearful smallness of the earth. She looked around at her drowsy, sun-drunken children, and her husband subdued in his nightly tinkering or his sporting magazines. Mitch had been home three weeks, and he had not yet appeared restless. Often he would read the papers to her; or when they had company in the evenings he would entertain them all.

But in the daytime the man was tacitly excluded from the house, save at meal times. It was not fair for him to come smelling around before a meal was ready. So all day Sister was the gay and truculent mistress of her home. Except at those occasional moments, growing rare now — such as during a wild gale or when she spied a beautiful ship with music in it throbbing toward the sea — she treasured her home above all things, the house without fear.

Mitch left their bed early mornings, sooner than even she got up. She would hear him below clumsily banging the utensils. She loved him for his ability to create more mess preparing coffee than she caused in fixing a Christmas dinner. Or she would hear him whistling out on the wharf. Like most Delta men, Mitch went to the river first thing each day to discover, for no reason, how the Old Man looked, and to scan the heavens for signs of E Pluvius Unum, as he called the rain.

'Get out of my way!' he yelled, pounding upstairs with her cup of coffee. Each morning Mitch's animal spirits bubbled over in such badinage. Sister glanced at Stephen's crib and patted her hair quickly, or she hid beneath the covers full of chills of delight.

'Get out my way!'

'Just because *you* sleep like a flead shoat,' she said under the covers, 'is no reason for your rousing the house in dark of morning. I don't want your coffee.' She loved this bit of homage, which prompted her to a pretense of scorn. She sipped the coffee in regal style, fastidiously like a bride. Mitch removed his boots and crept in with her. 'Hey! Don't *you* go to sleep again!' she warned. 'We've got hay to make!'

Her eyes dreaming down on the river through the insolent glory of the risen sun were dark and liquid, heavy with some sort of passion. The man rooted around under the covers and nibbled her knee.

She slid from the bed. Her body through the night garment was barely enlarged. A smaller child this time, perhaps. She fussed with her husband while dressing. It was so good to have Mitch back! He would be home until trapping time, some weeks. He had come home from alligator hunting so tender! He had been with her over three weeks, and not once had they profaned the innocent reunion with any quarreling. She hoped they would not sully his present stay. She seemed to be without weapons now, to be lacking the instinct to crouch and strike back, or to provoke the battle. She loved the many-sided man more than ever before.

Not with the old white lust, the blinding mists that had

twirled around and obliterated her will; because at this time, along with her flesh, in what she felt was a more honorable bestowal, she consciously *gave* her will, her strong tattered defiance, her secret core of hardness. So she loved him more deeply. She wanted him more tenderly and with greater insistence. He was her fickle partner in the now half-discerned creation of the vision which she was trying to realize. It was passing wonderful — loving him now as a wife, and slyly concealing from him the growing vision.

Then suddenly all of Mitch's tender and mocking sweetness fell away, and he went about in one of his sandy moods. He began to avoid her in the oblique, half-surly manner behind which he had hidden himself following the departure of the wild Irishman. Not that he was in any way offensive. He was simply not *there!* If he was surly, it was not toward her, but rather toward himself. He spoke to her with strange patience and courtesy — not coldly, but surely with no warmth. He finished the outbuildings he was making, and seemed proud of them. He kept her provided with firewood and piped the cistern water into her kitchen. But the more intimate attentions, those formerly tendered her in honor of her love, or her domestic stewardship, or the fact of her being with child — these abruptly ceased.

Let him alone! her heart counseled. She had no monopoly on the man. She wanted no monopoly. An overt rupture was infinitely preferable to this sort of game; but if it were a fated ordeal, let it do its worst! They were growing older, she reflected with quaint distaste but wholesome resignation. It was time they learned to ignore or endure each other's sandy spells.

Yet she wept long by herself, because the old freedom, laxness, disorderliness of the family routine were gone, and these she cherished, cherished. The very sounds of the household had changed in tenor. Between Sister and all of the sweet or rugged connotations of domestic things there lay a stern and lonely distance. And the fields — how clean, meaninglessly well-ordered; and the reddening fruit hung everywhere on the prim trees like stupid ornaments. In the silent house, meal followed meal without gusto. The dwelling seemed so tall and spotless, and levee stragglers bowed with such strained decorum!

They walked to the post-office in the evening, she and Mitch. Sister kicked at the dust, slashed the weeds with a stick, threw a shell at an impudent grackle — anything, anything to break the glassy nullity of the day! She was terrified now. They were lost! where were they going? They were no longer moving at all. Had they seen these same willows turn ruddy and die when they were children? A cold puff of wind from the northwest struck her back.

Now the cold came galloping. Thousands of willow leaves swirled around her. Her woolly shawl grazed her cheek with its coarse and goodly flapping. She tried to feel as though she were in a saddle. Grampaw's saddle. She looked at Mitch beside her. What a steady-going fellow! He had spent his day mending the roof. His face looked sober and well-fed. Was her fancy playing a joke? Was Mitch growing jowls? She could not endure it. All that she had loved in him was gone. It was an outrage! Scalding tears rose to her eyes. She must leave him — drive him away!

'Listen, I haven't tried to tame you,' she said vehemently.

Mitch turned in astonishment. At last! Some expression in his eyes. He looked away thoughtfully, then turned back to her.

'What are you trying to say?' he asked.

'Tame you! Tame you! I have not tried to do that!' She stopped in the road and stamped her foot. Her eyes were blazing. Mitch looked her up and down, still surprised. He glanced at the spot where her body showed a slight forward bulge. 'Don't hold it in for me!' the woman cried, looking quite distracted in the whirl of leaves. 'Don't go around holding it in for me!' Mitch looking at her was so concerned, so reasonable, that her tears came again. She would rather he struck her than to stand so mollified. It seemed to scotch the last vestige of her pride in him.

'Don't you want me to begin being a good husband?'

She snarled at his half-bitter grin, and shook his hand away.

'Go back to your other women,' she said. 'I'll not fatten you up or tame you!'

'And can I come and see you sometimes at night?'

'Yes! Will you go?'

He watched her a moment with level eyes. The old blue light flickered. She thrilled to it. Her flesh trembled.

'I'll go back,' he told her, 'in my own good time. You hear?'

'Go, then! Go! I have money saved, because I always knew we would part. Take it.'

'Thanks. And what sort of women will I go to? A blonde? Mulatto? Sabina Leboeuf?'

Sister walked away without answering. He followed her.

The river wind stung Sister's face, reddened her ears. Her lungs seemed awakening to clear their chambers of a month of dankness. The man and woman crossed their front yard, went around the side.

'Three years ago this place was not fitting for pigs,' said Mitch. 'A visitor had to wear boots in the dew — if any visitors should have come, which nobody did. The Kalaviches! The crazy Kalaviches!'

'You and your visitors! Why don't *you* go visiting? Perhaps that would put some life in you! You could stand some craziness now.'

'I'll go visiting, no bloody fear! I'll soon be in the marsh again, away from you and your brats and your poetry and your visions and your sighing all over the place!'

Sister turned away, biting her lip.

Bruce came in from the river-bank. They had supper in peace. But it was only a truce. While Mitch stared at the table like some scheming demon, Sister thought: I could submit to such a man. If only he were always like that!

Mitch ate more than usual, and went in and stretched himself on the sofa. She looked in at him. She felt that if he should go to sleep, she would be capable of shooting him. In a while, she passed through the room on her way to the levee with little Stephen. The man had dropped off. Asleep! Going out she banged the door so hard that he woke up, startled. When she returned later, Mitch passed her on the path, going out in his shirt-sleeves, and presently she heard him up the road singing.

Inside she locked the three doors and built a fire. She was working on a seine. The gauzy meshes grew slowly as frosty vapor. She tried not to think, but her mind kept turning on one harassing idea, the old hatred of being a woman, the one vain regret she seemed doomed to bear and combat forever.

Outside, the blinds were beginning to flutter and the river to seethe. The thermometer said thirty-seven degrees. People occasionally passed on the levee, hurrying home. She went out in the yard. There would be no rain: the wind-polished moon was high and lonely, having driven back all but the fiercest stars. She covered a coop of chicks with an old coat. The hen, wide awake, stared at her through the moonlit slats.

At ten o'clock there came a knock. She thought it was Mitch. She turned the key and walked away. Presently she came back to the door. It was Mr. Birchel, the storekeeper.

'No, I can't come in, Mrs. Holt. I passed by to tell you there's a killing wind on the way. A pilot steered close enough to holler to my son. We're expecting the lowest minimum in fifteen years. They forecast twenty-five degrees for the Delta by midnight.'

Sister thought of their baby oranges. She took off her woolens and lit a lantern, but the light was not needed. The moonlight threw shadows as bright as those of the sun. When she looked upward at the moon's frigid core, the shine glanced off her throat like water thrown. The air was full of pear leaves, and grit from the road.

She spied a man back in their young orchard. She went onward. It was her husband. He had returned through his neighbors' rear fields. He was shoveling dirt into a pile around the trunk of a tree, working against the approach of midnight like one possessed. He had covered but a few of the little trees' trunks. The trees were about two feet tall. The man did not look at his wife.

It was growing colder. The little trees would not stand a much lower temperature, because they had barely taken hold of their homes in the ground.

The dull gray earth sent up its bristling cold through the woman's soles. But she knew it was warm under the ground, where the baby roots were. The wind was very dry. She could feel endless areas of vegetation curling. She was aware of sap everywhere creeping downward. And there were busy voices in the adjacent fields, unseen men, women, and children frantically at work.

The woman hurried toward the house, and soon returned with a large glinting pitchfork. Fighting the wind, she dodged between the little trees to the haypile at the rear of the planted section. She plunged in the fork and brought away a black sagging heap of hay, and with this she marched to one of the trees her husband had sodded. The man scampered over to the ditch for a bucket of water to dip his shovel in, to make it better slice the sod.

The wind rose and rose, and the river was heard pounding

on its shores. The voices from the neighboring fields at times came plainly to the man and the woman:

'Move! Move out of my way! You're in the way!'

'More hay! Hurry up! More hay over here!'

'Put dis quilt over my lettuce plants! My lettuce, Jean!'

'Throw it! Throw duh mud, God damn it!'

'Break me another stick over there! A small one!'

'More hay!'

The husband dragged at his bucket of water across the frigid moonlight. Every time the man and the woman passed each other, they screamed ill-tempered words down the wind. Sometimes the strength of the wind made these hurled epithets heard only vaguely, like voices high in the heavens.

Mitch grasped his shovel and grunted deeply as he wedged the shining blade into the tough earth. The sod had a rank smell, like spring. Sister plunged her fork in vengefully, and straightened up with a triumphant forkful of hay. She piled hay around one of the trees near her husband, and stuffed it in tightly around the tender boughs. In a sudden rage, she advanced upon him with her pitchfork, bent on she knew not what rashness. The man's mouth in the moonlight was a sharp horizontal slit. His ears were gleaming in the moon. They seemed to be pointed at the tops. He waited for his wife to strike him, but a swishing onslaught of wind shouldered her bodily away from him. He laughed stridently.

'Once I was too wild and ill-mannered!' he shouted. 'Now I am too tame and dull!'

'Yes! And this is the last time I'll put my foot in these fields, Mitch Holt!' Her shrill voice raced away in the wind.

'Too tame and dull!' the man jeered, spitefully ramming his shovel into the ground which many suns had hardened. 'Too tame and dull! I suppose *you* are untamed!'

The woman ran nimbly after another load of hay. She lost her forkful of hay in the maddened wind. Before she could recover it, the last straw was scattered over the whole field. She cursed and hurled her fork at the haystack.

'I suppose you're never grouchy!' the man yelled at the top of his lungs as he frantically tamped a sodded tree with his boot. 'Not ever! Never dull! Never fretful! *You* haven't put on an ounce of flesh lately! You're slender as a mocking-bird, I reckon!'

But now their words were being jerked from between their cold lips by the wind and almost silenced before utterance. The woman panted heavily as she danced less and less nimbly back and forth, keeping up with the man's part of the labor. She was sweating under her light garments, but her freezing fingers had lost all sense of feeling. My God! The temperature must be down to twenty-five already! The man, plugging doggedly with his shovel, muttered on, but he was unheard, except when he pushed on the balky shovel; and then the words were shouted angrily. When she came near him, the woman heard the husky sound of his breathing. The other fields were quiet, now, except for an occasional yelp or roar, that was like sounds from the dens around an arena. The sky was filling with cursed clouds. Once the man and his wife were in complete darkness for a spell, and the woman heard her husband suddenly roar a long ejaculation of curious-sounding, unfamiliar profanity.

She herself fell to her knees in the dark, and herself cursed the cypress root that had tripped her up.

In time, they were almost finished. Nearly all the hay was gone. This stack had taken two men, working easily, a day to gather.... Only a row of trees remained to be sodded and covered. Once during a darkness the woman almost collided with the man. The moon came suddenly through the tattered clouds and he was revealed all shining with sweat, grown strangely heavy and tall. She stooped and rammed the armful of hay snugly among the branches of the little tree. It hurt her now to straighten her back. At the haystack she looked back and spied her husband resting, leaning on his shovel. Caught in the act, the sneaky loafer! His head was slightly drooped, his back curved thickly forward. He thumbed away the sweat and set to work again.

Now, after four hours of toil, they marshaled their bottom reserves of strength to complete the last six trees — sources of low-grade vitality never before called into play. Only six more! Only six more! Their knees were beginning to sag at unexpected moments. The woman found herself going in the wrong direction for the haystack. She turned round and round. She could not find it at all. She was floating in some kind of thick, numbing element. There was something heavy clinging to her belly, pulling it, dragging it downward. She heard her husband shouting. She collected her faculties and trudged toward the haystack. It was taking the man a long time to collect enough sod to cover the trunks of the final trees. The woman covered her last tree with hay, and three trees remained to be sodded. What was he doing? What *was* he doing? He was on one knee, lifting his shovel above his head and bringing it down before him in semicircles, but the clouds kept slowly putting the light on and off, giving a peculiar appearance to the man's movements. Why was he on his knees? Get up off your knees, silly! Stand up like a man!

Where was the house?

She sat on the ground. The contact burned her. She tried to fix her head. The wind was continually blowing it to one side. Stay where you are, head! Full of sleepiness and stupid searchings. No good . . .

The man was slapping her on the shoulder. '. . . on! Come on!'

She walked ahead. Her brain had cleared. The familiar openings in the old orchard. She looked behind. The husband was moving heavily, foot after foot dropping of its own weight.

Mouth open and underjaw slack. Black shoulders bunched thickly. And he was sideways, as though permanently mis-shapen, the upper half of his body turned sideways against the now deafening scream of the wind.

In the kitchen the bright kerosene light blinded them. The room seemed oddly neat. A strange place. The woman dragged out a chair and sat on it to light the fire in the stove. The husband squatted on his heels before the water faucet with a glass. He began drinking. One glass. Two glasses. Three. Four. He belched. He panted from the hard exertion of drinking.

The wife poured the man's coffee into his little bowl. She slid the sugarbowl over to him. He sipped the hot liquid while she drank hers with a smacking of the lips. He turned his head this way and that, and fixed his eyes on the several objects of the room rather stupidly. He looked at his wife. She was hugging her breasts, watching him too. They were angry at each other.

The woman climbed the stairs, followed by her husband. He assisted himself by grasping both the banisters. He un-dressed and threw himself into the bed at once. The woman brushed her hair. She lowered the top of the window carefully. She went in and tucked in the children, and kissed them. After a final glance about her, she blew down into the lamp. She felt her way to the bed. The noise of the river outside was a thunderous clamor. The woman lay with her back against her husband's. After several movements of her weary muscles, she settled into a position fitting along his body snugly. She wanted to cry. She waited to make sure he was asleep before giving way to tears. While she was waiting she fell asleep.

THE END